# KAJIRA OF GOR

I was thrust, in a sitting position, into the box. The ring at the back of the gag was snapped about a matching ring in the box. My head was thus held in place. For a moment the room seemed to go dark and then I gathered my wits again. My left wrist, to my horror, was fastened back and at my left side. My right wrist was secured similarly. Both of my ankles, too, had been fastened in position. I fought to retain consciousness. Then I was thrust back further in the box. A broad leather strap was then drawn tightly about me. I winced. Then it was buckled shut. I could hardly move. I looked at the men, from the box.

'She is secured,' said one of the men.

The man in charge nodded. 'Close the container,' he said. I was plunged into darkness.

Other titles in the

CHRONICLES OF COUNTER-EARTH

by John Norman

TARNSMAN OF GOR
OUTLAW OF GOR
PRIEST-KINGS OF GOR
NOMADS OF GOR
ASSASSIN OF GOR
RAIDERS OF GOR
CAPTIVE OF GOR
HUNTERS OF GOR
MARAUDERS OF GOR
TRIBESMEN OF GOR
SLAVE-GIRL OF GOR
BEASTS OF GOR
EXPLORERS OF GOR
FIGHTING SLAVE OF GOR
ROGUE OF GOR
GUARDSMAN OF GOR
SAVAGES OF GOR
BLOOD BROTHERS OF GOR

# KAJIRA OF GOR

**John Norman**

A STAR BOOK
*published by*
the Paperback Division of
W. H. ALLEN & Co. Ltd

A Star Book
Published in 1983
by the Paperback Division of
W. H. Allen & Co. Ltd
A Howard & Wyndham Company
44 Hill Street, London W1X 8LB

First published in the United States of America by
Daw Books, Inc., 1983



Printed and bound in Great Britain by
Anchor Brendon Ltd
Tiptree, Essex

ISBN 0 352 31432 X

# CONTENTS

# 1

# THE STUDIO

"Do you not see it?" asked the man.
"Yes," said the fellow with him.
"It is incredible," said another.
"The resemblance is truly striking," said the second man.
"Please turn your profile towards us, and lift your chin, Miss Collins," said the first man.
I complied.
I was in a photographer's studio.
"A little higher, Miss Collins," said the first man.
I lifted my chin higher.
"You may change in here," had said the man earlier, indicating a small dressing room off the studio. I had been handed a pair of clogs, a white silk blouse and a pair of black shorts.
"No brassiere or panties," he had said.
I had looked at him.
"We want no lines from them," he said.
"Of course," I had said.
The shorts were quite short, and, even without the panties, at least a size too small. The blouse, too, even without the brassiere, was tight.
"Please tie up the blouse, in front," he said. "We want some midriff."
I had complied.
"Higher," he had suggested.
I had complied.
I had then been, to my puzzlement, photographed several times, from the neck up, front view and profile, against a type of chart, on which appeared various graduated lines, presumably some type of calibrating or measuring device. The lines, as nearly as I could determine, however, correlated neither with inches nor centimeters.
"Now, please, step into the sand box," he had said.

I had then stepped onto the sand, in the wide, flat box, with the beach scene projected onto the large screen behind me. Then, for several minutes, the photographer moving about me, swiftly and professionally, sometimes almost intimately close, and giving me commands, the camera clicking, I had been posed in an incredible variety of positions. Men, I had thought, must enjoy putting a woman thusly through her paces. Some of the shots were almost naughty. I think, too, given the absence of a brassiere and panties, and the skimpiness and tightness of the shorts, and the tightness of the blouse, doubtlessly calculated features of my apparel, there would be little doubt in the minds of the observers as to the lineaments of my figure. I did not object, however. In fact I rather enjoyed this. I think I am rather pretty.

I was now standing in the sand, my left side facing the men, my chin lifted. The lights were hot. To my left were the lights, the tangles of cord, the men. To my right, in contrast, there seemed the lovely, deserted beach.

"She is pretty," said one of the men.

"She is pretty enough to be a Kajira," said one of the men.

"She will be," laughed another.

I did not understand what they were talking about.

"Do not see such a woman merely in terms of such predictable and luscious commonalities," said the first man. "You see clearly her potential for us, do you not?"

"Of course," said the second man.

I did not understand them.

"Turn on the fan," said the first man.

I then felt a cool breeze, blown by the large fan in front of me. In the heat of the lights this was welcome.

"This coin, or medal, or whatever it is, is very puzzling," had said the gentle, bespectacled man, holding it by the edges with white, cotton gloves, and then placing it down on the soft felt between us. He was an authenticator, to whom I had been referred by a professional numismatist. His task was not to appraise coins but to render an informed opinion on such matters as their type and origin, where this might be obscure, their grading, in cases where a collaborative opinion might be desired, and their genuineness.

"Is it genuine?" I asked.

"Who sold you this piece," asked the man, "a private party? What did you pay for it?"

"It was given to me," I said, "by a private party."

"That is extremely interesting," said the man.

"Why?" I asked.

"It rules out an obvious hypothesis," said the man. "Yet such a thing would be foolish."

"I do not understand," I said.

"Puzzling," he mused, looking down at the coin on the felt between us, "puzzling."

I regarded him.

"This object," he said, "has not been struck from machine-engraved dies. Similarly, it is obviously not the result of contemporary minting techniques and technology. It is not the product, for example, of a high-speed, automated coin press."

"I do not understand," I said.

"It has been struck by hand," he said. "Do you see how the design is slightly off center?"

"Yes," I said.

"That is a feature almost invariably present in ancient coins," he said. "The planchet is warmed, to soften the metal. It is then placed between the dies and the die cap is then struck, literally, with a hammer, impressing the design of the obverse and reverse simultaneously into the planchet."

"Then it is an ancient coin?" I asked.

"That seems unlikely," he said. "Yet the techniques used in striking this coin have not been used, as far as I know, for centuries."

"What sort of coin is it?" I asked.

"Too," he said, "note how it is not precision milled. It is not made for stacking, or for storage in rolls."

I looked at him. It did not seem to me he was being too clear with me. He seemed independently fascinated with the object.

"Such coins were too precious perhaps," he said. "A roll of them might be almost inconceivable, particularly in the sense of having many such rolls."

"What sort of coin is it?" I asked.

"You see, however," he asked, "how the depth of the planchet allows a relief and contrast of the design with the background to an extent impossible in a flat, milled coin?"

"Yes," I said.

"What a superb latitude that gives the artist," he said. "It frees him from the limitations of a crude compromise with the counting house, from the contemporary concessions which must be made to economic functionalism. Even then, in so small and common an object, and in so unlikely an object, he can create a work of art."

"Can you identify the coin?" I asked.

"This, in its depth and beauty, reminds me of ancient coins," he said. "They are, in my opinion, the most beautiful and interesting of all coins."

"Is it an ancient coin?" I asked.

"I do not think so," he said.

"What sort of coin is it, then?" I asked.

"Look here," he said. "Do you see how this part of the object, at the edge, seems flatter, or straight, different from the rest of the object's circumference?"

"Yes," I said. To be sure, one had to look closely to see it.

"This object has been clipped, or shaved," he said. "A part of the metal has been cut or trimmed away. In this fashion, if that is not noted, or the object is not weighed, it might be accepted for, say, a certain face value, the individual responsible for this meanwhile pocketing the clipped or shaved metal. If this is done over a period of time, with many coins, of course, the individual could accumulate, in metal value, a value equivalent perhaps to one or more of the original objects."

"Metal value?" I asked.

"In modern coinage," he said, "we often lose track of such things. Yet, if one thinks about it, at least in the case of many coins, a coin is a way in which a government or ruler certifies that a given amount of precious metal is involved in a transaction. It saves weighing and testing each coin. The coin, in a sense, is an object whose worth or weight, in standardized quantities, is certified upon it, and guaranteed, so to speak, by an issuing authority. Commerce as we know it would be impossible, of course, without such objects, and notes, and credit and such."

"Then the object is a coin?" I said.

"I do not know if it is a coin or not," said the man.

"What else could it be?" I asked.

"It could be many things," he said. "It might be a token or a medal. It might be an emblem of membership in an organization or a device whereby a given personage might be recognized by another. It might be a piece of art intended to be mounted in jewelry. It might even be a piece in some game."

"Can you identify it?" I asked.

"No," he said.

The object was about an inch and a half in diameter and about three eighths of an inch in thickness. It was yellowish, and, to me, surprisingly heavy for its size.

"What about the letter on one side?" I asked.

"It may not be a letter," he said. "It may be only a design." It seemed a single, strong, well-defined character. "If it is a letter," he said, "it is not from an alphabet with which I am familiar."

"There is an eagle on the other side," I said, helpfully.

"Is there?" he asked. He turned the coin on the felt, touching it carefully with the cotton gloves.

I looked at the bird more closely.

"It is not an eagle," he said. "It has a crest."

"What sort of bird is it?" I asked.

He shrugged. "Perhaps it is a bird from some mythology," he said, "perhaps a mere artist's whimsy."

I looked at the fierce head on the surface of the yellowish object.

It frightened me.

"It does not appear to be a whimsy," I said.

"No," he smiled. "It doesn't, does it?"

"Have you ever seen anything like this before?" I asked.

"No," he said, "aside, of course, from its obvious resemblance to ancient coins."

"I see," I said.

"I was afraid," he said, "when you brought it in, that you were the victim of an expensive and cruel hoax. I had thought perhaps you had paid a great deal of money for this, before having its authenticity ascertained. On the other hand, it was given to you. You were thus not being defrauded in that manner. As you perhaps know coins can be forged, just as, say, paintings and other works of art can be forged. Fortunately these forgeries are usually detectable, particularly under magnification, for example, from casting marks or filing marks from seam joinings, and so on. To be sure, sometimes it is very difficult to tell if a given coin is genuine or not. It is thus useful for the circumspect collector to deal with established and reputable dealers. Similarly the authentication of a coin can often proceed with more confidence if some evidence is in hand pertaining to its history, and its former owners, so to speak. One must always be a bit suspicious of the putatively rare and valuable coin which seems to appear inexplicably, with no certifiable background, on the market, particularly if it lacks the backing of an established house."

"Do you think this object is genuine?" I asked.

"There are two major reasons for believing it is genuine," he said, "whatever it might be. First, it shows absolutely no signs of untypical production, such as being cast rather than struck, of being the result of obverse-reverse composition, or of having been altered or tampered with in any way. Secondly, if it were a forgery, what would it be a forgery of? Consider the analogy of counterfeiting. The counterfeiter presumably wishes to deceive people. This end would not be well served by producing a twenty-five dollar bill, which was purple and of no familiar design. There would be no point in it. It would defeat his own purposes."

"I understand," I said.

"Thus," said the man, "it seems reasonable to assume that this object, whatever it is, is genuine."

"Do you think it is a coin?" I asked.

"It gives every evidence of being a coin," he said. "It looks like a coin. Its simplicity and design do not suggest that it is commemorative in nature. It has been produced in a manner in which coins were often produced, at least long ago and in the classical world. It has been clipped or shaved, something that normally occurs only with coins which pass through many hands. It even has bag marks."

"What are those?" I asked.

"This object, whatever it is," said the man, "can clearly be graded according to established standards recognized in numismatics. It is not even a borderline case. You would not require an expert for its grading. Any qualified numismatist could grade it. If this were a modern, milled coin, it would be rated Extremely Fine. It shows no particular, obvious signs of wear but its surface is less perfect than would be required to qualify it as being Uncirculated or as being in Mint State. If this were an ancient coin, it would also qualify as being Extremely Fine, but here the grading standards are different. Again there are almost no signs of wear and the detail, accordingly, is precise and sharp. It shows good centering and the planchet, on the whole, is almost perfectly formed. Some minor imperfections, such as small nicks, are acceptable in this category for ancient coins."

"But what are bag marks?" I asked.

"You may not be able to detect them with the naked eye," he said. "Use this."

From a drawer in the desk he produced a boxlike, mounted magnifying glass. This he placed over the coin, and snapped on the desk lamp.

"Do you see the tiny nicks?" he asked.

"Yes," I said, after a moment.

"Those are bag marks," he said. "They are the result, usually, of the coin, or object, being kept with several others, loose, in, say, a bag or box."

"There might, then," I asked, looking up from the magnifying device, "be a large number of other objects like this somewhere?" That I found a very interesting thought.

"Surely," said the man. "On the other hand, such marks could obviously have other causes, as well."

"Then all the evidence suggests that this is a coin?" I said.

"The most crucial piece of evidence," he said, "however, suggests that it cannot be a coin."

"What is that?" I asked.

"That it fits into no known type or denomination of coin."

"I see," I said.

"As far as I know," he said, "no city, kingdom, nation or civilization on Earth ever produced such a coin."

"Then it is not a coin," I said.

"That seems clear," he said. "No," he said. "Do not pay me."

I replaced his fee in my purse.

"The object is fascinating," he said. "Simply to consider it, in its beauty and mystery, is more than payment enough."

"Thank you," I said.

"I am sorry that I could not be more helpful," he said. "Wait!" he called after me. I had turned to the door. "Do not forget this," he said, picking up the small, round, heavy object on the felt.

I turned back to face him. I was angry. I had thought that the object might have had some value.

"It is only some sort of hoax," I said, bitterly.

"Perhaps," he said, smiling, "but, if I were you, I would take it along with me."

"Why?" I asked.

"It has metal value, or bullion value," he said.

"Oh?" I asked.

"Yes," he said. "Do you not understand what it is composed of?"

"No," I said.

"It is gold," he said.

I had hurried back and snatched the object, and put it in my purse. I had then, hurriedly, left his office.

"Turn up the fan," said the man, he who seemed in charge of those in the photographer's studio. The fan was turned up. "Keep facing as you are," he said, "your left side to us, your chin lifted. That's good." My hair was lifted and blown back. I felt the breeze from the fan, too, pressing my blouse back against me, even more closely. It rippled the silk at the sides. It tugged at the collar. The ends of the blouse, where I had tied them together, high on my midriff, as the man had requested, fluttered backward. "Now arch your back and lift your hands to your hair," he said. "Good, excellent," he said. I was not a professional model. I had often thought that I was beautiful enough to be one, but I was not one.

I heard the camera clicking. "Excellent," said the man. "Now look at us, over your left shoulder."

I had had the yellowish, metallic object assayed. It had indeed been gold. I had sold it to a bullion dealer. It would be melted down. I had received eighteen hundred dollars for it.

"Now, face us, crouching slightly, your hands at your hair," said the man. "Good."

These men, perhaps, wanted to train me as a model. Yet I suspected this was not their true purpose. I was not particular as to what might be their true purpose, incidentally. They obviously possessed the means to pay me well.

"Now smile, Tiffany," said the man. "Good. Now crouch down in the sand, your hands on your knees. Good. Now put your left knee in the sand. Have your hands on your hips. Put your shoulders back. Good. Smile. Good."

"Good," said one of the other men, too. I could see they were pleased with me. This pleased me, too. I now felt more confident that they might hire me. For whatever object they wanted me I could sense that my beauty was not irrelevant to it. This pleased me, as I am vain of my beauty. Why should a girl not use her beauty to serve her ends, and to get ahead?

"Now face the camera directly, with your left hand on

your thigh and your right hand on your knee," said the man, "and assume an expression of wounded feelings. Good."

"She is good," said one of the other men.

"Yes," agreed another.

"Now assume an expression of apprehension," said the first man.

"Good," said the second man.

I normally worked at the perfume and notions counter in a large department store on Long Island. It was there that I had been discovered, so to speak. I had become aware, suddenly, that I was the object of the attention of the man who was now directing this photography session. "It is incredible," he had said, as though to himself. He seemed unable to take his eyes from me. I was used to men looking at me, of course, usually pretending not to, usually furtively. I had been chosen to work at that counter because I was pretty, much like pretty girls often being selected to sell lingerie. Such employee placements are often a portion of a store's merchandising strategies. But this man was not looking at me in the same way that I was accustomed to being looked at. He was not looking at me furtively, pretending to be interested in something else, or even frankly, like some men of Earth, rare men, who look honestly upon a female, seeing her as what she is, a female. Rather he was looking at me as though he could scarcely believe what he was seeing, as though I might be someone else, someone he perhaps knew from somewhere, someone he would not have expected to have found in such a place. He approached the counter. He regarded me, intently.

I think I had never been so closely regarded. I was uneasy.

"May I help you?" I asked.

He said something to me in a language I did not understand. I regarded him, puzzled.

"May I help you?" I asked.

"This is incredibly fortunate," he said, softly.

"Sir?" I asked.

"You bear a striking resemblance to someone else," he said. "It is remarkable."

I did not speak. I had thought he might have begun by asking if he did not know me from somewhere. That stratagem, the pretext of a possible earlier acquaintance, hackneyed and familiar though it might be, still affords a societally acceptable approach to a female. If she is unreceptive, he may, of course, courteously withdraw. It was merely a case of mistaken identity.

"It was almost as though it was she," he said.

I did not encourage him. I did not, for example, ask who this other person might be.

"I do not think I know you," I said.

"No," he smiled. "I would not think that you would."

"I am also sure that I am not this other person," I said.

"No," he said. "I can see now, clearly, that you are not. Too, I can sense that you lack her incisive intellect, her ferocity, her hardness, her cruelty."

"I am busy," I said.

"No," he said, his eyes suddenly hard. "You are not."

I shrugged, as though irritated. But I was frightened, and I think he knew it. I was then terribly conscious of his maleness and power. He was not the sort of man to whom a woman might speak in such a manner. He was rather the sort of man whom a woman must obey.

"May I help you?" I asked.

"Show me your most expensive perfume," he said.

I showed it to him.

"Sell it to me," he said. "Interest me in it."

"Please," I said.

"Display it," he said. "Am I not a customer?"

I looked at him.

"Spray some of it upon your wrist," he said. "I shall see if it interests me."

I did so.

"Extend your wrist," he said. I did so, with the palm upward. This is an extremely erotically charged gesture, of course, extending the delicate wrist, perfumed, to the male, with the tender, vulnerable palm upward.

He took my wrist in both his hands. I shivered. I knew I could never break that grip.

He put down his face, over my wrist, and inhaled, deeply, intimately, sensuously.

I shuddered.

"It is acceptable," he said, lifting his head.

"It is our most expensive perfume," I said. He had not yet released my wrist.

"Do you like it?" he asked.

"I cannot afford it," I said.

"Do you like it?" he asked.

"Of course," I said.

He released my wrist. "I shall take it," he said. "Wrap it," he said, "as a gift."

"It is seven hundred dollars an ounce," I said.

"It is overpriced for its quality," he said.

"It is our best," I said.

He drew a wallet from his jacket and withdrew several hundred-dollar bills from its recesses. I could see that it held many more bills.

Trembling, I wrapped the perfume. When I had finished I took the money.

"There is a thousand dollars here," I said, moving as though to return the extra bills.

"Keep what you do not need for the price and tax," he said.

"Keep it?" I asked.

"Yes," he said.

"It is over two hundred dollars," I said.

"Keep it," he said.

While I busied myself with the register he wrote something on a small card.

"Thank you," I said, uncertainly, sliding the tiny package toward him with the tips of my fingers.

He pushed it back towards me. "It is for you," he said, "of course."

"For me?" I asked.

"Yes," he said. "When is your day off?"

"Wednesday," I said.

"Come to this address," he said, "at ten o'clock in the morning, this coming Wednesday." He placed the small white card before me.

I looked at the address. It was in Manhattan.

"We shall be expecting you," he said.

"I do not understand," I said.

"It is the studio of a friend of mine," he said, "a photographer. He does a great deal of work for certain advertising agencies."

"Oh," I said. I sensed that this might be the opening to a career of great interest to me, one in which I might be able to capitalize, and significantly, on my beauty.

"I see that you are interested," he said.

I shrugged. "Not really," I said. I would play hard to get.

"We do not accept prevarication in a female," he said.

"A female?" I said. I felt for a moment I had been reduced to my radical essentials.

"Yes," he said.

I felt angry and, admittedly, not a little bit aroused by his handling of me.

"I hardly know you. I can't accept this money, or this perfume," I said.

"But you will accept it, won't you?" he said.

I put down my head. "Yes," I said.

"We shall see you Wednesday," he said.

"I shan't be coming," I said.

"We recognize that your time, as of now," he said, "is valuable."

I did not understand what he meant by the expression 'as of now.'

He then pressed into my hand the round, heavy, yellowish object which I had later taken to the shop of a numismatist, and then, later, on the advice of the numismatist, to the office of a specialist in the authentication of coins.

"This is valuable," he said, "more so elsewhere than here."

Again I did not understand the nuances of his speech. I looked down at the object in my hand. I assumed, from its shape and appearance, it might be some kind of coin. If so, however, I certainly did not recognize it. It seemed alien to me, totally unfamiliar. I clutched it, then, however, for he had told me that it was valuable.

"You are a greedy little thing, aren't you?" he said.

"I shan't be coming," I told him, petulantly. He made me angry. Too, he made me feel terribly uneasy. He made me feel uncomfortably, and deeply, female. Such feelings were terribly stimulating, but also, in their way, terribly unsettling. I did not know, really, how to cope with them.

I decided I would take the beginning of next week off from work. I would try to find out something about the yellowish object. I would then try to think things out. Then, at my leisure, I would decide whether or not to go to the stipulated address on Wednesday.

"We shall see you on Wednesday," he said.

"Perhaps," I said.

"Wear the perfume," he said.

"All right," I said.

"Now kneel in the sand, facing the camera," said the man. "Kneel back on your heels. Place the palms of your hands down on your thighs. Lift your head. Put your shoulders back. Spread your knees."

"Excellent," said one of the men.

"Now assume the same position," said the man, "but in profile to the camera, your left side facing us. Keep your head up. Put your shoulders back more. Good. Splendid!"

"Splendid!" said another man.

"Now face the camera on all fours," he said. "Good. Now lift your head and purse your lips, as though to kiss. More. More sensuously. Now close your eyes. Good."

"Splendid," said another man.

"Open your eyes now and unpurse your lips, and turn, staying on all fours, so that your left side is facing us, so that we have your profile to the camera."

I complied.

"Now put your head down," he said.

I did so.

"Splendid!" said one of the men.

"Splendid!" said another.

I was keenly conscious of the radical submissiveness of this posture. I almost trembled with arousal. I dared not even think of the effect of such a posture upon a woman if she had been put in it by men who were truly in power over her.

"She will do very nicely, I think," said the first man.

"She will be ideal for our purposes," said another.

"You may get up, Tiffany," said the first man.

I rose to my feet. I gathered that the session was over. I was confident that they were pleased.

The fan, which had produced the surrogate of an ocean breeze, was turned off. The photographer began to extinguish his lights and put them to the side, in a line against the wall. One of the men turned off the projector and the beach scene which had been projected behind me vanished, leaving in its place a featureless, opaque, white screen.

"You are very pretty, Tiffany, Miss Collins," said the first man. "And you did very well."

"Thank you," I said.

"You may now change," he said.

"Very well," I said. I feared I might be being dismissed. I returned to the dressing room. I could hear them talking outside, but I could not make out what they were saying. In a few moments I emerged from the dressing room. I wore a man-tailored, beige blazer with a rather severe, matching pleated skirt, with a rather strict white blouse, of synthetic material, and medium heels. I had wished to present a rather businesslike look. I did not wish to wear particularly feminine clothes as men are inclined to see women who do this as females, and behave towards them and relate to them as such. Women are no longer forced, in effect, to dress as females, in particular ways, with all the dynamic, attendant psychological effects for both sexes which might accrue to such a practice.

I then stood before the fellow who seemed to be in charge. I saw that he did not particularly approve of my ensemble. I hoped this would not diminish my chances of meeting whatever requirements they might have in mind with respect to my acceptability. Perhaps I should have worn something more feminine. After all, I was a woman. Too, the shorts and blouse in which I had been placed, for the pictures, left little doubt in my mind that my femaleness, at least in some sense or another, might well be pertinent to their interests.

"Perhaps I should have worn something less severe?" I said, tentatively. I did want to be pleasing to them. Obviously they had a good deal of money to spend. Too, interestingly, they were the sort of men towards whom, independently, I felt a strong, disturbing, almost inexplicable desire to be pleasing.

"Your attire does seem a bit defensive," he said.

"Perhaps," I smiled. How interestingly, I thought, he had put that.

"Such defenses, of course," he said, "may be removed from a woman."

His remark, rightly or wrongly, struck me as being broader and deeper in its meaning than the mere bantering witticism it might have been taken to be. It suggested more to me, unsettling me, than a mere change of, or removal of, attire. It suggested to me, for a moment, a reference to a world in which a woman might be without defenses, fully, a world in which she was simply not permitted defenses.

"Perhaps I should have worn something more feminine," I said.

He regarded me, appraisingly. I sensed that he was looking past the severe man-tailored blazer, the rather strict blouse, the rather strict, beige pleated skirt. As they had had me pose in the shorts and blouse, and had had me move, I was sure they had little doubt, for most practical purposes, as to what I looked like.

"If you are selected," he said, "any apparel which you might receive, I assure you, will leave little doubt as to your femininity."

"If I am selected?" I asked.

"Yes," he said.

"It is my hope that I pleased you," I said. "I thought you were pleased." One of the men, I recalled, had thought that I might be ideal for their purposes.

"We are pleased," he said, "very. You did very well."

"When will you be able to make your decision?" I asked. "When will I learn whether or not I have been selected?"

"For one thing," said the man, "you have already been selected."

One of the men laughed.

"That decision we are empowered to make," said the first man. "The second decision, that with respect to the more important post, so to speak, of necessity, must be made elsewhere."

"May I call you?" I asked.

"We have your number," he said.

"I understand," I said. I was not really displeased, for he had told me that for one thing, at any rate, I had already been selected.

"Process the photos, immediately," he said to the photographer.

The photographer nodded.

They were apparently going to proceed expeditiously in the matter. This pleased me. I do not like to wait.

"When do you think you will know," I asked, "—about the more important post?"

"It will take at least several days," he said.

"Oh," I said.

"Come here," he said, beckoning to me. I went and stood quite close to him. "Put down your head," he said. I did so, and he, moving behind me, and pulling the collar of my blouse out a bit with his finger, put his head down, close to the side of my face, by my neck. He inhaled, deeply.

"Yes," I said, "I am wearing the perfume, as you asked."

"As I commanded," he said.

"Yes," I said, softly, rather startled at myself, "as you commanded."

I then left. I wore his perfume.

# 2

## THE CRATE

I turned off the shower.

It must have been about ten minutes after eight in the evening.

It was now some six weeks after my test, or interview, or whatever it had been, in the photographer's studio. On each Monday of these six weeks I had received in the mail, in a plain white envelope without a return address, a one-hundred-dollar bill. This money, I had gathered, was in the nature of some sort of a retainer. I recalled that the man who had first seen me at the perfume counter, he who seemed to be in charge of the group, had said that he recognized that my time, as of now, was valuable. I was still not clear on what he had meant by the phrase 'as of now.' These bills, until a few days ago, had been my only evidence that the men had not forgotten me. Then, on a Monday evening, a few days ago, the Monday before last, at eight o'clock, I had received a phone call. I had returned home to my small apartment only a few minutes earlier, from the local supermarket. I was putting away groceries and was not thinking of the men at all. I had, to be sure, taken the hundred-dollar bill from the mail box earlier and put it in my dresser. This had become for me, however, almost routine. I was, at any rate, not thinking of the men. When the phone rang my first reaction was one of irritation. I picked up the phone. "Hello," I said. "Hello?" Then I was suddenly afraid. I was not sure there was someone on the line. "Hello?" I said. Then, after a moment's silence, a male voice on the other end of the line spoke quietly and precisely. I did not recognize the voice. "You have been selected," it said. "Hello!" I said. "Hello! Who is this?" Then the line was dead. He had hung up. The next two nights I waited by the phone at eight o'clock. It was silent. It rang, however, on Thursday, precisely at eight. I seized the receiver from its hook. I was told to report the next evening to the southwest corner of a given intersection in Manhattan at precisely eight P.M. There I would be picked up by a limousine.

I was almost sick with relief when I saw that the man I knew, he whom I had met at the perfume counter, he who had seemed in charge of the others, was in the limousine. The other two were with him, too, one with him in the back seat and one riding beside the driver. I did not recognize the driver.

"Congratulations, Miss Collins!" he said, warmly. "You have been fully approved. You qualify with flying colors, as I had thought you would, on all counts."

"Wonderful!" I said.

The driver had now left the vehicle and come about, to open the door. The man I knew stepped out, and, while the driver held the door, motioned that I might enter. I did so, and then he entered behind me. The driver shut the door, and returned about the vehicle to his place. I was sitting between the two men in the back of the limousine.

"I had hoped I might qualify," I said.

"I was confident you would," he said. "You have the appearance, and, independently, the beauty and the dispositions. You are perfectly suited to our purposes."

"Am I to gather that I have been found acceptable for what you spoke of as the more important position, or post, or something like that, then?" I asked.

"Precisely," he said, warmly.

"Good," I said, snuggling back against the seat. I was quite pleased. These men, it seemed, were rich, or, at least, had access to considerable wealth. They would doubtless be willing to pay highly for the use of my beauty.

"I recall, you said," I said, "that I had already been selected for one thing, even at the photographer's studio."

"Yes," he said.

"But it was less important, I gather, than this other, more prestigious assignment, or position?"

"Yes," he said. "The other position, so to speak, could be filled by almost any beautiful woman."

"I see," I said.

"And if there should come a time in which your services

are no longer required for this more important post, as I have put it, you might still, I am sure, meet the qualifications for this other thing."

"That is reassuring," I said.

The man on my left smiled.

"Where are we going?" I asked.

"Were you given permission to speak?" asked the man I knew, he who had originally seen me in the department store, he on my right.

I looked at him, startled.

"Kneel down here," he said, pointing to the floor of the car, "your left side to the back of the front seat." I did so, frightened. I was the only woman in the car. "Get on your hands and knees," he said. I did so. I could then, facing as I was, see him, by lifting and turning my head. He was unfolding a blanket. "You will not speak," he said, "until five minutes after you have left the limousine." He then, opening the blanket, cast it over me. I, on all fours before them, covered by the blanket, hidden by it, was in consternation. The limousine drove on. No one outside the car could have told that I was in the car. I was silent.

As I knelt on all fours before them my mind was racing. Why had they done this? Perhaps they did not wish anyone to know that I was in the car with them. Perhaps they did not wish for me to be recognized with them, or they with me. Perhaps they were driving to some secret location, which they did not wish me to know. I was frightened. I did not know what their purposes were. After a time they let me lie down at their feet, with my legs drawn up, still covered with the blanket. I lay near their shoes. Once they even stopped for gas. "Do not move," I was told. I was perfectly quiet, at their feet. They drove about for at least four hours. It was all I could do to keep from rubbing my thighs together and moaning.

Then the limousine pulled to one side and stopped. The blanket was lifted from me.

"You may get out now," said the man who seemed in charge, pleasantly.

I rose to my feet and, crouching down, my muscles aching, stepped from the limousine. The driver had remained in his place. The man who had been to my right when I was sitting, he who seemed to be in charge of the others, had opened the door. I stood outside then, on the curb. There was traffic. The lights were bright. I was in the same place where I had originally been picked up, at the southwest corner of the intersection in Manhattan. It was a little after midnight.

I watched the limousine drive away, disappearing in the traffic. I did not really understand what they had done, or why they had done it. I stood back on the sidewalk then. I was extremely disturbed. I was almost trembling. Too, inexplicably, it seemed, I was terribly aroused, sexually.

Why had they done what they did?

For the first time in my life I had been put to the feet of men, and kept, uncompromisingly, in ignorance and silence.

They had dominated me. I almost trembled, filled with unfamiliar sensations and emotions. These feelings, these responses, were not simply genital. They seemed to suffuse, overwhelmingly, my whole body and mind.

I became aware of a man asking me for directions.

I turned away from him, suddenly, and hurried away. I had not yet been out of the limousine for five minutes. I could not yet speak.

I took my hand from the shower handle. A few drops of water descended from the shower head. It was warm and steamy in the bathroom, from the warm water which I had been running. It was about ten or eleven minutes after eight P.M. It was Tuesday. Yesterday, on Monday evening, at eight P.M., I had received another call. I had been instructed to take a shower at precisely eight P.M. this evening. I had done so. I slid back the shower curtain. There was steam on the walls and mirrors. I looked for my robe. I had thought I had left it on the vanity. It was not there. I stepped from the shower stall, and picked up a towel and began to dry myself.

Suddenly I stopped, frightened. I had thought I had heard a noise on the other side of the bathroom door, from beyond the tiny hall outside, perhaps from the tiny kitchen or the combination living and dining room.

"Is there anyone there?" I called, frightened. "Who is it?"

"It is I, Miss Collins," said a voice. "Do not be alarmed." I recognized the voice. It was he I took to be the leader of the men with whom I had been in contact, that of he who had first seen me at the perfume counter.

"I am not dressed," I called. I thrust shut the bolt on the bathroom door. I did not understand how he could have obtained entrance. I had had the door to the apartment not only locked but bolted.

"Have you cleaned your body?" he asked.

"Yes," I said. I thought he had put that in an unusual fashion.

"Have you washed your hair?" he asked.

"Yes," I said. I had done so.

"Come out," he said.

"Do you see my robe out there?" I called.

"Use a towel," he said.

"I will be out in a moment," I said. I hastily dried my hair and put a towel about it, and then I wrapped a large towel about my body, tucking it shut under my left arm. I looked about for my slippers. I had thought I had put them at the foot of the vanity. But they, like the robe, did not seem to be where I thought I had left them. I slid back the bolt on the bathroom door and, barefoot, entered the hall. There were, I saw, three men in the kitchen. One was he whom I now knew well. The other two, who wore uniforms much of a sort one expects in professional movers, I did not recognize.

"You look lovely," said the first man, he whom I recognized, he who was, by now, familiar to me.

"Thank you," I said.

"Make us some coffee," he said.

I proceeded, frightened, to do so. I was very conscious of my state of dishabille. Their eyes, I could sense, were much on me. I felt very small among their powerful bodies. I was conscious, acutely, how different I was from them.

"How did you get in?" I asked, lightly, when the coffee was perking.

"With this," he said, taking a small, metallic, penlike object from his left, inside jacket pocket. He clicked a switch on it. There was no visible beam. He then clicked the switch again, presumably turning it off.

"I do not understand," I said.

"Come along," he said, smiling, and getting up from behind the kitchen table. I followed him into the combination living and dining room. I noticed the coarse, fibrous texture of the rug on my bare feet. The other two men followed us into this room.

"There is my robe," I said, "and my slippers!" The robe was thrown over an easy chair. The slippers had been dropped at its base.

"Leave them," he said.

I knew I had not put them there.

He opened the door to the apartment and looked outside. He was seeing, I supposed, if anyone was in the hall.

He stepped outside. "Lock and bolt the door," he said.

I did so. I then stood, waiting, behind the locked, bolted door. I glanced back at the other two men, in their garb like professional movers. They stood behind me, in the apartment, their arms folded.

I heard a tiny noise. Fascinated, I saw the bolt turn and slide back. I then heard the door click. The man re-entered the apartment. He closed the door behind him. He returned the penlike object to his pocket.

"I did not know such things existed," I said. Inadvertently, frightened, I put my hand to my breast. I was very much aware that only a towel stood between me and this stranger.

"They do," he smiled.

"I didn't hear you enter," I said.

"It makes little noise," he said. "Too, you had the water running."

"You knew, of course," I said, "that I would not hear you enter."

"Of course," he said.

It had been in accordance with his instructions that I had been showering at the time.

"What are those things?" I asked. I referred to two objects. One was a large carton and the other was a weighty, sturdy metal box, about three feet square. The metal box looked as though it would fit into the carton, and, presumably, had been removed from it, after having been brought into the room.

"Never mind them now," he said.

The metal box appeared extremely heavy and strong. It reminded me of a safe. I wondered if it was. Too, I wondered why it had been brought to the apartment.

"Is that a safe?" I asked, indicating the box. It was sitting on the rug, like the carton. It was squat and stout, and efficient looking. Because of its weight it was impressed, with sharp lines, into the rug.

"Not really," he said. "But it may be used for the securing of valuables."

I nodded. There seemed little doubt about that. It appeared to me, indeed, that it might serve very well, in virtue of its strength and weight, for the securing of valuables. I conjectured that I, with my strength, would scarcely be able to move it about.

"What is in it?" I asked. I was curious. In the side of the box facing me I could see two small holes, about the size of pennies. I could not, however, because of the light, and the size of the holes, see into the interior of the box. The interior of the box was, from my point of view, frustratingly dark.

"Nothing," he said.

"I see," I said, in an acid tone. I was certain he was not being candid with me.

"Come over here," he said, pleasantly, beckoning to me.

I joined him.

I glanced over at my robe on the easy chair, and the slippers at its foot.

"My robe and slippers," I said, "were in the bathroom, were they not?"

"Yes," he said.

"You then entered the bathroom while I was showering, and removed them, did you not?"

"Yes," he said.

I had neither seen nor heard him doing this, of course. The water had been running. The shower curtain had been drawn.

"Why?" I asked.

"We decided that you would appear before us much as you are," he said.

"But, why?" I asked.

"It would be more convenient for us," he said. "Matters might then proceed somewhat more simply for us than might otherwise have been the case."

I was angry. Obviously I had been manipulated. I had been ordered to shower. Then, while I had showered, my apartment had been entered and my robe and slippers removed from the bathroom. I had been surprised in my own apartment. Then I had been given little alternative other than to present myself before them, doubtless as they had planned, well cleaned, fresh from the shower, and half naked.

"Are you angry?" he asked.

"No," I said, suddenly, "of course not." I was suddenly afraid that they might cease to find me pleasing. Doubtless their entry into my apartment had some purpose. I was then certain I understood their motivations. They had wished to take me by surprise, to observe my reactions, to see me as though I might be confused or startled, to see how fetching and exciting I might appear, captured, so to speak, in a moment of charming disarray. I hoped I had not disappointed them. Doubtless they were interested in testing me for a performance in some commercial, perhaps having to do with soaps or beauty products. I hoped that my responses had not jeopardized my chances for participation in whatever might be their intended projects. I did so want to please them. They paid well.

He was looking down at me. He was so large and strong. I was afraid he was not pleased. I smiled my prettiest up at him. I adjusted the towel a bit about my breasts, seemingly inadvertently, accidentally, pulling it down a bit, and then, hastily, with seeming modesty, tucking it securely, much higher, even more closely, about my body. "It is only," I smiled, "that you took me by such surprise. I did not know what to do."

"I understand," he said.

"It is not every day," I said, smiling, "that a girl finds herself surprised in her own apartment and then, in effect, forced to present herself before unexpected guests clad only in a towel."

"That is true," he said.

I smiled again.

"I hope that you are still interested in me," I said, teasingly, and, I am afraid, a bit anxiously.

"Perhaps," he said.

I would have preferred a more affirmative response.

There was a moment of awkward silence. I hoped they were not disappointed. I did not want to fail to please them. I would have been willing to do anything. I would even have been willing to let them hold me in their arms, or kiss me. I would even have been willing to let them make love to me. I knew such things were common. Why should a girl not turn her charms to her own profit? I did not want them to lose interest in me. They paid well.

"The coffee is ready," he said.

"Yes," I said, gratefully. I could no longer hear it perking.

I recalled I had been told to make it.

I hurried into the kitchen.

In a few moments I was serving them coffee, in white cups on the rectangular, black-legged, white-topped formica table. The kitchen tiles felt smooth and cool under my feet. They sat about the table. I felt aroused, and very feminine, serving them. I then poured myself a cup.

"Put your cup on the floor," said the man, "there, on the tiles."

Puzzled, crouching down, I did so.

"Now, kneel behind it," he said.

I knelt down on the tiles, behind the cup, the refrigerator to my right, the table, with the men seated about it, in front of me.

They sipped their coffee.

"You may drink," said the man.

I reached for the cup, before me, on the floor. I lifted it.

"No," he said. "Do not hold it by the handle. Hold it in your hands, as a bowl."

I then sipped the coffee in this fashion, the cup warm in my fingers. I then put it down. They were using the handles of their cups, I noted. And, too, of course, they were sitting at the table. Why should they be sitting, and I kneeling, I asked myself. Are we not the same? Are we not identicals? I watched them drinking in the customary fashion. Then I, again, sipped coffee from the cup, holding it in both hands, like a small bowl. I felt an urge to put the cup aside, tear off the towel, and put my body naked to the cool tiles before them, at their feet. I wondered what the tiles would feel like against me, against my breasts, my belly, my thighs.

The men finished their coffee.

"Have you finished your coffee?" asked he who seemed in charge.

I finished the coffee, holding the cup as I had been instructed to do. "Yes," I said.

"You may clear the table," he said.

I rose to my feet and put my cup in the sink. I then went to the table. I began to gather together their cups. "What is in the metal box?" I asked, lightly.

"I told you," he said. "Nothing."

I stacked the cups and carried them to the sink. "Really?" I asked.

"Yes," he said.

"I thought maybe you were delivering something to the apartment," I said.

"No," he said.

I rinsed off the cups.

"Is it really empty?" I asked.

"Yes," he said. I put the cups in the dishwasher.

"Do you want to store the box here for a time?" I asked. "Do you want me to keep it for you, for a time?"

"No," he said.

I turned to regard them, puzzled.

The man made a sign to his two assistants and they took the table and turned it, lengthwise, in the kitchen.

"Please sit on the table, Miss Collins," said the man.

I sat on the table, at one of the small ends, that nearest the dishwasher, puzzled, my feet dangling over the edge.

"No," he said, "sit on the table, completely, your feet on it, as well."

I slid myself back and then sat on the table, completely upon it. The formica top was cool and smooth. The sensations I felt were interesting and disturbing. I had never, of course, sat on the table in this fashion before. I held the towel tightly down by my thighs. I kept them closely together. The man in charge was by my feet, on my left. The other two men were behind me.

"We did not bring the box here to bring something to the apartment," said the man, "but to take something from it."

"But I have nothing of value here," I said, "or at least not of much value."

I saw the man then remove a heavy, sturdy steel anklet from the lower, right-hand pocket of his jacket. It was open. He then flipped it widely open. I then saw it, with a casual, expert gesture, snapped shut about my left ankle.

"What are you doing!" I cried.

Something rounded and leathery was then thrust in my mouth, something attached at the back of a broad, leather rectangle, by one of the men behind me. There were straps and buckles attached to this and, apparently, a heavy, slotted leather pad which went behind the back of my neck. I felt the leather rectangle drawn tightly back and felt, too, the apparently slotted leather pad, through which the straps apparently passed, one above, and one below, pressing against the back of my neck. Then I winced as I felt the straps drawn back, even more tightly. Then they were buckled shut. The apparatus was then fixed upon me. I had been effectively gagged.

I looked wildly at the man who had put the anklet on me. I tried, wildly, with my right foot, to slide it from my left ankle. I could move it, of course, only a tiny bit. I hurt the instep of my right foot. I scraped my left ankle. I looked again, wildly, at the man who had ankleted me. There was no doubt it was fastened on me, locked shut. There had been no mistaking the heavy, efficient snap with which the device's closure had been registered.

"Now," he said, to one of his fellows, "we need not listen to her blithering."

I felt my head pulled back. There was apparently a ring at the back of the leather pad now pressed so closely into the back of my neck.

I shook my head. I whimpered.

The man then jerked the towel from my hair. I looked at him. I shook my head. He then jerked away the towel I wore on my body. I was then turned and thrown on my belly, on the table, the two assistants pressing me helplessly against it, holding me tightly down by the arms. The men, when I had been stripped, had not even paused to look at me. They had seen, I gathered, many women.

I felt a piece of cotton or cloth touch my back, above and behind my left hip. It was wet. The area then felt cool. Then I whimpered. I felt a needle being entered into my flesh, in the center of that chemically chilled area. Tears sprang to my eyes. The needle was then withdrawn and I felt the area swabbed again with fluid. I was then drawn from the table and, by the arms, carried into the combination living and dining room of my small apartment. Their leader then, he who had ankleted me, opened the side of the stout, metal container. It had a heavy door. Inside were various straps, and rings.

I tried to struggle.

"Resistance is useless, Miss Collins," said the man.

I looked at him pleadingly.

Then I was thrust, in a sitting position, into the box. The ring at the back of the gag, doubtless sewn into the slotted leather pad, was snapped about a ring mounted at a matching height in the box. My head was thus held in place. For a moment the room seemed to go dark and then I gathered my wits again. My left wrist, to my horror, was fastened back, and at my left side, by straps attached to a ring. My right wrist was then secured similarly. In moments both of my ankles, too, had been fastened in position. I fought to retain consciousness. Then I was thrust back further in the box. A broad leather strap was then drawn tightly about me. I winced. Then it was buckled shut. I could hardly move. I looked at the men, from the box. My eyes pleaded with them.

"She is secured," said one of the men.

The man in charge nodded. "Close the container," he said.

I looked at the door. There was no handle or device for opening it on my side, and, even had there been, I could not, restrained as I was, have begun to reach it.

I whimpered piteously, as an utterly helpless, restrained woman. I looked at them, piteously. They must show me mercy!

Then the door was closed.

I was plunged into darkness, save for the tiny bits of light coming through the two small, round holes on my right, near my face.

When the door had closed two snap-fastenings had shut, one near the top of the door and one near its bottom. I then sat inside, helpless. I heard ten screw bolts twisted shut, unhurriedly. Three were along the top of the door and three were along the bottom of the door; two each were at the sides of the door, two between the hinges and two between the locks.

Earlier I had asked the man if the box might have been a safe. I had gathered from his response that it was not really a safe but that it might, indeed, upon occasion, be used in the securing of valuables.

I struggled in the straps, helpless.

I wondered if I might take some bitter consolation in his laconic response, which now seemed so ironic. Perhaps I, now so well secured within the box, might, at least, count as a valuable.

I pressed my head back against the iron behind me. I heard the movement of the two rings.

But how valuable could I really be, I asked myself. I doubted, frankly, that I could be of much value. If I were really of value, of much value, I did not think I would be fastened like this, strapped naked in a box.

I tried to peer out the small holes in the door.

I could see very little, a part of the upper wall in the apartment, a small framed print, of flowers, which had been there when I had rented the apartment.

The box was then lifted, apparently by handles.

I suddenly felt extremely faint. I fought against the loss of consciousness.

The box was then lowered into the cardboard carton.

I turned my head, moaning. I heard the clink of the two rings. I tried to move my wrists and ankles. I could hardly move them. The broad leather strap, buckled shut, pressed, too, deeply into my belly, holding me in place.

Outside of the two small holes now lay the cardboard. I could see a little light from the overhead lamp.

I turned my head and struck with the side of it against the iron behind me.

"Do not be stupid, bitch," said the man outside the box.

I sobbed.

I fought more fiercely to retain consciousness.

Because of the rings and straps, and the closeness with which they held me to the wall, I could gain little leverage. I could do little more than tap or rub my head against the iron.

I had indeed been stupid. Even under ideal conditions, fully conscious, and with an abundance of possible rescuers in the vicinity, any girl confined and gagged as expertly as I was would be able to do very little to call attention to her captivity. It was unlikely that even her fiercest and most desperate signals would be audible more than a yard or so from her tiny prison.

I began to moan and whimper. They must show me mercy!

The top of the cardboard carton was then closed.

I struggled, fiercely, for a moment, but then felt exhausted. I heard a segment of sealing tape torn from a roll and then, apparently, the top of the carton was sealed shut.

I put my head back against the iron. The two rings made a tiny sound. I became very conscious of the feel of the leather straps binding me. I pressed back. This eased the pressure of the strap at my belly. I felt my hair, still damp from the shower, between my back and the iron. Beneath my body, where I sat upon it, the iron felt cool, smooth and hard. I felt it this way, too, beneath my heels.

Then the carton was lifted, and was being carried. It would appear to be a carton in the care of professional moving men.

No one would think twice about it.

The thought crossed my mind that it was Tuesday evening. Tomorrow would be Wednesday, my day off at the store. I would not be missed until Thursday.

I then lost consciousness.

# 3

# CORCYRUS

It was warm in the room.

It seemed a lazy morning.

My fingers felt at the red-silk coverlet. I lay on my stomach on the soft, broad, red-silk surface. I tried to collect my wits. I moved my body, a little. I felt the soft silk move beneath it. I was nude. Too, I felt the warm air on my body and legs. I was not covered. I was lying nude, uncovered, on my stomach, on a wide, soft, silken surface.

I remembered the men, the straps and the box.

I turned and sprang to my hands and knees on the soft surface. I was on a vast bed, or couch. It was round and some fifteen feet in diameter. I was, half sunk in its softness, near the center of it. I had not realized such luxury could exist. A glance informed me, to my relief, that I was alone in the room. The room was a large one, and extremely colorful. The floor was of glossy, scarlet tiles. The walls, too, were tiled, and glossy, and covered with bold, swirling designs, largely worked out in yellow and black tiles. At one point there was a large, scarlet pelt on the floor. Against some of the walls there were chests, heavy chests, which opened from the top. There were mirrors, too, here and there, and one was behind something like a low vanity. I also saw a small, low table. It was near the couch. There were also, mostly near the walls, some cushions about. To one side there was a large, sunken basin. This was, perhaps, I thought, a tub. There was no water in it, however, and no visible faucets. I saw myself in one of the mirrors, on all fours in the great bed. I hastily looked away. To one side there appeared to be some sliding doors. On my right, and several feet away, there was, too, a heavy wooden door. It looked as though it might be very thick. I saw no way, no bars or locks, no chains or bolts, whereby its closure might be guaranteed on my side. It might be locked on the outside, I supposed. But, clearly, I could not lock it from the inside. I could not keep anyone out. I could, on the other hand, doubtless be kept in. At one point on the floor there was, fixed in the floor, a heavy metal ring. I also saw, in one wall, two such rings. One was mounted in the wall about a yard from the floor and the other, about a yard to its left, was mounted in the wall, about six feet from the floor.

I quickly, frightened, crawled back off the bed. It was not easy to do, given its softness. I felt the smoothness, the coolness, of the scarlet tiles on my feet. I saw that there was, anchored at one point in the couch, at what may have served as its foot, another such sturdy ring. Beneath it lay a coil of chain. Smaller rings, too, I noted, circling the couch, appeared at regular intervals about its perimeter, about every four or five feet, or so. Beneath these, however, there lay no chains. I fled to the window, which was narrow, about fifteen inches in width. It was set with heavy bars, spaced about three inches apart, reinforced with thick, flat, steel crosspieces, spaced at about every vertical foot. I shook the bars. They did not budge. I hurt my hands. I stood there for a moment, the shadows of the bars and crosspieces falling across my face and body. Then I fled back to the couch and, fearfully, crawled onto it.

There seemed something different, frighteningly so, about this place in which I now found myself. It seemed almost as though it might not be Earth. This did not have to do primarily with the room, and its appointments and furnishings, but rather with such things as the condition of my body and the very quality of the air I was breathing. I supposed this was the result of the lingering effects of the substance with which I had been sedated or drugged. The gravity seemed different, subtly so, from that of Earth. Too, my entire body felt alive and charged with oxygen. The air itself seemed vivifying and stimulating. These things, which appeared to be objective aspects of the environment were doubtless merely subjective illusions on my part, resulting from the drug or sedative. They had to be. The obviously suggested alternative would be just too unthinkable, just too absurd. I hoped I had not gone mad.

I sat on the bed, my chin on my knees. I became aware that I was very hungry.

One thing, at least, assured me that I had not gone mad. That thing supplied a solid reference point in this seemingly incredible transition between environments. It had been locked on me in my own kitchen. It was a steel anklet. I still wore it.

I looked over to one of the mirrors. I looked small, sitting on the great bed. I was nude. I wondered in whose bed I was.

I then heard a sound at the door.

Terrified I knelt on the bed, snatching up a portion of the coverlet on which I knelt, and held it tightly, defensively, about me.

The door opened, admitting a small, exquisite, dark-haired woman. She wore a brief, whitish, summery, floral-print tunic, almost diaphanous, with a plunging neckline. The print was a tasteful scattering of delicate yellow flowers, perhaps silk-screened in place. The garment was belted, and rather snugly, with two turns of a narrow, silken, yellow cord, knotted at her left hip. She was barefoot. I noted that she did not wear an anklet, such as I wore. There was something on her neck, however, something fastened closely about it, encased in a silken yellow sheath or sleeve. I did not know what it was. It could not be metal, of course. That would be terrifying. I noted that the door, which now closed behind her, was some six inches thick.

"Oh," said the girl, softly, startled, seeing me, and knelt. She put her head down, and then lifted it. "Forgive me, Mistress," she said. "I did not know whether or not you were yet awake. I did not knock, for fear of disturbing you."

"What do you want?" I asked.

"I have come to serve Mistress," she said. "I have come to see if Mistress desires aught."

"Who are you?" I asked.

"Susan," she said.

"Susan who?" I asked.

"Only Susan," she said.

"I do not understand," I said.

"That is what I have been named," she said.

"Named?" I asked.

"Yes, Mistress," she said.

"I am Tiffany," I said. "Tiffany Collins."

"Yes, Mistress," she said.

"Where am I?" I asked.

"In the city of Corcyrus," she said.

I had never heard of this city. I did not even know what country it was in. I did not even know in what continent it might be.

"In what country is this?" I asked.

"In the country of Corcyrus," she said.

"That is the city," I said.

"You are then in the dominions of Corcyrus, Mistress," she said.

"Where is Corcyrus?" I asked.

"Mistress?" asked the girl, puzzled.

"Where is Corcyrus?" I asked.

"It is here," she said, puzzled. "We are in Corcyrus."

"I see that I am to be kept in ignorance," I said, angrily, clutching the coverlet about my neck.

"Corcyrus," said the girl, "is south of the Vosk. It is southwest of the city of Ar. It lies to the east and somewhat north of Argentum."

"Where is New York City?" I asked. "Where are the United States?"

"They are not here, Mistress," smiled the girl.

"Where is the ocean?" I asked.

"It is more than a thousand pasangs to the west, Mistress," said the girl.

"Is it the Atlantic Ocean or the Pacific Ocean?" I asked.

"No, Mistress," said the girl.

"It is the Indian Ocean?" I asked.

"No, Mistress," said the girl.

I looked at her, puzzled.

"It is Thassa, the Sea, Mistress," said the girl.

"What sea is it?" I asked.

"That is how we think of her," said the girl, "as the sea, Thassa."

"Oh," I said, bitterly.

"Has Mistress noted certain feelings or sensations in her body, perhaps of a sort with which she is unfamiliar?" asked the girl. "Has Mistress noted any unusual qualities in the air she is breathing?"

"Perhaps," I said. These things I had construed as the lingering effects of the substance which had been injected into me, rendering me unconscious.

"Would Mistress like for me to have her bath prepared?" she asked.

"No," I said. "I am clean."

"Yes, Mistress," she said. I realized, uneasily, that I must have been cleaned.

"I have been perfumed, have I not?" I asked. I did not know if the room had been perfumed, or if it were I.

"Yes, Mistress," said the girl.

I pulled the coverlet up, even more closely, about my neck. I felt its soft silk on my naked, perfumed body. The perfume was exquisitely feminine.

"Am I still a virgin?" I asked.

"I suppose so," said the girl. "I do not know."

I looked uneasily at the heavy door, behind her. I did not know who might enter that door, to claim me.

"In whose bed am I?" I asked.

"In your own, Mistress," said the girl.

"Mine?" I asked.

"Yes, Mistress," she said.

"Whose room is this?" I demanded.

"Yours, Mistress," said the girl.

"There are bars at the window," I said.

"They are for your protection, Mistress," said the girl. "Such bars are not unusual in the rooms of women in Corcyrus."

I looked at the girl in the light, floral-print tunic, kneeling a few feet from the bed. It was almost diaphanous. It was not difficult to detect the lineaments of her beauty beneath it. It seemed a garment which was, in its way, demure and yet, at the same time, extremely provocative. To see a woman in such a garment, I suspected, might drive a man half mad with passion. I wondered what was concealed in the silken sheath about her neck.

"Why have I been brought here?" I asked. "What am I doing here?"

"I do not know, Mistress," said the girl. "I am not one such as would be informed."

"Oh," I said. I did not fully understand her response.

"Is Mistress hungry?" she inquired.

"Yes," I said. I was ravenous.

Smiling the girl rose lightly to her feet and left the room.

I left the bed and stood then on the tiles, near the bed, the coverlet still held about me, almost like a great cloak. The tiles felt cool to the bottoms of my feet. The weather seemed warm and sultry. I wondered if I might be in Africa or Asia. I looked at the rings on the couch, at the ring in the floor, and the two rings in the wall, one about a yard from the floor and one about six feet from the floor.

I looked at the door. There was a handle on my side of the door, but no way to lock or bar it, at least from my side.

I heard a noise, and stepped back.

The door opened and the girl, carrying a tray, smiling, entered.

"Mistress is up," she said. She then set the tray down on the small table. She arranged the articles on the tray, and then brought a cushion from the side of the room and placed it by the table. There was, on the tray, a plate of fruit, some yellow, wedge-shaped bread, and a bowl of hot, rich-looking, dark-brown, almost-black fluid.

"Let me relieve Mistress of the coverlet," she said, approaching me.

I shrank back.

"It is too warm for it," she smiled, reaching for it.

I again stepped back.

"I have washed Mistress many times," she said. "And Mistress is very beautiful. Please."

I let the coverlet slip to my hips. There was no mistaking the admiration in the eyes of the girl. This pleased me. I let her remove it from me. "Yes," she said, "Mistress is quite beautiful."

"Thank you," I said.

She folded the coverlet and placed it on the great couch.

"Susan," I said. "That is your name?"

"Yes, Mistress," smiled the girl.

"What are these rings?" I asked, indicating the heavy ring in the floor, and the two rings in the wall.

"They are slave rings, Mistress," said the girl.

"What is their purpose?" I asked, frightened.

"Slaves may be tied or chained to them," said the girl.

"There are slaves, then, in this place?" I asked. This thought, somehow, alarmed me, terribly. Yet, too, at the same time, I found it inordinately moving and exciting. The thought of myself as a slave and what this might mean suddenly flashed through my mind. For an instant I was so thrilled, so shaken with the significance of this, that I could scarcely stand.

"There are true men in this place," explained the girl.

"Oh," I said. I did not understand her remark. Did she not know that true men repudiated their natural sovereignty, forsook their manhood and conformed to prescribed stereotypes?

Was she not familiar with the political definitions? I wondered then if there might not be another sort of true men, true men, like true lions, who, innocent of negativistic conditionings, simply fulfilled themselves in the way of nature. Such men, I supposed, of course, could not exist. They, presumably, in the way of nature, would be less likely to pretend that women were the same as themselves than to simply relish them, to keep them, to dominate, own and treasure them, perhaps like horses or dogs, or, I thought, with a shudder, women.

"Would Mistress care to partake now of her breakfast?" asked the girl.

I was looking, fascinated, at the heavy ring set in the tiles.

"If Mistress wishes," said the girl, "she may tie me to it and whip me."

I looked at her, startled. "No," I said. "No!"

"I shall tidy the room," said the girl, "and prepare it for the convenience of Mistress."

She turned about and went to the side of the room. She began to take articles from the vanity, such as combs and brushes, and vials, and place them on its surface, before the mirror. She moved with incredible grace.

Glancing in the mirror she saw me behind her, watching her. "Mistress?" she asked.

"Nothing," I said.

She continued her work. She straightened pillows at the side of the room. She then went to one of the sliding doors at the side of the room and moved one back a few inches. She reached inside and, from the interior of the door, where it had doubtless been hanging, from a loop on its handle, removed an object.

I gasped.

"Mistress?" she asked.

"What is that?" I asked.

"A whip," she said, puzzled. Seeing my interest she brought it towards me. I stepped back. She held it across her body. Its handle was about eighteen inches long. It was white, and trimmed with yellow beads. Depending from this handle, at one end, were five, pliant yellow straps, or lashes. Each was about two and a half feet long, and one and a half inches wide.

I trembled.

I could scarcely conjecture what that might feel like laid to my body.

"Am I to be whipped?" I asked. I was terribly conscious of my nudity, my vulnerability.

"I do not think so, Mistress," laughed the girl.

I regarded the whip. I wished that she had been more affirmative in her response.

"Whose whip is it?" I asked.

"Yours, Mistress," said the girl.

"But for what purpose is it to be used?" I asked.

"It is for whipping me," she said. "It is my hope, however, that I will be so pleasing to Mistress that she will not wish to use it, or not often, on me."

"Take it away," I said. It frightened me.

The girl went to a wall and, near the large door, by a loop on its butt end, hung it from a hook. I had not noticed the hook before.

"There," said the girl, smiling. "It is prominently displayed, where we both, many times a day, may see it."

I nodded. I regarded the object. There was little mistaking its meaning.

"Susan," I said.

"Yes, Mistress," she said.

"Are there truly slaves here, in this place, in this city, or country?"

"Yes, Mistress," she said, "and generally."

I did not understand what she meant by "generally."

I felt the warm air on my body. I smelled the perfume, so delicately feminine, which had been put on me.

"You said you had been 'named' Susan," I said.

"Yes, Mistress," she said.

"The way you said that," I said, "it sounded as though you might have been named anything."

The girl shrugged, and smiled. "Of course, Mistress," she said.

"You are very pretty, Susan," I said.

"Thank you, Mistress," she said.

"These other rings," I said, indicating the rings about the couch, "are they also slave rings?"

"Yes," she said, approaching lightly, gracefully, "in their way, but most of them are only anchor rings, to which, say, chains or cords might be attached." She then crouched by the heavy ring, that with coiled chain beneath it, that fastened at what might, perhaps, count as the bottom of the couch. "But this," she said, "more appropriately, is the more typical type of ring which one thinks of as a slave ring. Do you see its resemblance to the others, that in the floor, those at the wall?"

"Yes," I said.

She lifted the ring. I could see that it was heavy. She then lowered it back into place, so that it again, in its retaining ring, fastened in a metal plate, bolted into the couch, hung parallel to the side of the couch. "By means of such a ring," she said, "a male silk slave might be chained at the foot of your couch."

The girl rose to her feet. "Surely Mistress is hungry," she said.

The light from the barred window was behind her. I also saw the shadows of the bars and crosspieces lying across the couch.

I turned and went to the low table where the tray had been placed.

"There are no chairs," I said.

"There are few chairs in Corcyrus," said the girl.

I turned to face her, almost in anguish. Something in this place terrified me.

"I have been unable to keep from noticing your garments," I said.

"Mistress?" asked the girl.

"Forgive me," I said, "but they leave little doubt as to your loveliness."

"Thank you, Mistress," said the girl.

"You are aware of how revealing they are, are you not?" I asked.

"I think so, Mistress," said the girl.

"By them the lineaments of your beauty are made publicly clear," I said.

"That is doubtless one of their intentions, Mistress," said the girl.

I suddenly felt faint.

"Mistress?" asked the girl, alarmed.

"I am all right," I said.

"Yes, Mistress," she said, relieved.

I then, slowly, walked about her, frightened. She stood still, very straight, her head up. She was incredibly lovely, and exquisitely figured.

"There is something on your left leg," I said, "high, on the thigh, just under the hip." I saw this through the almost diaphanous, white, floral-print tunic she wore.

"Yes, Mistress," she said. "It is common for girls such as I to be marked."

"Marked?" I asked.

"Yes, Mistress," she said. "Would Mistress care to see?"

Seeing my curiosity, my fascination, she drew up the skirt of the brief tunic, with both hands, and looked down to her left thigh.

"What is it?" I asked. It was a delicate mark, almost floral, about an inch and a half high and a half inch, or so, wide.

"It is my brand," she said.

I gasped.

"It was put on me in Cos," she said, "with a white-hot iron, two years ago."

"Terrible," I whispered.

"Girls such as I must expect to be marked," she said. "It is in accord with the recommendations of merchant law."

"Merchant law?" I asked.

"Yes, Mistress," said the girl. "May I lower my tunic?"

"Yes," I said.

She smoothed down the light tunic.

"It is a beautiful mark," I said.

"I think so, too," she said. "Thank you, Mistress."

"Did it hurt?" I asked.

"Yes, Mistress," she said.

"It doesn't hurt now though, does it?" I asked.

"No, Mistress," she said.

I reached out, timidly, toward her throat. I touched the object there.

"What is this?" I asked.

"The silk?" she asked. "That is a collar stocking, or a collar sleeve. They may be made of many different materials. In a cooler climate they are sometimes of velvet. In most cities they are not used."

Under the silk I touched sturdy steel.

"That, Mistress, of course," she said, "is my collar."

"Would you take it off," I asked, "please? I would like to see it."

She laughed merrily. "Forgive me, Mistress," she said. "I cannot take it off."

"Why not?" I asked.

"It is locked on me," she laughed. She turned about. "See?" she asked.

Feverishly I thrust apart the two sides of the silken sleeve at the back of the girl's neck. To be sure, there, below her hair, at the back of her neck, at the closure of the steel apparatus on her neck, there was a small, heavy, sturdy lock. I saw the keyhole. It would take a tiny key.

"You do not have the key?" I asked.

"No, Mistress," she laughed. "Of course not."

"Then you have, personally, no way of removing this collar?" I said.

"Yes, Mistress," she said. "I have no way of removing it."

I shuddered.

"May I ask you an intimate question, Susan?" I asked.

"Of course, Mistress," she said.

"Are you a virgin?" I asked.

The girl laughed. "No, Mistress," she said. "I was opened by men long ago for their pleasures."

"Opened?" I whispered.

"Yes, Mistress," she said.

"For their pleasures?" I asked.

"Yes, Mistress," she said.

"You have called me 'Mistress,' " I said. "Why?"

"That is the customary way in which girls such as I address all free women," she said.

"What sort of girl are you?" I asked.

"A good girl, I hope, Mistress," she said. "I will try to serve you well."

"Are you a slave?" I whispered.

"Yes, Mistress," she said.

I stepped back. I had tried to fight this understanding. I had told myself that it could not be, that it must not be. And yet, now, how simple, how obvious and plausible, seemed such an explanation of the girl's garb, and of the mark on her body, and of the collar on her neck.

"I am the slave of Ligurious, first minister of Corcyrus," she said. She slid the collar sleeve about the collar and, feeling with her fingers, indicated some marks on the collar. I could see engraving there. I could not read the writing. "That information," she said, "is recorded here."

"I see," I said, trembling.

She slid the collar sleeve back about the collar, arranging it in place. "I was purchased almost two years ago, from the pens of Saphronicus, in Cos," she said.

"The purpose of the collar sleeve is to hide the collar," I said.

"No, Mistress," she said. "Surely the collar's presence within the sleeve is sufficiently evident."

"Yes," I said, "I can see now that it is."

The girl smiled.

"The yellow fits in nicely with the yellow of your belt," I said, "and the yellow flowers on the tunic."

"Yes, Mistress," smiled the girl. The sleeve I saw now could function rather like an accessory, perhaps adding to, or completing, an ensemble. It did, in this case, at least, make its contribution to the girl's appearance. "The belt is binding fiber, Mistress," said the girl, turning before me. "It may be used to tie or leash me, or even, coiled, to whip me."

"I see," I said. It was a part of her ensemble.

"And the flowers," said the girl, "are talenders. They are a beautiful flower. They are often associated with love."

"They are very pretty," I said.

"Some free women do not approve of slaves being permitted to wear talenders," she said, "or being permitted to have representations of them, like these, on their frocks. Yet slaves do often wear them, the masters permitting it, and they are not an uncommon motif, the masters seeing to it, on their garments."

"Why do free women object?" I asked.

"They feel that a slave, who must love whomever she is commanded to love, can know nothing of love."

"Oh," I said.

"But I have been both free and slave," she said, "and, forgive me, Mistress, but I think that it is only a slave, in her vulnerability and helplessness, who can know what love truly is."

"You must love upon command?" I asked, horrified.

"We must do as we are told," she said. "We are slaves."

I shuddered at the thought of the helplessness of the slave.

"We may hope, of course," she said, "that we come into the power of true masters."

"Does this ever happen?" I asked.

"Often, Mistress," she said.

"Often?" I said.

"There is no dearth of true masters here," she said.

I wondered in what sort of place I might be that there might here be no dearth of true masters. In all my life, hitherto, I did not think I had ever met a man, or knowingly met a man, who was a true master. The nearest I had come, I felt, were the men I had encountered before being brought to this place, those who had treated me as though I might be nothing, and had incarcerated me in the straps and iron box. Sometimes they had made me so weak I had felt like begging them to rape or have me. I had the horrifying thought that perhaps I existed for such men.

"How degrading and debasing to be a slave!" I cried.

"Yes, Mistress," said the girl, putting down her head. I thought she smiled. She had told me, I suspected, what I had wanted to hear, what I had expected to hear.

"Slavery is illegal!" I cried.

"Not here, Mistress," she said.

I stepped back.

"Where Mistress comes from," said the girl, "it is not illegal to own animals, is it?"

"No," I said. "Of course not."

"It is the same here," she said. "And the slave is an animal."

"You are an animal—legally?" I asked.

"Yes," she said.

"Horrifying!" I cried.

"Biologically, of course," she said, "we are all animals. Thus, in a sense, we might all be owned. It thus becomes a question as to which among these animals own and which are owned, which, so to speak, count as persons, or have standing, before the law, and which do not, which are, so to speak, the citizens or persons, and which are the animals."

"It is wrong to own human beings," I said.

"Is it wrong to own other animals?" she asked.

"No," I said.

"Then why is it wrong to own human beings?" she asked.

"I do not know," I said.

"It would seem inconsistent," she said, "to suggest that it is only certain sorts of animals which may be owned, and not others."

"Human beings are different," I said.

The girl shrugged. "So, too, are tarsks and verr," she said.

I did not know those sorts of animals.

"Human beings can talk and think!" I said.

"Why should that make a difference?" she asked. "If anything, the possession of such properties would make a human being an even more valuable possession than a tarsk or verr."

"Where I come from it is wrong to own human beings but it is all right for other animals to be owned."

"If other animals made the laws where you come from," she said, "perhaps it would be wrong there to own them and right to own human beings."

"Perhaps!" I said, angrily.

"Forgive me, Mistress," said the girl. "I did not mean to displease you."

"It is wrong to own human beings!" I said.

"Can Mistress prove that?" she asked.

"No!" I said, angrily.

"How does Mistress know it?" she asked.

"It is self-evident!" I said. I knew, of course, that I was so sure of this only because I had been taught, uncritically, to believe it.

"If self-evidence is involved here," she said, "it is surely self-evident that it is not wrong to own human beings. In most cultures, traditions and civilizations with which I am familiar, the right to own human beings was never questioned. To them the rectitude of the institution of slavery was self-evident."

"Slavery is wrong because it can involve pain and hardship," I said.

"Work, too," she said, "can involve pain and hardship. Is work, thus, wrong?"

"No," I said.

She shrugged.

"Slavery is wrong," I said, "because slaves may not like it."

"Many people may not like many things," she said, "which does not make those things wrong. Too, it has never been regarded as a necessary condition for the rectitude of slavery that slaves approved of their condition."

"That is true," I said.

"See?" she asked.

"How could someone approve of slavery," I asked, "or regard it as right, if he himself did not wish to be a slave?"

"In a sense," she said, "one might approve of many things, and recognize their justifiability, without thereby wishing to become implicated personally in them. One might approve of medicine, say, without wishing to be a physician. One might approve of mathematics without desiring to become a mathematician, and so on."

"Of course," I said, irritably.

"It might be done in various ways," she said. "One might, for example, regard a society in which the institution of slavery, with its various advantages and consequences, was ingredient as a better society than one in which it did not exist. This, then, would be its justification. In such a way, then, he might approve of slavery as an institution without wishing necessarily to become a slave himself. In moral consistency, of course, in approving of the institution, he would seem to accept at least the theoretical risk of his own enslavement. This risk he would presumably regard as being a portion of the price he is willing to pay for the benefits of living in this type of society, which he regards, usually by far, as being a society superior to its alternatives. Another form of justification occurs when one believes that slavery is right and fit for certain human beings but not for others. This position presupposes that not all human beings are alike. In this point of view, the individual approves of slavery for those who should be slaves and disapproves of it, or at least is likely to regret it somewhat, in the case of those who should not be slaves. He is perfectly consistent in this, for he believes that if he himself should be a natural slave, then it would be right, too, for him to be enslaved. This seems somewhat more sensible than the categorical denial, unsubstantiated, that slavery is not right for any human being. Much would seem to depend on the nature of the particular human being."

"Slavery denies freedom!" I cried.

"Your assertion seems to presuppose the desirability of universal freedom," she said. "That may be part of what is at issue."

"Perhaps," I said.

"Is there more happiness in a society in which all are free," she asked, "than in one in which some are not free?"

"I do not know," I said. The thought of miserable, competitive, crowded, frustrated, hostile populations crossed my mind.

"Mistress?" she asked.

"I do not know!" I said.

"Yes, Mistress," said the girl.

"Slavery denies freedom!" I reiterated.

"Yes, Mistress," she said.

"It denies freedom!" I said.

"It denies some freedoms, and precious ones," said the girl. "But, too, it makes others possible, and they, too, are precious."

"People simply cannot be owned!" I said, angrily.

"I am owned," she said.

I did not speak. I was frightened.

"My Master is Ligurious, of the city of Corcyrus," she said.

"Slavery is illegal," I said, lamely.

"Not here," she said.

"People cannot be owned," I whispered, desperately, horrified.

"Here," she said, "in point of fact, aside from all questions of legality or moral propriety, or the lack thereof, putting all such questions aside for the moment, for they are actually irrelevant to the facts, people are, I assure you, owned."

"People are in fact owned?" I asked.

"Yes," she said. "And fully."

"Then, truly," I said, "there are slaves here. There are slaves in this place."

"Yes," she said. "And generally."

Again I did not understand the meaning of "generally." She spoke almost as though we might not be on Earth, somewhere on Earth.

My heart was beating rapidly. I put my hand to my bosom. I looked about the room, frightened. It was like no other room I had ever been in. It did not seem that it would be in England or America. I did not know where I was. I did not even know on what continent I might be. I looked at the girl. I was in the presence of a slave, a woman who was owned. Her master was Ligurious, of this city, said to be Corcyrus. I looked to the barred window, to the soft expanses of that great, barbaric couch, to the chain at its foot, to the rings fixed in it, and elsewhere, to the whip on its hook, to the door which I could not lock on my side. I was again terribly conscious of my nudity, my vulnerability.

"Susan," I said.

"Yes, Mistress," she said.

"Am I a slave?" I asked.

"No, Mistress," said the girl.

I almost fainted with relief. The room, for a moment, seemed to swirl about me. I was unspeakably pleased to discover that I was not a slave, and then, suddenly, unaccountably, I felt an inexplicable anguish. I realized, suddenly, shaken, that there was something within me that wanted to be owned. I looked at the girl. She was owned! In that instant I envied her her collar.

"I am a slave!" I said, angrily. "Look at me! Do you doubt that I am a slave? I am wearing only an anklet and perfume!"

"Mistress is not marked. Mistress is not collared," said the girl.

"I am a slave!" I said. I wondered, when I said this, if I was only insisting that I was a slave, that I must be a slave, because of such things as the barred window and the anklet, or if I was speaking what lay in my heart.

"Mistress is free," said the girl.

"I cannot be free," I said.

"If Mistress is not free," she said, "who is Mistress' master?"

"I do not know," I said, frightened. I wondered if I did belong to someone and simply did not yet know it.

"I know Mistress is free," said the girl.

"How do you know?" I asked.

"Ligurious, my master, has told me," she said.

"But I am naked," I said.

"Mistress had not yet dressed," she said. She then went to the sliding doors at the side of the room, and moved them aside. Thus were revealed the habiliments of what was apparently an extensive and resplendent wardrobe.

She brought forth a lovely, brief, lined, sashed, shimmering yellow-silk robe and, holding it up, displayed it for me.

I was much taken by it, but it seemed almost excitingly sensuous.

"Have you nothing simpler, nothing plainer, nothing coarser?" I asked.

"Something more masculine?" asked the girl.

"Yes," I said, uncertainly. I had not really thought of it exactly like that, or not consciously, but it now seemed to me as if that might be right.

"Does Mistress wish to dress like a man?" she asked.

"No," I said, "I suppose not. Not really."

"I can try to find a man's clothing for Mistress if she wishes," said the girl.

"No," I said. "No." It was not really that I wanted to wear

a man's clothing, literally. It was only that I thought that it might be better to wear a more mannish type of clothing. After all, had I not been taught that I was, for most practical purposes, the same as a man, and not something deeply and radically different? Too, such garb has its defensive purposes. Is it not useful, for example, in helping a girl to keep men from seeing her as what she is, a woman?

"Mistress," said the girl, helping me on with the silken robe. I belted the yellow-silk sash. The hem of the robe came high on the thighs. I looked at myself, startled, in the mirror. In such a garment, lovely, clinging, short, closely belted, there was no doubt that I was a woman.

"Mistress is beautiful!" said the girl.

"Thank you," I said. I turned, back and forth, looking at myself in the mirror.

I adjusted the belt, making it a little tighter. The girl smiled.

"Are such garments typical of this place?" I asked.

"Does Mistress mean," asked the girl, "that here sexual differences are clearly marked by clothing, that here sexual differences are important and not blurred, that men and women dress differently here?"

"Yes," I said.

"Yes," she said. "The answer is 'Yes,' Mistress."

"Sexuality is important here, then?" I said.

"Yes, Mistress," she said. "Here sexuality is deeply and fundamentally important, and here women are not men, and men are not women. The sexes are quite different, and here each is true to itself."

"Oh," I said.

"By means of different garbs, then," she said, "it is natural that these important and fundamental differences be marked, the garbs of men being appropriate to their nature, for example, to their size and strength, and those of women to their nature, for example, to their softness and beauty."

"I see," I said. I was a bit frightened. In this place, I gathered, the fact that I was a woman was not irrelevant to what I was. That I was a woman was, I gathered, at least in this place, something fundamentally important about me. This fact would be made clear about me even by the clothing which I wore. I glanced at the wardrobe. Deceit and subterfuge, I suspected, were not in those fabrics. They were such, I suspected, as would mark me as a woman and even proclaimed me as such. How would I fare in such a place, I wondered, where it might be difficult to conceal or deny my sex. How terrified I was at the thought that I might have to be true to my sex, that I might have little choice here but to be what I was, a woman, and wholly. I looked in the mirror. That is what I am here, I thought, a woman.

There was a sudden, loud knock at the door.

I cried out, startled. The girl turned white, and then, facing the door, immediately dropped to her knees. She cried out something, frightened. The door opened.

A large man stood framed in the doorway. He seemed agile and strong. He glanced about. His eyes seemed piercing. He had broad shoulders and long arms. His hair was cut rather short, and was brown, flecked with gray. He wore a white tunic, trimmed in red. He looked at me and I almost fainted. It was something in his eyes. I knew I had never seen a man like this before. There was something different about him, from all other men I had seen. It was almost as though a lion had taken human form.

"It is Ligurious, my Master," said the girl, her head now down to the floor, the palms of her hands on the tiles.

I swallowed hard, and then tried, desperately, to meet the man's gaze. I must show him that I was a true person.

"Get on the bed," he said. His voice had an accent. I could not place it.

I fled to the bed and crept obediently upon it.

He came to the edge of the bed and looked down at me. I half lay, half crouched on the bed. I was very conscious of the shortness of the robe I wore.

He said something to Susan and she sprang up and came to the edge of the bed. He said something else to her. I did not understand the language, or even recognize it.

"He says he thinks you will prove quite suitable," she said to me, in English.

"For what?" I begged.

"I do not know, Mistress," she said.

"Get on your back," he said.

Immediately, obediently, I lay supine before him.

"Raise your right knee, and extend your left leg," he said, "palms of your hands at your sides, facing upward."

I immediately assumed this position. I felt very vulnerable, particularly, interestingly, as the palms of my hands were exposed. I began to breathe deeply. I was terrified. I also realized, suddenly, that I was very aroused, sexually, obeying him.

The man glanced to the side. He said something to the girl. "He notes that you have not touched your breakfast," she said.

I moaned. I hoped that he was not displeased. It had been safe to displease the men I had hitherto known, or most of them. They might be displeased with impunity. I was afraid, however, to displease this man. I did not think he would accept being displeased. He, I was sure, would simply punish me, and well. He might even kill me.

He looked down at me.

I was much aroused. I whimpered. I expected him to rape me. I was even eager to be raped, anything to please him.

I felt his hand take my ankle. I was so charged with sensation that I almost fainted at the touch. Then I became aware that his grip was like steel. Then I saw him take a string from about his neck. On this string there was a tiny key. Startled, I felt the key inserted in the lock on my anklet. Then the anklet was removed. I lay trembling on the bed.

He stood there then, looking down at me, the anklet, string and key in his hand. I then realized, partly in relief, and, in a part of me, with disappointment, that I was not then, or at least not then, to be raped. I was not then to feel his strong hands on me, forcing me, as a woman, imperiously to his will.

"May I speak?" I whispered.

"Yes," he said.

"Who are you?" I asked. "Who is she? Where am I? What am I doing here? What do you want of me?"

"I am Ligurious, first minister of Corcyrus," he said. "She is unimportant. Her name is Susan. She is a slave."

"No," I said. "I mean, who is Ligurious? Who are you? I have never heard of you."

"You need know little more of me than that I am the first minister of Corcyrus," he said.

I looked at him. He must have some connection, of course, with the men who had come to my apartment. He had a key for the anklet.

"Where am I?" I asked.

"In Corcyrus," he said.

"But where is Corcyrus?" I begged. "I do not even know in what part of the world I am!"

He looked at me, puzzled.

The girl said something to him. He smiled.

"Am I in Africa?" I asked. "Am I in Asia?"

"Have you not noticed subtle differences in the gravity here," he asked, "from what you have been accustomed to? Have you not noticed that the air here seems somewhat different from that with which you have hitherto been familiar?"

"I have seemed to notice such things," I said, "but I was drugged in my apartment. Obviously such sensations are delusory, merely the effects of that drug."

"The drug," he said, "does not produce such effects."

"What are you telling me?" I asked, frightened.

"After a short while," he said, "you will no longer think of these things. You will not even notice them, or, at least, not consciously. You will have made your adjustments and accommodations. You will have become acclimated, so to speak. At most you may occasionally become aware that you are now experiencing a condition of splendid vitality and health."

"What are you telling me?" I asked, frightened.

"This is not Earth," he said. "This is another planet."

I regarded him, disbelievingly.

"Does this seem to be Earth to you?" he asked.

"No," I whispered.

"Does this seem to be a room of Earth to you?" he asked.

"No," I said.

"You have been brought here by spaceship," he said.

I could not speak.

"The technology involved is more sophisticated, more advanced, than that with which you are familiar," he said.

"But you speak English," I said. "She speaks English!"

"I have learned some English," he said. "She, however, speaks it natively." He turned to the girl. He said something to her.

"I have been given permission to speak," she said. "I am from Cincinnati, Ohio, Mistress," she said.

"She was brought to this world more than two years ago," he said.

"My original name was Susan," she said. "My last name does not matter. When I became a slave, of course, my name was gone. Animals do not have names, except as their masters might choose to name them. The name 'Susan' was again put upon me, but now, of course, I have it only as a slave name."

"Why was she brought here?" I asked.

"For the usual reason for which an Earth female is brought here," he said.

"What is that?" I asked.

"To be a slave," he said.

He then turned to the girl and said something. She nodded. He then turned again to me. "You may break position," he said.

I rolled to my stomach on the couch, clutching at it. I shuddered.

I was not on Earth.

"Why have I been brought here?" I asked. "To be a slave, to be branded, to wear a collar, to serve some man as though he might be my master."

"He would be your master," said the man, very evenly, very quietly, very menacingly.

I nodded, frightened. It was true, of course. If I were a slave then he who was my master would indeed be my master, and totally. I could be owned as completely, and easily, as Susan, or any other woman.

"But I think you will be pleased to learn what we have in store for you," he said.

"What?" I asked, turning to my side, pulling the robe down on my thighs.

"In time," he said, "I think things will become clearer to you."

"I see," I said.

"Do you have any other questions?" he asked.

I half rose up on the couch, my left leg under me, my palms on the surface of the couch. "Am I still a virgin?" I asked.

"Yes," he said.

This pleased me. I would not have wished to have lost my virginity while unconscious. A girl would at least like to be aware of it when it happens. Too, I was pleased because I thought that the possession of my virginity might make me somehow more valuable. Perhaps I could use it somehow to improve my position in this world. Perhaps I could somehow use it as a prize which I might award for gain, or as a bargaining device in some negotiation in which I might be involved. Then I looked into the eyes of Ligurious, first minister of Corcyrus. I shuddered. I realized then that my virginity, on this world, was nothing, and that it might simply be taken from me, rudely and peremptorily, whenever men might please.

Ligurious then turned and left the room. As he had left the room, though he had scarcely noticed her, Susan had knelt, with her head to the tiles. She now rose to her feet.

"Earlier," I said, "your master, when beside the couch, said something to you. What was it?"

"It is his desire," she said, "that you eat."

I quickly left the couch and went to the small table, on which the tray reposed. I did not wish to displease Ligurious. He was the sort of man who was to be obeyed, immediately and perfectly.

I loosened my robe and sat down, cross-legged, on the cushion before the table. I picked up a piece of the yellow bread.

"Oh, no, Mistress," said the girl, putting out her hand. "That is how men sit. We are women. We kneel."

"I will sit," I told her.

"Mistress understands, surely," said the girl, in misery, "that I must make reports to Ligurious, my master."

"I will kneel," I said.

"That is much more lovely," said the girl, approvingly.

I then began to eat, kneeling. This posture, to be sure, though I do not think I would have admitted it to the girl, did strike me as being much more feminine than that which I had earlier adopted. Certainly, at least, it made me feel much more feminine. I wondered if there was a certain rightness to women kneeling. Certainly we look beautiful, kneeling. The posture, too, at least if we are permitted to keep our knees closed, permits us a certain modest reserve with respect to our intimacies. Too, it is a position which one may assume easily and beautifully, and from which it is possible to rise with both beauty and grace. To be sure, the position does suggest not only beauty and grace but also submissiveness. This thought troubled me. But then I thought that if women should be submissive, then, whatever might be the truth in these matters, such postures would be appropriate and natural for them. In any event, the posture did make me feel delicately and exquisitely feminine. I was somewhat embarrassed, to be sure, by these feelings. Then it suddenly seemed absurd to me that I should be embarrassed, or should feel guilty or ashamed, about these feelings. I think I then realized, perhaps for the first time, fully, the power of the conditioning devices to which I had been subjected. How strange, and pernicious, I thought, that a woman should be made to feel guilty about being feminine, truly feminine, radically feminine! What a tribute this was to the effectiveness of contemporary conditioning techniques! In the world from which I came sexuality was not an ingredient but an accessory. Here, on the other hand, I suspected, men and women were not the same. Indeed, it seemed that here I would be expected to assume certain postures and attitudes, and genuinely feminine ones, perhaps merely because I was a woman. In this world it seemed that sexuality, and perhaps a deeply natural sexuality, was an ingredient, and not a mere accessory. It might lie at the very core of this world. An essential and ineradicable element in this world, culturally, appeared to be sexuality, with its basic distinctions between human beings, dividing them clearly into different sorts, into males and females. In a world such as this I realized that I might not only be permitted to express my natural, fundamental nature, but that I might be encouraged to do so. This was a world in which my femininity, whatever it was, and wherever it might lead, was not to be denied to me. I glanced at the whip on the wall. On this world, I suspected, I might even be given no choice but to be true to my sex, and fully. For a moment this made me angry. Surely I had a right to frustrate and deny my sex if I wished! If I was afraid to be a woman, truly and fundamentally, with all that it might entail, surely I should not be forced to become one! Yet I knew that in my heart I felt a sudden, marvelous surge of hope, a sense of possible liberation, that I might here, on this world, be freed, even if I were placed in a steel collar, to be what I truly was, not merely a human being, but the kind of human being I actually was, a human female, a woman.

"Mistress' drink is cold," said the girl. "Let me have it reheated or fetch you a fresh one."

"No," I said. "It is fine." I lifted the small, handleless bowl in two hands. I was excited that she had used the word "fetch." She was the sort of girl who might carry or fetch for Masters and Mistresses.

"No, Mistress," said the girl. "You are a woman. Drink more delicately."

I then sipped from the bowl.

"Yes, Mistress," she said. "That is more feminine." I then realized, even more profoundly than before, how deeply sexuality must characterize and penetrate this culture. The differences between men and women were to be expressed even in their smallest behaviors. What a significant and real thing it is in this culture to be a man or a woman.

"This is warmed chocolate," I said, pleased. It was very rich and creamy.

"Yes, Mistress," said the girl.

"It is very good," I said.

"Thank you, Mistress," she said.

"Is it from Earth?" I asked.

"Not directly," she said. "Many things here, of course, ultimately have an Earth origin. It is not improbable that the beans from which the first cacao trees on this world were grown were brought from Earth."

"Do the trees grow near here?" I asked.

"No, Mistress," she said. "We obtain the beans, from which the chocolate is made, from Cosian merchants, who, in turn, obtain them in the tropics."

I put the chocolate down. I began to bite at the yellow bread. It was fresh.

"Perhaps Mistress should take smaller bites," she said.

"Very well," I said. I then began to eat as she had suggested. I was a woman. I was not an adolescent boy. Again, even in so small a thing as this, I began to feel my femininity keenly. Too, again, I became very sensitive of the depth and pervasiveness of the sexuality which might characterize this world. Men and women did not even eat in the same way.

"Exceptions can occur under certain circumstances, of course," said the girl. "Mistress might, for example, in the presence of a man she wishes to arouse, take a larger than normal bite from a fresh fruit, and look at the man over the fruit, letting juice, a tiny trickle of it, run at the side of her mouth."

"But why would I wish to arouse a man?" I asked.

The girl looked at me, puzzled. "Perhaps the needs of Mistress might be much upon her," she said. "Perhaps she might wish to be taken and overwhelmed in his arms, and forced to surrender to him."

"I do not understand," I said, as though horrified.

"That is because Mistress is free," she said.

I had understood only too well, of course. But I was terrified to even think such thoughts.

"Slaves, I suppose, occasionally have recourse to such devices," I said. I was eager to learn.

"A device such as that with the fresh fruit," she said, "is more appropriate to a free woman. We do have at our disposal, as slaves, however, a number and variety of begging signals, such things as groveling and moaning, and bringing bonds to him in our teeth, wherewith we may endeavor to call our needs to his attention."

"Begging signals?" I said.

"We are at the complete mercy of our masters," she said.

"Are the masters then kind to you?" I asked.

"Sometimes they consent to content us," she said.

"How horrifying to be a slave," I said.

"Yes, Mistress," she said, putting her head down, smiling. I saw that, again, she was answering me in the fashion in which, doubtless, I wished to be answered, doubtless with deference to my dignity, status or freedom. Sorely then I envied her her collar. My feelings now began to alarm me. I decided that it would be safest to change the subject.

"Where are the spaceships?" I asked.

"Spaceships?" she asked.

"Yes," I said.

"I do not know," she said. "I have never even seen one."

"Oh," I said.

"Has Mistress?" she asked.

"No," I said. I gathered that Susan, like myself, had been brought to this world unconscious. We knew nothing, or almost nothing, of how we had come here.

"The people of this world have very little evidence," she said, "that such things even exist. The only evidence they have, for the most part, is that of certain objects brought from Earth."

"Objects?" I asked.

"Yes," she said. "Usually girls, in chains."

"You refer to them as 'objects'?" I asked, horrified.

"Yes, Mistress," she said. "They are slaves."

"I see," I said.

"This world is, as Mistress will discover," said the girl, "on the whole a very primitive and barbaric place. Do not expect to see complex machines and spaceships."

"Oh," I said.

"I do not even think that such ships are housed on this world," she said. "I think they merely visit it, from elsewhere."

"Surely men must come and go between here and Earth," I said.

"Perhaps, Mistress," she said. "But I know nothing of it."

"Have you no hope of returning to Earth?" I asked.

"Look at me, Mistress," she smiled. "I am half naked. I am branded. I am collared. I do not think I was brought to this world to be returned to Earth."

"But surely you wish to return to Earth," I said.

"No, Mistress," she said.

"But you are branded and collared," I said. "You are a slave!"

"It is my lot, Mistress," she said. "I am not discontent."

"But, why?" I asked.

"There are true men here," she said.

"I do not understand," I said.

"A thousand times better a collar on Gor than freedom on Earth," she said.

"I do not understand," I said.

"That is because Mistress is not a slave," she said.

"May I call you 'Susan'?" I asked.

"Of course, Mistress," she said.

"You need not call me 'Mistress,' " I said. "You may call me 'Tiffany.' "

"No, please, Mistress!" said the girl, turning white. "Please, no!"

"Very well," I said. I saw that she was under some strict and superb discipline.

"At the very least," I said, "I want us to be friends."

"No, Mistress, please," she said.

"But you are a girl from Earth," I said. "You are an American. I am an American."

"Please, no, Mistress," she begged.

"You are from Cincinnati, Ohio, in America," I said.

"I am a female slave," she said.

"Why can we not be friends?" I asked.

"You are free, and I am only a slave," she said.

I looked at her.

"I will try to serve Mistress well," she said. "Whip me, if I do not please you."

"Very well," I said. I thought that I was now beginning to

understand something of the discipline under which slaves might be held. I wondered what it would be like to be under such discipline. I shuddered.

"Does Mistress enjoy her breakfast?" asked the girl.

"Yes," I said.

"Good," she said.

"Susan," I said.

"Yes, Mistress," she said.

"This seems to be a very sexual world," I said.

"Yes, Mistress," she said.

"Are women safe here?" I asked.

"No, Mistress," she said. "Not really."

"You said earlier," I said, "that I was very beautiful." She had seen me naked.

"Yes, Mistress," said the girl.

"Do you think that men here, on this world, might find me of interest?"

"Do you mean *really* of interest," she asked, "as a female *slave?*"

"Yes," I said.

"Will Mistress open her robe?" she asked.

I did so.

"Will Mistress please stand and remove her robe, and let it dangle from one hand, and turn, slowly, before me?"

I did so. I waited, inspected.

"Yes, Mistress," said the girl.

I nearly fainted in fear, terrified, but not a little thrilled by this insight.

"Mistress would look well being sold from a block," she said.

Hastily, frightened, I pulled the robe on again, and belted it tightly.

"But I think Mistress has little to fear," she said.

I regarded her. In the girl's view, in some respects at least, as I had just learned, I was not unsuitable for slavery.

"Why?" I asked.

"You are well guarded," she said. "Your quarters, even, are in the palace of Corcyrus."

"This is the palace? There are guards about?" I asked.

"Yes, Mistress," she said.

"I am frightened by your master," I said.

"I, too, am frightened by him," she said.

"No doubt our fears are quite silly," I said.

"No, Mistress," she said.

"No?" I asked.

"No, Mistress," she said. "Our fears are fully justified. They are quite appropriate."

"Do you think he wants me?" I asked. I was terrified of Ligurious.

"I do not think so," she said.

"Why?" I asked, puzzled.

"If he wanted you," she said, "by now you would have been branded. By now you would be in his collar. By now you would have been chained naked at the foot of his couch. By now you would have felt his whip. By now you would have learned to beg to serve him."

"Oh," I said.

"It is not that he does not recognize your beauty," she said. "That any man could see at a glance."

"Oh," I said, somewhat mollified. I would have been outraged, or something in me would have been outraged, if I had not been thought worth a chain. I was sure I could prove to a man that I was worthy of a chain.

"His interest in you, merely, does not appear to be in that way," she said. "Too, of course, he has many beautiful women, and is a busy man."

"Many beautiful women?" I asked.

"Slaves," she said.

"More than you?" I asked.

"I am only one of his girls," she laughed, "and I am surely one of the least beautiful."

"How many slaves does he have?" I asked.

"He is an ambitious and abstemious man," she said. "He worked long hours in the service of the state. He has little time for the meaningless charms of slaves."

"How many slaves does he have?" I asked.

"Fifty," she said.

I gasped.

"Perhaps Mistress would like to finish her breakfast," said the girl.

I knelt down before the small table, as I had been taught. I was trembling.

Here, as I had just learned, one man might own as many as fifty women.

"Mistress is not eating," said the girl.

"I am not hungry," I said.

"Am I to report to my master, Ligurious," asked the girl, "that Mistress did not finish her breakfast?"

"No," I said. "No!"

"Every bit of it, please, Mistress," said the girl.

I nodded. I ate. I felt like a slave.

Then I had finished.

"Excellent, Mistress," said the girl. "I shall now dress Mistress. I will teach her the proper garments, and their adjustments, and the veils, and their fastenings. Then it will be time for her lessons."

"Lessons?" I asked, frightened.

"Yes, Mistress," she said.

"What sort of lessons?" I asked, apprehensively.

"Lessons in language," she said. "Lessons in our habits and customs. Lessons in the details of the governance of Corcyrus."

"I do not understand," I said.

"Who are you?" she asked.

"Tiffany Collins," I said.

"No, Mistress," she said.

I looked at her, puzzled.

"Put that identity behind you," she said. "Regard it as being gone, as much as if you were a slave. Prepare to begin anew."

"But, how?" I asked. "What am I to do? Who am I to be?"

"That much I know," smiled the girl. "I know your new identity. My master has told me."

"What is it?" I asked.

"From this moment on," said the girl, "accustom yourself to thinking of yourself as Sheila, Tatrix of Corcyrus."

"Sheila, Tatrix of Corcyrus?" I said.

"Yes," said the girl.

"What is a Tatrix?" I asked.

"A female ruler," she said.

I looked at her, disbelievingly.

"It is a great honor for me," said the girl, "to serve the Tatrix of Corcyrus."

I trembled, kneeling behind the small table. The brief robe of yellow silk did not seem much to wear. I was afraid of the world on which I found myself.

"Who are you?" asked the girl.

"Sheila?" I said. "Tatrix of Corcyrus?"

"Yes," she said. "Please say it, Mistress. Who are you?"

"I am Sheila, Tatrix of Corcyrus," I whispered.

"That is correct, Mistress," said the girl.

"I do not understand," I said. "I do not understand anything! I do not even know the name of the world on which I find myself."

"It is called Gor," she said.

## 4

# A NIGHT IN CORCYRUS

I awakened, sometime late at night. I had been dreaming in Gorean, the language spoken in Corcyrus, and, I had learned, in much of this world.

Several weeks had passed since I had been brought here. In this time I had been immersed, for hours, for Ahn, a day in studies and trainings pertinent to my new environment. I was still muchly imperfect in many things, but there was little doubt in my mind, nor I think in that of my numerous teachers, that I had made considerable progress.

I lay nude, late at night, on the great couch. The night was warm.

Supposedly I was Sheila, the Tatrix of this city, Corcyrus.

I could still feel the effects of the wine I had had for supper. I do not think that it was an ordinary wine. I think that it was an unusual wine in some respects, or, perhaps, that it had been drugged.

I had had a strange dream, mixed in with other dreams. It was difficult to sort these things out.

In the past few days, gradually, I had been entered into the public life of Corcyrus, primarily in small things such as granting audiences, usually with foreigners, and making brief public appearances. Always, in these things, Ligurious, happily, unobtrusively, was at my side. Often, had it not been for his suggestions, I would not have known what to do or say. I had even, the day before yesterday, held court, though, to be sure, the cases were minor.

"Let the churl be stripped," I had said, imperiously, "and a sign be put about his neck, proclaiming him a fraud. Then let him be marched naked, before the spears of guards, through the great gate of Corcyrus, not to be permitted to return before the second passage hand!"

This was the one case which I remembered the most clearly.

The culprit was a small, vile man with a twisted body. He was an itinerant peddler, Speusippus of Turia. I had found him inutterably detestable. A Corcyran merchant had brought charges against him. He had received a bowl from Speusippus which was purportedly silver, a bowl seemingly stamped with the appropriate seal of Ar. The bowl upon inspection, the merchant becoming suspicious as to the weights involved, had turned out to be merely plated. Further, since the smithies of Ar, those authorized to use the various stamps of Ar, will not plate objects without using relevant variations on the seal of Ar to indicate this, the object was not only being misrepresented but was, in effect, a forged artifact. This had led to a seizure and search of the stores and records of Speusippus. Various other discrepancies were found. He had two sets of weights, one true and one false. Too, documents were found recording the purchase of quantities of slave hair, at suitable prices, some even within the city of Corcyrus itself. This hair, as was attested to by witnesses, had been represented to the public as that of free women, with appropriate prices being expected. Hair, incidentally, is a common trade item in Gorean markets. It is used for various purposes, for example, for insect whisks, for dusters, for cleaning and polishing pads, for cushionings, decorations and ropes, particularly catapult ropes, for which it is highly prized. It is not unusual, incidentally, for slave girls, particularly for those who may not have proved superbly pleasing, as yet, to discover that their hair, even while it is still on them, is expected, like themselves, to serve various lowly, domestic purposes. For example, when a girl, serving at a banquet, hears the command, "Hair," she knows she is to go to the guest and kneel, and lower her head, that her hair may be used as a napkin or wiping cloth, by means of which the free person, either male or female, may remove stains, crumbs or grease from his hands. Similarly a girl's hair, if sufficiently long, may be used for the washing and cleaning of floors. In this she is usually on her hands and knees, and naked and chained. The hair is used in conjunction with the soap and water, in the appropriate buckets, being dipped in, and wrung out, and rinsed, and so on. Hair, incidentally, is not used for the application of such things as waxes or varnishes, because of the difficulty of removing such substances from the hair. Such a mistake could necessitate a shearing and a lowering of the market value of a girl for months. For similar reasons, a girl's hair, even within a cloth, if it is still on her, is seldom used for such purposes as buffing and polishing. Hair is common, of course, as a stuffing for pads used for such purposes, for example, for the purposes of cleaning, buffing and polishing.

I was pleased to see the odious Speusippus turned about by guards and dragged from my presence. How pleased I was, too, to see the awesome strength of men serving my purposes.

I lay on my back, on the great couch, in the hot Corcyran night.

Some things I did not understand. Even Susan, who knew much more of Gor than I, did not understand them.

In my audiences, and public appearances, for example, and even in the court, I appeared without the veils common to the Gorean free woman. I knew the veils, and Susan had instructed me in their meanings, arrangements and fastenings, but, publicly, at least, I seldom wore them. This omission seemed puzzling to me, from what I had learned of Gor, particularly in the case of a free woman of so lofty a station as a Tatrix, but I saw no real reason for objecting, particularly in the warm weather of Corcyrus. Indeed, Susan's being so scandalized, and her reservations about sending me forth unveiled from my quarters, she once of Cincinnati, Ohio, seemed to me exquisitely amusing. I did try to explain the matter to her, as Ligurious had explained it to me, when I had asked him about it. The important difference between myself and other free women, of high station, was precisely that, that I was a Tatrix and they were not. A Tatrix, Ligurious had informed me, has no secrets from her people. It is good for the people of a Tatrix to be able to look lovingly and reverently upon her. "Yes, Mistress," had said Susan, her head down. I had wondered if Ligurious was being candid with me. At any rate, there was little doubt that the features of their Tatrix had now become well known in Corcyrus, at least to many of her citizens. Indeed, only this morning I, unveiled, in a large, open, silken palanquin, borne by slaves, Ligurious at my side, had been carried through the streets of Corcyrus, behind trumpets and drums, flanked by guards, through cheering crowds. "Your people love you," had said Ligurious. I had lifted my hand to the crowds, and bowed and smiled. I had done these things with graciousness and dignity, as I had been instructed to do by Ligurious. It had been a thrilling experience for me, seeing the people, the shops, the streets, the buildings. It was the first time I had been outside the grounds of the palace. The streets were clean and beautiful. The smell of flowers was in the air. Petals had been strewn by veiled maidens before the path of the palanquin.

"It is good for you to appear before the people," had said Ligurious, "given the trouble with Argentum."

"What is the trouble with Argentum?" I had asked.

"Skirmishes have taken place near there," he said. "Look," he said, pointing, "there is the library of Antisthenes."

"It is beautiful," I said, observing the shaded porticoes, the slim, lofty pillars, the graceful pediment with its friezes.

"What is the problem with Argentum?" I asked.

"This is the avenue of Iphicrates," I was informed.

The people at the sides of the street did not seem surprised that my features were not concealed by a veil. Perhaps it was traditional, I gathered, as I had been informed by Ligurious, that this was the fashion in which the Tatrix appeared before her people. At any rate, whatever might have been the reason, the people, reassuringly, from my point of view, seemed neither scandalized nor surprised by my lack of a veil. If anything, they might have been saluting me, as though for my courage.

At one point the retinue passed five kneeling girls. They were barefoot and wore brief, sleeveless, one-piece tunics. Their heads were down to the very pavement itself. They wore close-fitting metal collars and were chained together, literally, by the neck. I gasped. "Do not mind such women," said Ligurious. "They are nothing. They are only slaves." I was shaken by this sight. My heart was pounding rapidly. I could scarcely breathe. It was not outrage which I felt, interestingly, nor pity. It was something else. It was a state of unusual sexual excitement, and arousal.

"Smile," suggested Ligurious, himself lifting his hand graciously to the crowd. "Wave."

I controlled myself, and then, again, favored the crowd with my attentions, with my smiles and countenance.

At one time, later, we passed by a set of low, broad, recessed-from-the-street, cement steps or shelves. Behind these levels, these shelves or steps, there was a high cement wall. There were several women, perhaps ten or eleven, on these steps or shelves. Most were white but there were at least two blacks and, I think, one oriental. Each was naked, absolutely. Too, chains ran from heavy rings to their bodies, to perhaps a lovely neck, or a fair wrist or ankle. They were fastened in place, literally, on the cement shelves. As the retinue passed, they oriented themselves to the street and knelt, their heads down to the warm cement. There were more rings than there were women on the shelves, and there were rings, too, set at various heights, in the wall behind the shelves. These rings, too, however, like many of the shelf rings, were not being used. There was an apparatus at one side, like a canopy wrapped about poles, but it, too, was not now in use.

I looked at the women, naked, kneeling, their heads down, chained on the shelves.

"More slaves," explained Ligurious.

Again I fought for breath. I clutched the side of the palanquin to steady myself.

"What is wrong?" he asked.

"Nothing," I said. "Nothing."

"It was only an open-air market," he said, "a small one. There are several such in Corcyrus."

"A market!" I said.

"Yes," he said.

"But what is bought and sold there?" I asked. I recalled the naked, chained beauties.

"Women," he said.

"Women!" I said.

"Yes," he said.

"I see," I said. How matter-of-factly he had put that! Such markets, clearly, like other sorts of markets, were a common feature of Gorean life.

"Bow, and wave," he suggested.

Again I lifted my hand to the crowds. Again I smiled forth from the palanquin.

But I began to tremble. I had seen owned, displayed human females, women who were merchandise, women who were literally up for sale.

"Put them from your mind," said Ligurious. "They are nothing, only slaves."

How terrifying, how horrifying, I thought, to be such a woman, one at the mercy of anyone who has the means to buy her. What a horrifying and categorical thing it would be, I thought, to be subject to sale.

"Hail Sheila, Tatrix of Corcyrus!" I heard.

"The people love you," said Ligurious.

On this world, I said to myself, a woman could be literally owned by a man. She could be as much his, literally, as a shoe or a dog. I fought the feelings within me. I strove against them. I tried to force the memory of the women chained on the shelves from my mind. I could not do so. I moaned. Then I could no longer deny to myself that I was aroused sexually, helplessly and terribly. The crowds, from time to time, surged closer to the palanquin. The guards, flanking the palanquin on both sides, pressed them back with the sides of spears. Among these guards, though he did not have a spear, was Drusus Rencius. He had been assigned to me, some weeks ago, as my personal guard. Behind the retinue, following it, came soldiers. Some of these had canvas sacks slung about their shoulders. From these sacks, from time to time, they would fling coins, and bits of coins, to the street. This was, I thought, a nice gesture. The people would scramble for these coins. It seemed they found them very precious. I continued to smile and wave to the crowd. From time to time, too, I stole a glance at Drusus Rencius. He, however, walking beside the palanquin, had eyes only for the crowd. Outside, perhaps, I seemed charming and benign. Inside, however, almost uncontrollable emotions raged within me. On what sort of world was this that I found myself! I had not known a woman could be so aroused! Again I looked at Drusus Rencius, and the others, guardsmen of Corcyrus. I wondered what it would be like to be owned by a man such as one of those. The thought almost made me faint with passion. I had no doubt they well knew how to teach a woman her slavery. I would be kept by them true to my womanhood, by the lash, if necessary.

"Is anything amiss, my Tatrix?" inquired Ligurious.

"No," I said. "No!"

Then I continued, again, to smile and bow, to nod and wave to the crowd.

I hoped that my condition was not evident to the stern, practical Ligurious, first minister of Corcyrus.

His maleness, and Goreanness, too, of course, were felt keenly by me.

At his least word I would have stripped myself in the

silken palanquin and presented myself publicly to him for his pleasures.

Soon the procession began to wend its way back to the palace. One incident, perhaps worthy of note, occurred. A man rushed forth, angrily, from the crowd, to the very side of the palanquin. Drusus Rencius caught him there and flung him back. I screamed, startled. In a moment, the retinue stopped, the man was held by the arms, on his knees, at the side of the palanquin.

Swords were held at the man's neck. "He is unarmed," said Drusus Rencius.

"Down with Sheila, not Tatrix but Tyranness of Corcyrus!" cried the man, looking angrily upward.

"Silence!" said Ligurious.

"You shall pay for your crimes and cruelties!" cried the man. "Not forever will the citizens of Corcyrus brook the outrages of the palace!"

"Treason!" cried Ligurious.

The man was struck at the side of the head by the butt of a spear. I cried out, in misery.

"This man is a babbling lunatic," said Ligurious to me. "Pay him no attention, my Tatrix."

The fellow, his head bloody, sagged, half unconscious, in the grip of the soldiers.

"Bind him," said Ligurious. The man's arms were wrestled behind his back and tied there.

He looked up, his head bloody, from his knees.

"Who are you?" I asked.

"One who protests the crimes and injustice of Sheila, Tyranness of Corcyrus!" he said, boldly.

"He is Menicius, of the Metal Workers," said one of the soldiers.

"Are you Menicius?" I asked.

"Yes," said the man.

"Are you of Corcyrus?" I asked.

"Yes," said he, "and once was proud to be!"

"What do you want?" I asked.

"Obviously it was his intention to do harm to his Tatrix," said Ligurious. "That is clear from his attack on the palanquin."

"He was unarmed," said Drusus Rencius.

"On a woman's throat," said Ligurious, coldly, "a man's hands need rest but a moment for dire work to be done."

I put my finger tips lightly, inadvertently, to my throat. I did not doubt but what Ligurious was right. Assassination so simply might be accomplished.

"Why would you wish me harm?" I asked the man.

"I wish you no harm, Lady," said he, surlily, "save that you might get what you deserve, a collar in the lowest slave hole on Gor!"

"It is treason," said Ligurious. "His guilt is clear."

"Why, then, did you approach the palanquin?" I asked.

"That the truth might be spoken in Corcyrus," he said, "that the misery and anger of the people might be declared!"

"Prepare his neck," said Ligurious. A man seized the fellow's head and pulled his hair forward and down, exposing the back of the fellow's neck. Another soldier unsheathed his sword.

"No!" I cried. "Free him! Let him go!"

"Tatrix!" protested Ligurious.

"Let him go," I said.

The man's hands were freed. He stood up, startled. The crowd about, too, seemed startled, confused. The face of Ligurious was expressionless. He was a man, I sensed, not only of power, but of incredible control.

"Have him given a coin!" I said.

One of the soldiers, one of those who had had a bag of coins, and coin bits, about his shoulder, came forward. He put a copper piece in the man's hand.

The man looked down at it, puzzled. Then, angrily, he spit upon it and flung it to the stones of the street. He turned about, and strode away.

I saw another man snatch up the coin.

There was a long moment's silence. Then this silence was broken by the voice of Ligurious. "Behold the glory and mercy of the Tatrix!" he said. "What better evidence could we have of the falsity of the lunatic's accusations?"

"Hail Sheila, Tatrix of Corcyrus!" cried the man who had snatched up the coin.

"Hail Sheila!" I heard. "Hail Sheila, Tatrix of Corcyrus!"

In a moment the retinue resumed its journey back to the palace.

"Is there anything to what the fellow said?" I asked Ligurious. "Is there unrest in Corcyrus? Is there some discontentment among our citizens?"

"You have surely received the reports of our officers," said Ligurious.

"Yes," I admitted.

"Heed them, then," said Ligurious. "They are objective, and official."

Such reports, I recalled, unequivocally attested to the hardiness and health of Corcyrus.

"Do not pay attention to the babblings of lunatics," said Ligurious. "They are not worth taking seriously. Too, you will always be able to find frustrates who, excusing themselves, will seek to lay their failures and shortcomings not at their own door but at the gate of their city."

"I need not concern myself with such charges, then?" I asked.

"No," said Ligurious. "Forget them. Dismiss them, completely."

I looked at him.

"If you need reassurance," he said, "listen to your people."

"Hail Sheila!" I heard. "Hail Sheila, Tatrix of Corcyrus!"

"You see?" he asked.

"Yes," I said. My heart, then, was flooded with elation, and with affection for the people of Corcyrus.

"You are loved," said Ligurious.

"Yes," I said. "I am loved." I waved happily at the crowd. I dismissed then the rantings of the lunatic from my mind.

"You did make a mistake," said Ligurious. He was smiling and waving to the crowd, but he was speaking to me.

"What was that?" I asked, waving to the crowd, speaking to Ligurious.

"You should have permitted us to execute Menicius," he said. "You did not. That was a mistake."

"Perhaps," I said. "But I am Tatrix of Corcyrus."

"Of course," said Ligurious.

I rolled onto my stomach on the silken coverlet. I touched it with my finger tips. It was exquisitely soft.

"May I present to you Drusus Rencius, Lady Sheila, my sovereign, he who is first sword among our guards?" Ligurious had inquired several days ago.

"The name seems not to be of Corcyrus," I said.

"Various mercenaries are within our services," said Ligurious. "We have soldiers from as far as Anango and Skjern."

"From what city does Drusus Rencius derive?" I inquired.

"Ar, Lady," said Ligurious.

"Our allegiances, I thought," I said, "are with Cos."

"Drusus Rencius is a renegade, Lady," said Ligurious. "Do not fear. He now serves only himself and silver."

I inclined my head to Drusus Rencius. He was a dark-haired, tall, supple, lean, long-muscled, large-handed man. He had gray eyes. He had strong, regular features. In him I sensed a powerful intelligence.

"Lady," said he, bowing before me.

He seemed quiet, and deferential. But there was within him, I did not doubt, that which was Gorean. He would know what to do with a woman.

"He is to be your personal guard," said Ligurious.

"A bodyguard?" I inquired.

"Yes, Lady," said Ligurious.

I looked at the tall, spare man. He carried a helmet in the crook of his left arm. It was polished but, clearly, it had seen war. The hilt of the sword in his scabbard, at his left hip, too, was worn. It was marked, too, with the stains of oil and sweat. His livery, too, though clean, was plain. It bore the insignia of Corcyrus and of his standing in the guards, that of the third rank, the first rank to which authority is delegated. In the infantry of Corcyrus the fifth rank is commonly occupied for at least a year. Promotion to the fourth rank is usually automatic, following the demonstrated attainment of certain levels of martial skills. The second rank and the first rank usually involve larger command responsibilities. Beyond these rankings come the distinctions and levels among leaders who are perhaps more appropriately to be thought of as officers, or full officers, those, for example, among lieutenants, captains, high captains and generals. That Drusus Rencius was first sword among the guards, then, in this case, as his insignia made clear, was not a reference to his rank but a recognition of his skill with the blade. That these various ranks might be occupied, incidentally, also does not entail that specific command responsibilities are being exercised. A given rank, with its pay grade, for example, might be occupied without its owner being assigned a given command. The command of Drusus Rencius, for example, if he had had one, would presumably be relinquished when he took over his duties as a personal guard. His skills with the sword, I suppose, had been what had called him to the attention of Ligurious.

These, perhaps, had seemed to qualify him for his new assignment. To be a proper guard for a Tatrix, however, surely involved more than being quick with a sword. There were matters of appearances to be considered. I felt a bit irritated with the fellow. I would put him in his place.

"The guard for a Tatrix," I said to Ligurious, "must be more resplendent."

"See to it," said he to Drusus Rencius.

"As you wish," responded Drusus Rencius.

Ligurious had then left.

Drusus Rencius looked down at me. He seemed very large and strong. I felt very small and weak.

"What is wrong?" I asked, angrily.

"It is nothing," he said.

"What!" I demanded.

"It is only that I had expected, from what I have heard, that Lady Sheila would be somewhat different than I find her."

"Oh," I said.

He continued to look at me.

"In what way?" I asked.

"I had expected Lady Sheila to seem more of a Tatrix," he said, "whereas you seem to me to be something quite different."

"What?" I asked.

"Forgive me, Lady," he smiled. "If I answered you truthfully I would fear that I might be impaled."

"Speak," I said.

He smiled.

"You may speak with impunity," I said. "What is it that I seem to be to you?"

"A female slave," he said.

"Oh!" I cried, in fury.

"Does Lady Sheila often go unveiled?" he asked.

"Yes," I said. "A Tatrix has no secrets from her people. It is good for her people to be able to look upon their Tatrix!"

"As Lady Sheila wishes," he said, bowing. "May I now withdraw?"

"Yes!" I said. He had seen me without my veil. I felt almost naked before him, almost as though I might truly be a slave.

"I shall be at your call," he said. He then withdrew.

I twisted on the couch and turned again to my back. I looked up at the ceiling.

The effects of the wine I had had for supper were still with me. I think it may have been drugged.

It was not easy to sort things out. I had had a strange dream, mixed in with other dreams.

"I am the Tatrix of Corcyrus," I had said to Ligurious, in the palanquin. "Of course," he had said.

How can I be the Tatrix of Corcyrus, I asked myself. Does this make any sense? Is it not all madness? I could understand how women could be brought to this world to be put in collars and made slaves, like Susan, for example, and doubtless others. That was comprehensible. But why would one be brought here to rule a city? Surely such positions of privilege and power these Goreans would reserve for themselves. The more typical position for an Earth girl, I suspected, would be to find herself at the feet of a master. I wondered if I were truly the Tatrix of Corcyrus. Surely I had seldom exercised significant authority. Too, at times, my schedule seemed a bit erratic or strange. At certain Ahn I was expected to be in the public rooms of the palace and, at others, even at the ringing of palace time bars, for no reason I clearly understood, I was expected to be in my quarters. "Certain traditions customarily govern the calendar of the Tatrix," Ligurious had informed me. At certain times I had been conducted to my quarters I had thought that sessions of important councils had been scheduled, councils at whose sessions it would be natural to expect the presence of the Tatrix. The matters to be discussed in certain of these meetings, however, I had learned from Ligurious, were actually too trivial to warrant the attention of the Tatrix. Thus it was not necessary that I attend. In certain other cases, I was informed, the meetings had been postponed or canceled. Protocols and customs are apparently extremely significant to Goreans. What seemed to me inexplicable oddities or apparent caprices in my schedule were usually explained by reference to such things. It is fitting that the proprieties of Corcyrus be respected by her Tatrix, even when they might appear arbitrary, had said Ligurious.

I looked up at the ceiling, in the hot Corcyran night.

Was I the Tatrix of Corcyrus?

Susan, I was sure, believed me to be the Tatrix of Corcyrus. So, too, I was confident, did my bodyguard, Drusus Rencius, once of Ar.

Too, I had not been challenged in the matter in my audiences, my public appearances, or even in court. By all, it seemed, I was accepted as the Tatrix of Corcyrus. Ligurious, first minister of the city, even, had assured me of the reality of this dignity. And had I wished further confirmation of my condition and status surely I had received it earlier today, from the very citizens of Corcyrus itself. "Hail Sheila, Tatrix of Corcyrus!" they had cried.

"I am the Tatrix of Corcyrus," I had told Ligurious. "Of course," he had said.

Inexplicable and strange though it might seem, I decided that I was, truly, the Tatrix of Corcyrus.

I closed my eyes and then opened them. I shook my head, briefly. The effects of the wine I had had for supper were still with me. I think that it might have been drugged. What purpose could have been served by such an action, however, I had no idea.

I had had a strange dream, mixed in with other dreams.

I whimpered on the great couch, lying in the heat of the Corcyran night.

I was Tatrix.

How extraordinary and marvelous this was! Too, I was not insensitive to the emoluments and perquisites of this office, to the esteem and prestige that might attend it, to the glory that might be expected to be its consequence, to the wealth and power which, doubtless, sometime, would prove to be its inevitable attachments.

In office, clearly, I acknowledged to myself, I was a Tatrix. I wondered, however, if there was a Tatrix within me, or something else.

I forced from my mind, angrily, the memory of the girls in brief tunics, chained by the neck, kneeling down, heads down, in the street. I forced from my mind, angrily, the memory of the women in the market, naked, chained in place, awaiting the interest of buyers.

I twisted on the great couch, in misery.

Nowhere more than on this world had I felt my femininity, and nowhere else, naturally enough, I suppose, had I felt it more keenly frustrated. I wondered what it was, truly, to be a woman.

I had had a strange dream. I had awakened into it, or had

seemed to awaken into it, from another. In the preceding dream I had been on my hands and knees on the tiles of a strange room. I was absolutely naked. There was a chain on my neck and it ran to a ring in the floor. Drusus Rencius, standing, was towering over me. He carried a whip. He was smiling. I looked up at him, in terror. He shook out the long, broad, pliant blades of the whip. It was a five-stranded Gorean slave whip. I looked at the blades, in terror. "What are you going to do?" I asked. "Teach you to be a woman," he said. I had then seemed to awaken into another dream. In this one was Ligurious. I felt portions of the coverlet being wrapped about me, between my shoulders and thighs. My arms were pinned to my sides, within the coverlet. I whimpered. It seemed that I was only partially conscious. Then I became aware of someone else in the room, bearing a small, flickering lamp. Ligurious held the coverlet with his right hand, holding it together, holding me in place, helplessly within it. With his left hand, it fastened in my hair, he pulled my head back painfully. This exposed my features to the lamp. I sobbed, responding to this domination.

"Do you see?" he asked. "Is it not remarkable?"

"Yes," said a woman's voice. I gasped. It was as though I looked upon myself. She, as I had earlier in the day, wore the robes of the Tatrix. She, too, as I had, wore no veil. In the madness of the dream, in its oddity, it was surely I, or one much like myself, who looked upon me. How strange are dreams!

"I think she will do very nicely," said Ligurious.

"That, too, would be my conjecture," said the woman.

Ligurious moved his right hand, grasping the rim of the coverlet, tight about my breasts.

"Do you wish to see her, fully?" he asked. I whimpered. I realized he could strip the coverlet away, baring me in the light of the lamp.

"You are not so clever as you think, Ligurious," she said. "Do you think I do not see that you, in stripping her, would be, in effect, and to your lust and amusement, stripping me, and before my very eyes?"

"Forgive me," smiled Ligurious, first minister of Corcyrus.

"Pull the lower portion of the coverlet down further," she said. "You have revealed too much of her thighs."

"Of course," he smiled, and adjusted the coverlet, drawing it down, over my knees.

"Men are beasts," she said.

"You well know my feelings for you," he said.

"They will go unrequited," she said. "Content yourself with your slaves."

I feared the woman bending over me. I could sense now that even if she seemed superficially much like me, at least in appearances, she was in actuality quite different. She seemed highly intelligent, doubtless more so than I, and severe and decisive. She seemed harsh, and hard and cold. She seemed merciless and cruel; she seemed arrogant, impatient, demanding, haughty and imperious. Such a woman I thought, as I am not, is perhaps a true Tatrix. Surely it seemed more believable that such a woman might hold power in a city such as Corcyrus than I.

The lamp again approached more closely. Again my head was pulled back, helplessly, firmly, forcibly.

"She is not as beautiful as I," said the woman.

"No," said Ligurious. "Of course not."

Then my hair was released and the two figures took their way from the room.

I had then twisted on the couch, freed myself of the confinements of the coverlet, and, sensible of the effects of the wine, or perhaps a containment of the wine, had fallen into a dreamless sleep.

I heard movements outside the door. The guard was being changed.

I could not lock the door from the inside. Yet I lay nude, on my back, on the great couch. I wondered if this was brazen. I rolled to my side and pulled my legs up. I bit at the silken coverlet. I wondered if there was a Tatrix within me. I did not think so. There was something else in me, I feared, something that I had only become clearly aware of on this barbaric world, this world in which I must be true to my femininity, and in which there were true men.

I then understood, I thought, the strange dream I had had. It was not contrasting now, I thought, perhaps two selves, or, more likely, two women, muchly resembling one another, but rather it had been calling to my attention, in its figurative imagery, in the symbolic transformations common to dreams, a discrepancy between what I in actuality was and what it was expected, doubtless, that a Tatrix should be. The contrast, I realized, had been clear, I helpless, sobbing under the domination of Ligurious, little better than a slave, and she above me, far superior to me, haughty, decisive, imperious, cold and powerful. I sobbed. I knew then from the dream, or from what had seemed a dream, that there was no Tatrix in me. I was not a Tatrix, not in my heart. I was, at best, something different. Angrily I arose from the couch. I went to the window. I put my hands on the bars. Many times, secretly, I had tried them. They were heavy, narrowly set, reinforced, inflexible. I laid my cheek gently against them. They felt cool. I then drew back and, my hands on the bars, looked out, across the rooftops of Corcyrus, to the walls of the city, and to the fields beyond. The city was muchly dark. Some of the major avenues, however, such as that Iphicrates, were illuminated, dimly, by lamps. In many Gorean cities, when men go out at night, they carry their own light, torches or lamps. I then looked upward, into the humid night. I could see two of the three moons of this world. I then, suddenly, angrily, shook the bars. They were for my own protection, I had been informed. But I could not open them, or remove them, say, with knotted clothing or bedding, to lower myself to the levels below. They might indeed serve to keep others out, perhaps climbing upward, or descending on ropes from the roof above, but they surely served as well, and as perfectly, to keep me within! What is this room, I asked myself, is it truly my protected quarters, or is it, rather, my cell?

I walked back to the center of the room, near the great couch. I looked back at the bars. Then I went to the long mirror behind the vanity. I looked at myself, in the mirror, in the dim moonlight, filtered into the room. She is rather pretty, I thought. She may be pretty enough, even, to be a slave. Susan, I recalled, had thought it possible that a man, some men at least, might find her of interest, really of interest, of sufficient interest to be worth putting in bondage. I wondered if she could please a man. Perhaps if she tried very hard to be pleasing some man, in his kindness, might find her acceptable. I turned before the mirror, studying the girl that I was thusly displaying. Yes, I thought, it is not impossible that she might be considered worthy of a collar. "Mistress would look well being sold from a block," Susan had said. "Are you free, Tiffany?" I asked the image in the mirror. "Yes," I told myself. "I am free." I turned my left thigh to the mirror, I lifted my chin. I studied the girl in the mirror. I wondered what she would look like, with a brand, with a collar. "You see, Tiffany," I said. "You are not branded. You are not collared."

I looked at the girl in the mirror. I wondered who I was, what I was.

"I am the Tatrix of Corcyrus!" I said.

But the girl in the mirror did not appear to be a Tatrix. She appeared, clearly, to be something else.

I forced from my mind the memory of the slaves I had seen earlier, the girls in the street, in their one-piece, skimpy garments, heads down, kneeling, chained together by the neck, the girls in the market, in their chains, stark naked, kneeling, too, their heads down to the warm cement, being publicly displayed for sale.

"What are you?" I asked. "Do you not dare speak? Then show me. Show me!"

Slowly, numbly, frightened, I turned about and went to the foot of the great couch. I knelt there, and, putting my head down, tenderly lifted up, in two hands, a length of the chain that lay coiled there. I kissed it. "No!" I cried out to myself, replacing the chain. But then I rose up and, timidly, softly, went to the wall where the whip hung. I removed the whip from its hook and knelt down with it. I wrapped its blades back about the handle. Then, humbly, my head down, submissively, near the point where the five long, soft blades join the staff, holding it in both hands, I kissed it. "No!" I wept, in protest. Then I replaced the whip on its hook. I went then again to the mirror. The vanity was low enough, meant to be used by a kneeling woman, and I was back far enough, that I could see myself on the tiles, completely. I saw the girl in the mirror kneel down. "No," I said. I saw her kneel back on her heels. I saw her straighten her back, and lift her chin, and put her hands on her thighs. "No!" I said. I saw her spread her knees. "No," I said. "No! No!" I had seen girls in the palace do that, for example, when a free man had entered a room. Sometimes, too, in identically this same position, they would keep their heads submissively lowered, until given permission to raise them. This variation, and similar variations, depend on the specific discipline to which a given girl is subjected. The head is usually kept raised; this precludes the necessity of a specific command to lift the head; in the head-lifted position she has no choice but to bare her facial beauty to the viewer; too, her least expression may be read; too, of course, she can see who is in the room with her and is thus better able, even from the first instant, to discern his moods, anticipate his needs, and respond to his commands.

I leaped to my feet, furious with the girl in the mirror. She lied! She lied! I fled to the wardrobe. I flung back the sliding doors. I was a Tatrix! I tore my yellow robe, that of brief silk, from its carved hanger. I put it on me, swiftly, angrily, belting it, tightly. I ran to the door leading from my quarters. I reached to the handle and jerked it wildly towards me. I had opened this door a hundred times. I cried out in surprise, in misery. This time it did not yield. I jerked twice again, both of my hands on the handle. The door, somehow, was fastened on the other side. It seemed, or something on it seemed, to strike against some obstacle or barrier.

I struck at it, pounding on it. "Let me out!" I cried. "Let me out!"

I heard two sliding sounds. On the other side, I knew, were four pairs of brackets. Never, however, as far as I knew, had they been used. Two of these pairs of brackets were on the door itself, one at the lower part of the door and one at the upper part. Matching them in height, but in the wall, were the other two pairs of brackets. One of these pairs, its members located on opposite sides of the door, corresponded to the upper-door brackets, and the other pair, its members opposite one another, one on each side of the door, corresponded to the lower-door brackets. The door was thus, if beams or bars were to be inserted through these brackets, prevented from swinging inward, its natural opening motion.

The door opened. Five guards were there. Two of them I noted, at a glance, were laying heavy beams against the wall. It was these, then, obviously, which had secured the door.

"The door was locked!" I said.

"Yes, Lady," said the leader of the guards. He was of the third rank, like Drusus Rencius. He, like the others, seemed surprised. Obviously he had not expected to see me at this time of night, or this early in the morning.

"Why was the door locked?" I demanded.

"It is always locked at this time of night," he said.

"Why?" I demanded.

"Orders," said he.

"Whose orders?" I asked.

"Those of Ligurious," he said.

"Why would such orders be given?" I asked.

"It is custom," said the guard.

"Why?" I asked.

"To protect the Tatrix, I suppose," said he. "Surely we would not want her wandering about the palace at night."

"There is danger in the palace?" I asked, angrily.

The guard shrugged. "Perhaps an assassin might have gained entrance," he said.

"I would be safe enough accompanied by guards, I am sure," I said.

"At this Ahn," he said, "it is customary for the Tatrix to be within her quarters."

"I am leaving them," I said. I made as though to brush past him. But his arm, like a bar of iron, barred my way. "No, Lady, forgive me," he said, "but you may not pass."

I stepped back. I was startled.

"I am Tatrix!" I said.

"Yes, Lady," said he.

"Get out of my way!" I said.

"I am sorry," he said. "You may not pass."

"Call Ligurious!" I said. I was determined to get to the bottom of this matter.

"I cannot disturb the first minister at this Ahn," he said.

"Why not?" I asked.

"He is with his women," said the man.

"His women!" I said.

"Yes, Lady," said the man.

"I see," I said.

"If you wish," said the guard, "I can call Drusus Rencius."

"No," I said. "No." I then withdrew into the room. I saw the door close. Then, a moment or so later, I heard the two beams, one after the other, slid into place.

"I am the Tatrix!" I screamed, angrily, from behind the door.

I then took off the robe, angrily, and threw it to the tiles. I could not go out. What need did I have of it?

Then, trembling, naked, with my finger tips, in the half darkness, in the moonlit room, I examined the door. I even felt the great hinges, with their pins, like rivets, on my side of the door. The lower ends of the pins had been spread, beaten wide, so that they could not be forced upwards, freeing them. I sank to my knees behind the door. I lifted my head and put my finger tips to the heavy wood. "I am the Tatrix," I whispered. Then I rose to my feet and went to the side of the great couch. I looked back to the mirror behind the vanity. I saw the frightened girl there. She was indisputably female, with all that that might entail on a world such as this.

"I am the Tatrix," I whispered.

Then I crept onto the great couch. I lay on my stomach on the couch, on the silk, near its foot. I supposed that sometimes girls might even be chained in such a place, like a dog at a man's feet, or perhaps even on the hard, cold tiles, under the slave ring.

If I were so chained, I thought, I would quickly learn to be pleasing.

What manner of world was this, I wondered, on which I found myself.

It was a world, I thought, on which men had never relinquished their sovereignty, on which they had never submitted to the knives of psychic castration.

From Earth, I could scarcely believe the men of this world, in their power and naturalness.

Where were such men on Earth, I asked myself. They must exist there, some few perhaps, somewhere.

Thousands, perhaps millions of women on Earth, I thought, must secretly pine for such men. How, without submitting themselves to such men, how without satisfying the complementary equations of sexuality, could their own femininity be fulfilled?

I had wished to go forth in the palace. I had not been permitted to do so, by men. I was angry! But, too, I knew that there were other emotions, deeper emotions, unfamiliar and troubling emotions, uncontrollable emotions, that were welling up within me. These emotions frightened me, and pleased me. I had not been able to do what I wished. It had not been permitted by men. My will had been overridden. I had been forced to comply not with my own wishes but with those of others. I had had to obey.

"I am a Tatrix!" I said, angrily. But I did not believe that it was a Tatrix which lay most deeply within me.

"What am I?" I wondered.

I rose on the couch to a position half sitting, half kneeling. I looked at the girl in the mirror, half sitting, half kneeling, as I was.

"What are you?" I asked. "Are you a Tatrix?"

She did not respond.

"You do not look like a Tatrix," I told her. Again she did not respond.

I then lowered myself to the couch and lay, again, on my stomach, near the foot of the couch. I recalled the girl in the mirror. I did not think she was so much different, truly, from the girls I had seen on the street, or those who had been chained on the cement shelves. I did not think that a man would think twice about it, for example, if he found her in a slave market.

I was angry with Ligurious. I had been told he was with his "women."

I wondered what it would be like to be one of his "women." Susan, I knew, was one of his women. She was half naked, branded and collared. She knelt before him, head down. She accorded him the utmost deference and respect.

I wondered what it would be to be the woman of a man such as Ligurious. Suppose I did not please him, I said to myself. Would I be whipped? Yes, I said to myself, I would be whipped.

"What am I?" I wondered.

"I am a Tatrix," I responded.

I saw then that it was near morning. I then fell asleep where I had lain down, near the bottom of the couch, near the chain and slave ring.

## 5

# MILES OF ARGENTUM; DRUSUS RENCIUS SPECULATES ON WHAT I MIGHT BRING AS A SLAVE; I HAVE OBTAINED GREATER FREEDOMS

"The arrogant knave now approaching the throne," said Ligurious, whispering in my ear, "is Miles, an ambassador, and general, from Argentum."

The fellow, approaching, coming up the long aisle toward

the great dais, on which my throne reposed, had indeed a bold stride. In the crook of his left arm he carried a helmet, crested with sleen hair. Behind him swirled a huge cape of trimmed, white fur.

"Remember that those of Argentum are our enemies, and the enemies, too, of our great ally, the island of Cos."

"I remember," I said.

"The men behind him," said Ligurious, "carry chests, filled with riches, to sue for your favor."

"He seems not to approach so humbly," I said.

"Brush back your robes a bit, so that he may better see you," said Ligurious.

I did this.

"Allow me," said Ligurious, "as these matters may be sensitive, to conduct this audience."

"Of course," I said. I was relieved that Ligurious would do this for me. I knew matters were tense between Corcyrus and Argentum. I did not wish to commit any blunders which might reflect adversely on the throne. Ligurious would know what to do.

I took an immediate dislike to the fellow approaching. He was from Argentum, our enemy.

I straightened myself on the great throne of Corcyrus, on the high dais, in the great hall of the palace. Men of high councils were about me. Guards, too, were plentiful. My own guard, Drusus Rencius, now in resplendent regalia, fitting for the guard of a Tatrix, was nearby. About the throne, here and there, spilled on the steps of the dais, in the manner of Corcyrus and some other cities, was a tasteful display of riches, rich cloths, golden coins and some chained female slaves. Susan, who was to me as my personal serving slave, kneeling, in a brief, white, see-through lace tunic, was chained on my right, her chain, fastened on her neck, running to a ring on the throne.

"Miles, Ambassador of Argentum, Miles, General of Argentum!" announced the herald.

The men behind Miles put down the boxes they had brought. Doubtless new riches would soon grace the steps of the dais.

"The throne of Corcyrus," said Ligurious, "greets the ambassador from Argentum, Miles, general of Argentum."

"On behalf of Claudius, Ubar of Argentum," said Miles, "I accept the greetings of Corcyrus."

"But do you not accept them for yourself, as well?" inquired Ligurious.

"Had I my will," he said, "I would have come to the walls of Corcyrus not with the scrolls of protest but the engines of war."

"Beware the quickness of your tongue," said Ligurious, "for you rant now not in one of Argentum's taverns but in Corcyrus, and before the throne of her Tatrix."

"Forgive me, noble Ligurious," said Miles. "I forgot myself. It was a natural mistake. In the taverns of Argentum we of Argentum are indeed accustomed to speaking freely before women such as your Tatrix. They are paga slaves."

There were cries of rage about me.

"Indeed," said he, "I have had many women far superior to your Tatrix in just such taverns. They served well in their chains, naked, in the pleasure alcoves."

More than one blade about me slipped swiftly, menacingly, from its sheath.

Miles did not budge, nor flinch, at the foot of the throne. He had a great shock of black hair. His piercing gray eyes rested upon me. I wished that I was veiled. I did not think he would ever forget what I looked like.

"Your scrolls have been examined," said Ligurious. "I, the Tatrix, and those of the high councils, have scrutinized them with more care than they deserved. Their evidences are false, their arguments specious, their claims fraudulent."

"Such a dismissal of their contents I expected," said Miles. "I myself would not have transmitted them. Better to have sent you the defiance of Argentum and a spear of war."

I myself had examined the scrolls only in a sense. Excerpts had been read to me, with criticism, by Ligurious. His analysis of their contents, I did not doubt, was sound. He was a highly intelligent man, and familiar, clearly, with the geographical and political features of the problems. The issues had to do primarily with our silver mines, which, unfortunately, lay near Argentum. Force, it seemed, was required to protect them. These mines were said to be almost as rich as those of Tharna, far to the north and east of Corcyrus. The claim of Argentum, of course, was that the silver mines were theirs. My education, so full and exacting in many ways, was incomplete in at least one obvious and glaring detail. I had not been taught to read Gorean. I was illiterate in Gorean.

"It is fortunate for Corcyrus, and for peace," said Ligurious, "that he with whom we truly have to deal is not Miles, general of Argentum, but with Claudius, her Ubar. He, I trust, is far less hotheaded. He, I trust, is more rational. He, I trust, may be expected to see reason and acknowledge, however reluctantly, the justice of our cause."

"Corcyrus is not feared by Argentum," said Miles.

"Yet," smiled Ligurious, "it seems that men with you have brought chests, bound with bands of iron, and intricately wrought coffers, to the foot of our throne."

"That is true," said Miles. These chests and coffers were behind him, on the floor.

"If the gifts are suitable," said Ligurious, "our Tatrix, after the cession of the mines, may be moved to deal somewhat less harshly with the miscreants of Argentum."

"I am sure that Claudius, my Ubar, would be relieved to hear that," said Miles.

Ligurious inclined his head, acknowledging these words graciously.

There was some laughter about me. I heard blades being returned to sheaths.

"I see," said Ligurious, lightly, "that you bring with you no male silk slaves, in chains, to be presented to the Tatrix."

"It is well known," said Miles, "that the Tatrix of Corcyrus is not interested in men, but only in gold and power."

"Beware," said Ligurious.

I did not understand, truly, the remark of Miles of Argentum. I was not interested in men, of course, I reassured myself, as a woman of Earth, but, on the other hand, I did not think that I was unusually greedy either. Such things, at any rate, were generally not uppermost in my mind. There was a difference sometimes, I supposed, between the true and reputed characters of public figures. How odd, sometimes, are fame and rumors. That I might conceivably be presented with male silk slaves took me aback for a moment but then I realized that, as a female ruler, it was not out of the question that I might be presented with such gifts. Typical gifts for a male ruler, I knew, might include beautiful female slaves, additional riches for his pleasure gardens.

"You may now open the chests and coffers," said Ligurious, eyeing them with interest.

"How is it," inquired Miles, "that the Tatrix of Corcyrus goes unveiled?"

"It is custom," said Ligurious.

"From our former messengers and envoys," said Miles, "I gather that the custom is a new one."

"Every custom has its beginning," said Ligurious. I was interested to hear this. I had not realized that the custom was a recent one. "There are many justifications for initiating such a custom. Foremost among them, doubtless, is that it is now possible for her subjects to gaze upon her with awe and reverence."

"I should think, rather," said Miles, smiling, "that you might fear that her subjects would gaze upon her not with awe and reverence, but interest."

"Interest?" asked Ligurious.

"Yes," said Miles, "wondering, perhaps, what she might look like in a collar."

"I think it is time," said Ligurious, "that you should improve your service to your Ubar. Let us see what gifts he proffers to Corcyrus, petitioning for our mercy and favor."

"Take no offense, Lady," said Miles to me, "for it is high commendation I extend to you. Though I have had many women far superior to you, and even in the alcoves of taverns, I am not insensitive to your beauty. It is not inconsiderable. Indeed, I have no doubt that in the middle price ranges you would prove to be a desirable buy."

I clenched my fists on the arms of the throne. How insolent he was! How I hated him! I wondered, too, if some men, indeed, might find me a desirable buy.

"Open the chests and coffers," said Ligurious, menacingly.

"Surely Corcyrus needs no more riches," said Miles. "Consider the lavishness of the appointments of this hall, the richness of the regalia of those here convened."

"Let us see what Claudius has sent us," said Ligurious.

"I see rich cloths here," he said, indicating the cloths spread tastefully about the steps of the dais. "I see that there is gold in Corcyrus," he said, indicating the coins in their plentitudes, seemingly casually spilled about the steps. "I see, too," he said, "that there are beautiful slaves in Corcyrus." His eyes rested then, fully, upon Susan, kneeling, chained by the neck to the side of my throne. This was not the first time that he had seen her, of course. Indeed, I had seen him picking her out more than once. I think he found her of interest. At any rate, clearly, she was not now being noticed in passing, as a mere component in a display, but was being attended to, observed, scrutinized, even studied, as a specific, individual slave, on her chain. She drew back, fearfully, with a small sound of the chain. She did not dare to meet his eyes. She clenched her thighs closely together. She was trembling; her breathing was rapid; doubtless her heart was pounding; doubtless she was aware of it in her small rib cage. Yet I had seen her looking at him. She had hardly been able to keep her eyes from him. I supposed it was difficult for mere female slaves, in their scanty garments, and in their lowly station, not to be excited by rich, powerful, handsome, resplendent free men, so far above themselves. It was much easier for one like myself, a free woman, and richly robed, to control, resist and fight femininity. In the case of the slave, on the other hand, femininity is actually required of her. Indeed, if she is insufficiently feminine she will be beaten. It is no wonder female slaves are so helpless with men. I noted the eyes of Miles of Argentum on Susan. She trembled, being appraised. I felt sudden anger, and jealousy. He had not looked at me like that! To be sure, she was a slave, and I was free. It would certainly be improper for anyone to look on me, a free woman, in that candid, basic way! Too, Susan had me at a disadvantage. Would not any woman look attractive if she were half naked and put on a chain? How could I compete with that? Let us both be stripped and chained, I thought, and then let men decide, examining us, which was most beautiful! But then I realized that Susan was, doubtless, far more beautiful than I. She was exquisite. It had been no mistake on the part of slavers that she had been brought to Gor. I then thought that tonight I might whip Susan. She could not resist. She was a slave. I could have her take off her clothes and then tie her to a ring. I could then whip her. That would teach her to be more beautiful than I! Then I thought how absurd that was. It was not Susan's fault if she were more beautiful than I, or my fault if I might not be, objectively, as beautiful as she. I felt ashamed of my hostility, my jealousy. But Susan's beauty, I realized, then, was not a matter merely of features and figure, exquisite though these might be. Her beauty had to do more intimately and basically I thought, somehow, with matters which were more psychological and emotional; it had to do, somehow, in its softness and femininity, with the slavery of her. I wondered if I might become more beautiful than I was. I wondered if I might become as beautiful, someday, as the women cited by Miles of Argentum as being so superior to me. I wondered if I might one day be so beautiful that he might see nothing to choose from, between me and them. I wondered if I might not, one day, even be their superior! But then I put such thoughts from my mind. Where was my pride and freedom!

"Let us see," insisted Ligurious, "what Claudius has sent us."

"Of course," said Miles of Argentum. He handed his helmet to one of the men about him. With a great key he unlocked the largest chest. The other chests and coffers, too, by others, were then unlocked.

Ligurious, and I, and the others, leaned forward, to glimpse the contents of these chests and coffers..

"In suit for the favor of Corcyrus, in deference and tribute to Corcyrus, Claudius, Ubar of Argentum," said Miles of Argentum, "sends this!"

He flung open the great chest, and turned it to its side. The other chests and coffers, by his fellows, were similarly treated.

"Nothing!" cried Ligurious. "There is nothing in them!"

"And that," said Miles of Argentum, "is what Claudius, Ubar of Argentum, sends to Corcyrus!"

"Insolence!" cried Ligurious. "Insolence!"

Cries of rage broke out from those about me.

Miles put out his hand and his helmet was returned to him. He put it again in the crook of his left arm. His great furred cape, by one of the men behind him, was adjusted on him.

"I now leave Corcyrus," he said. "When I return, I shall have an army at my back."

"You have insulted our Tatrix," said Ligurious.

"Your Tatrix," said Miles, "belongs in a cage, a golden cage."

There were further cries of rage from those about me. I did not understand, clearly, the nature of this insult, or the meaning of the reference to a golden cage.

"Here," said Miles, reaching into a pocket on his belt, "if you of Corcyrus are so eager for the silver of Argentum, I will give you some." He held up the coin. "This is a silver tarsk of Argentum," he said. He flung it to the foot of the dais. "I give it to you," he said. "It is about the worth of your Tatrix, I think, in so far as I am now able to assess her. It is, I think, about what she would bring in a slave market."

Blades flashed forth from sheaths. I saw Drusus Rencius restrain one man from rushing upon Miles of Argentum. In the small retinue of Miles blades, too, had leapt from sheaths.

"Strip him, and chain him to the slave ring of the Tatrix!" cried a man.

I shuddered. I would be terrified to have such a man chained at my couch. It would be like having a lion there. Too, I thought, surely it would be more fitting for women, in their softness and beauty, with their dispositions to submit and love, irreservedly and wholly, asking nothing, giving all, holding nothing back from the dominant male, their master, to be chained to a slave ring. This, in its way, is a beautiful symbol of her nature and needs. On the other hand, symbolic considerations aside, it must be noted that the chain is quite real. She is truly chained there.

Miles turned about and, followed by his retinue, left the great hall.

Those about the throne, most of them, began to take their leave.

"Do you think there will be trouble?" I asked Ligurious.

"No," he said. "Argentum, upon reflection, will think the better of her rash decision. Even Claudius knows that behind us stands the might and weight of Cos."

"The ambassador, he, Miles, the general of Argentum," I said, "seemed very firm."

"He is a hothead," said Ligurious. "In time, have no fear, when there is a more objective assessment of realities, cooler wisdoms will prevail."

"I would not like for there to be trouble," I said.

"Do not worry about it in the least," said Ligurious. "Put all such matters from your mind. I assure you that there will be no trouble whatsoever. You have my word on it."

"You relieve my mind," I said. "I take great comfort in your words."

"What did you think of Miles of Argentum?" asked Ligurious.

"I thought he seemed very strong, and handsome," I said.

"I see," smiled Ligurious. "Incidentally," he said, "would you like for me to have Susan whipped for you?"

"Why?" I asked. At the words of Ligurious there was a small sound from the chain of Susan. She shrank back, cowering beside the throne.

"Surely you saw her," said Ligurious, "when she knew herself to be under the gaze of the sleen from Argentum. She was dripping to the tiles before him. Forgive me. I did not mean to offend your sensibilities."

"She is only a slave," I said, lightly. Surely I could not admit to Ligurious that I, too, had been made uneasy by the presence of the ambassador from Argentum.

"True," laughed Ligurious. "I must take my leave now. Drusus Rencius will see you to your quarters."

I nodded, permitting Ligurious to take his leave.

"Thank you, Mistress," said Susan to me, kneeling beside the throne, "for not having me whipped."

"Is it true," I asked her, "that you might possibly have experienced feelings of a sexual nature before Miles of Argentum?"

"I cannot help myself, Mistress," she said. "Before such a man I begin to secrete the oils of submission."

"The oils of submission!" I said.

"Yes, Mistress," she said.

"I have never heard them called that," I said.

"It is what they are," she said, "at least in a slave."

"Oh," I said.

"Does Lady Sheila wish to return to her quarters now?" inquired Drusus Rencius.

"What of the treasures here," I asked, "and Susan, and the other slaves chained here?"

"Scribes from the treasure rooms will be along shortly," he said, "to gather in and account for the cloths and coins. The palace slave master will be along later, too, to release the girls and put them back about their more customary duties."

I then began to precede Drusus Rencius to my quarters. "Miles of Argentum is an arrogant knave, isn't he?" I asked Drusus.

"So it would seem, Lady," said Drusus.

I remembered the sight of the silver tarsk from Argentum, in the hand of Miles of Argentum, and the way it had looked, on the soft carpeting of the dais, on one of the broad steps leading up to the throne.

"Do you think," I asked, lightly, "that I might bring a silver tarsk in a slave market?"

"It would be difficult to say, without assessing Lady Sheila naked," he said.

"Oh," I said.

"Does Lady Sheila wish me to assess her naked in her quarters?" he asked.

"No," I said. "No, of course not!"

We continued to walk along the carpeted, ornamented corridors toward my quarters.

"But, from what you know of me," I said, "do you think that I might bring a silver tarsk?"

"As a Tatrix," he asked, "or only as another woman in the market, another mere female, up for vending, one about whom there is nothing politically or socially special, one who, like most others, will be priced and sold only on her own merits?"

"Like that," I said, "one whose price is determined merely by what she is, and nothing else."

"Are you serious?" he asked.

"Yes," I said, "as one whose value is determined only by herself."

"I would think, then," he said, "the price would be too high."

"Oh?" I said, angrily. "And what do you think I would go for?"

"Lady Sheila must remember," said Drusus Rencius, "that even if she might prove to be quite lovely, she is still untrained."

"Untrained!" I cried.

"Yes," he said.

"You speak as if slaves were mere animals!" I said.

"They are," he said.

I turned to face him, angrily. "And if I were such an animal, and for sale, what do you think I would bring?" I asked.

"May I speak with impunity?" he inquired, smiling.

"Yes," I said, "of course!"

"My remarks," he said, "will be based on the hypothesis that Lady Sheila's figure is acceptable, that her curvatures fall within suitable slave tolerances."

I looked at him.

"Am I entitled to assume this?" he asked.

"I suppose so," I said. I had no idea what these tolerances might be. I did regard myself as being rather pretty.

"We shall further assume," he said, "that Lady Sheila's figure is not merely acceptable, but quite lovely. This, I think, from what I know of her, would be a fair assumption. In any event, it will enhance the speculation."

"Very well," I said.

"Your face, for example," he said, "is quite delicate and

lovely. If your body matches it, I think you would clearly have the makings of a superb slave."

"Proceed," I said. It pleased me to have received this compliment from Drusus Rencius. Too, I had little doubt but what my body, which is slender and lovely, and not overly developed, well matched my face. Surely I would bring a high price.

"Let us further assume," he said, "that your beauty has been enhanced considerably, by being branded and collared."

"Very well," I said. I was beautiful. I would bring a high price indeed!

"Even so," he said, "you have had no previous owners, as I understand it."

"That is correct," I said.

"Having been unowned," he said, "it seems natural, then, to assume that you are inexperienced and untrained."

"Yes," I said.

"And there are many beautiful women," he said. "There is no dearth of them in the slave markets."

"And what, then," I asked, "do you think I would bring?"

He looked at me, smiling.

"What?" I asked.

"I would think," he said, "that you would bring somewhere between fifteen and twenty copper tarsks."

"Copper tarsks!" I cried.

"Yes," he said.

"Beast!" I cried. "Beast!"

"But remember," he said, smiling, "it is slaves who are assessed and have prices. Free women are priceless."

"Yes," I said, somewhat mollified, stepping back. "Yes!" I must remember that I was priceless. I was a free woman.

"Shall we continue on to your quarters?" he asked.

"Yes," I said, and then, turning about, once more preceded him down the corridor toward my quarters.

I had had matters out with Ligurious earlier, about such things as the barring on my door. My door, now, was no longer barred. The guards remained outside but that, of course, was an understandable precaution, one clearly in my own best interests, one pertinent to my personal security. Furthermore I was now free, almost whenever I wished, to go forth from my quarters. The only restriction was that I must be accompanied by my guard, Drusus Rencius. I could now leave my quarters even at night. Best perhaps, I was allowed to leave the palace whenever I might please, provided I did so incognito and in the company of Drusus Rencius.

## 6

# THE SIRIK

"There are places you have not taken me in Corcyrus," I said to Drusus Rencius.

We stood on the height of the walls of Corcyrus, on a stone riser behind the parapet, which permitted us to look out over the parapet, rather than through its apertures, on the surrounding fields.

"Not all places in Corcyrus," he said, "are safe, particularly at night, and not all are suitable for the sensibilities of a free woman."

There was a breeze blowing toward us, over the wall. It was welcome. I felt it move my veils back against my features. I reveled in its lightness and freshness.

"You should adjust your hood," said Drusus Rencius.

I had thrust it back, a few moments ago, to better revel in the breeze. To be sure, it was now possible to detect the color of my hair.

Angrily I readjusted the hood. Drusus Rencius was so protective!

He looked about, nervously. Why, I wondered, should he seem so tense or uneasy here.

I could smell the tarns, gigantic, crested saddlebirds, on their perches some hundred feet away, to our right. There were five of them.

"Do not approach them too closely," I had been warned by him.

"Do not fear," I had laughed. I had a terror of such things.

But why, then, if he were so wary of them, or fearful for my safety, had he wanted to come to this portion of the wall? It was he who had suggested that we come this close to those fearful monsters.

"I can still see your hair," said Drusus Rencius.

I drew the hood angrily even more closely about my features. Little more now could be seen of me, as is common with the robes of concealment, but a bit of the bridge of my nose and my eyes. It was five days ago that I had suggested we come to the height of the wall, that I might look out. He had originally been reluctant to bring me here, but then, almost too suddenly, it had seemed to me, had finally agreed. Now, here on the walls, he seemed nervous.

"You are still angry with me," I said, "about the Kaissa matches."

"No," he said.

"They were boring," I said.

"Centius of Cos was playing," he said. "He is one of the finest of the players on Gor." The appearance of a player of the stature of Centius of Cos at the matches in a city such as Corcyrus, I gathered, had to do with the alliances between Cos and Corcyrus. Otherwise it did not seem likely to me that he would have graced so small a tournament with his presence. He had won his games easily with the exception of one, with a quite minor player, which he had seemed to prolong indefinitely, as though attempting to bring about some obscure and particular configuration on the board. Then, apparently failing to achieve this, almost as though wearily, he had brought the game to a conclusion in five moves.

"You are still angry with me," I said.

"No," he said.

"Yes, you are," I said.

He did not respond.

"They were boring," I said. I had asked to be brought home early.

He did not respond.

The most exciting thing about the matches from my point of view was going in and out of the grounds. There were several slave girls there, just outside the grounds, fastened to various rings and stanchions. They had been chained there, to wait like dogs for the return of their masters.

"After you returned me to my quarters, I wager," I said, "you returned to the matches."

"Yes," he said. "I did."

"And did you get to see your precious Centius of Cos finish his final games?" I asked.

"Yes," he said.

"Please do not be angry with me, Drusus," I said.

"I am not angry with you," he said.

I wondered why I had spoken as I had. I was a Tatrix. Authority was mine, not his. He was only a guard, a mere guard. Yet I did not want him to be angry with me. There was something in me, something deep, I did not know what, that wanted to be pleasing to him.

I continued to look out over the fields. They were lovely. In a Gorean city it was not difficult for a woman to travel incognito. By the robes of concealment this is made easy. I wore the robes of a woman of high caste, today the yellow of the Builders. Drusus Rencius wore a nondescript tunic and a swirling maroon cape. The only weaponry he carried, that I could detect, was his sword. He might have been any mercenary, or armed servant, in attendance on a lady. I was pleased to travel incognito in the city, in this fashion. Otherwise, had I gone abroad in the robes of the Tatrix, we would have been encumbered by guards and crowds; we would have had to travel in a palanquin; we would have been forced to tolerate the annunciatory drums and trumpets, and put up with all the noisy, ostentatious, dreary panoply of office. To be sure I sometimes found such accouterments stimulating and gratifying but I certainly did not want them every time I wished to put my foot outside the palace gate.

I thought I heard a small noise, as of metal, from within the cloak of Drusus Rencius.

He had glanced to our right, to the tarns on their perches. They were saddled, and their reins were upon them. They were ready for investigatory excursions or, if the randomly selected schedules were appropriate, for routine patrols. The left foot of each tarn, by a spring clasp, which could be opened by hand, and a chain, was fastened to the perch. The birds, thus, for most practical purposes, could be brought to flight almost immediately. Their riders, or tarnsmen, were not in the immediate vicinity, but were, as is common, quite close, in this case in a guard station at the foot of the wall. In a matter of Ihn, given a command or the sounding of an alarm bar, they could be in the saddle.

Drusus Rencius looked back from the tarns. I heard again the small sound of metal from within the cloak.

He looked about, uneasily. This nervousness did not seem typical of him.

"Have you heard aught of the sleen of Argentum?" I

asked. It had been several days now since the return of Miles of Argentum to his city.

"No," said he.

"It is nice of you to bring me here," I said. "It is a lovely view."

He said nothing.

"I enjoyed the song drama last night," I said.

"Good," said he.

To be sure it had been difficult for me, at my present level in Gorean, to understand all the singing. Too, the amplificatory masks, sometimes used in the larger of the tiered theaters, somewhat distorted the sound. Some of the characters had seemed unnaturally huge. These, I had been informed, wore special costumes; these costumes had expanded shoulders and had exaggerated hemlines, long enough to cover huge platformlike shoes. These characters, thus, were made to appear larger than life. They represented, generally, important personages, such as Ubars and Ubaras. There had not been a great deal of action in the drama but movement on the stage was supplied in abundance by a chorus whose complex activities and dances served to point up and emotionally respond to, and interpret, exchanges among the principals. The chorus, too, sometimes singing and sometimes speaking in unison, took roles in the drama, such as first the citizens of one city and then of another, and then of another, and so on. It also was not above commenting on the activities and speeches of the principals, chiding them, calling certain omissions to their minds, offering them constructive criticism, commending them, encouraging them, and so on. Indeed, it was not unusual for the chorus and a principal to engage with one another in discourse. What I saw was clearly drama but it was not a form of drama with which I was familiar. The chorus, according to Drusus Rencius, in its various sections and roles, was the original cast of the drama. The emergence of principals from the chorus, of particular actors playing isolated, specific roles, was a later development. Some purists, according to Drusus Rencius, still criticize this innovation. It is likely to remain, however, in his opinion, as it increases the potentialities of the form, its flexibility and power. Such dramas, incidentally, are normally performed not by professional companies but by groups of citizens from the communities themselves, or nearby communities. Sometimes they are supported by rich citizens; sometimes they are supported by caste organizations; sometimes, even, they are sponsored by merchants or businesses, as a matter of goodwill and promotion; sometimes, too, they are subsidized by grants from a public treasury. Art in a Gorean city is taken seriously; it is regarded as an enhancement of the civic life. It is not regarded as the prerogative of an elite, nor is its fate left exclusively to the mercies of private patrons. The story in the song drama, in itself, apart from its complex embellishments, was a simple one. It dealt with a psychological crisis in the life of a Ubar. He is tempted, in the pursuit of his own schemes, motivated by greed, to betray his people. In the end he is convinced by his own reflections, and those of others, of the propriety of keeping the honor of his own Home Stone.

"What did you think of the drama?" Drusus Rencius had asked me last night. "The story of it," I had told him, seeking to impress him with my intelligence, "aside from the impressiveness of it, and the loveliness of its setting and presentation, is surely an unrealistic, silly one." "Oh?" he had asked. "Yes," I had said, "no true ruler would act like that. Only a fool would be motivated by considerations of honor." "Perhaps," had said Drusus Rencius, dryly. I had looked at him, and then I had looked away, quickly. I had felt like I might be nothing. He was regarding me with total contempt.

"I did enjoy the drama," I insisted to Drusus Rencius, standing on the riser, looking over the parapet, "really."

"Splendid," he said.

"I still think my comments were true, of course," I said, lightly. Surely it would not do to retreat on such a matter. Besides, for most practical purposes, I did regard them as true. Who, in these days, in a real world, could take anything like honor seriously?

"Perhaps," granted Drusus Rencius.

"You are a hopeless romantic, Drusus," I said to him, turning about, laughing.

"Perhaps," he said. He turned away from me. Again I heard the small sound in the cloak.

He looked at the tarns.

I turned away from him, hurt. I did not want him to be disappointed with me.

"The view here," I said, lightly, "is lovely. We should have come here before."

"Perhaps," he said.

I had seen much of Corcyrus in the past few days. Drusus

Rencius, for the most part, had been an attentive and accommodating escort. I loved the markets and bazaars, the smells, the colors, the crowds, the quantities and varieties of goods, the tiny shops, the stalls, the places of business which sometimes were so small as a tiny rug on the stones, on which a peddler displayed his wares. Drusus Rencius had even permitted me, with coins, helping me, to bargain. I had been very excited to come back to the palace with my small triumphs. I loved shopping, and looking, even when I was buying nothing. Trailing me about, while I satisfied my curiosity as to curious nooks and crannies, must have been tiresome for Drusus, but he had not complained. I had begun to fall in love with the Gorean city. It was so vital and alive. In particular I was excited by the female slaves I saw, barefoot, in their tunics and collars, not exciting much attention, simply being taken for granted, in the crowds. Such women were an accepted part of Gorean life. Sometimes, too, I would see a naked slave in the crowd, one sent forth from her house only in her collar. These women, too, did not attract that much attention. Their sight was not that uncommon in Gorean streets. One such woman, in particular, startled and excited me. She wore not only her collar. She also wore an iron belt. This belt consisted of two major pieces; one was a rounded, fitted, curved barlike waistband, flattened at the ends; one end of this band, that on the right, standing behind the woman and looking forward, had a heavy semicircular ring, or staple, welded onto it; the other flattened end of the waistband, looking forward, had a slot in it which fitted over the staple; the other major portion of this belt consisted of a curved band of flat, shaped iron; one end of this flat band was curved about, and closed about, the barlike waistband in the front; this produces a hinge; the flat, U-shaped strap of iron swings on this hinge; on the other end of this flat band of iron is a slot; it fits over the same staple as the slot in the flattened end of the left side of the barlike waistband. The belt is then put on the woman in this fashion. The waistband is closed about her, the left side, its slot penetrated by the staple, over the right side; the flat U-shaped band of iron, contoured to female intimacies, is then swung up on its hinge, between her thighs, where the slot on its end is penetrated by the staple, this keeping the parts of the belt in place. The whole apparatus is then locked on her, the tongue of a padlock thrust through the staple, the lock then snapped shut. I almost fainted when I first saw this thing. She actually wore it. It was on her! It was locked on her! The insolent mastery it bespoke made me almost giddy, the very thought that a woman might be subjected to such domination. She did not even control her own intimacies. They were controlled by he who owned her, and them.

"You seem interested in the iron belt," had said Drusus Rencius. "No," I had said. "No!" "There are many varieties of such belts," said Drusus. "You see a rather plain one. Note the placement of the padlock, at the small of her back. Some regard that arrangement as more aesthetic; others prefer for the lock to be in front, where it may dangle before her, constantly reminding her of its presence. I personally prefer the lock in the back. Its placement there, on the whole, makes a woman feel more helpless. Too, of course, its placement there makes it almost impossible for her to pick." "I see," I had said. How irritated I had been then with Drusus. He had discussed the thing as though it might have been a mere, inconsequential piece of functional hardware. Could he not see what it really was, what it meant, what it must teach the girl, how it must make her feel?

"There are wagons," I said, pointing over the parapet. There were some five wagons approaching the city, in a line. Each was being drawn by two strings of harnessed male slaves, about twenty slaves in each string.

"Those are Sa-Tarna wagons," said Drusus, "bringing grain to the city."

"What is that other wagon," I asked, "the smaller one, there near the side of the road, which has pulled aside to let the grain wagons pass?" I had been watching it approach. I thought I knew well what sort of wagon it was. It was the sort of wagon whose contents are of so little value that it must yield the road in either direction to any vehicle that might care to pass it. It was a squarish wagon. It was drawn by a single tharlarion, a broad tharlarion, one of Gor's quadrupedal draft lizards. It was covered by a canopy, mounted on a high, squarish frame, of blue-and-yellow silk.

"Lady Sheila is much too innocent, and her sensibilities are far too delicate," said he, "to inquire as to what sort of wagon that is."

"No," I said, "what?" I would pretend to an innocent ignorance.

"It is a slaver's wagon," he said, "a girl wagon."

"Oh," I said, as though surprised. After a time, I said, "I wonder if there are any girls in it."

"Probably," said Drusus. "Its canopy is up, and it is approaching the city."

"Are girls fastened in such wagons?" I asked.

"Usually," he said.

"How?" I asked.

"The most usual arrangement," he said, "involves a metal bar and girls who are independently shackled. The bar runs parallel to the length of the wagon bed. It is a liftable bar. It has a hinge at the end of the wagon bed near the wagon box. The bar is lifted, by means of the hinge, and the girls, by means of their ankle chains, are threaded upon it. It is then lowered and locked into a socket at the end of the wagon bed, near the gate."

"They are then well held in place," I said.

"Yes," he said.

"Are they clothed in such a wagon?" I asked.

"Sometimes they are, sometimes they are not," he said.

"I see," I said. I wondered what it might feel like to wear shackles, to have my ankles chained in proximity to one another, to have the chain looped about such a bar, so that I might not, even if I wished, be able to pull my ankles more than a few inches from it. I wondered what it might feel like, to know myself so helplessly and perfectly confined. My breath began to come more quickly.

"Lady Sheila seems much interested in the small details in the lives of female slaves," he said. Perhaps he had noticed the quickening of my breath, in the inward movements of the veil.

"Do not become presumptuous," I said.

"Forgive me," he said.

"I was merely curious," I said, irritably.

"Of course, Lady Sheila," he said. He need not know that I often, for no reason I clearly understood, in the loneliness of my quarters, slept at the lower end of the great couch, near the slave ring, and sometimes, seemingly almost unable to help myself, had knelt beside it in the darkness, and kissed it.

"The wagon is moving now," I said. The grain wagons had passed it. It was now, again, pulling toward the center of the road, the high iron-rimmed wheels trundling on the stone, seeking the long, shallow, shiny, saucerlike ruts, polished in the stone by the earlier passage of countless vehicles. I had been sure it was a slave wagon, of course, from the blue-and-yellow silk. Outside the establishments of slavers there often hung streamers and banners in these colors, and sometimes, on the walls, or doors, or posts near the doors, these colors, in diagonal stripes or slashes, were painted. When I had seen signs or emblems of this sort I had often, as though interested in something else, requested that we take our way down that street. Generally I had been able to see little or nothing, usually only the narrow, gloomy doors, often of iron, of grim, almost fortresslike buildings, but, sometimes, there would be an open-air market or some girls, as displays, would be chained outside. Inside some of these buildings I had learned there were display courtyards where girls, for example, might be examined in natural light. In the open-air markets, or in the outside displays, the girls, seeing me viewing them, had usually knelt, immediately, putting their heads down, exhibiting total deference and respect before a free woman. Some, seeing me looking at them, had actually thrown themselves, trembling, to their bellies. "They are afraid of you," Drusus Rencius had explained. "Why?" I had asked. "Because you are a free woman," he had said. "Oh," I had said. They must have had, I gathered, some of them at least, unfortunate experiences with free women. I watched the wagon trundling slowly down the road. I wondered what it felt like to ride in such a wagon, not as its driver, of course, but as its cargo. I considered the lack of springs in such a vehicle, the high, iron-rimmed wheels, with their lack of cushioning, the primitiveness of the roads it must traverse. I did not think the ride would be a smooth one. How much protection might be afforded a girl chained on the boards in the wagon bed of such a vehicle by the single layer of the fabric of a slave tunic, if, indeed, she were permitted one?

"Are such wagons padded?" I asked.

"No," he said.

"Oh," I said.

"But sometimes cloths are thrown in them," he said. "That way the goods will not be so bruised when they come to the market."

"I see," I said. If I were such a girl I would not wish to be brought bruised to the market. That way I might bring a lower price. That way I might get a master who was less well fixed.

"It is natural for slavers to wish to get the highest possible prices for their girls," he said.

"Of course," I said.

I could not see the wagon now. It was somewhere below the wall.

I straightened myself on the riser, behind the parapet. I drew a deep breath. How pleased I was that I was free! How dreadful, how horrifying, it would be to be merely a lowly slave!

"You seem nervous today, Drusus," I said.

"Forgive me, Lady Sheila," he said.

"Is there anything wrong?" I asked.

"No," he said.

"What is that sound from within your cloak," I asked, "as of metal?"

"Nothing," said he.

One of the tarns moved on the perch, several feet to our right. I did not wish to approach too closely to such things. I wondered why Drusus had brought me to this particular place on the wall. The proximity of the tarns made it less pleasant than it might otherwise have been. The view, however, as I had remarked, was lovely.

"You do not think much of me, do you, Drusus?" I asked.

"I do not understand," he said, startled.

"You think that I am pretty and ignoble, don't you?"

"I receive my fees for guarding Lady Sheila," he said, "not for forming opinions as to her character."

"Do you like me?" I asked.

"Having suggested that I might think little of you, and might regard you as pretty and ignoble, now you inquire if I might like you?" he smiled.

"It is not impossible," I said.

He smiled.

"Do you?" I asked.

"Does it matter?" he asked.

"No," I said, angrily. "Of course not!"

"Then," he smiled, "there is no point in answering."

"Do you?" I asked, angrily.

"I am paid to guard you," he said, "not to consider any personal feelings, one way or another, which I might have towards you."

"One way or another?" I asked, angrily.

"Yes," he said.

"You despise and hate me!" I said.

"I could find it easy to despise you," he said, "and, at one time, from all that I had heard of the Tatrix of Corcyrus, and know of her governance of the city, I would have thought it would also be easy to hate you, but now, now that I have met you, I could not honestly say that I hate you."

"How flattering!" I remarked.

"Your official self and your personal self, or your public and private selves, seem quite different," he said.

"Perhaps," I said, irritably.

"It is doubtless that way with many people," he said.

"Doubtless," I said.

He looked from one side to the other, along the walk behind the parapet. For most practical purposes we were alone on the wall. The nearest people, a couple, were better than a hundred yards away, to our left. He looked again then to the tarns. Then he looked at me. Then, angrily, he looked out, over the parapet. His fists were clenched.

I, too, looked out, over the parapet. I could feel tears in my eyes. I wanted to please Drusus Rencius. I wanted, desperately, for him to like me. Yet everything I did or said seemed to be wrong. Then I was very angry with myself. It did not matter. I was not a slave at his feet, half naked in a collar, fearful of his whip, piteously suing for the least sign of his favor. I was a Tatrix. He was only a guard, nothing! I wondered, shuddering, what it would be to be the slave of such a man. I did not think he would be weak with me. I thought that he would, like any typical Gorean master, keep me under perfect discipline.

"I enjoyed the czehar concert," I said, lightly.

"Good," he said.

The czehar is a long, low, rectangular instrument. It is played, held across the lap. It has eight strings, plucked with a horn pick. It had been played by Lysander of Asperiche. The concert had taken place two nights ago in the small theater of Kleitos, off the square of Perimines.

"The ostraka were quite expensive, weren't they?" I asked.

"Yes," he said.

It was quite commonly the case, I had learned, that for a concert by Lysander one could not buy admission at the gate, but must present ostraka purchased earlier in one of the market places or squares. These were apparently originally shells or pieces, shards, of pottery, but now were generally small clay disks, with a hole for a string near one edge. These were fired in a kiln, and glazed on one side. The glazing's colorations and patterns are difficult to duplicate and serve in their way as an authentication for the disk, the glazings differing for different performances or events. The unglazed back of the disk bears the date of the event or performance and a sign indicating the identity of the original vendor, the agent authorized to sell them to the public. Some of these disks, also, on the back, include a seat location. Most seating, however, in Gorean theaters, except for certain privileged sections, usually reserved for high officials or the extremely wealthy, is on a first-come-first-served basis. These ostraka, on their strings, about the necks of their owners, make attractive pendants. Some are worn even long after the performance or event in question, perhaps to let people know that one was fortunate enough to have been the witness of a particular event or performance, or perhaps merely because of their intrinsic aesthetic value. Some people keep them as souvenirs. Others collect them, and buy and sell them, and trade them. If the event or performance is an important one, and the ostraka are limited, their number being governed by the seating capacity of the structure or area in question, it is unlikely that they will be publicly displayed until after the event or performance. It is too easy to snatch them from about the neck in the market place. Too, sometimes rich men have been known to set ruffians on people to obtain them. Needless to say some profiteering occasionally takes place in connection with the ostraka, a fellow buying a few for a given price and then trying to sell them for higher prices later outside, say, the stadium or theater.

"How much did they cost?" I asked.

"Together," he said, "a silver tarsk."

"That is more, I recall," I said, "than you thought I might go for if I were sold for myself alone, as a slave."

"Yes," he said.

I stiffened, somewhat angrily.

"Lady Sheila must remember that she is not trained in the intimate and delicious arts of the female slave."

"Arts?" I inquired.

"Yes," said he, "the complex, subtle and sensuous arts of being pleasing, fully, to a man."

"I see," I said.

"It is natural," he said, "that some women will bring much higher prices than others."

"Of course," I said, irritably.

"Some women," he said, "do not even know the floor movements of an aroused, pleading slave."

"They must indeed be stupid," I said. I had no idea, of course, what they might be.

"I do not think they are necessarily stupid," he said, "merely ignorant, perhaps because untrained, or perhaps merely because they have not yet been awakened sexually, have not yet been forced to feel the slave fires in their belly, have not yet, by strong men, been made the helpless victims of their own now-enkindled needs."

"I thought Lysander played well," I said.

"He is regarded as one of the finest czehar players on all Gor," said Drusus Rencius, dryly.

"Oh," I said. I felt so stupid. It seemed I could do nothing right with Drusus Rencius.

I looked out, again, over the fields.

"Is Lady Sheila all right?" inquired Drusus Rencius.

"Yes," I said.

The last few days had been full ones. Aside from the markets and bazaars, and the theaters in the evening, I had seen much else of Corcyrus as well. It had been pleasant to walk through the cool halls of the libraries, with their thousands of scrolls organized and cataloged, and through the galleries on the avenue of Iphicrates. The fountains in the squares, too, were impressive. It was almost hard for me to remember that they were not merely ornaments to the city but that they also, in the Gorean manner, served a very utilitarian purpose. To them most people must come, bearing vessels, for their water. Some of the smaller fountains were worn down on the right side of their rim. That was where right-handed people would rest their hand, leaning over to drink. I particularly enjoyed the public gardens. Given the plantings flowers in them, of one sort or another, are in bloom almost all of the year. Here, too, are many winding and almost secluded paths. In them, combined, one finds color, beauty and, in many sections, if one wishes it, privacy. I knew few of the flowers and trees. Drusus Rencius, to my surprise, whenever I was in doubt, could supply me with the name. Goreans, it seemed, paid attention to their environment. It means something to them. They live in it. How few children of Earth, I thought, are taught the names and kinds of the trees and shrubs, the plants, the insects and birds, which surround them constantly. I was also surprised to find that Drusus Rencius seemed genuinely fond of flowers. I would not have expected, given my Earth background, that a man of his obvious power and competence could care for anything, and so deeply, as innocent, delicate and soft as a flower. At one secluded point in one of the gardens I had paused and, pretending to adjust my veil, had stood quite close to Drusus Rencius, but he had stepped back, and looked away. He had not kissed me. I had then, angrily, refastened my veil. I wondered why he had not kissed me. Was it because I was a Tatrix? I wondered what it would be like to be kissed by him. I wondered if he might, touching my lips, I in his arms, helplessly held there, suddenly rape my lips with his kiss, and then, unable to help himself, hurl me to his feet, crouching over me then ferociously, to remove my robes and force me to his service.

I felt the wind, over the parapet, move my veil.

I had enjoyed these days with Drusus Rencius but, at night, returned to my quarters, I would often be restless and lonely. At such times, though I did not confess this to Drusus, nor even to Susan, I would feel helpless, weak and needful. I had formed the habit, for no reason I clearly understood, of sleeping near the foot of the couch, near the slave ring. I would sometimes lie there miserably, twisting and turning, almost sobbing, afflicted with helpless feelings and strange, troubling emotions that I could scarcely begin to understand. I did not know what was wrong with me. I knew only that I felt empty, miserable and unfulfilled.

Drusus Rencius occasionally took me to see various portions of local games. These involved such things as races, javelin hurling and stone throwing. I would usually stay for an event or two and then leave. On the whole I found such games boring. When I wished to leave, or change my location, to see something different, he always deferred to my wishes. I was, after all, the Tatrix and he was, after all, only my guard. From one set of contests, however, I could not, to his surprise, be budged. I had sat on the tiers, close to the fenced enclosure, thrilled. These were contests of sheathed swords, the sheaths chalked with red, so that hits might be noted. The contestants were sturdy men, stripped to the waist, in half tunics, bronzed and handsome, with rippling muscles.

As they thrust at one another and fended blows, moving with great speed and skill, in their swift passages, under the watchful eye of the referee, backed by two independent scorers, I could scarcely conjecture what would be involved in actual swordplay, with steel unencumbered with sheaths. I was terrified to consider it. And women, I thought, must abide its outcome. On a cement disk, about a foot high and five feet in diameter, on the opposite side of the enclosure, as though in symbolism of this, a young, naked woman was chained. The chain was on her neck and ran to a ring anchored in the center of the disk. It was long enough to permit her to stand comfortably which, sometimes, she did. Most of the time, however, she sat or lay, almost catlike, on the disk, watching the fighting. Her body was slim and well formed. Her hair was brightly red and, when she stood, it fell almost to her knees. When the contests had begun she had not seemed particularly interested in them, but, as they had proceeded, she had become more and more attentive. She was now watching them with great closeness. She was the prize. She would be given to the victor. "Do you wish to leave now?" Drusus Rencius had asked once, during an interval between passages. "No!" I had said. He had regarded me, puzzled. "I want to see who wins her," I said, angrily. He looked over to the woman. She was then standing, the chain on her neck dangling down to the ring. She had one hand at her bosom. She was frightened. "She is only a slave," he had said. But he had sat down, patiently, beside me, content, it seemed, to wait until I was ready to leave. How angry I was with him them. Could he not conjecture the feelings, the trepidation, of the poor girl? She had a chain on her neck. She was a prize. She did not know to whom she would be awarded. She did not know who it would be whom she would have to serve, who it would be to whom she would belong! The poor, soft, helpless chained thing! How callous and stupid are men! Too, I like she, as fortunes shifted in the matches, as points were won and lost, was torn back and forth in my conjectures and anticipations. Doubtless the men in the audience were intent on the bouts, observing the styles and skills of the contestants, tallying points, and assessing the play. Surely they seemed to have little mind for the chained prize. Surely they seemed eager to applaud, striking their left shoulders, particularly fine thrusts or particularly tight, fierce passages. I, on the other hand, I am sure, tended to see the bouts rather differently. I saw them, I think, almost as though through the eyes of the prize. This was natural. I was a woman. Accordingly, I, too, in a sense, was a prize in such matters. Then the bouts were ended. I almost fainted with relief. He whom the girl had favored, and whom I had favored, had won, a swift, lithe, bronzed giant of a youth. After the men, and his opponents, had swept about him, congratulating him, she was unchained. She crept to his feet and kissed them. Then she fetched him a dipper of water and, kneeling, head down, lifting her arms, holding the dipper with both hands, proffered it to him. He drank and then she returned the dipper to the bucket, near the fence. She then returned to where he stood on the sand, talking with men, and, crouching down, or kneeling or standing, as was most efficient at the time, lovingly, kissing him meanwhile, softly and timidly, wiped his body clean of sand and sweat with her long hair. When he left the pit she followed him, a bit behind him and on his left, heeling him. I was much aroused and was almost trembling as Drusus Rencius, who seemed unaware of my condition, conducted me back to the palace. In a deserted corridor, before we would turn into the corridor leading to my door, and come into the view of any guards there, I stopped. I would give Drusus Rencius another chance to kiss me. "This veil," I said, irritatedly, "is loose," reaching to it, fussing with it, taking a pin from it, with the result that the cloth, as though temporarily disarranged, fell to my left. I then stood quite close to Drusus Rencius. "It is hard for me to see," I said to him. "Could you please fasten it for me?" "Of course," he said, and took the pin. I lifted my head to him. He was tall and strong. As he reached to the right of my face I gently stayed his hand. "I give you my permission to kiss me," I whispered.

"Does Lady Sheila command me to kiss her?" he asked.

"No," I said. "Of course not."

"I do not require a woman's permission to kiss her," he said. Then he repinned my veil, closing my lips away behind it. He had then escorted me to my quarters.

After supper, when I was alone in my quarters, I was furious and miserable.

I stripped myself and threw myself on the great couch. I lay on it for hours, sometimes pounding it in anger, clawing at it with my fingers, biting at it in misery, dampening it with hot tears, squirming on it in misery.

I had been rejected by Drusus Rencius. I had thrown myself at him like a tart, and had been rejected! How could I have done that? Was I only a little tart, or was I a desperate, needful woman, one who had dared to be true to her needs? How I hated him! I was a Tatrix, a Tatrix! He was only a soldier, a mere guard! I had power. I could have my vengeance on him! I could tell Ligurious that he had become fresh with me, that he had dared to try to kiss me. Surely he might be broken in rank for that, or whipped, or even slain! I wondered why he had not kissed me. Was it because I was a Tatrix? But I did not think that that thought, momentous though it might be, would have deterred a man such as Drusus Rencius. Was it then because I was not sufficiently attractive? Perhaps. But on Earth I had been thought to be very pretty. Too, Miles of Argentum had speculated that I might bring as much as even a silver tarsk in a market. Was it then because I was free? Were Gorean men spoiled for free women by those collared, curvacious little sluts they had crawling about their feet, desperately eager to please them? Given such luscious alternatives it was natural enough, I supposed, that men would see little point in subjecting themselves to the inconvenience, frustration and pain of relating to a free woman, with her demands, inhibitions and rigidities. Perhaps they could not be blamed for not choosing to reduce the quality of their lives in this fashion. To be sure, if slaves were not available, then it was understandable how men might relate to free women. Sexually starved, and driven by their needs, they would then be forced to make do with whatever might be available, the best in such a case perhaps being the free woman. But on Gor alternatives, real alternatives, slaves, were available. It was no wonder free women, as I had heard, so hated slaves. How could they even begin to compete with a slave, those dreams come true for men? Perhaps that is it, I thought, perhaps that is why he did not kiss me. Perhaps he did not kiss me because I was free, or, I added, in my thinking, not truly understanding the qualification, because he thought I was free. I lay there in the darkness, in the heat of the silks. I wondered why I had made that qualification in my thinking—"because he thought I was free." Could he have been wrong, I asked myself. Could he have been mistaken? How absurd, I thought. What could you possibly mean, I asked myself. The meaning is perfectly clear, I told myself, irritably. Are you stupid? I am a Tatrix, I cried out to myself. I am free! Of course, I am free! "Go now to the slave ring," a voice seemed to say to me. I got up and, almost as though in a trance, scarcely understanding what I was doing, went to the slave ring, that at the foot of the couch. I knelt there. "Are you positioned at the ring," the voice seemed to say. "Yes," I whimpered, to myself. "Take it in your hands, Tiffany," it said, "and kiss it." I took the heavy ring in my hands, lifted it, and kissed it. I then put it back gently, lovingly, against the couch. I then felt it would be permissible for me to return to the couch. I crawled again upon it, to its center. "Get where you belong," said the voice, a bit impatiently. I crawled then to the bottom of the couch and lay there, near its foot, by the slave ring. I wondered if Drusus Rencius would have refused to kiss me if I had not been a free woman, but a slave. If I had been a slave, say, perhaps, a fifteen-copper-tarsk girl, that amount for which he had once suggested a slaver might let me go, I think I might have received a somewhat different treatment at his hands. "It is fortunate for you," said the voice within me, "that Drusus does not know that you are a slave." "I am not a slave," I said, aloud. "I am not a slave!" "Remain where you are, at the foot of the couch, until morning," said the voice within me. "I will," I said, frightened. I had then fallen asleep. To my embarrassment I was still there in the morning when I awakened, Susan having entered the room. "I must have moved about in my sleep," I said to Susan. "Yes, Mistress," she had said, her head down, smiling. I had considered whipping her, but I had not done so. "What is it like, being owned, and having a master," I had later asked Susan, while being served breakfast, as though merely curious. "Consider yourself as having a master, and being owned," said Susan, "that you are totally his, and that he may do with you, fully, whatever he wants." I shuddered. "It is like that," she said, "only it is real." "I see," I had whispered.

I stood on the riser, behind the parapet. I looked out over the fields.

"I hear it again," I said, "that sound, as of metal, from within your cloak. What is it?"

"Nothing," he said.

On Gor my entire mind and body, in the fullness of its femininity, had come alive, but yet, in spite of my new vitality and health, I was in many ways keenly miserable and unfulfilled. On Earth, in its pollutions, surrounded by its crippled males and frustrated women, exposed to its antibiological education and conditionings, subjected to the perversions of unisex, denying their sexuality in its fullness to both sexes, the nature of the emptiness in my life, and its causes, had been, in effect, concealed from me. I had not even been given categories in terms of which I might understand it. Where I had needed reality and truth I had been given only lies, propaganda and false values. Here on Gor, on the other hand, I was becoming deeply in touch with my femininity. Never on Earth had I felt it as keenly and deeply, never on Earth had I been so deeply sensitive to it, so much aware of its needs, delicacy and depth. But here on Gor I was clearly aware of my lack of fulfillment, instead of, as on Earth, usually only vaguely or obscurely aware of it. What had been an almost unlocalizable malaise on Earth, except at certain times when, to my horror, I had understood it more clearly, on Gor had become a reasonably clearly focused problem. On Earth it had been as though I was miserable and uncomfortable without, often, really knowing why, whereas on Gor I had suddenly become aware that I was terribly hungry. Moreover, on Gor, for the first time, so to speak, I had discovered the nature of food, that food for which I so sorely hungered, and the exact conditions, the exclusive conditions, perhaps so humiliating and degrading to me, yet exalting, under which it might be obtained. Such thoughts I usually thrust quickly from my mind.

"You are right, Drusus," I said, suddenly. "Slaves are unimportant. They are nothing."

"Of course," he said. "But what has brought this to mind?"

"A conversation I had this morning with that little chit of a slave, Susan."

"Oh," he said.

"It is unimportant," I said.

He nodded.

"Do you know her?" I asked.

"I have seen her, yes, several times," he said.

"What do you think she would bring?" I asked.

"She is a curvaceous little property," he said, "and seems to understand herself well, and the fittingness of the collar on her neck."

"Yes?" I said.

"Three tarsks, perhaps," he said.

"So little?" I asked, pleased.

"Three silver tarsks, of course," said he.

"Oh," I said, angrily.

"There is little doubt what she would look like at the slave ring," he said, "and, too, she has doubtless received some training."

I did not doubt but what Susan, the little slut, had received some training. There was not a detail about her which did not seem, in its way, a perfection.

This morning she had again, in entering my quarters, discovered me near the foot of the couch. Usually, early in the morning, before she entered, I would try to be elsewhere.

"I do not know what is wrong with me," I confessed to her, desperately needing someone to talk to, as she served my breakfast. "I sometimes feel so empty, so miserable, so uncomfortable, so meaningless, so restless."

"Yes, Mistress," she had said, deferentially.

"I just do not know what is wrong with me," I had lamented.

"No, Mistress," she had said.

"You," I said, "on the other hand, seem contrastingly content and serene, even fulfilled and happy."

"Perhaps, Mistress," she smiled.

"What is wrong with me?" I asked.

"Your symptoms are clear, Mistress," she said.

"Oh?" I said.

"I have seen them in many women," she said.

"And just what is wrong with me?" I asked, irritably.

"I would prefer not to speak," she said.

"Speak!" I had said.

"Must I?" she asked.

"Yes!" I said.

"Mistress needs a master," she said.

"Get out!" I had screamed, leaping to my feet, kicking aside the small table, sobbing. "Get out! Get out!"

The girl had fled from the room, terrified.

I had sobbed then in the room, and thrown things about and run to the wall, and struck it with my fists, weeping. "No!" I had cried. "That is stupid, stupid! She is wrong, wrong, wrong, wrong, wrong!"

Only later had I been able to wash and compose myself, and prepare to accompany Drusus Rencius to the height of the walls, to enjoy the view, as we had planned. I had recalled that he had not, initially, wished to take me to the walls, and then, rather suddenly, it had seemed, had agreed to do so.

"I am a larger woman than Susan," I informed Drusus Rencius, on the wall, acidly. "I am taller, and my breasts are larger, and my hips are wider."

"Other things being equal, such things might somewhat improve your price," he admitted.

"I scorn slaves," I said. "I despise them."

"Quite properly," said he.

I looked out, over the wall.

How pleased I was that I was free! How frightful, how terrible, it would be, to be a slave!

"Is Lady Sheila crying?" he asked.

"No!" I said.

I fought the wild needs within me, seeming to well up from my very depths, needs which seemed to be to surrender, to submit and love, totally, irreservedly, giving all, asking nothing. How superficial, suddenly, seemed then the dispositions to selfishness and egotism in me. From whence could these other emotions, so overwhelming within me, have derived, I asked myself. Surely they, frightening me in their way, seemed directly at odds with the Earth conditionings to which I had been subjected. I feared they could have their source only in the very depths of my nature and being.

I dabbed at my eyes with the corner of my veil. "I am not crying," I said. "It is the wind." I then turned about, to look back from the wall over the city of Corcyrus. "There," I said. "That is better."

The tarns on their perches were now on my left.

I looked over the roofs of Corcyrus. I could see, among trees, the various theaters, and the stadium. I could see the palace from where we stood. I could see, too, some of the gardens, and the roof of the library, on the avenue of Iphicrates.

"The city is beautiful," I said.

"Yes," he said, joining me in surveying it.

I was in love with the Gorean world, though I found it in some ways rather fearful, primarily, I suppose, because it permitted female slavery.

I wondered if Susan were right, if I needed a master. Then I put such thoughts from my mind, as absurd.

I was not a cringing, groveling slave, a girl locked in a collar, who must hope that some brute might see fit to throw her a crust of bread. I was quite different. I was a woman of Earth. I was proud and free. Indeed, on this world I even enjoyed a particularly exalted status, one a thousand times beyond that of my imbonded sisters in the city below. I was a Tatrix!

I looked down from the wall, over the many roofs of Corcyrus.

Why was Susan happy, and I miserable? She was only a collared slave. I was free.

I surveyed Corcyrus. In the Gorean world, and I sometimes still had difficulty coping with this comprehension, female slavery was permitted. How horrifying! Yet something deeply within me, undeniably, was profoundly stirred and excited by this comprehension. This stirring within me troubled me. It did not seem to be a response which I had been taught.

"There is the palace," said Drusus Rencius, pointing.

"I see," I said.

Given the sovereignty of males in nature, general among the mammals and universal among the primates, it was natural enough, I supposed, that in a civilization congenial to nature, rather than in one opposed to it, that an institution such as female slavery might exist. This might be regarded as the civilized expression of the biological relationship, a recognition of that relationship, and perhaps an enhancement, refinement and celebration of it, and, within the context of custom and law, of course, a clarification and consolidation of it. But why, I asked myself, irritatedly, should a civilization be congenial to nature? Is it not far better, I asked myself, for a civilization to contradict and frustrate nature; is it not far better for it to deny and subvert nature; is it not far better for it to blur natural distinctions and confuse identities; is it not far better for it, ignoring human happiness and fulfillment, to produce anxiety, guilt, frustration, misery and pain?

"There is the theater of Kleitos," said Drusus Rencius, "the library, the stadium."

"Yes," I said.

But whatever might be the truth about such matters, or the optimum ways of viewing them, female slavery, on Gor, was a fact. There were, as I had long ago learned, slaves here. I looked out, over the city. In the city, within these very walls, there were women, perhaps not much different from myself, in collars, who were literally held in categorical, uncompromised bondage. I had seen several of them, in their distinctive garb, in their collars. I had even seen one who, naked and in her collar, had been locked in an iron belt. Such women were owned, literally *owned,* with all that that might mean.

"There, where you see the trees," said Drusus Rencius, "is the garden of Antisthenes."

"How many slave girls do you suppose there are in Corcyrus?" I asked, as though idly.

"I do not know," he said. "Probably several hundred. We do not count them."

"Do such women seem happy?" I asked.

"As they are only slaves," said Drusus Rencius, "their feelings and happiness are unimportant."

"Of course," I said. Men are such brutes! How helpless are the slaves!

"There, where you see the trees," said Drusus Rencius, again, "is the garden of Antisthenes."

"Yes," I said. We had visited it twice. It was there, on our second visit, that I had first tried to entice Drusus Rencius to kiss me. The second time had been after we had witnessed the fencing matches. I had been rejected both times. I wondered if I would have been rejected had I been a collared slave. To be sure, he might have made me whimper and beg for his kiss.

I rejected an impulse to kneel before Drusus Rencius. How I hated him!

"There are places you have not taken me in Corcyrus," I reminded him.

"Perhaps," he granted me.

"There was a place two days ago," I said, "which we passed in the afternoon."

"Surely you heard the music which was coming from within?" he asked.

"Yes," I said. It would not be easy to forget that music, so melodious, so exciting and sensual.

"A girl was dancing within," he said. "It was a paga tavern."

"You did not let me enter," I said.

"Such girls often dance in little more than jewels, or chains," he said. "It is better, I think, too, that free women not see how they look at men and how they move before them."

"I see," I said. "And how do men find such women?"

"It is in the best interests of the woman," said he, "that the men find her pleasing, very pleasing."

"I see," I said, shuddering. I wondered if I could be pleasing to a man in that way, dancing before him, and then, later, if he had paid my owner my price, in an alcove. Most girls in such a place, I had heard from Susan, but generally not the dancers, came merely with the price of the drink itself. I supposed that if one were a dancer, and was then serving in an alcove, an additional price having been paid for one's use, one would have to strive to be particularly good. Gorean men, I was sure, would see to it that they got their money's worth.

"Sometimes I feel sorry for slaves, mere slaves," I said.

"Do not," he said.

"Why not?" I asked.

"As you suggest," he said, "they are merely slaves."

"Of course," I said, bitterly.

"Does Lady Sheila identify with slaves?" he asked.

"No," I said. "Of course not!"

"Good," he said.

"Why is it good?" I asked.

"It is said," he said, "that she who identifies with slaves wants the collar on her own neck."

"No!" I cried.

"It is only a saying," he said. "Another such saying is that she who identifies with slaves is a slave."

"Absurd!" I said.

"Doubtless," he said.

"But if I were a slave," I said, poutingly, "I suppose I would have to obey. I would have to do what I was told." I stood quite close to him. I was quite small compared to him. His size and masculinity made me feel weak.

"Yes," he said, looking down into my eyes. "In such circumstances, you would have to obey. You would have to do what you were told."

I turned away from him, suddenly, frightened, and looked again out over the wall, toward the fields. The tarns, now, were again on my right.

"It is fortunate that I am not a slave," I laughed.

"Yes," he said.

"Soldiers, too, are to obey, are they not?" I asked.

"Lady?" he asked.

"Hereafter," I said, "when I wish to go somewhere, or do something, I shall expect you to respect my wishes."

"If Lady Sheila is dissatisfied with my services," he said, "she need only call this to the attention of Ligurious, first minister of Corcyrus. A replacement, perhaps one more pleasing to her, may then be assigned."

"While you are assigned as my guard," I said, "you will obey me. I shall decide if, or when, you are relieved of your duties, or even if you are to be discharged entirely from the service of Corcyrus."

"Yes, Tatrix," he said.

"Your services are not entirely displeasing to me," I said, "but it is my intention to see that they are improved. I am Tatrix of Corcyrus."

"Yes, Tatrix," he said.

"Should I wish to enter a paga tavern, for example," I said, "you will accompany me."

"In most paga taverns," he said, "free women are not permitted. In some they are."

"I see," I said. To force an entry to such a place, I then understood, might necessitate an altercation, one perhaps ensuing in the exposure of my identity as the Tatrix. A common free woman, for example, might simply be forbidden to cross certain thresholds.

"Too," he said, "even if commanded, I could not knowingly lead you into danger, for example, into certain sections of the city at night. It is my duty to protect the Tatrix, not to place her in jeopardy."

"You are an excellent guard, Drusus," I said. "You are right, of course."

"I could take you to a tavern in which families are served," he said.

"It was not such a tavern I had in mind," I said.

"Oh," he said.

"Slaves can enter taverns, can they not?" I asked.

"If on an errand, or in the company of a free person," he said.

"There seems little concern for their sensibilities," I observed.

"Sometimes," said he, "they are even taken to such places by their masters, that they may see the paga slaves, and the dancers, and thus learn from them how to serve even more deliciously and lasciviously in the privacy of their own quarters."

"What if I were clothed as a slave?" I asked.

"It is unthinkable!" he said.

I was pleased that this thought, obviously, had touched a nerve in him. I wondered if he had speculated, privately, on what I might look like clad as a slave, or perhaps, in chains, not clad at all. Many men had probably wondered what I looked like, naked. I had always been rather jealous, rather private, about my body, though. I had never had a master who might simply order me to strip. I had been seen naked, of course, by the men in my apartment, when they had removed the towel from me. I remembered how casually and efficiently they had handled me, how I had been injected with the contents of the syringe, how I had been secured with leather straps, helpless and gagged, in the heavy metal box, with air holes.

"Too," he said, "in so public a place you might, unveiled as is a slave, be recognized. Your resemblance to the Tatrix, at least, would surely be noted."

"You are right again, of course," I said. He was.

He was silent.

"Drusus," I said.

"Yes," said he.

"I would like to see a slaver's house, inside. I would like to see the 'pens.' "

"Such are not fit for the sensibilities of a free woman," he said.

"I would like to see them," I said. "That would not be dangerous, would it?"

"No," he admitted, reluctantly. Such places, I gathered, might be among the safest on Gor. I could scarcely conjecture the effectiveness of the security that might be practiced within them, how helplessly the slaves might be confined. Too, a free person on Gor is almost never in any danger from a slave unless it be a guard slave, and he is attacking its master. In some cities a slave can be slain for so much as touching a weapon. Insurbordination, slaves are quickly taught, is not acceptable, in any way, to the Gorean master.

"Then," I said, triumphantly, "I shall expect you to arrange a tour."

"Are there any particular pens of interest to Lady Sheila?" he asked.

"The choice," I told him, airily, "may be yours."

"Did you merely wish to see girls in the grated pits, or chained in their kennels, or at their rings," he asked, "or did you wish, perhaps, to gain also an idea of what goes on in such a house?"

"What do you mean?" I asked.

"How, for example," he said, "girls might be trained."

"That might be interesting," I said, as though considering it, trying to keep the excitement out of my voice. The thought of women being trained, actually trained, as Susan might have been trained, almost made me faint with excitement. I wondered if I might train well. I supposed I might be punished if I did not. Under such conditions I suspected I would train quite well. I would do my best to be a diligent and apt pupil.

"Your presence, of course," he said, "as you may be aware, may inhibit the slaves."

"You are an intelligent man," I said. "Perhaps you can figure out a way to prevent that."

"It might be possible," he said, "in the privacy of the house, where few would know you."

"What do you have in mind?" I asked.

"Do you have pretty legs?" he asked.

"Yes!" I said. I thought I had very pretty legs.

"It might be possible," he mused.

"Tomorrow!" I said.

"So soon?" he asked.

"Yes," I said.

"Why should you wish to see such a place?" he asked. "Why should it be of interest to you?"

"I am merely curious," I said, tossing my head.

"Tomorrow?" he asked.

"Yes," I said.

"I shall attempt to make the arrangements," he said.

"Do so," I said. "I shall be totally cooperative." I then heard again that small sound, as of metal, from within his cloak.

"Why did you wait so long to bring me to the height of the wall?" I asked. That small sound of metal had reminded me of his reticence with respect to its origin. That had puzzled me. Too, I recalled his earlier nervousness, though now that had seemed to pass. Too, I had not understood why he had brought me to this particular place on the wall. Its proximity to those fearful tarns, only feet away, had been unsettling.

He shrugged. Too suddenly, it had seemed, after earlier demurrings, he had brought me to the wall. It had almost been as though he had decided on some action. His nervousness, too, had seemed uncharacteristic. What was there here, other than the tarns, which need not be closely approached, to be nervous about?

"You seem strange today, Drusus Rencius," I said. "You seem less communicative than usual. There are many things here I do not understand. I do not know why you hesitated so long to bring me here. It is a lovely view. Then why would you have so suddenly, so belatedly, have found my suggestion agreeable? Had something happened to make you change your mind? Why, too, earlier, did you seem so distracted, as though your thoughts were elsewhere? Too, of all these places on the wall, why did you bring me here, so close to those terrible birds. They frighten me."

"I am a poor guard, Lady Sheila," he said. "Too, I am poor company this day. Forgive me. Worse, I fear I am a poor soldier."

"Why should you say that?" I asked. That genuinely puzzled me.

"I had long considered bringing you to this place, Lady Sheila," he said, "even before you yourself expressed an interest in the walls, but, again and again, I forced the thought from my mind. This thought I resisted further, even more tenaciously, when you yourself broached it, now and again. Then, finally, after much troubled thought, it seemed to me that perhaps it was best that I let myself accompany you here."

"I do not understand what you are saying," I said.

"Here I would be alone with the Tatrix of Corcyrus, near saddled tarns," he said. "It seemed then that I knew what I should do. It seemed then that a given course of action would be appropriate. It would be easy enough to execute. Indeed, I could undertake it now. It is perhaps what I should do. I shall not, however, do it. I contravene no orders. Rather I will let the game take its course."

"You speak in riddles," I chided him.

"Let us now descend from the wall," he said. "Let us now return to the palace."

I glanced at the tarns. They were gigantic, fierce birds. Drusus Rencius stood close behind me. I thought for a moment he might take me in his arms. I felt faint. I wanted him to do so.

"What is that sound from within your cloak?" I asked.

"Nothing," he said.

"Show me," I said. I turned. He held open the side of the cloak, it then like a curtain between me and the city. The parapet was at my back.

There, held by a snap catch against the silken lining of the great cloak, looped, in coils, there hung a set of light chains. I could not determine the exact arrangement of the chains, coiled as they were. There seemed, however, to be a longer chain, which was a base chain, and two smaller, subsidiary chains. At one end the base chain was attached to a rather small neck ring, but suitable for closing about a woman's neck; at the other end it was attached to one of the subsidiary chains, about a foot long, and terminating on each end with a ring; those rings looked as though they might fit snugly about a woman's ankles; the other subsidiary chain seemed to be placed about two feet or so below the neck ring; at its terminations were smaller rings, which looked as though they might close snugly, locking, about a woman's wrists.

"What is that?" I asked.

"It is called a sirik," he said.

"Do men carry such things?" I asked.

"Sometimes," he said.

I wondered what chains like that would feel like on my body. They looked very graceful. They were doubtless flattering. Too, they would hold me quite well.

"Let us descend from the wall," said Drusus Rencius. "Let us return to the palace."

"Very well," I said.

# 7

# BRACELETS

"It is so skimpy," I said, "so tiny."

"Retire behind the screen," he said, "and put it on."

I hurried behind the three-part screen in one corner of the large, well-lit room in the inn of Lysias, off the square of Perimines, on the street of Philebus. It is not far from the house of the slaver, Kliomenes, on Milo Street. We had entered the inn through its front door. We would leave it through its back door, which opened onto an alley. Later, we would return to it through this same back door. We would then take our final exit, once again, later, through the front door.

I put the small garment on the broad, dark-stained, polished boards of the floor near my feet, behind the screen. I then began to remove the veils and robes of concealment. "There is no place back here," I said, "to put my garments."

"Put them on the top of the screen," he said. "I will fold them and place them on the chest." I did this, reaching above my head to place them on the top of the screen. He then removed them from this location.

"You are to be barefoot," he said.

I removed my slippers and put them to the left side of the screen. I saw his hand take them.

I then removed the remainder of my garments, and saw them, from the top of the screen disappear. Now, behind the screen, I was naked. Only an inch of wood separated me from such a man. I wished that I had retained some of my other garments behind the screen, if only for psychological security. I felt the dark, polished floor beneath my bare feet. I felt the air of the room, behind the screen, on my body. I touched the screen lightly with my finger tips.

"Are you ready?" he asked.

"No!" I said. I hastily, trembling, crouched down and seized up the small bit of cloth I had placed at my feet. I moaned, inwardly. It was so light, tiny and short. It would be dismayingly revealing. Surely such garments are an insult to a woman, I thought, forcing her to show how beautiful she is, to anyone who might care to look upon her. I drew it over my head and pulled it down, desperately, about my body. It was a gray, beltless, one-piece garment of rep cloth, with inch-wide straps over the shoulders. I tugged it down, at the hem, at the sides, trying to make it cover more of my thighs.

"Are you ready?" he asked.

"Yes," I said, faltering.

"Step forth," he said.

I came forth, from about the edge of the screen.

"Aiiii," he said, softly, to himself.

This response pleased me.

"Stand there," he said, indicating a place on the floor.

I went to where he had indicated.

"Now turn, slowly, and then face me," he said.

I did so.

"Are my legs pretty?" I asked.

"Yes," he said. "But your face and figure, as a whole, are also quite pretty."

"You find my pleasing, then?" I asked.

"Yes," he said. "Indeed, I had not supposed that the Tatrix of Corcyrus would prove to be such a beauty."

"Surely, then," I smiled, "I would be worth at least a silver tarsk."

"There are many beautiful women in the markets," he said. "You are untrained."

"Oh," I said.

"Come here," he said, "and remove my cloak. Then fold it, and place it on the chest."

I did so.

"Now return to where you were, facing me."

I did so.

"The Tatrix of Corcyrus does not often remove cloaks for gentlemen," I informed him. I did not tell him, of course, how I had almost trembled being so near him, and how pleased I was to have performed this small service for him.

He did not respond but continued to gaze upon me, as though studying me. My scanty garb, of course, I understood, invited such scrutiny.

"Few men," I said, "have looked upon the Tatrix of Corcyrus clad in this fashion."

"Stand straighter," he said.

I did so.

"Doubtless they would think of her somewhat differently, if they saw her clad like this," I said.

"Or any woman," he said.

"Of course," I said. I shuddered to think how men might think of women clad like this.

"The garment," he said, "is perhaps too modest."

"Too modest?" I asked.

"Yes," he said, "but it will perhaps do. I tried to find a garment which would be both serviceable for our purposes and, at the same time, considerate, within the limitations of our project, of your modesty. That explains the neckline which does not plunge to your belly, revealing much of the beauty of your breasts, and the hemline, which is surely something less than slave short.

I pulled down the sides of the garment. It seemed quite short to me.

"It does not even have a nether closure," I said to him.

"In that it is authentic," he said. "Such a closure, or the lines of a lower garment, affording such a closure, would be instantly detected by slaves."

"I see," I said.

"The slave, at any instant," he said, "is to be available to the master."

"I see," I said.

"Do you wish to continue with this project?" he asked.

"Yes," I said.

"I will take you into the house as though you might be a new girl or a fresh capture. This will explain why you are not yet in a collar. It will also make plausible your lack of a brand, should the matter arise. Your garment, incidentally, is long enough to cover most common brand sites. That you are a totally free woman, and not a slave, or a capture enroute to the collar, will be known to several members of the staff. They will, accordingly, refrain from handling you as though you were such a slave or capture, for example, stripping you, hurrying you through the halls with whips, and so on. Certain other members of the staff will not know that you are free. I shall take it upon myself to protect you from them. The pose of a jealous captor should suffice. The slaves, of course, will not know you are free. They will think you are merely a new girl, either a slave or one who, optionless, will soon be reduced to their status, one who will then be no more than they."

"No one will know, even high members of the staff, will they," I asked, "that I am actually the Tatrix of Corcyrus."

"No," he said. "They will know only that you are a free woman."

"Good," I said.

"Come here," he said, pointing to a place before him. I went there and stood there, before him. It was not far from the couch, behind him. The couch was a large, square one, with, in its foot, the slave ring, an almost inevitable feature, it seemed, in Gorean domiciles. There was a small mat, and blanket, both rolled up, beneath the slave ring. They would doubtless be used there by a chained slave, if the master permitted it.

I glanced about the room. It was spacious, well-lit, comfortable and private. I wondered if free men and free women ever met in such places, for affairs. But then I glanced again at the slave ring. It seemed more likely that a man might a totally free woman, and not a slave, or a capture en route to evening. I looked at Drusus Rencius. How could a free woman, I thought, ever compete with a slave?

"Drink this," said Drusus Rencius.

"What is it?" I asked, startled. It seemed he had produced this almost by magic. It was a soft, leather botalike flask, drawn from within his tunic.

"Slave wine," he said.

"Need I drink that?" I asked, apprehensively.

"Unless you have had slave wine," he said, "I have no intention of taking you through the streets clad as you are. Suppose you are raped."

I put the flask, which he had opened, to my lips. Its opening was large enough to drink freely from. "It is bitter!" I said, touching my lips to it.

"It is the standard concentration, and dosage," he said, "plus a little more, for assurance. Its effect is indefinite, but it is normally renewed annually, primarily for symbolic purposes."

I could not believe how bitter it was. I had learned from Susan, whom I had once questioned on the matter, the objectives and nature of slave wine. It is prepared from a derivative of sip root. The formula, too, I had learned, at the insistence of masters and slavers, had been improved by the caste of physicians within the last few years. It was now, for most practical purposes, universally effective. Too, as Drusus Rencius had mentioned, its effects, at least for most practical purposes, lasted indefinitely.

"Have no fear," said Drusus Rencius. "The abatement of its effects is reliably achieved by the ingestion of a releaser."

"Oh," I said. I knew this, of course. Susan had told me. When a female slave is given the releaser she knows that she may soon expect to be hooded, and bred.

"Could it not be sweetened?" I asked.

"I have chosen that you drink it as it is," he said, "as it is normally drunk."

"You would have the Tatrix of Corcyrus drink unsweetened slave wine?" I asked.

"Shall we return to the palace?" he asked.

"I will drink it," I said. I was a bit irritated with Drusus Rencius. Clad as I was before him, he had seemed to become much more domineering, much more aggressive with me, than he had before. Something in me resented this, but I felt something else, something deeper within me, how deep I did not know, excited and deeply moved, responding to it.

"Do you wish help in drinking it?" he asked.

"How could you help me drink it?" I asked, puzzled.

"The female is put on her knees," he said. "The man crouches behind her. Her head and body are bent back. Her nostrils are pinched shut. The liquid is then poured into her mouth. Before she can breathe, she must swallow. In this way even a frightened or stubborn girl, early in her bondage, learns that she must, if her master wishes it, accept nourishment."

"What if she keeps her mouth closed, her teeth clenched?" I asked. "What if she chooses to expel the nourishment later?"

"A mouth may be forced open," he said. "Too, it is difficult to induce gagging if the hands are tied behind one."

"I see," I said.

"To be sure," he said, "this method, for its best results, requires two men. Do you wish help?"

"No, thank you," I said. "I shall manage very nicely by myself."

I then, grimacing, forcing myself, a little at a time, and then, desperately, tears in my eyes, hurrying, in great swallows, downed the foul beverage.

"Very good," he said.

I thrust the soft leather flask back to him. Gasping, half choking, I wiped my mouth with the back of my forearm.

"Go stand there," he said, pointing to a place near the door, "facing me."

I went to where he had indicated and turned, then, facing him.

He tossed the soft flask to the top of the chest, atop his cloak, which I, earlier, bidden, had folded and placed there.

"Why did you make me drink unsweetened slave wine?" I asked.

"Stand straighter," he said.

I stood straighter.

"Why did you make me drink unsweetened slave wine?" I asked.

He looked me over, casually, not hurrying, from my head to my toes, and then, slowly, back.

"It was fitting," he said.

I gasped. The arrogance of him!

"What do you have there!" I said.

He had removed a pair of light bracelets, joined by about five inches of light chain, from his pouch.

"Slave bracelets," he said. "Turn around, facing the door, your hands behind your back."

Almost numbly I did so. I heard him approach me. Then he stood behind me, quietly, not moving. Perhaps he was looking at me. Then, suddenly, I felt the two bracelets flung about my wrists, striking them, encircling them and snapping shut.

I was suddenly very frightened.

I tried, tentatively, behind my back, to separate my hands. They could move only to the ends of their short chain.

"You are braceleted," he said.

I leaned against the door, terrified, almost fainting, using it for support. I was breathing deeply. My heart was pounding. I was braceleted! He was busying himself elsewhere in the room. I do not think he noted my condition.

How helpless I felt, braceleted.

In a moment he had returned to my vicinity, by the door. I now straightened my body. I was struggling to regain my composure.

"You braceleted me easily," I observed, lightly.

"It is not hard to bracelet a woman," he said.

It had been done so casually, so expertly, with apparently so little thought. Too, it had seemed to me to happen very suddenly, very decisively. In one instant I was free, and in the next I was held helplessly, the prisoner of bands and a chain. I was still shaken, perhaps even visibly so, with the enormity of what had been done to me. I had been made helpless.

"You have braceleted other women, haven't you?" I asked. He had done it so easily, so nonchalantly.

"Yes," he said. I hated those other women. I tried again to separate my wrists. I could not do so, of course. How short, how strong, seemed the chain that held them in proximity to one another. Suddenly I felt very weak. I, like the other women before me, perhaps women who were mere slaves, wore the steel of Drusus Rencius.

"We shall leave now," he said.

"Yes, Master," I said. "Oh!" I said. "I did not mean that! Forgive me! It slipped out. I did not mean it."

"Do not worry about it," he said. "It is difficult for a woman clad as you are, and braceleted, not to think of a man as her master."

"Thank you, Drusus," I said. "You are very kind. Such a mistake, as you might imagine, is very embarrassing."

"Doubtless," he granted me, indulgently.

I wondered what it would be like to be owned, and to have to call a man "Master." But, of course, owned, it would be quite suitable and proper for one to do so, for he would be, in fact, in such a situation, one's Master. My mind was racing. How could it be that I had called Drusus Rencius "Master"? How inadvertently, how naturally, it had slipped out. I wondered if I were actually a proud, free woman, as I thought, or was something else, perhaps only a slave.

"If Lady Sheila is ready," he said, "perhaps we should leave now."

I put up my head.

I reminded myself that I was not really, in a sense, braceleted. Oh, I wore the steel. It was locked on me, and well, but I was the Tatrix of Corcyrus. I could order Drusus Rencius to remove it from me at any moment I wished, and he would. Thus, in that sense, it was not truly on me. I did shudder, for a moment, at the thought of what it would be to be truly in such bonds, but then I hastily dismissed such fearful and unsettling thoughts from my mind.

"Lady Sheila?" he asked.

"Yes," I said. "Let us go."

He then opened the door and, holding me by the left arm, conducted me from the room.

## 8

# I HAVE BEEN IN THE HOUSE OF KLIOMENES; THE ROOM IN THE INN OF LYSIAS; WAR

"Perhaps now," said Drusus Rencius, "you have a better idea of the nature of the pens."

I could not even answer him, accompanying him back through the alleys to the inn of Lysias. I feared that my head might begin to swirl, that I might lose consciousness. I was scarcely aware of my surroundings, of where I was or what I was doing, or even of my feet touching the ground. I felt light-headed. I was trembling. I was filled with wild, turbulent emotions. I would never have believed that women could be subjected to such domination. I hoped that Drusus Rencius could not smell my arousal.

"Leading position," said Drusus Rencius.

I put my head down to his waist and he fastened his left hand in my hair.

"Tal, Citizen," said Drusus Rencius to the fellow passing us in the alley.

"Tal," said he.

It was in this fashion, my head down, his hand in my hair, my head turned to the side, hair, too, about my face and features, obscuring them, that Drusus Rencius had chosen to convey me past strangers in the alleys, coming and going to the house of Kliomenes. There was little danger I would be recognized. When we had passed the stranger he released my hair and I again straightened up. I was following him, generally, a little behind and on his left. It seemed appropriate that I, in my disguise, might seem to heel him, as though I might be a mere slave. It seemed to me that he had held my hair more tightly than he had needed to, when we had passed the stranger. I still wore the slave bracelets. He had declined to remove them when we had left the house of Kliomenes. In his steel, heeling him, occasionally being put into leading position by him, I felt much in his power.

"Did you enjoy the pens?" asked Drusus.

"Please do not make me speak," I whimpered. I was terribly conscious of the heat in my body, and the absence of a nether closure in my garment. Had Drusus Rencius so much as snapped his fingers I think I might have thrown myself to my back in the alley, begging for his touch.

"This is the house of Kliomenes," had said Drusus Rencius, climbing the stairs to the narrow, heavy iron portal, recessed some feet back, at the end of a narrow tunnel, in the wall. It was on the street of Milo. Above the entrance to the tunnel, and on its right, in the wall, hanging from an iron projection, was a narrow, blue-and-yellow banner. I followed Drusus Rencius carefully, that I might not fall. "This is one of the better, and more respectable of the slave houses in Corcyrus," he said. "That is one of the reasons that I have selected it for your visit, that your sensibilities, those of a free woman, not be excessively offended."

"I see," I said.

"On the other hand, do not expect it to compromise overly much with its women. Such would be a violation of the ethics of the slavers. Its women, you will find, all things considered, are held rather close to the standards of slave perfection."

"I see," I said.

He beckoned and I joined him in the narrow tunnel leading to the door. I regarded the iron door, apprehensively. "There are truly slaves in there?" I asked.

"Of course," he said. "If you enter, you will be, probably, the only free woman in the house, unless there is a new girl in there, in chains, awaiting, say, the iron and the collar."

"Oh," I said.

"Do you wish to enter?" he asked.

"Yes," I said.

"You are a woman, and it is the house of a slaver," he said.

"I will enter," I said.

He then struck on the iron door. He then thrust me in front of him, so that I, in the tunnel, was between him and the door.

There was a small, rectangular, iron observation panel, now shut, in the door.

I felt the stone of the tunnel beneath my feet, the steel holding my wrists helplessly behind me.

The observation panel slid back. I saw eyes looking at me, and then, beyond me, at Drusus Rencius.

The panel slid shut with a click.

I wanted to turn and run. I could not do so, of course, because of the walls of the tunnel, and Drusus Rencius behind me.

"They are expecting us," said Drusus Rencius, sensing my sudden terror.

I heard chains and bars behind the door, bolts being freed. Then the door swung open. "Enter," said a pleasant-enough-looking young man in the threshold. I entered, followed by Drusus. Beside the young man there was a guard, too, within. I heard the door, with its various devices, being refastened behind me. We were in a tiny torchlit room. Only a few feet before us was another door, also iron, similar to the outside door.

"Bracelet check," said the young man to me, pleasantly.

"Turn your back to him, and lift your wrists," said Drusus Rencius.

I did this and the young man quickly, expertly, checked the bracelets. They were locked on me. I was helpless.

I then turned again, to face the interior door.

I cried out, startled.

The guard, crouching beside me, had taken my left ankle in his left hand and run his right hand beneath my foot.

"No," said Drusus Rencius, deterring the guard, "there is nothing taped to her instep, nor is there anything else of the sort for which you might be searching concealed about or in her body or hair. She is to be exempted from slave search." I then realized, shuddering, just how thorough slave search might be.

The guard looked at the young man, who nodded. The guard then stood up.

The young man then tapped a complex signal on the inner iron door. In a moment I heard it being freed of its fastenings. It then swung open and we, the young man, Drusus Rencius and myself, were admitted to the corridor beyond. The guard there refastened the door and then took his place on a stool behind a small table.

"We need a pass and a license," said the young man to the guard.

I looked at Drusus Rencius.

"The license is only a formality," he said. "No free woman, unless a capture, may proceed beyond this point unless she is in the charge of a free man who is responsible for her and has a current license for her. This is a device to control the movements of free women in the house and a precaution against the attempted escape of slave girls pretending to be free women."

"Here is your pass," said the young man, handing a small disk to Drusus Rencius. It was not unlike one of the ostraka used as tickets or tokens for admission at the theater or other such events. The guard, meanwhile, was writing something down on a small, rectangular form. I had little doubt what it was. "And here," said the young man, taking the form from the guard and handing it to Drusus Rencius, confirming my speculations, "is your license for the female." I was a woman. Accordingly, I had to be licensed in the house of Kliomenes. How humiliating! The Goreans have a saying, "There are only two kinds of women, slaves, and slaves." I pulled at my wrists. They were well held in the bracelets.

"Is she really free?" asked the young man.

"Yes," said Drusus Rencius, putting the pass and license in his pouch.

"Interesting," said the young man.

"Do you find it surprising?" asked Drusus Rencius.

"Yes," said the young man.

The guard then stood up and came about the table. I backed away a foot or two.

He crouched down near me, and then stood up, regarding me. "Those are slave curves," he said, "and rather lovely ones."

I blushed, helpless.

"Such curves," he said, "should not be wasted on a free woman."

"I do not think Publius will believe she is free," laughed the young man.

I looked at Drusus Rencius.

"Publius," said Drusus Rencius, "is the house master. I know him from Ar."

"He would like to see you, after your tour," said the young man, "to drink a cup of paga."

"I shall be delighted," said Drusus Rencius. He did not ask me for my permission to do this, I noted.

"She is truly free?" asked the guard.

"Yes," averred Drusus Rencius.

"It is a shame," said the guard. "Curves like that should be up for sale."

"From what I have heard of her," said Drusus Rencius, smiling, "she is the sort of a woman who has her price." I wondered what he meant by that.

"Hermidorus will accompany you in the house," said the young man, "if we can tear him away from his scrolls."

"He understands, does he not," asked Drusus Rencius, "that the woman is free and, accordingly, certain things are not to be seen."

"Of course," smiled the young man. "Hermidorus!" he called, loudly.

In a few moments, from a side door, a few yards farther down the corridor, another young man emerged. He was dark-haired and dark-eyed, and had a rather scholarly look about him. He did not seem much different to me than some young men I had seen about universities. He seemed an improbable inhabitant of such a place.

"This is Drusus, a soldier of the city," said the first young man. "He is known to Publius."

Drusus Rencius and the newcomer inclined their heads to one another.

The newcomer then looked me over.

"Do you think she could pass as a slave?" asked the first young man.

"Easily," smiled the second. I realized then the question had been rhetorical. I flushed. Why did Gorean men, seemingly so naturally, look upon me as a slave?

"Follow me," said the young man, turning about.

"Leading position," said Drusus Rencius.

Swiftly I put down my head again and winced as Drusus fastened his hand in my hair.

Thus again was I led past a stranger in the alleys. As we passed the stranger, he approaching us, he was on our right. Goreans commonly pass in this fashion, the sword arms of right-handed individuals being thus on the side of the approaching stranger.

I saw some girls rummaging through a garbage can. They wore short tunics but they were not slaves. Goreans sometimes refer to such women as "strays." They are civic nuisances. They are occasionally rounded up, guardsmen appearing at opposite ends of an alley, trapping them, and collared.

"Buy me, Master," begged the girl, kneeling before Drusus Rencius. "I will give you much pleasure."

"Next!" barked the trainer, in the house of Kliomenes.

The next girl hurried forward and knelt before Drusus Rencius, kissing his feet, and then lifting her head, piteously, to him. "Buy me, Master," she said. "I will give you much pleasure."

"Next!" barked the trainer.

The next woman then hurried to Drusus and threw herself to her belly before him, kissing his feet. She then rose slowly to her knees, kissing him from the ankles to the waist. Kneeling before him, then, close to him, holding his legs she looked up at him. "Buy me, Master," she whispered. "I will give you much pleasure."

How furious I was that these women were being sent to the feet of Drusus Rencius. They were naked and beautiful, but who would want to buy them? They were only slaves. That could be told by the collars they wore, bars of rounded iron which, here, in the house, had been curved about their necks and hammered shut. I stood in the background, angry, braceleted, helpless.

"You!" said the trainer, gesturing to another girl with his whip. "To his feet! Beg for love!"

This girl hurried forward and knelt before Drusus Rencius. "I beg for love, Master," she whispered.

"You!" said the trainer, indicating another girl. She, too, hurried forward. She knelt before Drusus Rencius, her palms on the floor, her head to the very tiles. "I beg for love," she whispered. "I beg for love, Master."

I was startled. I realized, suddenly, that these two women, indeed, were begging for love. "Beg elsewhere, sluts!" I thought. "Leave Drusus Rencius alone!" And how offensive that a woman should beg for love! Surely her intimate, desperate needs for attention, for affection and love were better concealed even from herself, if possible, and certainly, at least, from others! And if they must beg, the helpless sluts, did they not know how a woman begs, by looks, by glances, by small, hopeful services. Surely a woman should not be expected to speak honestly in such matters. What brute would force her to such extremities? Too, how vulnerable a woman would make herself, placing herself so at the mercy of men, subject to being spurned, subject to his scorn and rejection. Yet how simple, how straightforward and liberating might be such a confession. How beautiful it might be to so express one's vulnerability, and femininity, so tenderly, so piteously, so openly. To be sure, one would expect such a confession only from a woman whose needs were both desperate and deep, a woman who had needs such as might characterize slaves.

"Come along," said Hermidorus.

"Please, Drusus," I said. "My hands have been braceleted long enough. I am beginning to feel too helpless, too much like a slave. Please release me."

"I will release you in the room," he said.

I then continued to follow him, still braceleted, through the alleys, toward the inn of Lysias.

"Slowly, more humbly," cautioned the trainer, half crouching over, watching carefully, moving slowly beside the girl. Then he moved about her, more quickly, varying his perspective. Then he moved to the end of the room, where he might wait for her to approach. "Head lower," he said. "Better, better." I watched her approach him, head down, on her hands and knees, her breasts depending beautifully. Then she dropped the whip from her teeth before his booted feet. She then remained there, head down, in position. "Better," he said. He then picked up the whip and tossed it across the tiles. "Again," he said. She then rose lightly to her feet and hurried to the whip, where, once more, she dropped to her hands and knees. She picked up the whip delicately in her teeth, and looked at him. He snapped his fingers. Again, then, head down, slowly, she approached him, the whip held in her mouth.

"Kneel, back on your heels," said the trainer to the dark-haired woman. "Straighten your back, suck in your gut, put your shoulders back, thrust out your breasts, spread your knees, widely, lift your chin, put your hands on your thighs. You are not going to be sold as a tower slave, Lady Tina. You are going to be sold as a pleasure slave."

The whip cracked, and I jumped. But it had not touched the girl, only startled her.

She knelt behind the dark, smooth post, facing it, her knees on either side of it, her belly and breasts against it, her hands embracing it.

"This may be done to music," said Hermidorus, "and, as you know, there are many versions to the post dance, or pole dance, singly, or with more than one girl, with or without bonds, and so on, but here we are using it merely as a training exercise."

The whip cracked again and the girl, suddenly and lasciviously, became active.

I gasped.

She began to writhe about the pole. "Kiss it, caress it, love it!" commanded the trainer, snapping the whip. "Now more slowly, now scarcely moving, now use your thighs, and breasts more, moving all about it, holding it. Touch it with your tongue, lick it! Use the inside of your thighs more, your breasts, turn about it, slowly, sensuously. Lift your hands above your head, palms to the pole, caressing it. Turn about the pole! Twist about it! Now to your knees, holding it!" He then cracked the whip again. "Enough!" he said. She was then as she had been before, kneeling behind the post, her knees on either side of it, her belly and breasts pressed against it, her hands embracing it. The girl was looking at me. She was wondering, perhaps, if I were the next to be put to the post. I looked away, angrily. Did she not know I was not a lowly thing like she? Did she not know I was free?

"It is a useful exercise," said Hermidorus to Drusus. "It helps a girl learn how to address herself, naked, to a standing master."

"Obviously," agreed Drusus.

I looked back at the girl. She was now looking away. I

looked at the post. It was dark, and shiny. It had been polished smooth, apparently, by the bodies of many girls.

The girl looked suddenly at me. There was a hostility in our looks toward one another. She saw, I think, in my eyes, that I thought I could have done better at the post than she. Then I looked away. What would I care for her opinions! Were we competitive women?

"Come along," said Hermidorus.

"These women," said Hermidorus, "are practicing their floor movements."

A trainer stood among them, with a whip. Occasionally he would snap this whip near a girl. I did not doubt but what the girls on the tiles, if they were found sufficiently displeasing to the trainer, or too frequently required the admonitory signal of the cracking leather, would soon hear the snap of the lash not in their mere vicinity but on their own bared bodies. Two of the girls, I saw, had stripes on them, one on the thigh, and one on the side. The trainer was not now paying them much attention. They were now, apparently, doing well.

"Come along," said Hermidorus.

"How beautiful!" I breathed.

Drusus Rencius looked sharply at me. I feared for a moment I might be struck.

Hermidorus, on the other hand, did not seem to notice. My exclamation, perhaps, had seemed sufficiently inadvertent, involuntary and irrepressible, to be ignored; or perhaps it was to be ignored because I was not a slave, but a free woman. I did not meet Drusus Rencius's eyes. It was not like I had just decided to speak and had spoken. In a place like this I did not know if I was subject to discipline or not. I did not think so, for I was a free woman. On the other hand I knew I was here on the sufferance of the house of Kliomenes. Indeed, on these premises, I knew that Drusus Rencius even held a license on me.

The drummer and the flautist prepared once more to play.

The girl in the long, light chain smiled at me. She, at any rate, was pleased by my response.

A wrist ring was fastened on her right wrist. The long, slender, gleaming chain was fastened to this and, looping down and up, ascended gracefully to a wide chain ring on her collar, through which it freely passed, thence descending, looping down, and ascending, looping up, gracefully, to the left wrist ring. If she were to stand quietly, the palms of her hands on her thighs, the lower portions of the chain, those two dangling loops, would have been about at the level of her knees, just a little higher. The higher portion of the chain, of course, would be at the collar loop.

The musicians began again to play. There is much that can be done with such a chain. It was a dancing chain. Its purpose was not to confine the girl but to allow her to incorporate it in her dance, enhancing the dance with its movements and beauty. It is, of course, symbolic of her bondage, this adding fantastic dimensions of significance to the dance. It is not merely a beautiful woman who dances, but one who can be bought and sold, one who is subject to male ownership. Too, of course, the wrist rings, and the collar, are truly locked on her. There is no doubt about it. It is a slave, with all that that means, who is dancing.

I watched her, my breath almost taken away by her beauty.

"She is a valuable woman," said Hermidorus.

I did not doubt it.

"Come along," he said.

"We are readying her for her sale," said Hermidorus.

I watched her naked on the block, under the tutelage of a whip-carrying trainer. It was small, rounded room, with mirrors. He was putting her through slave paces.

"She is to be auctioned in five days," said Hermidorus.

My eyes and those of the girl met. At that instant her weight was on the palms of her hands, her arms straight, and the sides of her feet, her body lifted from the block, her legs straight and spread widely behind her.

I realized then, with a shock, that she was going to be sold.

Then she was being put through further slave paces.

"Come along," said Hermidorus.

I wondered what it would be like to be sold. That girl was going to be sold. Susan had been sold. The other girls, too, or many of them, I supposed, and countless others like them, passing through just such houses as this, would be sold. Such sales would not be uncommon on Gor. They would take place with little more thought than might attend the vendings of horses or cattle.

I was trembling. The hand of Drusus Rencius on my arm drew me, bodily, from the room.

"I have changed my mind!" wept the girl. "I will be pleasing! I will be pleasing!"

I looked through the heavy bars of the cell, some three inches in thickness, reinforced with flat crosspieces, to the opposite wall. It was hard to see. There, kneeling on straw, trying to pull towards us, her wrists tied behind her back to a ring set in the wall, was a blond girl. "I will be pleasing!" she wept. "I will be pleasing! I will be pleasing!"

I then turned away from her, following Hermidorus and Drusus Rencius.

"She is not yet begging to be pleasing," said Hermidorus to Drusus.

"Correct," he said.

I looked behind myself, following them, at the dark cells, most of them empty, along the corridor. This was certainly not my favorite part of the house. It was dark, and cold, and clammy. Occasionally my bare feet stepped in puddles of cold water, seeped to this level, and caught in concavities or irregularities in the corridor flooring. And, here and there, I could see passages, narrow, crooked and dark, leading to even lower levels. I was pleased that we were not going to traverse them. It had seemed frightening enough to me to come even to this level. Sometimes, in our descent, on catwalks, we had even passed over pit cells, little more than holding holes, ceilinged with locked iron gates, sunk in the floor of the corridor. I had cried out with misery and terror in passing over one of these for a large hand, emerging suddenly through the grating, had seized my ankle. Drusus Rencius had pried open the fingers and thrust the hand away. I then kept closely to the center of the catwalks. There were male slaves in this house, too, I had learned. Had the slave known I was free, I do not think he would have touched me. He might have remained crouching in his hole, thinking what thoughts he might, but I do not think he would have dared to touch me. A male slave can be slain for touching a free woman. "She is not here for punishment," Hermidorus had informed the dark shapes beneath the grating. I then realized that a slave girl, perhaps for purposes of her discipline, might be lowered through the grating hole, doubtless into eager hands, the grating then being resecured.

In the corridors, in our movements through them, particularly in the upper levels, we would sometimes encounter slaves, usually employed in domestic tasks, such as running errands, carrying burdens, dusting or cleaning. These women were usually naked, except for their collars, which, I gathered, was the way women were usually kept in a slaver's house. At the approach of the free men, Hermidorus and Drusus, they would immediately position themselves, usually with their knees wide, kneeling back on their heels, their heads up, their hands on their thighs, in the position I had come to understand was that of the pleasure slave, but sometimes, instead, kneeling with the palms of their hands on the tiles, their heads down, too, to the same tiles.

There was one temporary, partial exception to this, which I will mention. After we had left some carpeted corridors, higher in the house, and were moving to the lower levels, and traversing heavy, flagstonelike tiles, we approached a slender, dark-haired girl who, on her hands and knees, in chains, with a bucket of water, cloths and a brush, in that portion of the corridor, was scrubbing tiles.

As we approached, she oriented herself towards us, palms of her hands on the floor, and put her head to the tiles. But, as we neared her, she lifted her head, desperately.

"Hermidorus!" she cried, suddenly. "Hermidorus!"

He stopped before her, a few feet from her, and we stopped, too, behind him.

"Do you not know me?" she begged. The chain she wore was a work sirik. It resembles the common sirik but the wrists, to permit work, are granted about a yard of chain. Like the common sirik, it is a lovely chain. Women are beautiful in it. "Deirdre!" she cried. "Deirdre! Two years ago in Ar we lived in the same building!"

He looked at her, not speaking.

"Deirdre," she whimpered.

"In the instant you were imbonded, you ceased to be Deirdre, Girl," he said.

"Girl?" she said.

"What is your house name?" he asked.

"Oh, no," she said. "Not you! Not you, of all people! You do not see me as a slave! You could not see me as a slave! I know you. That would be impossible! You could not relate to me as though I might be a slave! You could not! One such as you would never enforce my slavery upon me! One such as you could never do so!" Then she looked up at him, her lower lip trembling. " 'Renata' is my house name," she said.

He then removed the belt from his tunic. The accouterments on it he handed to Drusus Rencius.

"You lifted your head from the tile position before free persons had passed you, Renata," he said. "You also addressed a free man twice by his name. Similarly your speech has been inadequately deferential. It has not been interspersed, at appropriate points, for example, by the expression 'Master.' You have also referred to yourself as though you might still be 'Deirdre.' Such falsifications of identity are not permitted to slaves. Deirdre is gone. In her place there is now only a slave, an animal, who must wear whatever name masters choose to put on her. Similarly, when asked a question, that pertaining to your house name, you did not respond with sufficient promptness. Do you understand all that I am saying, fully and clearly, Renata?"

She looked up at him, tears in her eyes. "Yes, Master," she said.

"On all fours, Renata," he said.

"Yes, Master," she sobbed, assuming this position.

"Perhaps you should precede us a few paces down the hall," said Drusus Rencius to me.

I moved, frightened, a few feet down the hall, not looking back. Then, suddenly, I heard the belt beginning to fall, sharply, on the girl. I turned in time to see her on her side, in her chains, receiving the last few blows. She had not been pleasing. She was a slave. Of course she was being punished.

Then Hermidorus, without further ado, took back his accouterments from Drusus and slipped them on his belt. He then fastened the belt again about his waist.

I was startled that one such as he, seemingly so scholarly and gentle, possessed such uncompromising strength. The female had learned, to her sorrow, that in his presence she would not be permitted the least slackness in her discipline.

"I am sorry for the interruption," Hermidorus apologized to Drusus Rencius.

"That is perfectly all right," said Drusus.

The girl lay on her stomach, in her chains, in the water on the tiles. She lifted her head, gazing in pain, disbelief and awe at Hermidorus. She was a slave who had not been pleasing. She had been put under his belt.

We then continued down the hallway.

"Master," she called out, "I want to lay for you! I want to lay for you! Please have me sent to your rooms! I want to lay for you!"

Hermidorus did not look back.

I looked back. I saw in the girl's eyes that she now knew she was a slave, and helplessly so, and that she loved him.

We continued on our way.

I wondered if he would have her sent to his rooms. The decision was his. She was a slave.

"As the house opens to the public at the tenth Ahn," said Hermidorus, "perhaps I should now take you to the office of Publius, who wished to greet you before you left the premises." The tenth Ahn is the Gorean noon.

"Splendid," said Drusus Rencius.

We were then making our way upward from some of the lower pen areas.

I had not realized the complexities of a slaver's house, and this house was not an unusually large one. We had seen the baths and the sales yard, which is also used for exercise; we had seen various holding areas, ranging from silken, barred alcoves for superb pleasure slaves, through cells and cages of various sorts more fit for medium-priced women, to incarceration chambers that were little more than grated pits or gloomy dungeons, areas in which a slave might be terrorized to find herself placed; other holding areas, ranging from good to bad, were no more than a ring position, in a wall or on a floor; we also saw kitchens, pantries, eating areas, some with mere troughs or depressions in the floor, storage areas, guard rooms, offices, and places for the keeping of records; there were also a laundry and an infirmary; too, there were rooms where such subjects as the care and dressing of hair, the application of cosmetics, the selection and use of perfumes, manicure and pedicure, and slave costuming were taught, and even rooms where inept women, usually former members of the upper castes, could be instructed in the small domestic tasks that would now be expected of them, small services suitable for slaves, such as cleaning, cooking and sewing. Certain areas of the house, however, I was not shown, presumably because I was a free woman, such as the lowest pens, the branding chamber, the discipline room, and the rooms where girls were taught to kiss and caress, and the movements of love.

"I will be good! I will be good!" I heard a girl cry, from within a low, steel, rectangular box, shoved against the side of the passage, presumably that it would not be in the way. I stopped, startled. It had not occurred to me that a girl could be held within those small confines. Indeed, in the half-darkness of the lamp-lit passage I had hardly noticed the box. It was about four feet long and three feet wide, with a depth of perhaps eighteen inches. It was of steel and opened from the top. In the lid, at each end, there was a circle, about five inches in diameter, of penny-sized holes. It was locked shut, secured by two flat, steel bars, perpendicular to its long axis, padlocked, in front, in place. "I will be good!" wept the girl, from within.

"It is a slave box," said Hermidorus.

"I beg to be pleasing, Masters!" cried the girl, from within.

"Surely she must be a very tiny woman," I said, horrified, to Drusus Rencius.

"She is the former Lady Tais of Farnacium," said Hermidorus. "Her house name is Didi. She is, as I recall, a normal-sized slave."

"The box is so small," I said.

"It is supposed to be small," said Drusus Rencius.

"But consider the cramping, the tightness, the girl's helplessness," I said.

"Those are among its purposes," he said.

"But it is so small!" I protested.

"It is not really so small," he said.

I looked at him.

"It would be, for example," he said, "more than large enough for you."

"I will obey lovingly and with total perfection, Masters," averred the woman from within the box. "I beg only to be permitted to be fully and totally pleasing to my Masters!"

"Come along," said Hermidorus.

We then, once again, followed him.

"I beg to be pleasing!" cried the woman from within the box. "I beg to be permitted to be totally pleasing!"

"She is almost ready to leave the box," said Hermidorus.

"Let me see the license on her," said Publius. "I see," he smiled, surveying the scrap of paper given to him by Drusus

Rencius, "the Lady Lita." He looked at me. "A pretty name," he said.

I thought so, too.

He smiled at me, as though amused by the name. I did not understand this.

"It is not her true name, of course," said Publius to Drusus Rencius.

"Of course not," said Drusus Rencius.

"Doubtless, in the circles in which you travel, Lady Lita," said Publius to me, "it would not do for your friends to know how you were brought half naked and braceleted into a slaver's house."

I looked away from him. I did not deign to respond to such a remark.

"It would be quite a scandal doubtless," he said, "and make a quite good story in the telling."

I looked away, loftily, still braceleted.

"Here, Lady Lita," he said, "let us stand you over here, in the light, where we can get a better look at you." He conducted me to a pool of light, at the foot of a shaft of light, falling from a high, barred window.

I stood there, and the men stood back, looking at me.

"She is very pretty," said Publius. " 'Lita' would be a good name for her."

"I think so," said Drusus Rencius.

I stood there, being inspected. I had been afraid that Publius, when he had been conducting me to the pool of light, and placed me here, might have touched me. I could not have prevented it, in such a brief garment, with no nether closure, my hands braceleted helplessly behind my back, but he had not done so. Had he done so, of course, my condition of arousal would have been made humiliatingly and embarrassingly evident to him. I hoped that my need was not somehow evident, subtly so, in my appearance and behavior, perhaps through body cues. I hoped, too, they could not smell it.

"Kneel down here, Lady Lita, in the light," said Publius.

I knelt down, in the pool of light. I kept my knees closely together. I was confused, and frightened. I was kneeling before men.

"Are you sure she is free?" asked Publius.

"Yes," said Drusus Rencius.

"Interesting," said Publius. He then walked slowly about

me, looking at me, and, then, again, stood a few feet before me, looking down at me.

"Look at her," he said.

"Yes?" said Drusus.

"Closely," said Publius.

"Yes?" inquired Drusus.

"Do you not see?" asked Publius.

"What?" asked Drusus.

"She has the softness, the femininity, the look of a slave about her," he said.

"I assure you," smiled Drusus, "she is far from a slave."

"I do not think so," said Publius. "I think she is a natural slave, and would train superbly to the collar."

Drusus threw back his head and laughed at the absurdity of this thought. I myself did not find it so amusing.

"Does anyone know she is here?" asked Publius.

"No," said Drusus.

"Why do we not then enslave her?" asked Publius. "No, Lady Lita," he said, "do not rise to your feet." I had almost leapt up. My wrists wildly, suddenly, had jerked against the bracelets. They had not yielded, of course. They were not made to yield. I knelt back then, in the light, on my heels.

"It would not be difficult," said Publius. "We could transport her from the city. Then, elsewhere, when she is suitably branded, and her neck is locked in a proper collar, when she is fully and inescapably a slave, absolutely rightless, and in your power, we might make test of the matter."

"This woman is not a slave," said Drusus Rencius.

"A silver tarsk says she is," laughed Publius.

"How are things in Ar?" asked Drusus Rencius. "I have not been there for a long time."

"I will get the paga," said Publius.

The men then drank, and spoke of small things. Meanwhile I knelt in the light, braceleted, and was seldom, I think, in their mind or attention. Once I noticed that my knees had opened somewhat, without my really thinking about it. I quickly closed them. I hoped no one had noticed. I wondered if I was a slave. Publius thought so, and he was a slaver. He had been willing to put a silver tarsk on the matter. I looked at Drusus. Something in me seemed to say, "You lose your tarsk, Drusus Rencius. She is a slave."

Then I hastily thrust such a horrifying thought from my mind.

"Please, Drusus," I had said. "My hands have been braceleted long enough. I am beginning to feel too helpless, too much like a slave. Please release me."

"I will release you in the room," he had said.

I had then continued to follow him, still braceleted, through the alleys, toward the inn of Lysias.

Why did he not release me now? Why did he still keep me braceleted, like a slave? Could he not see that I was almost overcome with emotion? Could he not see my misery, my distress? Could he not see how overwrought I was? Could he not see the difficulty I was having, fighting myself?

We were approaching closer and closer to the inn of Lysias. This exicted and thrilled me, but, too, it frightened and terrified me. There I would be alone with Drusus Rencius, a Gorean male, in the room. What would I do? How would I act?

I moaned to myself.

I wished to run to the room, and I wished to hang back, almost as though against a leash.

Emotions raged within me, furies and resentments lingering from my Earth conditionings, residues of masculine values which I had been encouraged to espouse and exemplify, and, released on Gor, welling up from deeply within me, from what sources I could scarcely dare conjecture, alarming me, disconcerting me, almost overpowering feelings of helplessness, vulnerability and femininity.

I did not know what to do. I did not know how to act.

"I am free," I cried to myself, "I am free! Free!"

But I was half naked and my hands were braceleted behind me. Each step, too, was taking me closer to the room!

I wished that I had never seen slaves, and the house of Kliomenes. I wished I had never known how beautiful they were, and how they were dominated by men, and must obey! I wished that I had never felt these powerful emotions, in all their irresistibility, profundity and depth! But then I knew that this was false. It is better to feel than not to feel. I was overwhelmingly moved by having seen slaves, and thrilled to have been permitted, even on a license, to see the house of Kliomenes. Even though I myself was surely not a slave my life, I knew, was a thousand times richer for having realized that such things existed, for having seen such basic, deep, human and real things.

"How do you know that you are not a slave, Tiffany?" I

asked myself. "How do you know that you are different from those other girls? How do you know that you are not, as Publius suggested, a natural slave? How do you know the collar would not be quite appropriate for you? How do you know it does not, in fact, rightfully belong on you?"

"No," I said to myself, almost poutingly, "I am free!"

Then something within me, frightening me, seemed to laugh, derisively. "You are a slave, Tiffany," it said. "You know you are a slave. You have known it, in one way or another, in your heart, for years."

"No!" I said to myself. "No!" "But, yes, Slave," said the voice within me, insistently, derisively, mocking me. "No!" I said. "Yes," it whispered. "Yes, yes."

I wondered if I was a slave. The thought thrilled me, and terrified me.

Why had Drusus Rencius not freed me from the bracelets! We were not now in the house of Kliomenes!

"I will release you in the room," he had said.

Why would he not release me now? Why could he not be of help to me? Could he not see how I was fighting myself!

I wondered if she who was helpless in his bracelets was a slave.

Oddly enough I had felt most a slave, most dominated, in the house of Kliomenes when, in the office of Publius, the men had talked, and I had knelt alone and to one side, my head down, in the light, neglected, braceleted, waiting for the men, the masters, to finish.

I hurried along in the alley behind Drusus Rencius.

I tried to fight the emotions rising in me, welling up, irresistibly, from my very depths. I was confused and torn. In me conditioning warred with nature. Men were the masters. Did they not know that? Why did they not enforce their power, their will on us? Could they not see what we wanted, what we needed? Were they so inattentive and insensitive? Were they so stupid, so blind? Could they not see that I, in order to attain my perfection, needed the weight of a chain, the taste of a whip? Could they not see that I could not be perfect until my will was taken from me, and I must serve will-lessly? Could they not see that this was what I wanted? I was not a man. I was a woman! I wanted to surrender to nature, but I feared, mightily, to do so. I sensed what a woman might become if she surrendered to nature. I scarcely dared think it, let alone speak it. How categorical, how fearful, how absolute such a thing would be! Yet I longed for it. I wished a man would throw me to my belly and lock a collar on my throat. I wished to lie trembling at his feet, in the shadow of his whip, knowing that thenceforth, whether I wished it or not, I existed for love, passion and service.

"Leading position," said Drusus Rencius. I swiftly put my head down and felt his fingers lock themselves deeply in my hair. I turned my head and pressed my lips suddenly, helplessly, to his thigh, kissing him. He twisted my head cruelly to the side, holding it there, turned, so that my lips could not touch him. My eyes brimmed with tears, not only from the pain, but more so, from the fact that I had been rejected.

We had then passed the stranger, approaching, in the alley. Drusus Rencius released my hair, and I straightened up, continuing to follow him.

We were almost at the back entrance of the inn of Lysias. I had been rejected!

How furious I was at the girl who had so helplessly kissed at the leg of Drusus Rencius. How she had humiliated and embarrassed me, the shameless tart! I hated and despised her. Where had she come from? Who was she? Surely she could not have been I!

We were then at the back entrance of the inn of Lysias.

"Kneel here," said Drusus Rencius, indicating a place near the back entrance, near some garbage cans.

I knelt, immediately, obediently.

He entered the inn. He would see if anyone was about, or if we might, unobserved, make our way up the back stairs to the room.

I moaned softly, with need.

I knelt near the back entrance of the inn, near the garbage cans. I pulled weakly against the bracelets.

I looked up, suddenly, startled. A man was standing there, looking at me. He had come, apparently, from down the alley. I put down my head, swiftly, so swiftly that it almost startled me, showing submission. I had seen his eyes. I was terribly frightened.

The back door of the inn opened and Drusus, to my relief, emerged.

"She is not out for use?" asked the man.

"No," said Drusus. "Sorry." He then snapped his fingers and I leaped up and, at a gesture, preceded him into the inn, and up the rear stairs.

I was trembling. I was sure that in another moment or two I, utterly helpless, might have been seized and penetrated in the alley.

In a moment, then, we were again in the room, and Drusus had locked the door behind us.

I leaned back against the door, my head back, breathing deeply.

"He thought you had been put out for raping," said Drusus, chuckling to himself.

I looked at him.

"Did you enjoy the house of Kliomenes?" asked Drusus.

How absurd to me seemed the lightness, the casual cast, of his question. The experience had been an incredibly meaningful one for me. Scarcely never before, I think, had I been so in touch with my femaleness. It was hard to conceive of how one could be more in touch with one's femaleness, unless, of course, one were oneself a slave.

Drusus Rencius looked at me. Then I went to where he stood, and knelt down before him.

He looked down at me, angrily, startled. "What are you doing!" he asked.

"Kneeling down before you," I said, "helpless, braceleted, as a woman before a man."

His fists were clenched.

"If you want me," I said, "have me."

"Get up!" he cried. Then he seized me by the upper arms and pulled me to my feet. He held me before him.

"Taste the slave in me," I begged.

He looked down into my eyes, fiercely. His grip on my arms, holding me absolutely helplessly; was like iron.

"Oh, would that you were a slave," he whispered, intensely. "Would that you were a slave!"

He then, lifting me from my feet as though I might have been no more than a doll, suddenly, violently, with a cry of rage, flung me from him, yards from him, to the surface of the bed. On the bed I scrambled to my knees. The wall was at my back.

There were sounds from outside the window, cries in the street.

Drusus Rencius went to the window, listening. "Corcyrus," he said, "has seized the mines of Argentum. It has begun."

"What has begun?" I asked, frightened.

"War," said Drusus Rencius.

I looked at him, frightened.

"I will return you to the palace, immediately," he said. He indicated that I should lie on my belly on the bed before him. I did so and, lying on the bed, my head turned to the side, sunk partly in its softness, felt the bracelets removed from me.

I rose from the bed, pulling down the edges of the brief, one-piece garment I wore. Drusus Rencius returned the slave bracelets to his pouch. "My garments, please," I said. I would have him serve me. He handed me my garments. I retired behind the screen and, in a few moments, re-emerged.

"Lady Sheila will require a new guard," he said.

"No," I said. "I will not."

He looked at me, surprised.

"You are not relieved of your duties," I said. "You are still my guard, and will continue to serve me as such."

"Lady Sheila well knows how to torture a man," he said.

"Yes," I said. "I do."

He regarded me, bitterly.

"Return me now to the palace," I said.

"Yes, Tatrix," he said.

# 9

# I DETERMINE TO TAKE COGNIZANCE IN THE CITY

I stood by the barred window in my quarters, looking out. I could see portions of the courtyard below, sections of the inner walls and the first of the two gates leading to the outside. I could also see, back from the walls, a portion of the square outside the gates. Most of the crowd outside the gates I could not see. I could see some men and women moving across the square, presumably to join it. It was the second such crowd in the past week. I saw some men, across the square, perhaps seeing someone in my window, stop, and shake their fists. I moved away from the window.

"Mistress!" cried Susan, entering with a tray, stopping suddenly, spilling wine. She looked at me, with the sudden terror of a slave who had been clumsy. "Forgive me, Mistress!" she cried. "I will clean it up immediately!"

I watched her while she put down the tray, picked up the goblet, and hurried to fetch cloths and water. In a moment she was on her hands and knees, frightened, cleaning the floor. I myself, of course, a woman of wealth and position, a Tatrix even, was above such tasks. They were properly to be performed by lesser women. Ideally, of course, they fell to those women for whom they were perfectly suited, slaves.

"Susan," I said.

"Yes, Mistress," she said, looking up from her hands and knees, frightened.

"Why did you spill the wine?" I asked.

"I am sorry, Mistress!" she said.

"Why did you spill it?" I asked. She had seemed surprised.

"I was startled, Mistress," she said. "I had not expected to find you here. I had thought that I had seen you in an anteroom off the great hall, only some Ehn earlier."

"You were mistaken," I said.

"Yes, Mistress," she said.

"There is another crowd outside the gate this evening," I said.

"Yes, Mistress," said the girl.

"It is an angry crowd again, is it not?" I asked.

"I fear so, Mistress," said the girl.

I went to the barred window, and looked out. I could hear the crowd but, because of the walls and gates, could see very little of it.

"I think guardsmen will soon issue forth to disperse it," said Susan.

"Can you make out what they are shouting, what they want?" I asked, lightly.

"No, Mistress," said Susan, putting down her head.

"I can make it out quite clearly, from the window," I said, irritably.

"Forgive me, Mistress," said Susan.

"Speak," I said.

"They call for the blood of the Tatrix of Corcyrus," she said, "whom they call tyranness and villainess of Corcyrus."

"But, why?" I asked. "Why?"

"I do not know, Mistress," said Susan. "There are scarcities in the city. They may be angry about the progress of the war."

"But the war goes well," I said.

"Yes, Mistress," said Susan, putting her head down.

There was then a heavy knock at the door. "Ligurious, first minister of Corcyrus," announced a voice, that of a guard.

"Enter," I said.

The door opened and Ligurious, with his imposing stature, yet leonine grace, entered. He bowed to me, and I inclined my head to him.

At his entrance Susan put the palms of her hands on the floor and lowered her head to the tiles, assuming a position of slave obeisance common with her in the presence of her master. I wondered if Ligurious's slave master required this position of all of his women. I supposed so.

Ligurious looked down at her, irritably. It was clear what she had been doing.

"Was it she who spilled the wine?" he asked.

"Yes," I said.

"If you do not wish to exert yourself," he said, "I can have her whipped for you."

"It is all right," I said. "She is only a stupid, meaningless slave."

"Run along, Susan," I said. "You can finish later."

"Yes, Mistress," said Susan, leaping up, darting away.

"Tonight," said Ligurious, "I will give her to guardsmen. She will dance the whip dance, naked." There are many whip dances on Gor, of various sorts. In a context of this sort, presumably not in a tavern, and without music, the girl is expected to move, writhe and twist seductively before strong men. If she does not do well enough, if she is insufficiently maddeningly sensuous, the whips fall not about her, but on her. When one of the men can stand it no longer he orders her to his mat where, of course, she must be fully pleasing. If she is not, then she is whipped until she is. Then, when one man is satisfied, the dance begins again, and continues in this fashion until all are satisfied, or tire of the sport.

"How goes the war?" I said.

"I have come to report another glorious victory," said Ligurious. "This one has occurred on the Plains of Eteocles."

"The enemy, then," I said, "is east of the Hills of Eteocles, and is through the Pass of Theseus."

"You have been examining maps?" inquired Ligurious.

"I made inquiries," I said. He knew I could not read. I was illiterate in Gorean.

"I see," he said.

I heard men shouting, and the rattle of weaponry outside, down in the courtyard.

I hurried to the barred window.

"Those will be guardsmen," said Ligurious, "issuing forth to disperse the rabble."

"Yes," I said. I could see a double line of guardsmen, with shields and spears, exiting through the gates. In a moment, too, I could see men and woman fleeing across the square.

"Those are small groups of dissidents," said Ligurious. "Pay them no mind. You are loved in Corcyrus."

"Each of our victories," I said, "seems to occur closer to Corcyrus."

"Surely you saw the silver brought in from Argentum?" he asked.

"Yes," I said. "It was prominently displayed in the victory parade several weeks ago, that over which we presided."

"Over which you presided, my Tatrix," said he, modestly.

"Yes," I said.

I recalled this parade well. Ligurious had been in the palanquin with me. He had been, in his force and presence, both visible and prominent. I, as earlier, apparently in accord with the public customs of Corcyrus, had been unveiled. My features, it seemed, would be well known to thousands.

"It seems little more silver has been forthcoming," I said.

Ligurious was silent.

"Did your troops enter Argentum?" I asked.

"Our generals did not feel it was necessary," said Ligurious.

"It seems that our first victory, after the seizure of the mines, occurred on the Fields of Hesius," I said.

"Yes," said Ligurious.

"Our second occurred on the shores of Lake Ias," I said, "and our third east of the Issus." This was a northwestward-flowing river, tributary to the Vosk, far to the north.

"Yes, my Tatrix," said Ligurious.

"Now we have been victorious once more," I said, "this time on the Plains of Eteocles."

"Yes, my Tatrix," said Ligurious.

"They lie within a hundred pasangs of Corcyrus," I said.

"It is part of a plan, my Tatrix," said Ligurious. "We are stretching their supply lines. Then, when we wish, soon, now, we will strike like a tarn, cutting them. We will then subject a starving, demoralized enemy to devastating attacks. Have no fear, Lady. They will soon be helpless. We will soon have them beneath our swords."

"Are there scarcities in the city?" I asked.

"There are none in the palace," said Ligurious. "Did Lady Sheila enjoy her spiced vulo this evening?"

"In the city?" I said.

"In a time of conflict," said Ligurious, "there are always some privations."

"Are they minor?" I asked.

"Yes," he said. "With your permission," he said. He then bowed, and withdrew.

I watched him withdraw. I wondered what it would be like to have to do obeisance to such a man, and what it would be like to be in his arms.

I then turned again to the barred window. From where I stood, sometimes, I could see tarn wire, as the light struck it, in its swaying movements. It was strung about, over the courtyard, between the palace and the walls. Too, it had been strung elsewhere, I had heard, in the city.

The door opened and Susan entered, and knelt down and lowered her head. It is common for slaves to kneel when entering the presence of free persons. It is common, too, of course, more generally, for them to kneel whenever they find themselves in the presence of a free person, for example, if they are in a room and a free person enters.

"You may finish your work," I informed the slave from Cincinnati, Ohio.

"Yes, Mistress. Thank you, Mistress," said the girl. In a moment, then, she was again, on her hands and knees, with water and cloths, her head down, rinsing and cleaning the tiles, thoroughly and carefully removing the residue of sticky, half-dried wine from them.

"Susan," I said.

"Mistress?" she asked, raising her head.

"Did Ligurious speak to you?" I asked.

"Yes, Mistress," she said.

"You know that tonight you are to—to dance?"

"Yes, Mistress," she said. "Before selected guardsmen. The whip dance."

"It was not my idea, Susan," I said. "I did not ask Ligurious to have you punished. It was his idea. I want you to know that. I am sorry."

"It had not even occurred to me that it might have been your idea, Mistress," smiled Susan. "You did not even want me punished. Mistress has always shown me incredible lenience. Mistress has always shown me incredible kindness. It is almost as if—"

"Yes?" I said.

"—almost as if Mistress has some idea of the helplessness and vulnerability of the slave."

"And how," I asked angrily, "would I, a free woman, have any idea of that?"

"Forgive me, Mistress," said Susan. "Of course you, as a free woman, could not!" I was angry. I considered whipping the little, collared slut. She put her head down, quickly, and continued her work, menial work, work suitable for such as she, a slave.

"Susan," I said.

"Yes, Mistress?" she asked.

"Is it hard to learn the whip dance?" I asked.

"I am not a dancer, Mistress," said Susan, "nor are most who perform the dance. It is not even, really, a dance. One simply has one's clothes taken away, and then one moves before strong, powerful men as such men would have a woman move before them. Then when one is sufficiently pleased, he indicates this and you serve his pleasure."

"How do you know what to do?" I asked.

"Sometimes one tries different things," she said, "for example, about or on the furniture, on the floor, about their bodies, at their feet, on your back, on your belly, hoping to find something that they will respond to. Sometimes they give you explicit instructions or commands, as when a woman is put through slave paces. Sometimes they guide you, or help you, sometimes by the whip, sometimes by expressions or cries. At other times the girl listens, so to speak, to the slave fires in her belly, and seems to become one with them and the dance, and then, soon, must beg the brutes, in her dance, and by her piteous expressions and gestures, to relieve the merciless tensions in her body, allowing her to complete the cruel cycle of arousal, allowing her to receive them and submit to them, the masters, in the spasmodic surrender of the helpless slave."

"But the whip," I said. "Do you not fear it?"

"I fear it," she said. "But I do not think I will feel it."

"Why?" I asked.

Susan suddenly looked me directly in the eye. "I dance well," she said.

I turned away from her. When I looked at her again, she had finished her work.

"Will Mistress be needing me further for this evening?" she asked.

I looked at Susan.

How chaste, how modest, how demure she seemed in her brief tunic, and collar, with her lovely face and beautiful little figure! How dainty, how exquisite! How deferential, how shy! Surely she was a woman's slave, and only that, attentive, knowledgeable, efficient, respectful and self-effacing.

But a man such as Ligurious had bought her naked off a slave block in Cos.

What a sweet, bashful girl she was.

But tonight she would dance naked for guardsmen.

"Mistress?" asked Susan.

"You do not seem distressed that tonight you will dance," I observed. Indeed, it seemed she might be looking forward to it.

"No, Mistress," she said.

"Why?" I asked.

"Must I speak?" she asked.

"Yes," I said.

"I love men, and wish to serve them, fully," she said.

"Lewd and shameless slut!" I cried.

"I am a slave," she said. "Forgive me, Mistress. Too, I have not been given to a man in eleven days. My fingernails are bloody from scratching at the tiles in my kennel."

I shuddered. I had not thought much about where slave girls might be kept at night. To be sure, I knew that they were not wandering freely about the palace. Now, it seemed, that some, at least, might be locked in kennels. This made sense, of course, considering that, like the shameless, little slut, Susan, they were animals.

"It does not seem that the whip dance, truly, would be much of a punishment for you," I said.

"Ligurious has several women," she said. "He does not know me that well. He has had me only a few times, and I have improved my skills, considerably, since then."

"He thinks, then, that it will be a terrible punishment for you?" I asked.

"I would suppose so," she said. "Doubtless he expects that I will be muchly lashed."

"What is it like to be in the arms of a man such as Ligurious?" I asked, as though not much interested, really.

"He devastates a woman," she said, "turning her into a tormented, whimpering animal, and then he makes her yield to him, fully, and as a slave."

"Did you spill the wine on purpose?" I asked.

"No, Mistress," she laughed. "I did not know that Ligurious was coming to your quarters. It occurred before his arrival. Too, I know you would not be so cruel as to assign a girl to the whip dance. Too, the common punishment for such a clumsiness is not the uncompromising, degrading severity of the whip dance but disciplines more prosaic in their nature, such as a restriction or change in rations, close chains or, most often, a switching or whipping."

"I see," I said.

I wondered what Susan would look like, her body glistening with a sheen of sweat, twisting and writhing before men, pleasing them as a naked slave, theirs then to be exploited and used however they might wish. She seemed such an ideal woman's slave, such an efficient, bashful, modest girl, it was hard to imagine her in such a context. But she had told me that her fingernails were bloody from scratching at the tiles in her kennel. It seemed then that quiet, sweet, withdrawn, retiring Susan actually had sexual needs and powerful ones. These needs, too, presumably, given her appearance and curvatures, bespeaking a richness in female hormones, would be deeply feminine ones. I wondered in how many girls like Susan there might lie a pleasure slave, waiting to be uncaged and commanded.

"I dance well," she had told me.

How startled I had been when she had said that. I had turned away. She had looked into my eyes, in that instant, not as a slave into the eyes of a free woman, but as one woman into the eyes of another. I had felt then, in that instant, that we were both, ultimately, only women, that we were identical in our femaleness, that we were united in the bonds of a common sisterhood and what, in relationship to men, it entailed. We were both, ultimately, only women; we were both, ultimately, though I was free and she was a slave, representatives of the slave sex.

I wondered if I, too, could dance well. I knew that if I did not, I would be lashed.

"I will have no further need for you tonight, Susan," I said. "I think that you should soon report to your masters of the evening."

"Yes, Mistress," she said. "Thank you, Mistress."

"Susan," I said.

"Yes, Mistress?" she said.

"Is there unrest in the city?"

"I do not know, Mistress," she said. "I am seldom outside the grounds of the palace."

I had resolved upon a bold plan.

"Before you report to your temporary masters," I said, "inform Drusus Rencius that I wish to see him. He is to report to my quarters within the Ahn."

"Yes, Mistress," she said.

"It will not be necessary to inform Ligurious of this action on your part," I said.

"As Mistress wishes," she said.

"It is my recommendation," I said, "that in reporting to your temporary masters you are a little late, but just late enough to increase their eagerness, not late enough that you are lashed for tardiness."

"Yes, Mistress," smiled Susan. "Thank you, Mistress!" She then sped from the room.

I then went again to the barred window, and looked out, over the city.

I myself had been outside of the palace grounds only infrequently in weeks, since my visit to the house of Kliomenes. I had been out, of course, in the grand victory parade, staged shortly after the seizure of the mines.

I then turned away from the window. I would now await the arrival of Drusus Rencius. I had seen him privately scarcely at all since the house of Kliomenes and the inn of Lysias. Our relationship was totally professional. Twice he had requested to be relieved of his duties, to be assigned to a new post, but I had refused to grant this request. That he might be restless, tortured or bitter in my presence meant nothing to me. I was a Tatrix. He was a soldier. He would obey me.

I considered his apparent discomfort in my presence. I smiled. It pleased me. Let him suffer.

## 10

# I HAVE TAKEN COGNIZANCE IN CORCYRUS; WE ARE RETURNING TO THE PALACE

Through the darkened street, along the crooked way, Drusus Rencius and I were making our way back to the palace. He carried a torch. The smaller streets of Gorean cities are often dark at night. The pedestrians carry their own light.

"I would prefer," said Drusus Rencius, "that we had kept to the main thoroughfares."

"I wished to speak to citizens in lesser known districts, as well," I said.

"Is Lady Sheila satisfied?" he asked.

"Yes," I said, "on the whole, though the people often seemed reticent, or frightened."

"Times are troubled," said Drusus Rencius.

I had stopped many passersby, particularly in the larger streets, making inquiries. I had even stopped in some of the more respectable taverns, those in which free women, without difficulty, might enter. The people seemed enthusiastically appreciative of the governance of the Tatrix and made light of shortages. They discounted and belittled rumors of discontentment or unrest in Corcyrus. Things in Corcyrus, it seemed, were much as Ligurious had assured me. The people were supportive of the policies of the palace, loyal to the state and personally devoted to their beloved Tatrix.

"Many of the shops," I said, "are boarded up."

"Many merchants have left the city," said Drusus Rencius, "taking their goods with them."

"Why?" I asked.

"They are afraid," he said. "The Street of Coins is almost closed." This was actually a set of streets, or district, where money changing and banking were done. There are other types of establishments in the area, too, of course. "Private citizens, too, many of them," said Drusus Rencius, "their goods on their back, have taken their leave of the city."

"Craven rabble," I said. "Why can they not be brave like the others?"

"Wait!" said Drusus Rencius, stopping. He lifted the torch, which he carried in his left hand, increasing the range of its illumination, and put out his right hand, holding me back, a barrier to my advance.

"What is it?" I asked.

"I heard something," he said. "Stay back."

I stepped back. The sword of Drusus Rencius left its sheath. I now understood why he, though right-handed, had been carrying the torch in his left hand. It facilitated an immediate draw.

"I do not hear anything," I said.

"Be quiet," he said.

I suddenly saw, emerging from the darkness, three shapes. "Tal, Soldier," said one of them.

"Tal," said Drusus Rencius. He backed against a wall. I stood very near him, frightened.

"We are lost," said one of the shapes, ingratiatingly. He drew a sheet of paper from within his tunic. "I have directions here, on a sheet of paper. You have a torch."

"Do not approach," said Drusus Rencius.

The fellow smiled and, slowly, in his fingers, wadded up the sheet of paper, and dropped it to the street.

Three swords then left their sheaths.

"Give us the woman," said the man.

"No," said Drusus Rencius.

I suddenly cried out, seized from the side, and I saw Drusus Rencius, the torch flung to the side, lunge toward the man who had been in the center of the first two. One man, one of two who had been approaching us from the side, threw me back against a wall. I could not move because of his presence. My veil, not even unpinned, was wadded and thrust back, deeply in my mouth. I heard swords clashing. I was turned to the side and my robes of concealment were pulled forward and down, over my head. A narrow strap was then slung about my head and pulled back, deeply between my teeth, and tied tightly behind the back of my neck. This secured the entire arrangement. I then, in my own garments, had been effectively gagged and hooded. I was then turned to the wall and my hands were jerked behind my back. In a moment, with two or three loops of cord, they were fastened in place. I then felt myself lifted to the shoulder of a man. I was utterly helpless. I heard another sword, quite near me, sliding from its sheath. "Run!" I heard a man cry. I was flung then from his shoulder, striking my own shoulder against a wall, and sliding down to the street. I heard feet running away.

"They are gone," I heard Drusus Rencius say.

I whimpered as loudly as I could. Only such tiny, piteous noises were permitted me by the gag.

I felt a hand on my shoulder. "There you are," said Drusus Rencius.

I heard a sword laid on the stones behind me. Then, feeling about my head, Drusus Rencius undid the strap that held my gag and hood in place. The fresh air felt good on my face. I could hardly see him, but inches from me. The torch had gone out. He, in the darkness, adjusted my veil.

"Are you all right?" he asked.

"Yes," I said. "Who were they?"

"Probably slavers," he said. "I do not know. They are gone now."

"Slavers?" I whispered, in horror.

"Probably," he said. "It was you they were interested in. They did not appear to be young ruffians out for an evening's sport. Too, they seem to have handled you with an efficiency that comes with training and practice."

I was then silent, trembling.

"They are gone now," said Drusus Rencius.

"My hands are tied," I whimpered.

"Forgive me," he said. He then, after a moment, had freed my wrists. He then picked up his blade. He then rose to his feet. I was on my knees, then, before him. I held him about the legs, and put my face against his leg. I was terrified from what had occurred. I was still trembling.

"Get up," he said, angrily. "Your behavior seems too much like that of a woman."

"I am a woman," I said.

"No," he said. "You are a Tatrix."

I sobbed.

"Get up," he said.

"I could have been carried into slavery," I said, frightened, holding him.

"You torturing slut," he snarled, suddenly, "I am tempted to put chains on you myself."

"Are you so attracted to me, Drusus?" I said, startled. "So attracted to me that you would be satisfied with nothing less than my total ownership?"

"Torturing slut!" he said. "Get up!"

"You do desire me!" I said. "You desire me with the most powerful desire with which a man can desire a woman, that he own her completely, that she be his total slave!"

"I hate you, and despise you!" he said.

"And want me!" I said.

"Let us return to the palace," he said, "before I leave you here in the darkness, a prey to those who, more than I, would see to it that you get what you deserve."

"And what is it that I deserve, Drusus," I asked, at his feet.

"A marked thigh," he said, angrily, "and a collar-encircled neck."

"Do you think that I am a slave?" I cried.

"You would make an ideal slave," he said.

"Insolence!" I cried.

"Truth," he said.

I cried out in rage.

"But you are not a slave," he said. "Get up."

"It is fortunate for me that I am not a slave, isn't it," I asked, "at the feet of a man such as you?"

"Yes," he said, "it is very fortunate for you."

"And what would you do with me," I asked, "if you did own me?"

"That," he said, "own you, and as a woman is owned, fully."

"Give me your hands," I said.

He then helped me up.

I smoothed my robes. "It is interesting to know that you desire me," I said.

He was silent.

"Indeed," I said, "it is quite amusing. Perhaps I should have you whipped for insolence. Do not aspire above your station, Drusus. I am a Tatrix. You are nothing, only a guard."

"Yes, Tatrix," he said.

"I hold you in contempt," I said. "I scorn you. I am worlds above you."

"Yes, Tatrix," he said.

"And do not forget it," I said.

"No, Tatrix," he said.

"What are you doing?" I asked. I had seen his arm move, with the blade.

"I am cleaning the blade, wiping it on my tunic," he said.

"Cleaning it?" I asked.

"In driving the men off, I wounded two of them," he said.

"Are you all right?" I asked.

"Yes," he said. I resisted an impulse to kneel before him, begging to lick the blood from the blade, begging him then to dry it in my hair.

"Is it clean?" I asked.

"Yes," he said.

"Do not sheathe it until we reach the palace," I said. "The streets are dark."

"I have no intention of doing so," he said.

"At least," I said, "I have satisfied myself as to the condition of the citizenry and the status of the city."

"How is that?" he asked.

"You heard, surely," I said. "The people make light of privations. They are loyal. They are devoted to their Tatrix."

"Such are the answers to be given to such questions in Corcyrus," he said.

"I do not understand," I said.

"The people are afraid," he said. "You have inspired terror. Your rule is one of iron."

"I do not understand," I said.

"Too, your spies are everywhere," he said. "The people to whom you spoke probably mistook you, ironically enough, for one of your own spies."

"I have no spies," I said.

"I can name seven," said Drusus Rencius. "How many you have, of course, I do not know."

I shuddered, confused. These spies, if, indeed, there were any, must be reporting to someone else, perhaps to Ligurious.

"Will we light the torch on the way home?" I asked.

"I think it will be safer to move silently in the darkness," said Drusus Rencius.

"Perhaps you are right," I said, shuddering.

"Please follow me, a bit behind," said Drusus Rencius. "I mean this as no insult to you."

"I understand," I said. I certainly had no objections, under the circumstances, to heeling him like a slave.

"Are you coming?" he asked. He turned about.

"It is so dark," I said.

"I do not think it will be safe to remain here," he said. "Try to follow me."

"I am afraid," I said. I could not see my footing.

"Do you wish for me to carry you?" he asked.

"And how would you do that?" I asked, apprehensively.

"In my arms, with honor," he said. "Did you think I would throw you over my shoulder like a bound slave?"

I was silent. How did I know how Drusus Rencius would carry a woman, particularly a woman such as I sensed I might be. I did know how the other fellow had carried me, over his shoulder, bound, absolutely helpless, perhaps, indeed, like a slave.

"It would be better for you to walk," said Drusus Rencius. "In that fashion my sword arm would be unencumbered."

"Are these streets not supposed to be patrolled by guardsmen?" I asked.

"Most of the guardsmen," said Drusus Rencius, "have been sent to the west, to the front."

I was silent.

"The forces of Ar will be difficult to hold," said Drusus Rencius.

"Of Ar!" I said.

"Yes," said Drusus Rencius. "Forces of Ar entered the fray after the seizure of the mines. Argentum, as you know, is an ally of Ar."

I had not known this, basic though it might be. Many things, it seemed, had not been made clear to me. I did know that we were supposed to have strong ties of one sort or another with the island ubarate of Cos. Susan, I knew, had been bought in Cos. I knew almost nothing of Ar. I did know that Drusus Rencius had once been of that city. Too, I knew it was one of the most powerful, if not the most powerful, city on Gor. In known Gor, it was rivaled only by Turia, in Gor's southern hemisphere.

"Our forces will be victorious," I assured Drusus Rencius.

"The enemy is already within twenty pasangs of Corcyrus," he said.

"Take me back to the palace," I said, "swiftly, please."

"Yes, Lady Sheila," he said.

He then turned about, and started off, through the darkness. I hurried along behind him, heeling him like a slave.

I felt miserable, and terrified and sick.

In the palace I would be safe.

## 11

## SUSAN HAS BEEN BEATEN; LIGURIOUS SPEAKS WITH ME; THERE IS NOTHING TO FEAR; I AM SAFE IN THE PALACE

I was thrust into my quarters by a guard, and the door was shut behind me.

A lamp was lit in the room. I heard whimpering.

"Susan!" I cried.

The girl lay on her belly, naked on the tiles. Even the silken collar sheath, of one color or another, which was usually worn, selected to match a tunic, was gone. Her neck was encircled by the bared, unadorned steel alone. She had been terribly whipped.

I knelt beside the girl. "The brutes!" I cried, softly. I touched her hair, gently. Tonight I knew she had danced the whip dance.

"This was not done to me by guardsmen, Mistress," she said. Then she began to sob.

"By whom, then?" I demanded.

"It was done to me by the slave master of Ligurious, on the orders of Ligurious," she said.

"But, why?" I asked.

"Because I did not inform Ligurious that you had had Drusus Rencius summoned tonight to your quarters."

"How did he learn of this?" I asked.

"Doubtless from a guard, and, too, that you had left the palace," she said.

"I am sorry, Susan," I said. It had been I, I recalled, in the prosecution of my own plans, and in my desire for secrecy, who had suggested to Susan that the summoning of Drusus Rencius to my quarters need not be made known to Ligurious.

"Why have you been put here?" I asked.

"That you may see me, Mistress," she sobbed.

"It is all my fault," I said.

"No, Mistress," she said. "It is my fault. I was not pleasing to my master."

Ligurious apparently had been disturbed, particularly that I had left the palace. He, with guardsmen, with lanterns, had met Drusus Rencius and I at the small postern gate in the east wall of the palace grounds, that through which we had returned. Drusus Rencius had been detained there, and I had been hurried to my quarters.

There were suddenly two blows on the door, loud knocks. "Ligurious, first minister of Corcyrus," announced a guard, from the other side of the door.

I stood up, and went to the center of the room. I tried to stand very straight, very regally.

"Enter," I said.

Ligurious entered.

Susan, frightened, with an effort that must have been painful for her striped body, knelt, with her head down to the tiles, the palms of her hands on the floor, in that form of obeisance apparently required by Ligurious of his women.

"To your kennel, Slave," said Ligurious.

Susan lifted her head. "Yes, Master!" she said.

"Get out, Slut!" he said.

"Yes, Master!" she cried, and, springing to her feet, fled from the room.

"You are up late," observed Ligurious.

"I was in the city," I said, defiantly.

"It can be dangerous in the city," he said, "especially in these times, and at night."

I tossed my head. He need not know what had happened on the darkened street.

"You must understand," he said, "that I have a responsibility for your safety."

"It was not necessary that you treated Susan as you did," I said.

"Do not attempt to interfere in the relationship between a man and his slave," he said. "That relationship is absolute."

"I see," I said. I stepped back, frightened.

"In the future," he said, "you are not to leave the palace without my permission. In the meantime, you will remain here, confined to your quarters."

"No!" I cried.

"Remove your veil," he said, "and your outer robes, and slippers."

Frightened, I did so. I then stood before him in a long, off-the-shoulder, yellow, silken sliplike garment.

"You now stand before a man, Lady Sheila," he said, "as barefoot as a slave."

"I shall call the guards!" I cried.

"And whom do you think they will obey?" he asked.

"I will call Drusus Rencius!" I cried.

"He has been relieved of his duties," said Ligurious. "He is no longer your guard."

"Oh," I said.

"And he seems pleased to be done with you."

"Oh," I said. Now I could no longer torture Drusus, with my nearness and inaccessibility.

"And I cannot say that I blame him," said Ligurious. "For you seem to be a frigid little slut."

"Slut!" I cried.

"Do not form an over-exalted opinion of yourself," he said. "You are only a slut from Earth and no better than a female slave."

I looked at him with horror. He stepped toward me, and I shrank back. Then I whimpered as I felt his strong hands grasp me by the upper arms. He looked down into my eyes. "Displease me in the least," he said, "and I will put a brand in your hide and a collar on your neck. Do you understand?"

I could not begin to free myself of his grasp. "Yes," I said. "Yes!" I was terrified.

He did not release me. He continued to look down into my eyes. He seemed to me terribly strong and large.

"I wonder if I should subject you to rape discipline," he mused.

"No," I said. "Please, no." But I felt heat between my legs, and weakness and helplessness. I knew that my body was lubricating itself, preparing to receive him, if he should choose to have me.

"You are so much like her," he said, looking down into my eyes.

"Who?" I asked.

"One who makes me weak," he smiled, "one with whom I am smitten."

"I am only a barbarian," I said.

"She, too, is a barbarian," he said, "like yourself a barbarian beauty."

"Who is she?" I asked.

"You do not know her," he said. Then he removed his hands from me. "In character, of course, you are quite different. She is superior, lofty, noble, regal and fine. Girls like you, on the other hand, can be found in any market. Too, I think she is probably even more beautiful than you, though the resemblance is truly striking. And in intellect, in brilliance and decisiveness, of course, there is no comparison."

"Perhaps she should be Tatrix of Corcyrus, and not I," I said, angrily.

"Perhaps," he smiled.

I turned away from him. "I am the Tatrix of Corcyrus, am I not?" I asked.

"Yes," he said.

"You know that I am from Earth," I said. "How is it that I was brought here, to be Tatrix?"

"We wished to go outside the city," he said, "to find one from the outside, free of all connections and factions, to rule over us with wisdom and objectivity."

"I see," I said. "Then I am truly the Tatrix of Corcyrus."

"Of course," he said.

"How is it, then," I asked, "that I have been treated with rudeness, that even now I am barefoot in your presence?" I did not, of course, make an effort to put my slippers back on. I did not know if he would permit it. He had, of course, ordered me to remove them.

"You are useful," he said, "and you have your purposes. You are not, however, indispensable. It would be well for you to remember that. It might encourage you to be more cooperative."

"I suppose," I said, "I should be pleased that you did not order me to strip completely and kneel before you."

"You are, of course," he said, "a free woman."

"Yet it seems," I said, "if only implicitly, you have threatened me."

"Suitable disciplines and punishments may be arranged for a free woman," he said, "suitable to her status and dignity."

"I am sure of it," I said, ironically.

He then approached me, and stood quite close to me. I was facing away from him.

"And yet," he said, "I sense that such disciplines and punishments, those suitable for free women, would not be suitable for you."

"And what sorts of disciplines and punishments would be suitable for me?" I asked.

He held me from behind, by the arms. I was helpless. "Such that would be appropriate for slaves," he said.

I stiffened, but I could not free myself.

"You are so different from her," he said. I felt his breath on the left side of my neck. "Your dispositions, your responses, the way you carry yourself, the way you move, how you speak." I felt weak. "I sense," he said, "wherein your deepest fulfillments would lie. I sense what it is that you need and want, what it is that without it you will never achieve your most perfect and complete self."

"What?" I asked.

"The collar," he said.

"No!" I cried.

"Fight it and deny it, if you will," he said. "Have your sport. But it is true."

"No," I wept.

"Consider your incredible femininity," he said. "You have the curves, the softness, the instincts, the helplessness of the slave."

"No!" I said. "I will try to be less feminine, and thus more of a woman!"

"Words from the insane asylums on Earth," he laughed. "This is Gor. It is fortunate you are not a slave, or your true womanhood, the marvelous softness and depth of your femininity, revealed and manifested, would in all its fullness be required of you, and without compromise, even to the whip, by masters."

He then put his right hand in my hair and held my left

wrist in his left hand. He drew my head back, painfully, until even my back was bent backwards.

"It is interesting," he said, "how different she is from you. Yet, too, you seem in many ways so similar." I whimpered, helplessly held. "Do you know that women such as you are born to the chain?" he asked.

"No," I said, strained. "No."

"Yes," he said, "and you will not be complete until it is on you."

I whimpered helplessly. Why did he not drag me to the bed and take me?

I understood then what true womanhood was. It was not the denial and frustration of femininity but the full surrender to it, being true to, and honest to, my deepest nature and needs. Femininity was not incompatible with womanhood. It was its expression.

What insanities, what perversions, what sickness, I had been taught on Earth!

"Ah, forgive me, Lady Sheila," said Ligurious, as though concerned. "I almost forget, holding you in this fashion, that you are a free woman."

He then released me.

I straightened up, and, turning about, pulled away from him, as though I had managed to free myself.

Ligurious bowed to me, from the waist, as though in deep apology. But he was smiling.

I was horrified. I realized then that I must fight my femininity. I had learned, of course, that in doing this, far from expressing womanhood, I was frustrating and denying it, but that, in my terror, was what I then wished to do. I then, terribly, feared my womanhood, and that to which it might lead. I thus, then, decided that my femininity, and thereby my womanhood, must be denied and fought. I could no longer be so simple as to pretend to myself that my womanhood was best served by its own frustration, suppression and denial. I was no longer victimized by that propagandistic stupidity. The danger, I now understood clearly, was womanhood itself. Openly, honestly, must it be repudiated and denied. That was what was most to be feared, that was the great danger to women, their own womanhood, that which was what they were, in their deepest heart and belly. I was afraid to look deeply into myself. I was afraid of what I might find there.

"I am a free woman," I said. "I am free! I am free!"

"Of course you are," he said.

"I am now going to put on my slippers," I said.

"Have you received permission to do so?" he asked.

I looked at him, frightened.

"You may do so," he said.

I slipped into the slippers. I then felt more secure. There is something about being barefoot before a man who is shod that tends to make a woman feel more like a slave before him. These sorts of feelings are intensified, of course, if the woman is naked, or partially clothed, as I was, according to his dictates, before him. Slaves, of course, are often commanded to nudity before their masters and their clothing, if any, is always subject to his approval.

In the slippers, interestingly, I felt again the Tatrix of Corcyrus.

"Are there spies in the city?" I asked.

"Doubtless Argentum has spies in the city," he said.

"Our spies," I said. "Ones who spy on our own people."

"Of course," he said. "That is a realistic precaution in any city."

"And to whom do these spies report?" I asked.

"To the proper authorities," he said.

"I am not aware of receiving the reports of these spies," I said.

"You are still being trained in the governance of Corcyrus," he said.

"How goes the war?" I asked.

"As I reported earlier," he said, "well."

"The enemy," I said, suddenly, almost faltering, "is within twenty pasangs of Corcyrus."

"That information is, I believe," he said, "approximately correct."

"That is too close!" I said.

"Such matters need not concern the Tatrix," he said. "They need concern, rather, our generals."

"That is too close!" I said.

"We shall soon cut their supply lines," he said. "Do not fear, Lady Sheila. Our forces will be victorious."

"Ar is in the war!" I said.

"That is true," he said. "But momentarily we are expecting reinforcements from Cos."

"I am afraid, Ligurious," I said.

"There is nothing to fear," he said. "The city is secure. The palace is impregnable."

"I do not want the war," I said. "I want the fighting stopped. I am afraid. I want a truce!"

"Such matters," he said, "need not concern you. Leave them to others."

"Surely the enemy will consider a truce!" I said.

Ligurious looked at me and, suddenly, laughed. His laughter unsettled me. I felt that perhaps I had said something inutterably naive or stupid.

"That is out of the question?" I asked.

"Yes," said Ligurious. Was the enemy so bitter, so determined? What had driven them to these passions of war? What was it that they desired in Corcyrus?

"Sue for peace!" I said.

"Everything is planned for," said Ligurious. "We have anticipated all contingencies."

"I want us to sue for peace," I said.

"That decision is not yours," said Ligurious.

"Am I not the Tatrix of Corcyrus?" I demanded.

"Of course," smiled Ligurious.

"Do I not rule in Corcyrus?" I asked.

"Of course," said Ligurious.

"I rule in Corcyrus," I said.

"Yes," said Ligurious.

"And who rules me?" I asked.

"I do," said Ligurious.

I shuddered.

"Did Lady Sheila enjoy her spiced vulo this evening?" he asked.

"Yes," I whispered.

He then left.

I went to the barred window, looking out. I was confined to my quarters. Out there, somewhere, in the darkness, beyond the walls, was the enemy.

Apparently they were such that they would not even consider a truce.

I wondered what it was that they wanted, so keenly, so determinedly, in Corcyrus.

I was frightened. Perhaps the troops of Cos would come to our rescue. I was pleased that I was safe in the palace.

# 12

# I SIT UPON THE THRONE; I WAIT IN THE HALL

"Dress her in her most regal robes," commanded Ligurious.

"Yes, Master," said Susan, fumbling with the garments.

I stood before the mirror in my quarters. I watched the glorious robes of state being placed about my shoulders.

Earlier I had stood frightened behind the door, now kept locked, my ear to the wood.

"They are within the city!" I had heard cry.

"Impossible!" had cried a guard.

"How was it done?" inquired another, insistently, bewilderedly.

"It seems a Sa-Tarna wagon was fleeing before the approaching enemy, seeking to reach the city before being overtaken," said a man. "There was time, happily, it seemed, though the matter would be close, for the wagon to win its race, and sorely, as you know, did we need the grain. The gate was opened to admit the wagon. Surely there would then be time, and time enough, given the distances involved, to close the gate. The wagon seemed to be drawn by two strings of male slaves, twenty in each string, as is common. These men, however, were not slaves. The wagon within the portal, they threw off their harnesses and from beneath the grain drew forth swords. They prevented the closing of the gate. In moments the vanguard of the enemy had arrived."

I had hurried then to the barred window. I could see smoke rising from the city.

Shortly thereafter Ligurious and Susan had arrived at my quarters.

Ligurious wore soldierly garb, but of a sort with which I was not familiar. I did not know the insignia, the markings.

"Put her in the veil of state," said Ligurious. Susan brought forth a long, lovely veil, intricately embroidered. She adjusted my robes about me, concealing, in the fashion of the robes of concealment, now not thrown back, but drawn up, my hair and much of my head. She then pinned the veil in place. It was very beautiful. It was opaque. Little could now be seen of me but my eyes and a bit of the bridge of my nose. I had not even known such a veil existed. Hitherto I had generally worn veils only when intending to travel incognito in the city, and I had never worn them on official occasions of state.

"Come along," said Ligurious. He took my arm and, half dragging me, conducted me from my quarters.

In moments we were hurrying through the halls. Falling in behind Ligurious were some five or six men, not my guards, who were dressed much as he was.

The halls seemed, for the most part, oddly deserted. Occasionally a man ran past. At one point, crouching down, then kneeling, as we passed, by hangings at the side of the corridor, was a slave girl. She was terrified. She wore some twists of silk about her. She wore a collar of a sort, rather high and ornate, which is often jeweled. No jewels, however, caught the light as we passed. They had been, I gathered, pried from their settings.

Susan was not with us. I did not know where she was. Apparently she had been left behind.

I was thrust into an anteroom, one off the great hall. In this room there were some four or five men and a woman. The woman wore a robe, hooding her, and was turned away from me. She was about my height. Interestingly she was barefoot and the robe she wore came only a bit below the knees. I thought she had nice calves and ankles. Mine, I thought, might be better, A man, dressed rather in the fashion of Ligurious and the others, was lifting a sheet about her. She clutched this sheet about her, drawing it even about her head, and holding it together, before her face, effectively veiling herself with it. She turned to face me. Then she turned away. Her eye color, I noted, was not dissimilar to mine.

Ligurious turned me, so that I faced the door to the great hall, where, on the lofty dais, reposed the throne of Corcyrus.

"Is all ready?" asked Ligurious.

"Yes," responded a man.

"The tarns?" asked Ligurious.

"Yes," said the man. "Everything is ready."

I turned. I saw that the sheet, now, had been drawn completely over the woman, as though thrown over her. As it hung about her, its hem fell midway between her ankles and knees. I was startled. It was almost as though, under the sheet, she might be naked. I gasped. Something was being fastened about her throat, over the sheet, under her chin. It was round. There was a long strap connected with it. It was a slave collar and leash!

Ligurious took me by the arm and turned me about, again, facing me toward the door to the great hall.

I did not know who the woman was, but I suspected that she might be she with whom Ligurious had confessed himself to be so smitten, she to whom I apparently bore some resemblance. It seemed odd to me, almost incomprehensible, that Ligurious, a man such as he, who must have had some fifty women at his feet, women such as Susan, women kneeling in terror and awe about him, for he was their total master, should be so much like a callow youth, should be so weak, with this woman. Did he not know, I asked myself, scornfully, that she, too, ultimately, was only a woman, that she, too, ultimately, needed only the whip and a master?

I was then conducted into the great hall by Ligurious. It was empty. The two great entrance doors, at the far end, were locked from the inside, with the great beams in their brackets. It took ten guardsmen to move those beams. I could not begin to budge them.

"Is there any sign of the men of Cos?" I heard a man ask behind us, from the anteroom.

"They are not fools," said another man. "They will not meet Ar on the land."

"Do the people resist the enemy?" I heard another man ask.

"No," said another man. "They abet them."

I ascended the steps of the dais, conducted by Ligurious. At his indication I took my place on the throne.

"The doors of the anteroom will be locked behind us," said Ligurious. "You will not be able to open them."

"What is going on?" I asked.

"You will soon serve your purpose," said Ligurious.

"What purpose?" I said.

"That purpose which we feared might one day have to be served, that purpose, or major purpose, why you were brought to Gor."

"I do not understand," I said. I did recall that last night I had been assured that everything had been planned for, that all contingencies, according to Ligurious, had been anticipated. I wondered if I still had a role to play in these contingencies.

"You still need me, then?" I said. "I still figure in your plans?"

"Of course," he said.

I was relieved to hear this. I was afraid as to what might prove to be my fate if a man such as Ligurious no longer had any particular or special use for me. I was pretty. I could conjecture what fates might lie in store for me.

"Listen," said he. "Do you hear it?"

"Yes," I said. It was a dull, striking sound, coming as though from a great distance. It had a rhythm to it.

"It is a ram," said he, "doubtless slung from a cradle, drawn by ropes, doubtless with a will by citizens of Corcyrus."

"It sounds far away," I said.

"It is at the outer gate," he said.

"The citizens of Corcyrus love me," I said.

"Do not doubt it," he said. "I must now take my leave. I fear there is little time."

"But what of me?" I said. "I am afraid. Will you come back for me?"

"Have no fear, Lady Sheila," he said. "You will be come for."

"Soon?" I asked.

"Yes," he said. He then backed down the stairs. He bowed deeply. "Farewell, Lady Sheila, Tatrix of Corcyrus," he said.

He then withdrew.

I heard a splintering in the distance, and then, in a moment, a new striking, doubtless on the interior gate.

I heard the closing of the anteroom door behind Ligurious, and then the dropping in place of beams, the sliding of bolts. It had been locked from within, from the other side.

I sat on the throne, clutching its arms, alone in the great hall.

# 13

# THE GOLDEN CAGE; MILES OF ARGENTUM SPEAKS WITH ME

The great beam cracked, and then splintered, and the doors burst in at the far end of the aisle, leading towards the throne.

I clutched the arms of the throne in terror.

Before this I had heard the screams of the crowd outside the doors, their shouting and pounding, then the striking of a heavy beam against the door.

Men and women, many in rags, brandishing knives and implements, mixed with soldiers, poured into the great hall. The doors were open, and one hung awry on its hinges. The mob, with the soldiers, swirling about the heavy beam, now dropped, which had been used to breach the doors, flooded toward the dais. At the foot of the dais, shaking fists, shouting angrily, some restrained by soldiers, the crowd stopped. "Cut her to pieces!" I heard. "Tear her to pieces!" More than one man, brutally by soldiers, was struck back. I shrank back, on the throne.

The crowd seemed to part, scurrying to the sides about the central aisle.

Down the aisle, now, approaching, his sword in his right hand, his helmet in the crook of his left arm, came a large, sturdy figure. Others followed behind him. I recognized him.

"Miles, General of Argentum, Victor over Corcyrus!" announced a soldier.

He ascended the first two steps of the dais. He was sweaty. He had dirt on the side of his face. There was blood on his legs.

"Greetings, Sheila," he said, "Tatrix of Corcyrus."

"I am from Earth," I cried out. "My name is Tiffany Collins!"

"She is Sheila, Tatrix of Corcyrus!" cried men in the crowd. "It is Sheila, Tatrix of Corcyrus!" "It is she!" "It is Sheila!" "It is Sheila, the Tatrix of Corcyrus!"

I moaned. I was terrified that they should know that.

Miles of Argentum sheathed his sword. He handed his helmet to one of the men with him.

He approached the throne.

"Please, don't," I said.

Then he jerked away the veil of state from my features. I, though a free woman, had been face-stripped before free men. My face was as bare to them as though I might be a slave. Face-stripping a free woman, against her will, can be a serious crime on Gor. On the other hand, Corcyrus had now fallen. Her women, thusly, now at the feet of her conquerors, would be little better than slaves. Any fate could now be inflicted on them that the conquerors might wish, including making them actual slaves. The hand of Miles of Argentum then brushed back my robes, that my whole head and features, to the throat, might be revealed to the crowd.

"This is the way in which I am more accustomed to seeing you," he said. "Greetings, Lady Sheila, Tatrix of Corcyrus."

"I am Tiffany Collins," I said, weakly. "I am from Earth."

"Your features," said Miles of Argentum, "are surely well known to hundreds, if not thousands."

"Cut her to pieces!" cried men in the crowd. "Tear her to pieces!" cried women in the crowd.

"I am from Earth!" I cried. "I am Tiffany Collins!"

"Bring forth the palace slave called Susan," said Miles of Argentum.

Susan, from somewhere in the back, was thrust forward. I gasped. She was absolutely naked, save that she still wore the collar of Ligurious. Her hands were bound behind her back. In her nose there was a small, circular, wire apparatus which had apparently been held open, thrust through her septum, and then permitted to spring shut. Attached to this apparatus, tied through it, dangling, was a looped thong, about two feet in length. It was clearly a device by means of which a slave, or perhaps any female, might be led.

"You are Susan, are you not," inquired Miles of Argentum, "who was as personal serving slave to Sheila, the Tatrix of Corcyrus?"

"Yes, Master," she said.

He indicated that she might kneel before the throne.

"Is this she who was to you as Mistress?" inquired Miles of Argentum, addressing himself to the terrified slave from Cincinnati at his feet.

"Tell them I am Tiffany Collins, from Earth!" I told Susan.

"She is truly from Earth, I think, Master," wept Susan, "and that is what, I recall, she told me her name was."

I almost cried out with relief.

"And putting aside such former names and worlds," said Miles, "as whom do you know her here?"

Susan began to tremble.

"You know the penalties for a slave who lies," said Miles. "Think carefully and well, my small, nose-ringed beauty."

"She is she who was to me as Mistress," said Susan, sobbing, "she whom I served, Sheila, Tatrix of Corcyrus."

There was a cry of elation from the crowd.

"Forgive me, Mistress!" cried Susan. She then, at a sign from Miles, led by the thong, in the grip of a soldier, hurrying, almost running, that she did not place the least stress on the device in her nose, was being conducted rapidly from the room. I supposed she would be placed with other women, perhaps wearing similar devices. They can be tied about slave rings, fastened to other such thongs, and so on. Just before the soldier had grasped the thong I had seen her wildly look at Miles of Argentum. Doubtless she remembered him well from the audience, so long ago. Too, I thought it quite likely that he remembered her. In that audience he had looked upon her as though she might not be likely to quickly slip his mind. Too, he had had her summoned to the dais by her palace name. She had tried to read in his countenance, in that brief, wild instant, before she was removed from the dais, her fate, but she had been unable to do so. He was not, perhaps by intention, even looking at her. She did not know then if, when the collar of Ligurious was removed from her, she would be sent to his headquarters or not. There, of course, if she were found sufficiently pleasing, after perhaps a closer examination and trial, another collar might be put on her. She would, in any case, wear one collar or another, somewhere. She was a slave.

"Call the captain from Ar," said Miles of Argentum.

A tall, lean figure entered the hall, and approached now down the long aisle. Then he stood on the dais, almost with Miles of Argentum.

"No," I whispered. "No."

"Drusus Rencius, Captain of Ar, on detached service to the forces of Argentum," said Miles of Argentum. "I believe you two have met."

I shook my head, disbelievingly. I had been told he was a renegade from Ar. Twice, I knew, suddenly realizing it now, he could have stolen me from Corcyrus, delivering me to Argentum, once when we were on the walls near the tarn perches and once, later, when, my whereabouts unknown to Ligurious and others, I had been in the house of Kliomenes, braceleted, half naked and helpless. But he had not abducted me, nor attempted to do so. It seemed rather he had, for whatever reason or reasons, preferred, as he had once remarked on the walls of Corcyrus, to let the game take its course.

"Do you know this woman, Captain?" asked Miles, general of Argentum.

Drusus Rencius handed his helmet to a soldier and climbed then to the height of the throne.

He put out his hands and lifted me to my feet before the throne. He then held me by the upper arms and looked down, deeply, into my eyes.

I shuddered. This was not a matter in which he wished to risk any mistake.

"Yes," he said.

"How do you know her?" asked Miles of Argentum.

"I was, for several weeks," he said, "her personal bodyguard."

"You know her then quite well?" asked Miles.

"Yes," said Drusus Rencius.

"Can you identify her?" asked Miles.

"Yes," said Drusus Rencius.

"Who is she?" asked Miles of Argentum.

"She is Sheila, Tatrix of Corcyrus," said Drusus Rencius.

There was a sudden cry of pleasure and victory from the crowd. Drusus Rencius released me, and turned about, and, descending from the dais and making his way through the crowd, left.

I watched him leave.

"Strip her," said Miles of Argentum, "and put her in golden chains, and put her in the golden cage."

I felt the hands of soldiers at my clothing. It was torn from me, before the very throne. Then, when I was absolutely naked, a golden collar, to which a chain was attached, with wrist rings and ankle rings, was brought. It was a chaining system of that sort called a sirik. My chin was thrust up and I felt the golden collar locked on my throat. Almost at the same time my wrists, held closely together before me, were locked helplessly in the wrist rings. In another instant my ankles, held, were helpless in the ankle rings. A chain then ran from my collar to the chain on my wrist rings and from thence, the same chain, to the chain on my ankle rings. My ankle-ring chain was about twelve inches in length, and my wrist-ring chain was about six inches in length. The central chain, where it dangled down from the wrist rings, lay on the floor before the throne, before it looped up to where it was closed about a central link of the ankle-ring chain. This permits the prisoner, usually a slave, to lift her arms. She is thus in a position to feed herself or better exhibit her beauty to masters in a wider variety of postures and attitudes than would otherwise be the case. The point of the sirik is not merely to confine a woman, but to confine her beautifully.

Two guards then held me, one by each arm, before the throne. I was naked. I was chained. I wore the sirik.

They lifted me up, then, at a sign from Miles of Argentum. I was absolutely helpless. My feet must have been some six or seven inches from the floor before the throne. Even by pointing my toes I could not couch the carpeting. I was held there, being exhibited to the crowd, chained in the sirik.

"Behold the Tatrix of Corcyrus," called Miles of Argentum, indicating me with a sweeping gesture, "helpless, and in chains!"

There was a wild cheer from the crowd, almost a shriek, as though for blood.

"Will you come back for me?" I had asked Ligurious.

"Have no fear, Lady Sheila," he had said. "You will be come for."

"Soon?" I had asked.

"Yes," he had said. Then he had bade me farewell, and left.

I looked down on the crowd, into the wild eyes, the upraised fists. I saw, too, the soldiers. I moved helplessly in the chains, held before the crowd. Ligurious and the woman, and the others, had doubtless, by now, on tarns, made good their escape. The uniforms the men had worn were not unlike that in which I had just seen Drusus Rencius, and not unlike those of certain others about the dais, soldiers. They were, I took it, habiliments of Ar. The woman in the slave collar and on the leash, covered by the sheet, her bare feet and ankles visible beneath it, would presumably be assumed to be merely a naked captive.

I struggled in the chains. The words of Ligurious, that I would be come for, now took on a new and frightful meaning for me.

I looked down into the crowd.

Now it seemed, truly, I had been come for.

"Make way! Clear the way!" called Miles of Argentum. Soldiers began to clear the aisle of men and women, that we might have a clear exit from the great hall. I was lowered to my feet.

"What are you going to do with me?" I asked Miles of Argentum.

"We are going to take you into the courtyard," he said, "and put you in the golden cage. You may recall that I told you once that you belonged in a cage, a golden cage."

Tears sprang into my eyes. I did not want to be put into a cage. I was not a slave, or another type of animal. Too, I did not understand the meaning of a golden cage.

At a sign from Miles of Argentum a soldier picked me up, lightly, in his arms. He held me as easily as though I might have been a child. Then, in his arms, I was carried rapidly down the steps of the dais and down the aisle, between the halves of the parted crowd.

In a matter of but moments I was blinking against the sunlight in the courtyard. Too, I felt the heat and the sun on my bared skin. I was put on my feet near a tall, narrow, cylindrical cage with a conical top. The height of this cage was about seven feet; its rounded floor was perhaps a yard in diameter. In the top of the cage, at the top of the cone, on the outside, there was a heavy ring.

I was thrust into the cage and the door was locked shut behind me. It had two locks, one about a third up from the floor and the other about a third down from the top.

"In this cage, Lady Sheila," said Miles of Argentum, "you will be paraded through the streets of Corcyrus, exhibited in our triumph. Doubtless you will enjoy receiving the love and devotion of your people. You will, thereafter, be transported in this same cage to Argentum. I might mention to you that the bars of this cage, like the chains you wear, are not of pure gold, but of a sturdy golden alloy. Similarly, portions of the cage, like the floor and the interior of the top, and the gilded cone ring, are of iron. You will find that the holding power of these various devices is more than adequate, by several factors, to hold ten strong men. Incidentally, allow me to commend you on how well you look in chains. You wear them beautifully enough to be a slave."

I clutched the golden bars, in order not to fall.

"Your body, also," he said, "is beautiful enough to be that of a slave."

I moaned. I could see men approaching, with rope. Too, behind them, drawn by two tharlarion, came a flat-topped wagon. At the back of this wagon was an arrangement of beams, with a projecting, supported, perpendicularly mounted beam that extended forward, some fifteen feet in the air, toward the front of the wagon. At the forward portion of this projecting beam there was a ring, not unlike the one on the top of the cage.

Miles of Argentum surveyed me, and the chains, and the cage.

"Yes," he said, "these arrangements all seem suitable and efficient. I think we may count on your arriving in Argentum in good order."

A rope was being passed through the ring at the top of my cage. The flat-topped wagon was being drawn near. I gathered that the cage would be suspended from the ring on the projecting beam on the wagon, that it would hang suspended over the surface of the wagon, some feet from the flat bed of the wagon. From within the cage, it suspended thusly, I would not even be able to touch anything outside of the cage.

I was totally in their power.

I was inutterably helpless.

"What are you taking me to Argentum for?" I asked.

"For impalement," he said.

## 14

# THE CAMP OF MILES OF ARGENTUM; TWO MEN

"No," I whimpered. "No!" I awakened, my legs drawn up, cramped, in the tiny cage. I lay on my side. I heard the chains move on the small, circular floor of the cage. I twisted to my back, my knees raised. I could feel the chain from the collar lying on my body. My manacled hands were at my belly. The chain joining them I could feel, too, on my belly. I could feel the extension of the central chain, below the manacles, too, on my body, and then it passed between my legs, lying on the iron floor, then making its rendezvous with my shackled ankles. I had been dreaming that I was again being carried in the cage through the streets of Corcyrus. Because of the width of the wagon bed and the height of the cage, some five feet or so above the surface of the wagon bed, I had been reasonably well protected from the blows of whips, the jabbings of sticks. Soldiers, too, patrolled the perimeters of the moving wagon. More than one man, pressing between the soldiers and clambering onto the wagon, sometimes unarmed, sometimes with a whip or stick, sometimes even with a knife, was seized and thrown back into the crowd by soldiers. The crowds cheered Miles of Argentum and his men. And, as my wagon passed them, they seemed to go mad with hatred and pleasure, crying out and jeering me, and shrieking with triumph to see me so helplessly a captive. The people of Corcyrus, it was clear, had welcomed the men of Argentum, and their allies from Ar, as liberators. The colors of Argentum and of Ar, on ribbons and strips of cloth, dangled from windows and festooned, even being stretched between windows and rooftops overhead, the triumphal way. Such colors, too, were prominent in the crowd, on garments and being waved, fluttering, by citizens and sometimes even by children, perched on the shoulders of adults. I had stood in the cage, frightened, bewildered and confused. I had not been able to even begin to understand the hatred of the people. I had stood in the cage that I might be better seen. If I did not do so, Miles of Argentum had informed me, simply, I would be beaten like a slave.

I had now awakened in the cage, frightened. I had dreamed I was being again carried through the streets of Corcyrus. I had recoiled, fearfully, from the sting of a fruit rind hurled at me. Often in that miserable journey, suspended in the cage, carried between jeering crowds, I had been pelted with small stones, garbage and dung.

I whimpered, chained in my tiny prison. At least I was alone now, and it was quiet. The cage creaked a little, moving in the wind. I crawled to my knees and, with my fingers, parted the opaque cloth which had been wrapped about the cage for the night, before it had been raised to its present position. I looked out through the tiny crack. I could see fires of the camp, and several tents. I heard music from the distance, from somewhere among the tents, where perhaps girls danced to please masters. We were one day out of Corcyrus, on the march to Argentum. I looked down to the ground. It was some forty feet below. The cage was slung now not from the ring on the wagon beam but from a rope which had been thrown over a high stout branch of a large tree. The cage had then been hoisted to this height and the rope secured.

"Villainess of Corcyrus! Tyranness of Corcyrus!" the people had cried.

I lay back down then in my chains, on the small iron floor of the cage, my knees pulled up high, and looked upward at the hollow, conelike ceiling of the cage. It seemed I had no more tears to cry.

I did not want to die.

I heard the music in the distance.

I wished that I were a slave, that I might have a chance for life, that I might have an opportunity to convince a master somehow, in any way possible, that I might be worth sparing.

But I was a free woman and would be subjected only to the cold and inhuman mercies of the law.

I was being transported to Argentum for impalement.

I could not cry any more.

Then, suddenly, I felt the cage drop an inch, and then another inch.

I scrambled to my knees, looking out, as I could. But, because of the opaque covering of the cage, its fastenings and the difficulty of moving it, I could see very little.

Then the cage was still. Then, after a time, it dropped another inch, and then another. I knelt in the cage, holding my chains, to keep them from making noise.

Slowly the cage was lowered. Then it rested on the ground.

My heart was beating wildly. I now seemed very much alive. The stealth, and the gradualness, which seemed to characterize what was going on, did not suggest the activities of authorized representatives of Miles of Argentum. It did not even occur to me to scream. From whom would I summon help, and to what purpose? If these nocturnal visitors wished to steal me, perhaps to make me a slave or sell me, I would go only too willingly into whatever bondage they chose to inflict upon me. I would enter it joyfully. I would revel in it. I would, in my gratitude, see to it that I proved to be to them a slave beyond their wildest dreams. Then suddenly I was terrified. What if these visitors were not opportunists or slavers. What if they were men of Corcyrus who wished to return me to the city, there to subject me to secret and horrifying tortures which might shame the agonies of an impaling spear on the walls of Argentum?

I did not know whether to cry out or not.

The cover on the cage was unlaced, and thrust back, around the cage. Two men were there. They were dressed entirely in black. They wore masks. One of them held an unshuttered dark lantern and the other opened a leather wrapper containing keys and tools on the ground. He, then, with a variety of keys and picks, and small tools, swiftly, expertly, trying one thing and then another, addressed himself to the upper lock. He was skillful, and apparently a smith in such matters, perhaps a skilled specialist within his caste. In fifteen Ehn both locks had yielded. The cage door was opened and I was pulled out. I was put on my back and the man, swiftly, with numerous small keys, and some of the other tools, addressed himself to my collar lock. I felt the collar pulled away. Then, in a few Ehn, I had been freed, too, of the manacles, and then the shackles. I was turned to my stomach. My right wrist was tied to my left ankle, I struggled about, turning my head. I saw the golden sirik put back in the cage; it was not the sort of thing, I gathered, which these fellows would care to have found in their possession; I then saw the cage closed and the cover readjusted about it; then, together, the two men, with the rope, drew it slowly upward; in a few moments it hung quietly where it had before, when it had been occupied. If its lowering and raising had not been noticed, I did not think that now anyone would be likely to find anything amiss until morning, when it would be lowered and found empty. The cord which had fastened my wrist to my ankle was then removed and I was drawn to my feet. I was startled that I was put in no bonds. A cloak was handed to me. I drew it swiftly about my body and over my head, grasping it closed with my fists beneath my chin. Over my head as it was, and it being a short cloak, too, it fell midway, as I held it about me, on my calves. I was grateful not only for the disguise it afforded me, but, too, because it gave me some way to conceal my nakedness. I felt a hand at my back and I was conducted from the area of the tree and the suspended cage. As we removed ourselves from that area we passed the slumped figures of two guards, an overturned flagon near them.

"Hold!" called a drunken voice, as we passed between tents.

We stopped. My left upper arm, now that we had left the area of the tree and cage, under the cloak, was in the custody of the man on my left. He had taken it in charge almost immediately upon leaving the cage area. He did not wish to accept the risk, it seemed, that I might attempt to escape, perhaps impulsively attempting to dart away into the darkness. There was little danger of that now. His grip was like iron. I still held the cloak together, and about my face, with my right hand. I attempted to pull the cloak forward more, and averted my face, that my features might not be seen.

"Masks, eh?" said the newcomer. "So she is a free woman, is she? But perhaps not for long!"

He laughed drunkenly, and staggered about, in front of us. He tried to reach for the cloak I held clutched about my face. I turned my face away, clutching the cloak about it.

"A modest pudding," he said, surprised. "Forgive me, Lady," he said, bowing low. Then he staggered about, behind us, again. Then I suddenly felt the cloak being lifted behind me. "She has legs good enough to be those of a slave," he said. We then proceeded on our way. I was shaking. Too, I now had some idea of the publicness of a slave's body.

I was pulled back into the shadows between some tents.

Two guardsmen, with a lantern, passed. Then, again, we threaded our way amongst the canvas-lined lanes of the camp of the men of Argentum.

Most of the tents were dark. Within some were small fires. When men passed between the fires and the canvas wall of the tent we could see their shadows on the canvas. In one tent a girl danced slowly, sensuously, before a seated male. Her skills suggested that she might be a camp slave, a girl from one of the strings of camp slaves, strings of girls owned by authorized merchants, holding contracts for certain seasons or campaigns, kept within the camp, and traveling with it, for renting out to soldiers at fees stipulated in the contracts. Too, of course, she might be a girl even from Corcyrus, or another community, perhaps a paga girl. Such as these are sometimes brought to the camps on speculation. The fees for their use are not contractually controlled, as are those of the regular camp slaves, but the fees of the camp slaves, of course, being fixed and almost nominal, tend to exert a considerable, informal influence on the market; they set competitive standards, ensure realistic pricings and reduce the risk of excessive local profiteering. On Earth it is not unusual for a free woman to attempt to take a profit on her own beauty, using it, for example, if only in mate competitions, to advance herself economically. On Gor, however, if that same woman should be enslaved, she will soon discover that the profits accruing from her beauty redound now not to her, but to her master. This is quite appropriate. It, like she herself, is his.

As we passed another tent, a darkened one, I heard the sounds of chains from within. "Oh, more, Master, I beg you, please, more," I heard, "more, more, please, oh, my Master, more, please more, please more, my Master, I beg you!" How scandalized I was! What was it within, a harlot, a whore! But I feared it was far worse, something a thousand times lower, something a thousand times more despicable and helpless, a slave.

In a few moments we stopped, between some darkened tents. I was then lifted from my feet and placed, sitting, on the ground.

"Why are we stopping here?" I whispered. "Who are you? What are you doing!"

My last question was prompted by the fact that one of the men, the larger of the two, he who had held my left arm, had now crossed my ankles. He was now wrapping a long piece of binding fiber about them, sometimes looping them both, sometimes taking it about only one ankle, sometimes snaking it about both ankles and securing it between both with tightly drawn loops. He even, occasionally, threaded an end through other, already secured loops. He then pulled the entire tie tight. What he had done was far more elaborate and complex than was required to hold a girl's ankles. A loop or two, properly knotted, I did not doubt, would be adequate for the perfect accomplishment of such a task. Then, to my surprise, he placed the two loose ends of the binding fiber in my hands. I held them, puzzled. He had not knotted the tie. Similarly no move had been made to secure my hands.

"Wait!" I whispered. "No!" I then understood what they intended.

The smaller of the two men, he who had been so expert with the locks and chains, placed his fingers across my lips.

"No!" I whispered. "Don't leave me! Who are you? Why have you done what you have done?"

He increased the pressure of his fingers on my lips, and I was silent.

He leaned close to me and whispered. I did not recognize the voice.

"We have brought you here," he said. "It is a half of a pasang from the cage."

I nodded, miserably.

"The camp will be awake in three Ahn," he said.

I nodded.

He withdrew his fingers from my lips.

"Do not leave me!" I begged.

"The camp will be awake in three Ahn," he said.

"Who are you?" I begged.

He was silent.

"Why have you done what you have done?" I asked.

"Once you did me a kindness," he said. "I have never forgotten."

"What kindness?" I asked.

"Our accounts are now squared," he said. "It is done. The matter is finished."

"And what, then, is his motivation?" I asked, indicating the larger man.

"It is other than mine," said the smaller man.

The larger man then drew his cloak away from me. I was

then sitting in the dirt, naked, with my ankles fastened together, the two ends of the fiber clutched in my hands.

"Do not leave me," I begged. "Keep me. I am prepared even to be your slave!"

The larger man suddenly, angrily, reached for my throat. I felt those large hands close about it. For an instant things went black. I knew he could crush the life from me at his whim.

"Do not kill her," said the other.

The hands left my throat.

I gasped. I swallowed painfully. The larger man retrieved his cloak.

The two men stood, preparing to take their leave.

"Do not leave me here, I beg you!" I whispered.

"Already, in this," said the smaller man; "you have been granted more than a hundred times the lenience and favor that you deserve."

"Are you not my friends?" I asked.

"No," said he. "We are your enemies."

I looked up at him, in misery.

"Farewell," said he, "Lady Sheila, villainess and tyranness of Corcyrus."

"Wait!" I whispered.

But they were gone, and gone in different directions. I thought of crying out, but doubtless they would be away by the time men would come, and with their masks doffed, who would know them? I would succeed in doing little more than calling attention to myself.

"Wait!" I whispered softly, piteously. But they had vanished.

"The camp will be awake in three Ahn," the smaller man had said.

Feverishly I began to unwind and unthread the binding fiber on my ankles. It took me better than an Ehn to do so.

I saw a lantern approaching, held by one of two guardsmen. I cast aside the binding fiber, and then crept to the side, to lie on my belly in the shadows behind a tent. I felt one of the tent ropes on my shoulder. I heard someone inside the tent stirring in sleep. The lantern of the guardsmen had then passed.

I rose to my feet, wildly, frightened, and then hurried away between the tents.

# 15

# ALARM BARS

"Hold! Who goes there?" called a voice. I heard the snarling of the patrol sleen, its jerking at its chain.

Weeping, I fled back among the tents. The guardsman did not release the sleen. He would probably not want it loose among the tents.

I crouched behind a tent, in the darkness. This was the third time I had tried to leave the camp. Once there had been stakes and wire; another time there had been a deep ditch; each time there had been guardsmen with sleen. The sleen, I had little doubt, had been able to detect my approach, and had led the guardsmen to my vicinity. The perimeter of the camp seemed ringed with guards and sleen. The camp was heavily guarded. This was perhaps because it was still within the range of Corcyrus, and perhaps, too, because of a special captive, a Tatrix, thought to be chained in a suspended cage.

I looked up. I moaned. In the moonlight, not more than a hundred yards away, I could see the cage slung from its branch. In my running, and fear, disoriented, and once pursued by drunken soldiers, I had inadvertently returned to its vicinity. If I were caught I did not doubt but what I would soon again find myself the prisoner of those cramped quarters, though doubtless in fresher, sturdier bonds, probably of iron, and not locked, but hammered closed about my neck and limbs. The cage, too, then would probably be closed with plates and rivets, and the guards doubled or tripled about it. I crouched down, my head in my hands. In a little more than an Ahn, I feared, the camp would be awakened. Already it seemed to me that there were more people about than before, more men to avoid.

I shrank back into the shadows. Two men, cooks, I think, from their conversation, were passing.

I heard wings overhead. Looking up I saw a tarn. It was flying northwest. Behind it, on long ropes, dangled a tarn basket. Sleen were no problem for it, I thought bitterly. It was not the first such departure, or, indeed, arrival, I had noted in the camp.

I had hitherto avoided the more lit, busy portions of the camp, generally about the areas for tradesmen, suppliers and sutlers, and the storage, delivery and mess areas.

There were too many men there, and it would be, surely, too easy to be detected.

I, then, stealthily, my heart pounding, began to follow, keeping in the shadows, the two men who had just passed. I was terribly frightened. They were moving toward the center of the camp.

"What are you doing there, Slut, skulking about?" called a man. I had not seen him, between the tents. He had some gear slung over his shoulder. He was apparently waiting there. I backed away from him. "Let her go," said another man, emerging from a tent. He, too, carried some gear. "You can see she is a slave, returning to her master." I then hurried away. In the darkness they had not detected that I lacked a brand. Too, they had not noticed that my neck was not encircled by a slave collar.

I was now in consternation. I did not see how I could proceed. People seemed to be getting up now about the camp.

"Ena!" called a girl, hurrying to catch up with another.

I stepped back into the shadows.

A tall, slim girl, naked, turned about. A bit of slave silk dangled languidly from her left hand.

The new girl was short and lusciously bodied. She wore a brief, silken slave tunic, fastened with a single tie at her bosom. A single tug frees the tie and allows the garment to be parted for the view and pleasures of a master. Both women wore collars.

"And how did the night go?" asked the new girl. "Were you well used?"

"Yes," responded the taller girl, dreamily. "And you?"

"Superbly," said the shorter girl.

The two girls then began to walk down the lane between the tents. I, my head down, my hair about my neck and shoulders, hopefully tending to conceal the bareness of my neck, the absence there of a steel circlet, fell into step behind them, seemingly, I hoped, only another slave on her way back to her master.

I soon became aware that this must be a lane leading to the chains. Other girls, soon, here and there, entered it, before and behind me, and between me and those who had been directly before me.

"And what of the resistance you intended to offer?" one girl was asking another.

"It was crushed," said the other. "He did not choose to accept it. Then he made me serve him well."

"It is the fifth time you have served in his tent since we left Argentum," said the first girl.

"Yes," said the second.

"I think he likes you," said the first girl.

"Perhaps," said the other.

"Do you think he will buy you?" asked the first girl.

"It matters not to me," said the other. "I do not care, one way or the other."

"There are stains on your face as though you had been crying," said the girl. "And it does not seem to me that you have been beaten."

"Oh?" asked the other.

"You pretentious tarsk sow," laughed the first girl, "you were begging him to buy you!"

"What if I was!" said the other, tossing her head.

"And when did you beg this?" asked the girl.

"After my resistance had been crushed, and he made me serve him without compromise as a slave," said the other, "and again this morning, before we parted."

"You seem pleased enough now," observed the girl.

"Tassy," said the other, "he is going to make an offer for me!"

"That is marvelous, Yitza!" said the first girl.

"But will Myron let me go?" asked the second girl.

"I do not know," said the first. "Such matters are between the men."

The second girl moaned.

"Look at it this way," said the first girl. "If we did not wear collars we would not even know the touch of such men as Rutilius. Too, if we were not slaves and sent to their tents, we would not even know what to do. We would be only ignorant free women."

"How I sometimes pity free women!" laughed the second girl. "They are so stupid!"

"But fear them, Yitza," said the first girl, "for they are free and you are enslaved."

"Of course," said the second girl, shuddering.

"And remember that they hate you," said the first.

"I know," said the second.

A man stepped out, into the center of the lane. I stopped, frightened. But his attention was on another.

"Yeela," said he.

A girl, addressed by a free man, fell to her knees before him.

"I have paid fee for you," he said.

"It is early, Master," she laughed. "Would you lie to a poor slave?"

"Perhaps," he said.

"If you have not, know that you will be charged," she laughed. "I am not for free!"

But then he had crouched down and taken her in his arms. She was thrown beneath him, grasping at him, to the dirt. Frightened, I took my way about them. I tried to hide among other girls. I hoped that no man would decide to pull me out from among them.

"What is for breakfast?" I heard one girl asking another.

"I have heard," said the other girl, who was a shorter one, "that each of us will have five berries put in our gruel this morning."

"Good," said the first.

"If no bad reports are received on any of us," added the second.

"I was pleasing," said the first.

"So, too, was I," averred the second.

"If Jasmine is not fully pleasing again," said the first girl, "I think I will pull her hair out."

"And so, too, will the rest of the chain!" laughed the second girl, the shorter one.

Jasmine, I suspected, would soon learn to be pleasing. Certainly it would be in her best interests to be so. She would probably have to spend at least a portion of every day within the reach of her chain sisters. Doubtless soon she would be begging them for counsels in sensuality, for tricks and techniques, that she might improve herself and become less inadequate as a slave.

"He took away my clothes," one girl was telling another, "but then he did not so much as touch me. He made me serve him, rather, in small and menial ways. I must cook sullage for him. Then I must launder and iron a tunic. Then I must dust his goods and clean and tidy his tent. Then I was made to sew, and then clean and polish his leather."

"And how did you feel," asked the girl to whom she was speaking, "performing these small tasks for him, suitable for a slave?"

"Gradually, serving him helplessly, then lovingly in these fashions, I became more and more aroused," she said. "Then, finally, after the polishing of the leather, I could stand it no longer. I threw myself to my belly before him, juicing like a larma."

"Did he then content you?" asked the other girl.

"Yes," said the girl, "though the brute made me squirm a little first."

How well that master had understood sex, and the sexuality of the female, I thought. He apparently understood something of the pervasiveness and totality of female sexuality. They had been, in their way, having sex together for hours, before he even touched her. Well had he understood the woman, and her needs and desires to be pleasing, and to submit and serve in many ways. It was the total woman, in her wholeness, which he, to her joy, had chosen to dominate.

How terrible, I thought, to be a slave!

"Would you like to be sent again to his tent?" asked the other girl.

"Yes," said the girl. "Yes! Oh, yes!"

What a meaningless slut she was! How pleased I was that I was not a slave!

"You, Slave!" called a voice.

I stopped in my tracks. I put my fists before my mouth, in terror, but, too, to hide my neck.

"Not you, you!" said the voice.

I quickly hurried on, trembling. It seemed that any moment I must be discovered

"I must see him again," the girl in front of me was saying.

"Why?" asked the other.

"I think he is my love master," she breathed.

"It is more likely that you are his love slave," laughed the other.

"He must call for me again!" said the girl.

"You are, of course, entitled to hope that," said the other, "when you lie alone, chained in your place."

"He must!" she wept.

"Perhaps he will have you summoned again to his tent," said the second girl.

"I must see him again!" she said.

"That will be decided by masters," said the second girl. How horrifying to be a slave, I thought. How pleased I was that I was not a slave.

Swiftly, then, seeing more men waiting further down the lane, some with loops of chain in their hands, I slipped to the side between the tents. I could see women lining up down there, too, being put in wrist or throat coffle, each one doubtless reporting in, and in the proper position, to the appropriate slave master.

I skirted a large cooking area. I could smell freshly baked bread, and the cooking of eggs and meat.

I made my way among tents, every sense alert, sometimes crawling on my hands and knees.

It was still quite dark. Here and there there were morning fires. The moons were down.

I cried out in misery. A sleen, snarling, leapt toward me, but was stopped by its chain.

I continued on my way, treading narrow valleys between mountains of sacks, narrow aisles separating cliffs of boxes.

"Where are you going, little lady?" called a fellow from above me. He was standing on boxes, carrying a box. I had not even seen him. "The chains," he said, "are behind you and to your right."

Swiftly I sped away, in the general direction he had indicated. Then, when I was confident I was out of his sight, I resumed, as nearly as I could, given the bundles, the boxes and crates, my original direction.

Then I found myself in a blind alley, a place where the passage was closed by a sheer wall of boxes, several feet over my head. I hurried back and tried another passage. It, too, to my misery, was blocked. Then I suddenly realized I had lost my direction. Between the boxes, at places, darknesses in the darkness, there were narrow cracks. I did not know which were passages and which were mere places where several boxes had been removed. I struck with my fists at the wall of boxes.

Then, suddenly, I heard a tarn scream, and not more than two or three hundred yards away.

Too, I saw a lantern approaching behind me.

I darted through an opening, came to a wall, and crouched between two boxes.

I saw the light of the lantern on the boxes ahead of me, as it was lifted at the passage I had entered.

"She came this way," said a voice.

I heard the two men entering the passage.

"There she is!" said one of them. I gasped, in terror.

Then I heard a sudden scrambling. "I've got you, you little she-sleen!" he said.

I heard a small body flung to the dirt. Then I heard the snapping on of slave bracelets.

"Turn her over," said a voice.

I heard a body moved.

"She's a pretty one," said a voice. "Read her collar."

"Our little thief is Tula, of the chain of Ephialtes," said another voice.

"I stole nothing, Master!" cried the girl.

"Thrust up her tunic," said the first voice. "Now split your legs, Tula. Good girl. Now, what were you saying?"

"It was only one pastry, Master," said the girl. "Forgive Tula! Do not beat her!"

"Keep those legs wide, Tula," said the first voice.

"Yes, Master," whimpered the girl.

I then listened, with misery, while the two men, one after the other, in the narrow passageway between the boxes, used the slave.

Worse, I felt heat between my own thighs. Their casual, brutal, forceful use of her almost overwhelmed me psychologically. How helpless, how dominated are slaves! I touched myself. To my horror, I, too, was wet. I gritted my teeth. I hoped they could not smell me. I trembled. I tried not to feel. It was almost as though they, in inflicting themselves on that pathetic slave, were subjecting me, as well, to those insolent, debasing, masterly thrusts. Yet, of course, they were not, and in this, to my scandal, I felt keen frustration. I found myself envying her. I wondered what it would be like to be helpless in the arms of such brutes, a cringing vessel for their pleasure, choiceless but to rhapsodically succumb. Then I forced such thoughts from my mind. Surely I must not think such thoughts. Surely they were appropriate only for a slave!

I looked up, miserably. The sky was becoming gray now. In a few minutes, perhaps, the cage would be lowered. Then my absence would be noted.

The entire camp, then, and its vicinity, I did not doubt, would be subjected to an inch-by-inch search, one that it would be impossible to elude.

I had failed to escape.

"On your feet, Tula," said one of the men.

"Tula has served you well, has she not?" begged the girl. I heard her pull at the slave bracelets.

"Put down her tunic," said the first man.

"There," said the second.

"When we called to you to stop, Tula," said the first man, "you ran. Have you ever run away before?"

"I was not really running away," said the girl. "I just did not want you to catch me."

"Must a question be repeated?" asked the first man.

"No, Master," she said, quickly. "I have never run away before!"

"That is fortunate for you," said the man.

I shuddered, crouching between the boxes. The first time a girl runs away she is commonly only beaten. Many girls, when they first go into a collar, do not realize that escape, for all practical purposes, is impossible for them, or how easily, commonly, they can be picked up and caught. The practical impossibility of escape is a function of several factors. Perhaps one of the most important among them is the closely knit nature of Gorean society. In such a society it is difficult to establish false identities. Other factors which might be noted are the support of the society for slavery, the absence of a place to run, so to speak, and the relentlessness with which slaves are commonly sought. Other factors are such things as the distinctive garb of the slave, the encirclement of her neck with a collar and the fact that her body is marked with a brand. The best that a slave can commonly hope for is that she might fall into the power of a new master. The usual punishment for a girl's second attempt at escape is hamstringing, the severing of the tendons behind the knees. This does not completely immobilize the girl, for she may still, for example, drag herself about by her hands. Such girls are sometimes used as beggars, distributed about a city by wagon in the morning, and then picked up again at night, with whatever earnings they may have managed to obtain during the day.

"You will not beat me though, will you?" wheedled the girl.

"No," said the first man.

"Thank you, Masters!" said the girl.

"You have, however," said the man, "stolen a pastry, lied about it to us, and run away."

"You said you would not beat me!" protested the girl.

"We shall not," said the man. "Ephialtes might."

"Do not tell him, I beg you!" she cried.

"Do you really think that you can do the things you have done with impunity, you, a slave?" asked the man.

"No, Master," she wept.

"We have discovered you have a taste for sweets," said the man. "Ephialtes will discover if you have a taste for leather."

"Have pity on me, Masters," she wept. "I am only a helpless, braceleted slave!"

"Turn about, Tula," said the man. "You are on your way back to your master."

As I heard them leaving, I looked about the corner of my hiding place. I saw two large men. Preceding them, her hands locked behind her in slave bracelets, was a beautifully shaped little slave. She had dark hair. Her slave tunic, which was extremely short, was red.

I followed the men down the passageway. I stopped once, when they stopped, to extinguish the lantern.

Following them I came to an opening between the boxes, through which they had taken their way.

They had led me out of the maze.

I then saw many wagons and could smell tharlarion, and straw. I made my way swiftly through this area.

I then stopped, startled. The great cry of a tarn smote the air.

I fell to my hands and knees as two men passed, on the other side of a wagon.

I rose up and sped as furtively and swiftly as I could toward the area from which I had heard the bird's scream. I stopped, seeing a bird take to the air, a tarn basket, on long ropes, trailing behind it. I put out my hands. There seemed to be a platform in front of me. It must have been fifty yards long. On it there seemed to be two broad, leather skids. On these skids, some twenty yards or so in front of me, there were four or five tarn baskets. I heard the snapping of wings. I crouched down beside the platform. A tarn, with its rider, alighted on the platform. There were men there, one fellow with a board and papers, and two others, who seemed to be aides. I saw ropes being fastened between the tarn and the basket now first in the line. I crawled forward and, as the men were concerned with the tarn, it moving about and occasionally stretching and snapping its wings, crawled into the last basket. Within that basket was a blanket, one which had probably been used to cover some cargo brought to the camp. I drew the blanket over me and lay quietly in the bottom of the basket.

It was becoming lighter now, and I was becoming more and more afraid.

I gave myself little chance to escape, but I could do nothing more. I had done all that I could.

It seemed I lay there for an Ahn. The heavy fiber of the basket cut into my skin. I did not, however, so much as move. Then other tarns were brought, one by one, to the platform. The other baskets were lofted away. Mine only, it seemed, remained.

"So where is Venaticus?" said a man.

"Sleeping one off," said another fellow.

"Tangled up in the chains of some slave," suggested another.

"I think it will be another warm day," said a fellow.

"Good," said one of the men. "Then they may have the covers down on the slave wagons."

"When we dismantle," said a man, "you could always drift back in the march and see Lady Sheila. She is a pretty little vulo in her cage."

"They are all pretty in chains and behind bars," said another man.

"I hate to think of them shoving an impaling spear up her ass," said a man.

"I know an impaling spear I'd like to shove up her ass," said another man.

There was laughter.

Men may do with us what they wish, I thought. Our only chance is to turn them against themselves, and use them for our purposes. But in this we frustrate nature, that of men and of ourselves. How can we win, then? Perhaps, I thought, only by losing. But these thoughts were more appropriate to Earth than Gor. It did not seem possible to turn the men of Gor against themselves. Perhaps they were less simple than the men of Earth, or more simple, more basic and natural. They had, at any rate, never permitted themselves to be tricked out of their natural rights and powers. The conniving woman on Gor, she who would seek to control and manipulate men, is likely to soon find herself at the feet of her would-be victim, naked, kissing them, locked in his collar.

There seemed suddenly a storm of wings in the air, and I heard the striking of tarn talons on the platform. Men, almost immediately, began to work about the basket. I felt the basket move as ropes were fastened on it and jerked tight. There was a tiny space between two folds of the blanket, through which I could see, looking then through an opening in the weaving of the basket. With two fingers I drew the blanket more together.

"Your face is smeared with lipstick," said a man, "and you stink of slaves and paga."

"I cannot explain that," said a fellow, as though puzzled, "for all night I have rested comfortably in the tent of the cargo riders."

"The company will not be pleased," said a fellow. "If you slept a wink last night I am a purple urt."

"It is lucky for you then," said the newcomer, concernedly, "that indeed I neglected to slumber."

"Are you in a condition to fly?" asked a man.

"I shall sleep in the saddle," said the man.

"You have a long flight, of several stages," said a man.

"I shall be well rested then by the time of my arrival in Ar," said the newcomer.

"I am sure the paga slaves will be pleased," said a man, "all several hundred of them."

"Do not neglect to fasten your safety strap," said a man.

"I shall do so, unless perhaps I chance to fall asleep first," the newcomer assured the fellow.

"What is that sound?" asked a man.

"It sounds like an alarm bar, back in the south part of the camp," said a man.

"I wonder what is wrong," said another.

"Will I see Bemus in Ar, or Torquatus?" asked the newcomer.

"No, luckily for the paga slaves," said a man. "You are the only rider this morning bound for Ar. Bemus has a pickup to make in Lydius, and Torquatus in Bazi."

"It is an alarm bar," said a man, "clearly."

"I hear another, too, now," said a man.

"I wonder what is going on," said the newcomer.

"You will rendezvous with us in ten days, on the south bank of the Issus," said a man. "You will be bringing another shipment of Ka-la-na for the officers."

"I wonder what is going on," said the newcomer.

"You are late," said a man, with a rustle of papers.

"I am never late," said the newcomer. "It is only that sometimes it takes me longer to be on time than others."

"I hear other alarm bars, too, now," said a man.

"Do you think the camp is under attack?" asked a man.

"No," said a man.

"It is probably a fire," said a man.

"I do not see any smoke," said a man.

"Perhaps Lady Sheila has escaped," suggested a fellow, lightly.

This suggestion was greeted with raucous laughter. The little vulo, doubtless, was still safe in her cage.

"It is probably a fight between companies or platoons," said a man, "probably over gambling or a slave."

"I think I will go see," said the newcomer.

"Into the saddle!" said a man.

"But a fight!" said the newcomer.

"Venaticus," cautioned the man.

"Very well," he said.

"It must be important," said a man. "Hear the alarm bars now."

"If it were only a fight, there would not be that many alarm bars," said a man. "Indeed, there probably would not be any. It would not be necessary to alarm the whole camp over an incident of that sort."

"It is probably a drill," said a man.

"That is it," said another. "It must be a drill."

Suddenly there was a storm of wings and the basket, a moment later, was jerked forward, slipping along the leather skids and then, in another instant, taking my breath away for an instant, it was lofted like the others high into the air. Through tiny cracks between the woven fibers of the deep, sturdy basket I could see the ground slipping away beneath us. Wind seemed to tear through the fibers of the basket. I clutched the blanket, it being torn in the wind, more closely about me. The ropes and the basket creaked. The rider took the tarn once about the camp, doubtless to satisfy his curiosity. He could make out little, however, I suspected, from the air. I could see men below moving about in the camp, emerging from tents and such, but there seemed to be no clear pattern to their activity. Certainly the camp was not under attack, nor did there seem to be any fire. The absence of a clear pattern to the activity, too, suggested that a drill, or at least a general drill, was not in progress. Perhaps it was merely a testing of the crews of the alarm bars. He then turned the tarn about and began to take his way toward the northwest. I lay in the bottom of the basket. I pulled my legs up, and pulled the blanket about me. I was cold. I hoped that I would not freeze. I was frightened. I saw the camp disappearing in the distance. Only faintly now could I hear the ringing of the alarm bars. The fiber of the basket would be temporarily imprinting its pattern on my skin. I hoped that the ropes would hold.

# 16

# I AM ON THE VIKTEL ARIA, IN THE VICINITY OF VENNA

I felt a hand on my shoulder. It shook me, gently. I could also feel the warm sun on my back. There was grass under my belly. I had been awakened on an incline. There was muddy water about my feet.

I had been three days the unsuspected guest of the tarnsman from the camp of Miles of Argentum. On the first two nights he had camped in the open. On the first night I had crept forth and, from his pack, after he was asleep, stole some meat and Sa-Tarna bread. I also took a drink from his canteen. I partook sparingly in these things for fear of being discovered. If he detected any tiny shortages in his supplies perhaps he put them to the accounts of straying vagrants. On the second day I noticed, to my uneasiness, more dwellings below us. Too, I noted more tended fields. On the second night I stole fruit from an orchard and drank from a pool. I decided to risk a third day in the basket, to put even more hundreds of pasangs between me and Argentum and Corcyrus. On this third day, however, to my dismay, I could see roads below, and many dwellings and fields. We passed over, even, two towns. On the third night, frightening me, he landed within the palisade of a fortified inn. The tarn basket was left within the palings of a special enclosure within this general palisade. Now it was time, I knew, to take my leave. Surely I was not interested in being delivered to Ar, the very ally of Argentum, where, presumably, it would be impossible to escape detection. I could not, however, to my consternation, climb the palings of the enclosure or find a space between them to squeeze through. I hid among the tarn baskets, of which there were several there. When a new basket, that of a late arrival, unhitched from its tarn, was being dragged within the palings from the landing area outside, within the larger palisade, while it was being put in its numbered space, I slipped out. I hid among garbage boxes behind the inn. No sleen patrolled the inner yard, probably because of the danger to guests. I fed from the garbage, ravenously. It had rained recently and there was water in various discarded containers and lids. I drank greedily. Muchly did I envy the people in the inn, with their viands and beverages, their clean rooms, their clothing and warm beds. I envied even the slaves that might be within. They, at least, were secure and well fed. What had they to worry about, other than being pleasing to their masters? I cried out, suddenly, softly, as the fur of a scurrying urt brushed my leg. I crawled about the inn, keeping to the brush at its side. I moved leaves out of the way with my hand. Leaves brushed my back. Then I could see the main gate of the palisade. A wagon, drawn by a tharlarion, was entering. It tipped to the left, its wheels sinking into the ruts, on the left almost to the hubs, in the soft ground, from the rains. The driver cracked the whip and called out to the tharlarion. "Do not make so much noise," he was cautioned by the porter. "People are sleeping." The porter then went to the tharlarion and pushing at it and striking it, urged it forward. The great beast grunted and threw itself forward, against the harness. The wagon was drawn through the gate, water from the ruts dripping from its wheels. To my dismay I then saw the porter close the gates and thrust the great beam across, through its brackets, behind them. This he secured in place with a lock and key. He then accompanied the teamster to the stables. I hurried forward and ran to the gate. I felt under the palings of the gate. I began to dig there in the softness of the ground, and in the muddy water pooled in the ruts. I tried to thrust my body down, under the gate. There was not enough room. I heard the creaking of another wagon, this one coming about the inn. I hid back in bushes to the side. In moments the porter had returned to the gate. I was in misery. I could not slip under the gate, or dig out under it, if the porter was there. He was a man and would simply stop me, and capture me. I did not know when, or if, another wagon would arrive before daylight, one that might take the porter again from his post, giving me time to dig out under the gate. Risking much I slipped back to the enclosure where the tarn baskets were. As I feared, it was now once more locked. I hurried back about the inn. The porter was engaged in a discussion, and not a particularly aimiable one, with the driver. The driver had apparently criticized the porter for not being at the gate, and the porter, in response, was being officiously careful about checking the driver's ostrakon of payment. "I am not sure that is the mark of Leucippus," said the porter. "It does not look much like his mark." "Awaken him, then," said the driver, "and certify that it is so." "I do not care to awaken him at this Ahn." "I am to be on the road by dawn." "You will have to wait." "I do not have time to wait!" In the end the porter opened the gate and let the man proceed. By that time I was in the back of the wagon. An Ahn or so later, when it was nearly dawn, I eased myself silently from the back of the wagon and crouched down on the road. It continued on its way. I then left the road and ran across the fields.

"Are you awake?" asked a voice.

The hand on my shoulder shook me again, again gently.

My body stiffened. "Yes," I whispered.

I lay on the slope of a ditch, as it ascended to a road. There was a trickle of water at my feet. The grass was very green here, because of the water.

When I had left the wagon, by means of which I had accomplished my escape from the inn, I had fled across the fields. I had run and walked until perhaps noon, and had then, fearful of discovery, hidden near a small pool in a brake of ferns until nightfall. I had washed in the pool and drunk from it. I had set out again in the moonlight. I had eaten almost nothing and I was terribly hungry. I had been afield for only an Ahn or so when the winds had risen and clouds had obscured the moons. Rain had begun to fall, as it apparently had the night before. I stumbled on through the darkness, my legs lashed to the thighs by the knives of the wind-whipped grass. I soon grew weak and exhausted. I sought a dwelling, or a road, which I might follow to a dwelling, that I might there, like an urt, skulk about and, as at the inn, piteously seek some sustenance from their refuse. Twice I fainted, probably from hunger. The second time I recovered consciousness the storm had worsened and the sky was bursting with lightning and thunder. As I crouched in the grass I saw, in a valley below me, in a flash of lightning, like a wet stone ribbon, a road. I crawled toward it. At its edge there was a deep ditch. Had I not been crawling, I might, in the darkness, between flashes of lightning, have come on the ditch unawares and fallen into it. As it was I lowered myself down its slope with the intention of then climbing the other side and attaining the surface of the road. In the bottom of the ditch there was, at that time, a flow of water some six inches deep, from the storm. I knelt in this, the cold fluid rushing about my legs, and, cupping my hands, drank from it. I then started to climb toward the road. I was suddenly frightened. The incline was steeper than I had anticipated. I slipped back, into the water. I tried again, inching myself upward. Grass pulled out of the slope, clutched in my hands. I slipped back. I was weak and miserable. I waded at the bottom of the ditch and, in two or three places, again tried to climb out of it. I was not successful. The storm, meanwhile, had subsided. I could now see the moons. In the moonlight I found an ascent which I, though with difficulty, could manage. Gasping, holding at the grass, inching my way upward, I drew my body from the grass to the road. I looked at the road, from my belly. I felt out with my hands. It seemed constructed of large, square stones. It was not an ordinary road, I thought. Like most Gorean roads, however, a single pair of ruts marked its center. Gorean vehicles, commonly slow moving, tend to keep to the center of a road, except in passing.

In the distance I heard the sound of bells, harness bells. It might be a wagon, or a set of wagons, which had pulled to the side of the road during the storm and now, with the passing of the storm, had resumed its journey. It must be near morning, I thought, that they are on the road. Gorean roads are seldom traveled at night. The bells were coming closer. I moaned and slid back from the road, again into the ditch. I slipped back a yard or so down the grassy slope, and then, clinging to grass, held my position. I could not see the surface of the road. I would wait here until the wagons had passed. They would not, I was sure, at night, in the moonlight and shadows, detect my presence. I clung there until the first wagon had passed. I could hear others approaching, too. I let myself slip down further in the ditch. I must not be discovered. I put my cheek against the wet grass. I was very tired. It was a good hiding place, the ditch. In the darkness, in the moonlight and shadows, I would not be detected. I was safe. I dreaded the climb again to the surface of the road. The ditch was so steep. I did not understand the need for such a ditch at the side of the road. But I was safe now. There were other wagons, too, coming. There must be many wagons. I must wait. I would rest, just a little bit. It would not hurt to close my eyes, only for a moment. I was so hungry. I was so tired. I was so miserable. I would rest, just for a little bit. I would close my eyes, only for a moment.

"What are you doing here?" asked a voice.

"I am a free woman," I said.

I lay on the incline, the grass under my belly. It was warm now. The sun felt hot on my back. Muddy water was about my feet. A man was behind me. At least one other, I could hear him moving about, was above and in front of me, up on the surface of the road.

"I was attacked by bandits," I said. "They took my clothes."

"Hold still," said the voice behind me.

I heard the clink of a chain.

My body stiffened, my fingers clutched at the grass.

A chain was looped twice about my neck and padlocked shut.

"What are you doing?" I whispered.

"Hold still," said the voice.

The chain was then taken under my body and down to my ankles. My ankles were crossed and the chain was looped thrice about them, holding them closely together. Another padlock then, its tongue passing through links of the chain, was snapped shut. My ankles were now chained tightly together. I could not even uncross them. It is common to run a neck chain to the ankles in front of a woman's body, rather than behind it. In this fashion any stress on the chain is borne by the back of her neck rather than her throat. It is also regarded as a more aesthetic chaining arrangement than its opposite, the neck chain, for example, with its linearity, and its sturdy, inflexible links, affording a striking contrast with the softnesses, the beauties, of her lovely bosom. This arrangement is also favored for its psychological effect on the woman. As she feels the chain more often on her body in this arrangement, brushing her, for example, or lying upon her, she is less likely to forget that she is wearing it. It helps her to keep clearly in mind that she is chained. It reminds her, dramatically and frequently, of that fact.

"What are you doing?" I asked. "I am a free woman!"

"How is it, did you say," asked the man behind me, "that you are unclothed?"

"Bandits took my clothes!" I said.

"And left you?" he asked.

"Yes," I said.

"If it had been up to me," said the fellow behind me, "I think I would have taken you along and left the clothes."

I was silent.

"I suppose," he said, pleasantly enough, "they might have been poor of eyesight, or perhaps it was just very dark."

I did not speak.

"What is your Home Stone?" he asked.

I thought quickly. I did not want to identify myself with Corcyrus, of course, or any cities or towns in that area, even Argentum. Too, I knew we had flown northwest. I then took, almost out of the air, a city far to the north, one I had heard of but one, unfortunately, that I knew little about. The name had been mentioned, I did recall, on the tarn platform, in the camp of Miles of Argentum. Perhaps that is what suggested it to my mind.

"That of Lydius," I said.

"What is the location of Lydius?" he asked.

"North," I said. "North."

"And where in the north?" he asked.

I was silent.

"On what lake does Lydius lie?" he asked.

"I do not know," I said.

"It does not lie on a lake," he said.

"Of course not," I said.

"On what river does it lie?" he asked.

"It doesn't lie on a river," I said.

"It is on the Laurius," he said.

I was silent.

"What is the first major town east of Lydius?" he asked.

"I don't remember," I said.

"Vonda," he said.

"Yes," I said.

"No," he said. "Vonda is on the Olni. It is Laura."

"Yes," I said, sick and hungry, chained.

"You are certain that you are a free woman?" asked the man.

"Yes," I said.

"Where is your escort, your guards?" he asked.

"I was traveling alone," I said.

"That is unusual for a free woman," he said.

I was silent.

"What were you doing on this road?" he asked.

"Traveling," I said. "Visiting."

"And where did you think you were going?" asked the man.

"I don't know," I sobbed. I did not even know what towns lay along this road. I did not even know where I was.

"Look here," said the fellow. He turned me about. I saw he was a brawny, blond youth. He did not seem angry or cruel. He crouched down and, with one finger, near the bottom of the ditch, made a precise marking, or drawing, in the mud.

"What letter is that?" he asked.

"I do not know," I said.

"Al-ka," he said.

"I cannot read," I said.

"Most free women can read," he said.

"I was not taught," I said.

"You have a luscious body," he said.

"Please unchain me," I said.

"It has delicious slave curves," he said.

"Unchain me, please," I begged.

"Your body does not suggest that it is the body of a free woman," he said. "It suggests, rather, that it is the body of a natural slave."

"I beg to be unchained," I said. "You can see that I am a free woman. My body is unbranded. I do not wear a collar!"

"Some masters," said he, "are so foolish as not to brand and collar their women."

"That would be stupid," I said.

"I think so," he said.

"So you can see, then," I said, "that I, uncollared, unbranded, must be free."

"Not necessarily," he smiled.

"Unchain me," I begged.

"What is your name?" he asked.

"Lita," I said. I remembered this name from the time that Drusus Rencius had taken me to the house of Kliomenes in Corcyrus. It was the name he had chosen for me there, Lady Lita, of Corcyrus. It had sprung into my mind probably because of that trip. Too, I recalled that both Publius and Drusus Rencius had thought that it would be a good name for me.

Both of the men then laughed, he standing now before me as I sat on the bank, and he, who was apparently alone, on the surface of the road.

"What is wrong?" I asked.

"That is a slave name," he said.

"No!" I said.

"It is a common slave name," he said. "Indeed, it is one of the names popular with the masters for unusually juicy and helpless slaves."

"It is also the name of some free women," I said.

"It is possible, I suppose," said the man.

"Please unchain me," I begged.

"Lita," said the man.

"Lady Lita," I said.

"Lita," said he.

I looked at him in misery.

"It seems clear you are a slave, Lita," he said. "You are naked. You apparently have no Home Stone. You do not know where you are. You cannot even read. Your name is even that of a slave."

"No!" I said.

"But it is," he said. "Therefore, since it seems clear that you are a runaway slave, you will henceforth address us as 'Master.' "

"Please, no," I said.

"If you are actually a free woman, as you claim," he said, "no great harm will be done. On the other hand, if you should prove to be a slave, as you doubtless will, this will save you some whippings for disrespect."

I stared at him in misery.

"Do you understand?" he asked.

"Yes," I said.

He continued to look at me.

"Yes—Masters," I said.

"The word sounds very natural on your lips, Lita," he said.

"Yes, Masters," I said.

"You may thank us," he said.

"Thank you, Masters," I said.

He then scooped me up and, standing on the slope, threw me over his left shoulder. My head faced behind. In this fashion a girl cannot see where she is being carried. In this fashion, too, it is her bottom which is first being presented for the view of those whom her carrier approaches. It is thought useful for her to understand this. It is, of course, a common way of carrying female slaves. He then, slipping, crouching down, putting out his hand, scrambled up the slope.

In a moment they had put me on a blanket in the wagon bed of an open tharlarion wagon. They were not ungentle with me.

"I am very hungry, Masters," I said. "May I have something to eat?"

"Surely," said the fellow who had carried me up the slope. Then, while the other fellow took his place on the wagon box and started the ponderous draft beast into motion, he gave me two generous pieces of bread, two full wedges of Sa-Tarna bread, a fourth of a loaf. Such bread is usually baked in round, flat loaves, with eight divisions in a loaf. Some smaller loaves are divided into four divisions. These divisions are a function, presumably, of their simplicity, the ease with which they may be made, the ease with which, even without explicit measurement, equalities may be produced. He also gave me a slice of dried larma, some raisins and a plum. Twice he poured me water from a bag into a cup. He indicated the side of the cup from which I might drink. When a cup is shared masters and slaves do not drink from the same side of the cup.

"Do not eat so quickly," he cautioned me, as I tore piteously at the bread. "How long is it since you have eaten?" he asked.

"Since last night," I said, "before the bandits attacked."

He laughed. I continued to bite and tear at the bread. I had hardly eaten in four days. At the inn I had eaten even garbage.

"Eat more slowly, little Lita," he said, "or you will make yourself ill."

"Yes, Master," I said.

In a time, my repast was finished. He put aside the cup from which I had drunk.

"You look much better now," he said, "now that you have been fed and watered."

"Thank you, Master," I said. "May I speak?"

"Yes," he said.

"Where am I?" I asked.

"You are on the Viktel Aria," he said, "north of Venna, moving south."

I realized, then, I had stayed longer with the tarnsman than perhaps I should have. I was closer to Ar than I cared to be. On the other hand he, obviously, had not gone directly to Ar. I was grateful for that. He was the sort of fellow who tended to be rather casual about his commercial obligations, I gathered. He had come well north of Ar, it seemed. It probably had to do with the inn at which he had stopped. Doubtless he had stopped there for a reason, probably one of the inn slaves, girls who, for an additional fee, are supplied to the guests, to see to their needs and comforts. His cronies, Bemus and Torquatus, as I recalled, were not in Ar to meet him, having been dispatched, respectively, as I recalled, to Lydius and Bazi. Thus he might well have looped north for a rendezvous with some favorite slave. I did not think he would be bothered mightily if he arrived late in Ar, or if, as he might put it, it took him a little longer, once again, to be on time. Venna, I recalled, was some two hundred pasangs or so north of Ar. The expression "Viktel Aria" means "Ar's Triumph" or "The Triumph of Ar." In its more northern lengths this road is commonly thought of as the Vosk Road.

"Why are there such deep ditches at the sides of the road?" I asked.

"It is that way for more than a hundred pasangs in this area," he said, "except for crossroads and turn-offs. It makes it difficult, then, to bring supply wagons across the road, either from the east or west, the road acting then rather as a wall."

"Its purpose is defensive, then," I said, "military."

"Yes," he said.

"Where are you going?" I asked.

"Venna," he said.

"When will you arrive?" I asked.

"Tomorrow morning," he said.

"Tonight," I said, "when you sleep, you do not need to keep my legs chained. I will not run away."

"On your belly, pretty Lita," he said, "and put your hands, wrists crossed, behind you."

I did this. He tied my wrists together.

"Not only will your ankles be chained tonight," he said, "and your wrists bound, as they are, but, too, you will be chained by the neck to a wagon wheel."

"What are you going to do with me?" I asked.

"Turn you over to the office of the Archon, in Venna," he said.

# 17

# THE CEMENT PLATFORM

My chin was thrust up, rudely, with a thumb. "No," said a voice. "It is not my Tutina."

The man, then, with the Archon's man, stepped down from the circular cement platform, and rejoined the crowds coming and going in the busy street. The street was apparently an important one in Venna, and led down to a market square. My platform was on the left side of the street, looking down toward the square, and at the forward corner, nearest the street, of a public slave market, some fifty feet in length, along the street, and some fifty feet in depth. Behind this area, at the back of the display area, was a gloomy building with barred windows. It was in this building that the slaves were kept at night. The Archon's man also had his office in this building. From where I was I could see some of the girls, reclining, or sitting about, on their chains. When someone came to examine them, usually only to look at them more closely, they would kneel. The Archon's man would then, sometimes at least, come about and join the prospective customer, praising the girl, and seeing if he could elicit a bid. They were for sale. I was not, or at least not yet. I had been given to understand that if I were not claimed within ten days, I, too, would be put up for sale, even if I might be a free woman, if only to cover the cost of my keep. It had been determined that my Home Stone, if I had one, was not that of Venna, or Ar, or of one of their allies. I was then, in any case, it seemed, without money, without credentials, fair game for the slaver's block.

It was hot standing on the cement platform, my wrists in loose, but unslippable shackles, chained over my head. My shackle chain went through a ring, itself suspended from another chain and ring, fixed in an outjutting beam, extending forth at a right angle from the sturdy upright. There was a supporting beam, too, braced at its lower end against the upright and at its upper end against the outjutting beam. The entire structure was quite strong and solid. It would have held, I was sure, a dozen men. At the front of the outjutting beam, a piece of paper containing a legend, or advertisement, was nailed. I had seen it before it had been put up but I, being illiterate, could not read it. I was very curious to know what it said.

I saw a man pause in the crowd, to look upon me. I feared for a moment he might recognize me as Sheila, the Tatrix of Corcyrus. But then I saw that he was only looking upon me, idly, casually, as a man might examine a female slave. I wished that I had been given clothing. I trembled in the shackles. I was not used to being looked upon in that fashion, so straightforwardly, so candidly, so obviously.

I looked away. When I looked back, he was gone. I did not know if he had been wondering what I might look like, licking and squirming for him, or if his interest had been more speculative, more theoretical or academic, wondering what I might bring, if I were sold.

"Lady, kind lady!" I called to a gentlewoman passing by, in her robes and veil. I would try to get her to read the legend for me. "Please, kind lady!"

The woman, who had been keeping her eyes straight ahead, as though not wishing to see any of the girls in the market, suddenly, angrily, stopped. I saw her eyes, over the veil. They were not pleasant.

"Forgive me, kind lady," I said.

"You spoke to me," she said.

"Yes," I said. "Forgive me, kind lady. No one has read to me the legend posted over my head. I beg you to do so."

She lifted her robes and climbed to the cement platform. She was about two inches taller than I. She stood then before me.

"You spoke to me," she said.

"Yes, kind lady," I said.

"Where you come from," she said, "do slaves not address free women as 'Mistress'?"

"I am a free woman, too," I said. "I am not a slave."

"Naked, lying slave!" hissed the woman.

"I beg you for kindness," I said. "Even if I were a slave, which I am not, we share the same sex. We are both women."

"I am a woman," she said. "You are an animal."

"Take pity on me," I said. "We have in common at least that we are females."

"Do not dare to see me in terms of such a denominator," she said. "It is not my fault that I share a sex with she-sleen and she-tarsks, and, lower than either, with she-slaves."

"I am not a slave," I said. "I am free. I am not collared. I am not branded!"

"If I owned you," she snapped, "you would soon be collared and branded, and then you would be sent to the stables or scullery, where you belong!"

"Forgive me," I said.

"Forgive you, what?" she said, in fury.

"—Mistress!" I said.

"I know your type," she said, in fury. "You are the sort for whom my companion forsakes me! You are the sort he runs panting after in the taverns, the sort whose bodies their masters sell for the price of a drink!"

"No," I said. "No!"

"You are the sort of woman who likes men, aren't you?" she said.

"No, Mistress," I cried. "No! No!"

"Why aren't you kneeling, Slut?" she asked.

"I'm chained," I cried. "I can't!"

"Kneel," ordered the free woman, coldly.

"I can't, Mistress!" I wept. I let myself hang from the shackles, my knees bent, piteously.

"You should not have accosted a free woman," she said.

She then removed her gloves and, with them, struck me across the face. Tears sprang to my eyes.

"You must also address her as 'Mistress,' " she said. I was then struck again.

"You have denied your slavery," she said. "You have dared to compare yourself with me, insulting me by calling to my attention that we are both females. You have denied that you are of the category of the sensuous slut! You have denied, lyingly, that you are eager to serve men!" She then struck me four times. "Do you think I cannot see what you are?" she asked. "Do you think it is unclear to anyone who looks upon you? Do you think I am stupid? Anyone could see that you are a slave! It is obvious!" Then she lashed me across the face and mouth with her gloves, several times. It did not really hurt so much, but it did sting, and, of course, it was terribly humiliating. I began to cry. "And you did not kneel!" she cried. She struck me twice again. I hung in the shackles, sobbing. I was most afraid that she might call the Archon's man. He might, if requested, I feared, use a whip on me. She then, angrily, withdrew from the platform and resumed her journey down the street.

"What was that all about?" asked the Archon's man.

"I spoke to her, Master," I said. I called him "Master" for he, like the young men who had caught me at the edge of the Viktel Aria, had made it clear to me that I was to address him, whether I was free or not, with a slave's respect.

"But she is a free woman," he observed.

"Yes, Master," I said. With a rustle of chain I again got my feet under me.

"It was foolish of you," he said.

"Yes, Master," I sobbed.

"Your face is red," he said.

"Yes, Master," I said.

Later in the afternoon, after I had been fed and watered, standing in the shackles, I decided to once again essay the decipherment of the legend on the post. This time, having learned my lesson, I would not trouble a free woman in the matter. I knew that I was pretty and I had little doubt, even though I was tired and my arms were now sore, that, chained as I was, displayed as I was, my attractions might be of interest to passing males. Men of Earth, I knew, would often strive to please even a scantily clad woman, for example, one wearing a sun suit or a bathing suit. I, for example, had had this experience on summer weekends and at the beach.

"Sir, Master!" I called to a man. He seemed a friendly enough looking fellow.

He approached me, climbing to the platform. "Yes?" he inquired.

"I am a free woman," I said, "but nonetheless I will call you 'Master.' " I hoped that this would flatter him.

"Whatever you wish," he said.

"And you are surely a very handsome Master," I said. He was, as a matter of fact, very handsome. On the other hand, I was out to get my way. Men, incidentally, will believe anything they are told.

"Why, thank you," he said.

"There is a legend over my head," I said.

"Yes, there is," he agreed.

"Can you read it?" I wheedled.

"Why, yes," he said. "I can."

"Please, please," I wheedled. "Please read it for little Lita." I referred to myself by this name. It was the name I had given to the two young men on the road, and also, if only to be consistent, to the Archon's man. On the other hand I did not mind the name. I rather liked it. It excited me.

"It says," said the man, " 'Whip me, if I speak without permission.' "

I turned white.

He smiled.

"It does not really say that, does it?" I asked, frightened.

"No," he said.

"Please tell me what it says," I said.

"We shall assume, for purposes of this discussion, that you are a slave," he said.

"Very well, Master," I said, puzzled.

"Do you believe that slaves should serve free persons," he asked, "or that free persons should serve slaves."

"I believe it is the slaves who should serve the free persons," I said, hastily, "not the other way around." I certainly did not want to have the flesh whipped off my bones.

"And if I read that legend for you," he said, "I would be serving you, wouldn't I?"

"Yes, Master," I said.

"And you would not want that, would you?" he asked.

"No," I said.

"Then," he said, "you do not want me to read the legend for you."

"No, Master," I said, miserably.

"Very well," he said and, chuckling, left.

I shook the chains in frustration. He seemed to be a very kind man. If I had not tried to be so clever, if I had not tried to trick him, he probably would have read the legend for me.

I watched him walking off.

He had not seemed eager, even desperate to please me, in spite of the fact that I was naked. I then realizd, with a strang feeling deep within me, something akin to fear and excitement, that on this world it was the naked women, or scantily clad women, women who would be slaves, or would be presumed to be slaves, women such as I, who must serve and please the men. This was not Earth; it was Gor.

"Oh, Lady!" I called. "Please, Lady!"

The slave, alone, in the brief, sleeveless red tunic, with sides split to the waist, turned, to see whom I might be addressing.

"Lady!" I called to her.

"I am not a lady," she said. "I am a slave."

"Please," I said. "Can you read the legend posted over my head?"

"Cannot you read?" she asked.

"No," I said. I looked at her. She was nicely curved, with brown hair and eyes. She wore a close-fitting steel collar.

"I am sorry," she said. "I cannot either. I was never taught." She then sped on her way.

"What is going on?" asked the Archon's man.

"Nothing, Master," I said.

"If you delay slaves in their errands, and they are late," he said, "they might be whipped."

"I am sorry, Master," I said.

"Why did you delay her?" he asked.

"I wanted her to read the sign posted over my head," I said.

"Why didn't you ask me?" he asked.

"I was afraid," I said. "You did not read it to me. I thought then perhaps you did not want me to know what it said."

"And, without determining whether that was true or not," he said, "you nonetheless sought, perhaps thereby circumventing my will, to determine its contents?"

"Yes, Master," I said. "Forgive me, Master!"

"You should be whipped," he said. He unclipped the coiled slave whip from his belt.

"I am a free woman!" I told him.

"You have a slave's body," he said.

"Even so, I am a free woman," I said.

"Perhaps you are a free woman," he said. "It is hard to imagine a slave being so stupid."

"Do not whip me," I begged.

I saw him recoiling the blades of the whip. I viewed this action with unspeakable relief.

He then thrust it before my face. "Lick it, and kiss it," he said.

"Please," I begged.

"You will do so now," he said, "or after you have been beaten with it."

I then reached my head forward and, delicately, licked and kissed the whip. He then replaced the stern, supple disciplinary device on his belt.

"Master," I said.

"Yes," he said.

"Why did you not tell me what the sign said?" I asked.

"I showed it to you," he said. "It did not occur to me that you could not read."

"But I cannot," I said. "Please tell me what it says!"

"Not now, pretty Lita," he said. "Not now." He then walked away. I stomped with my right foot. I shook the chains, angrily. Tears came to my eyes. I was being frustrated, as though I might be a slave.

The afternoon wore on.

My body and arms began to ache miserably.

From time to time one man or another in the crowd would pause to gaze on me. I usually looked away from them, but, even so, it seemed I could sometimes sense their eyes on me, roving me with impunity. I, chained as I was, was exposed to their gaze as any stripped slave. Sometimes they would come up to the platform, to examine me more closely. The Archon's man, however, would not permit them to touch my body or test my slave reflexes. Similarly, I was not required to respond to certain sorts of commands, for example, to make "slave lips," pursing my lips for kissing, or to writhe slowly before my viewers. It was still regarded as a theoretical possibility, I gathered, that I might be free. "She is not for sale," the Archon's man told one fellow. "Too bad," had said the fellow. "Not now," had added the Archon's man. "Perhaps later," said the fellow. "Perhaps," had agreed the Archon's man.

It was late in the afternoon when, suddenly, my body stiffened in terror. I put my head down, swiftly, trembling. I wanted to hide but, of course, I was held perfectly where I was, exposed, helpless in the shackles.

He must not have seen me! He must not have seen me!

I turned away a little, in the chains, as though merely to change my position.

My heart was pounding in terror.

He, of all people!

Surely he had not noticed me. Surely he had not seen me. He must not have seen me!

"Let the churl be stripped," I had said, imperiously, "and a sign be put about his neck, proclaiming him a fraud. Then let him be marched naked, before the spears of guards, through the great gate of Corcyrus, not to be permitted to return before the second passage hand!"

But I could not run now. I, helpless, naked, chained in place, was being publicly displayed.

A Corcyran merchant had brought charges against him, a matter having to do with a bowl, purportedly silver, but only plated, and one bearing a forged mark, misrepresenting it as the work of the silversmiths of Ar.

Surely he must now have passed by.

Further inquiries had been made and it was found that he had among his goods a set of false weights.

He must now have gone. He must!

Too, it had been discovered that he had sold slave hair to the public, representing it as that of free women.

I was safe. He must have gone by now.

How pleased I was to have sentenced him to his humiliation, pronouncing the judgment of the Tatrix against him! How pleased I was to have seen him dragged by guards from my august presence. How splendid, too, to have men serving one, obeying one, in this fashion! He had been an itinerant peddler, an obsequious, cringing, ugly, small, vile man with a twisted body. Surely he was one of the most detestable human beings I had ever seen.

I stiffened, again, in terror. Someone had joined me on the

cement platform. I kept my head down. Then, as had happened two or three times before, I felt a thumb under my chin. My head was pushed up.

I found myself looking into the eyes of the peddler, Speusippus of Turia.

## 18

## THE LEASH

Speusippus stepped back and regarded me. I kept my head up, looking at him.

He glanced up at the sign over my head. He could doubtless read it.

He then looked me over possessively, and slowly and with pleasure. He began to rub his hands together.

"Sir?" I asked.

"Sir!" he laughed. "It is now 'Sir,' is it? 'Sir' for Speusippus. Excellent!"

I moved in the shackles. I felt so helpless!

"It seems that our fortunes have changed somewhat," he said. "Excellent."

"I do not understand," I said.

"How did you get here, so far away?" he asked. "How did this delightful shift in your circumstances come about?"

"I do not know what you are talking about," I said. "I do not know you. I have never seen you before in my life."

"Now it is you who are naked and helpless," he said. "Splendid!"

"I think you have me confused with someone else, Sir," I said. "I have never seen you before in my life."

I then shrank back. He stood quite close to me. I felt his breath on my cheek.

"I am not stupid," he whispered. "Do not play games with me."

"Sir?" I asked.

"I know who you are," he said.

"Who?" I asked.

"Sheila," said he, whispering in my ear. "You are Sheila, Tatrix of Corcyrus!"

"No," I whispered. "No!"

"The office of the Archon will doubtless be pleased to learn the identity of its lovely prisoner," he said.

"They will not believe it," I said.

"They will conduct inquiries," he said, "with rather clear consequences, I think, for yourself."

"Do not tell them, I beg you," I said. "They will take me back to Argentum for impalement!"

He smiled.

"Please, do not tell them, Speusippus," I begged.

" 'Sir'?" he asked.

"Please, do not tell them, Sir," I begged.

"It is pleasant for one such as I to be called 'Sir' by the Tatrix of Corcyrus," he said.

"Please do not tell them," I begged, "—Sir!"

"Who are you supposed to be?" he asked.

"The Lady Lita, of Lydius," I said.

" 'Lita'?" he grinned. "That is a splendid name for you. Excellent."

I trembled. That name, especially when not prefixed by 'Lady', I felt, somehow, did seem to have a certain rightness for me. I wondered if, in some sense, I was a "Lita," or, say, a "Tuka," or a "Lana," other common names for slaves on Gor. Earth-girl names, too, incidentally, are commonly used as slave names on Gor, such as Jean, Joan, Priscilla, Sally, Deborah, Lois, Sandra and Stacy. At any rate the name did make me feel slightly uneasy, and excited, and rather like a slave. This was perhaps a function of its simplicity, loveliness and femininity. I hardly dared speculate what I might feel like if it were actually put upon me and I were then to discover that, by a master's will, I had become "Lita." The name was originally given to me, I recalled, by Drusus Rencius, put upon me as a part of my disguise, and for the purposes of my licensing, in the house of Kliomenes. I felt momentarily angry. The beast must have known that it was a common slave name.

"Where were you caught?" he asked.

"North of Venna," I said, "on the Viktel Aria."

"Well," said Speusippus, "I think I will now call the Archon's man and tell him who you are."

"Please, do not, Sir," I begged.

"And if I do not," asked Speusippus, "what will you do?"

"Anything," I whispered.

"Anything?" he asked, smiling.

"Anything!" I whispered.

"You may now begin to call me 'Master,' " he said.

" 'Master'?" I asked, in horror.

"Yes," he said. "It will be useful in your disguise."

"I do not understand," I said.

"You will be a free woman," he said. "I would have it no other way. But your disguise will be quite thorough."

"I do not understand," I said.

"It will be delicious," he said, "having the Tatrix of Corcyrus, a free woman, serve me as though she might be a mere slave, and with the full offices and services of the slave."

"Do not so shame me," I said. "If you must, simply enslave me."

"No," he said. "It is as a free woman that you will so serve me."

"Never as a free woman!" I said.

"Very well," he said. "I shall now call the Archon's man."

"No," I said. "No."

"Does Lady Sheila accept my terms?" he asked.

"Yes," I said.

"Yes, what?" he asked.

"Yes—Master," I sobbed.

"I see you have caught her," Speusippus called to the Archon's man. "Good work!"

"Do you know her?" asked the man, coming over to the platform.

"Yes," said Speusippus. "She ran away a few days ago."

"Who owns her?" asked the Archon's man.

"I do," said Speusippus. "She is mine."

"What is her name?" asked the Archon's man.

"Lita," said Speusippus.

"It is not improbable that that is her name," said the Archon's man. "She was using it."

"That was foolish, wasn't it, Lita?" asked Speusippus.

"Yes, Master," I said.

"Where did you lose her?" asked the Archon's man.

"North, on the great road," said Speusippus.

"That is where she was caught," said the Archon's man. "She is apparently yours. Do you have papers on her?"

"No," said Speusippus.

"Do you have friends who can vouch for you, that she is yours?"

"I am from Turia," said Speusippus. "I am a stranger in this beautiful city."

"Things, then, are not so simple," said the Archon's man. "As you can see she is not even collared or branded. She is claiming to be a free woman."

"No, Master," I said.

"Perhaps I could hold her for ten days," said the Archon's man, "and then, if there are no other claimants, turn her over to you." He looked at me. "What did you say?" he asked.

"I am not a free woman, Master," I said. "I am a slave."

"There are still problems," said the Archon's man. "She will deny that she is your slave."

"No, Master," I said. "I am his." I almost choked on the words. Too, the words themselves frightened me, terribly. I knew that I was lying, of course, but still they frightened me. How fearful it would be, I thought, to say such words and know that they were true, that one did belong, fully, to a man.

"Do you admit that you are his slave?" the Archon's man asked me. "Do you acknowledge that, and freely, and not under torture?"

"Yes, Master," I said. "I am his slave."

"Then you were lying to us before," he said.

"Yes, Master," I said.

He unclipped the whip from his belt.

"No, no," smiled Speusippus. "That will not be necessary. I am sure that little Lita has learned her lesson. Haven't you, Lita?"

"Yes, Master," I said. I twisted in the chains, making sure that the Archon's man had returned the whip to his belt. He had done so, I noted with relief.

"You have not even had her branded and collared," said the Archon's man. "If I were you I would see to these details promptly. If she escapes from you again, you might not recover her so easily. Someone else, having her properly marked and collared, might decide to keep her."

"I shall take all of these matters under the most serious consideration," said Speusippus, nodding soberly.

I smiled to myself. I saw that Speusippus had no intention of doing anything so cruel as putting a brand on me or anything as degrading as putting my neck in a collar. Too, he had not let the Archon's man whip me. I saw that Speusippus would treat me with lenience, kindness and deference. I saw that I had nothing to fear from Speusippus. After all, I was a free woman, and the Tatrix of Corcyrus.

"Thank you, Master," I said, in relief, to the Archon's man, as he released my wrists from the shackles. It felt so good to put my arms down. I almost fell on the platform.

"Poor little Lita," said Speusippus, sympathetically. He patted me, tenderly, on the shoulder. "This has been such a terrible experience for you. But do not worry now, little Lita. It is over. I will take you away with me now."

"Thank you, Master," I whimpered, playing my role.

But then I felt my hands tied behind my back, with a wire-cored cord. I was tied, and well.

Then I was leashed like a dog, or less than a dog. It was a slave leash. I was leashed like a slave.

"May I reimburse you for her keep?" inquired Speusippus.

"No," said the Archon's man. "Such services are furnished by the city."

"Splendid," said Speusippus. "Come along, Lita." I felt the tug of the leash. I was leashed!

"Do not spoil her," cautioned the Archon's man.

"We would not want to spoil you now, would we, Lita?" asked Speusippus.

"No, Master," I whispered. I shuddered. Gorean slaves, I suspected, were seldom in any danger of being spoiled. They were commonly held under disciplines of iron.

I followed Speusippus down from the platform. I did not want the leash to be pulled taut.

"Master," I said.

"Yes?" he said.

"Can you read the sign that was posted over my head, please?"

"Yes," said he. "It says, 'Who owns this slave? Who can identify her?' "

"That is all?" I said.

"Yes," he said.

"Thank you, Master," I said. For so little I had been struck by the free woman, and tricked and frustrated in the chains!

He pulled me closer to him by the leash. I did not want to stand so close to him.

On the sign, it seemed, it had been presupposed that I was a slave. To be sure, Gorean men tended to look upon me, it seemed, as though I belonged in that degraded category, or as though it might, in fact, be mine.

"Have no fear," grinned Speusippus. "They are well satisfied. From their point of view the slave has been identified and her owner has been located. Indeed, he has even come and claimed her."

"Yes, Master," I said.

He then took up the slack in the leash until he held me, by the leash, but inches from him.

"I, Speusippus," he said, whispering intimately to me, "have the Tatrix of Corcyrus naked and on a slave leash."

"Yes, Master," I said.

"Say that word again," he whispered, "and more slowly, pronouncedly and beautifully."

"Master," I said.

"And she addresses me, Speusippus, the lowly peddler, as 'Master,' " he said.

"Yes, Master," I said.

He turned about, slackening the leash, and I followed him.

I was led through the streets. The people of Venna paid me little attention. Such sights, I gathered, were not that uncommon in a Gorean city, that of a naked, leashed slave in the care of her master. But could they not see that I was not branded, that I was not collared? But this seemed to make little difference. Clearly my status was either bond or that of a captive. Indeed, perhaps I was being conducted even now to the shop of a metal worker, there to be marked and receive, and have locked upon me, measured and fitted, a suitable, inflexible, identificatory circlet of bondage.

I followed Speusippus of Turia through the streets of Venna, even through the great market square. I was naked, barefoot and bound. I followed him whether I wished to or not. I was leashed.

## 19

# THE TRUNK

"Now we are alone, Lady Sheila," he said.

He had turned from the door, after locking it and depositing the key in his pouch.

I stood with my back against the wooden wall. I watched him put the pouch, on its strap, in a far corner of the room, with other articles. It was a small, bare, largely unfurnished room. It had a common wall with a small stable, beyond which was a small stable yard. His tharlarion was in the stable, and his wagon, outside, in the yard, chained. His goods, in various crates and trunks, had been brought into the small room. It was one of several such small dwellings, with attached stables and yards, in a line, habitations rented out to teamsters and itinerant merchants. It was on the southern outskirts of Venna.

I had scrubbed down the tharlarion, cleaning and washing its scales and claws. I had then, under his supervision, cleaned out its stable and brought in fresh greens for it to feed upon.

After this he had taken me to the public trough where I, under his instructions, washed. We had then returned to the small dwelling in the complex where I, over a small grill in the yard, cooking not allowed in the shacks, had cooked for him. He had thrown me one piece of meat. In front of some of the other shacks in the line, in the yards, I could see girls cooking for masters, too. They, of course, were clearly slaves. After I had cleaned the grill and washed the paraphernalia connected with his meal we had come indoors. He had now locked the door.

I felt the roughness of the wall at my back.

He opened a chest and drew forth, from somewhere within it, apparently from under several other objects, a brief gray tunic, and threw it to me. I caught it, eagerly. I had not had clothing since shortly after my capture in Corcyrus. Even so tiny and despicable a scrap of clothing as a mere slave tunic, I then realized, can be a precious treasure to a woman. He sat down on a box, watching me, his hands on his knees, across the room from me. Swiftly, elatedly, gratefully, I drew the tiny garment over my head. It was sleeveless, scandalously short and its neckline plunged to my belly, but I welcomed it as though it might have been the most splendid gown in the wardrobe of a Tatrix.

"Thank you, Master!" I cried. "Thank you. Oh, thank you, Master!"

"Now take it off," he said.

Slowly, numbly, I took the garment off, and dropped it to the side.

"Now kneel before me, Lady Sheila," he said.

I dropped to my knees before him.

"Open your knees," he said.

"I am a free woman," I protested.

Then I saw his eyes, and opened my knees before him.

"Excellent, Lady Sheila," he said. "Now say, 'I, Lady Sheila, the Tatrix of Corcyrus, kneel naked, my knees open, before Speusippus of Turia.' "

"I, Lady Sheila, the Tatrix of Corcyrus," I said, "kneel naked, my knees open, before Speusippus of Turia."

"Excellent," he said. "Do you remember sentencing me, in Corcyrus?"

"Yes, Master," I said.

"You seemed very proud then," he said. "You do not seem so proud now."

"No, Master," I said.

"You are sorry for having sentenced me, aren't you?" he asked.

"Yes, Master," I said.

"And you wish to atone for it, don't you?" he asked.

"Yes, Master," I said.

"And I will see that you do so," he said.

"Yes, Master," I said.

"On your belly, Lady Sheila," he said. I lowered myself to my belly before him.

"Do you wish to be taken to Argentum for impalement?" he asked.

I lifted my head to look at him, my eyes wild. "No," I cried. "No!"

"We are going to get along very well, aren't we?" he asked.

"Yes, Master," I said.

"And we are going to get to know one another very well, aren't we?" he asked.

"Yes, Master," I sobbed.

"You may now beg to please me," he said.

"Whip me!" I begged him. "Enslave me! Give me no choice! Do not make me do this of my own will!"

"Say," he said, " 'I, Sheila, Tatrix of Corcyrus, naked and on my belly, of my own free will, beg to please Speusippus of Turia.' "

"I, Sheila, Tatrix of Corcyrus," I said, "naked and on my belly, of my own free will, beg to please Speusippus of Turia."

" 'And as a slave,' " he added.

"And as a slave," I sobbed.

I lay there on the floor, sobbing, and, to my horror, watched him unroll wretched, stinking sleeping furs.

He then removed his tunic and reclined on the furs, watching me, leaning on one elbow.

"I do not even know how to please a man," I said, "let alone with the sensuous intimacies of a slave."

"Have no fear," he said. "I know that you are an ignorant free woman."

"Yes, Master," I said.

"But I shall expect you to show marked and rapid improvement in these matters," he said.

"Yes, Master," I said.

"If you do not," he said, "you will be punished."

"Yes, Master," I said.

"You do not want to be punished, do you?" he asked.

"No, Master," I said.

"You will endeavor, then, to make rapid progress in the arts of intimacy, won't you, Lady Sheila?" he asked.

"Yes, Master," I said.

He then beckoned that I should approach him.

"I am a virgin!" I cried.

"Excellent," he said. "Then, before the night is done you will be opened by Speusippus of Turia for the uses of men."

I then, on my belly, sobbing, began to crawl toward him.

"Stop," he said.

I stopped, puzzled. My body was still on the floor. I had not yet even come to the edge of those stinking furs.

"You are a free woman," he said, "and you have much to learn. We will begin with simple things."

"Master?" I asked.

"Lie at my feet," he said, "and lick, and kiss and suck at them. When you have managed to learn to do that properly, I will give you further instructions."

"Yes," I wept.

"Yes, what?" he asked.

"Yes—Master!" I sobbed.

"You did not do badly, Lady Sheila," he said. "If I did not know better, I would have thought that you had had some-training. Perhaps it is natural in a woman. Get in." He held open the lid of the large trunk.

I crawled into the large, deep trunk, and lay down in it, on my side, with my legs drawn up.

"Did I please Master?" I asked.

"You speak like a slave," he sneered.

"Forgive me, Master," I said. Interesting enough, and I hardly understood this, and it seemed almost incredible, I did, clearly, want him to find me pleasing.

"Are you hungry?" he asked.

"Yes, Master," I said. For my supper I had received only one piece of meat. It had been thrown to me, as though I might have been a dog.

He went somewhere in the room and returned with a piece of dried meat. He dropped it into the trunk, near my face. I seized it in my hands.

"Thank you, Master," I said.

He was looking down into the trunk. I looked up at him.

"If I had not been pleasing," I asked, "would you have given me this?"

"No," he said.

I then realized that it was truly in the best interest of a female captive, or slave, to be pleasing. If she was not pleasing, and perhaps even quite pleasing, she might not be fed. By superb performances a girl might, I thought, encourage a master to believe that she was worth feeding, and, perhaps, even feeding well.

"What are you going to do with me?" I asked.

"What I please," he said.

"Yes, Master," I said.

"In the morning we are going south," he said.

"Not to Ar!" I said.

"No," he said. "We will be turning west."

He looked down at me, huddled in the trunk. I bit a little at the meat. I was ravenously hungry.

"Were you given permission to feed?" he asked.

"Forgive me, Master," I said. I hoped he would not take the food from me.

"What do you know?" he said. "You are only a stupid free woman."

"Yes, Master," I said.

"You may feed," he said.

"Thank you, Master," I said. I bit hungrily at the meat.

"You eat like a starving slave," he said.

"Forgive me, Master," I said. I then took smaller bites, bites perhaps somewhat more conformable to the dignity of a free woman, a lady and a Tatrix. Still, when one is naked and in a trunk, and half starved, it is difficult to eat with dignity. For most practical purposes, as he had treated me, even though technically I might be the Tatrix of Corcyrus, I was a half-starved slave.

"I never thought to have the Tatrix of Corcyrus naked and in my trunk," he said.

"Can I breathe in here, Master?" I asked.

"There are air holes," he said. "You are not the first woman who has been in this trunk. To be sure, this is the first time it has ever held a Tatrix."

"There is a blanket in here," I said. "Thank you, Master."

"That is to keep the prettiness of its occupants from being bruised," he said. "The sweat and stink on it is from female slaves. It will serve for you as well, Lady Sheila. As it floored this trunk, serving as their kennel, so, too, it floors it now, when it serves as yours."

"As Master wishes," I said.

"Do you remember in my trial," he asked, "the matter of the hair, how it was discovered that I might inadvertently have sold some slave hair as that of free women?"

"Yes, Master," I said.

"In the morning," he said, "I am going to obtain some hair from a free woman."

"Master?" I asked.

"In the morning," he said, "you are going to be shorn."

"Master knows my secret," I said. "He has power over me. He may do with me what he wishes."

"And I shall," he said.

"Yes, Master," I said.

"Sleep tight in your kennel, Lady Sheila, lofty Tatrix of Corcyrus," he said. "It is where you are going to be spending quite a few nights."

I looked up at him.

"Pleasant dreams," said he, "Slut." Then he shut the heavy lid of the trunk. In another moment I heard the turning of keys in two heavy locks. Then he walked away.

With the trunk shut I could see the air holes. Some of them, tiny perforations, I could see through. I saw him extinguish the lamp. I then heard him lie down on the sleeping furs. I then lay back in the trunk, my legs pulled up. He had called me "Slut." Was it my fault if I had responded well to his instructions, if I had done what I was told! I wondered if I had done too well. Next time he would surely want at least that, and probably a good deal more. I smiled to myself. He had seemed surprised. I, too, had been surprised. My tongue, and lips and fingers, after a few Ehn, astounding me, had been ready and eager, and quick, subtle and delicate. I was grateful for his instruction, and I sought to improve upon it. Interestingly, I found that I was pleased to touch him. To be sure, I was crude and unrefined. I was uninformed in subtleties of technique and I had too simple a sense of pacings and rhythms, of when to make him, and me, wait, of when to be languorous, of when to be merciless. I was unaware, even, of the fuller possibilities of sound, of speaking to him, and of vocalizing my emotions and sensations in a variety of ways, adding a whole additional dimension to the totality of the experience. To be sure, some masters, at least at some times, desire to be served, in so far as the girl can, in absolute silence. "What has a slave to say?" they sometimes ask. Forced to perform, humiliatingly, under the ban of silence, enforcing as it does the male's total domination of her, can be very thrilling for a woman. Also, it helps her to keep clearly in mind that it is a mere animal who is serving. Also, I was unaware, more seriously, of many of the aesthetic and psychological aspects of what could be done. I did not make the most of the visual dimension, for example. Too, more naively, in my almost exclusive concern with touching, a common error, incidentally, with new slaves, I neglected by expressions and attitudes, to acknowledge and confess the deeper realities of our relationship, that I was, in the final analysis, his obedient captive. I was probably insufficiently alert, too, to the deeper ranges of his desires, of what he wanted, fully, from a woman. The master is to be served, of course, by the total slave. On the other hand, within my limitations, and within the ranges within which I was operating, I seemed to have an almost instinctual sense for what I was doing. I seemed to have a natural sense of timing and a capacity to anticipate, on many occasions, probably from subtle body cues, what he might desire, or what might please him. I discovered that I had talents I did not know I had, and I found myself thrilled to apply them. Though it was I, in the final analysis, who was in his total power, yet I found, to my gratification and astonishment, that I could turn him into a twisting, writhing slave under my touch. Then, angrily, he would seize me and throw me beneath him, making me helpless. I was then well reminded who, ultimately, was in command. I lay in the trunk, my legs pulled up. He had called me a "slut." I did not really mind this. Indeed, something in me relished it. I remembered how I had behaved in the furs. The expression was, perhaps, I thought, with a shudder, quite appropriate. Certainly he had not permitted me to relate to him, in the least, in the inhibitory modalities of dignity and respect; accordingly, I had found myself relating to him in a deep, real, primitive, sexual, natural, biological manner, in a manner certainly not that of a free woman, but rather of a slave or a slut. Doubtless this was supposed to be a part of his vengeance on me, but I, nonetheless, found it quite fulfilling. Something in me found it quite rewarding to relate to a man in this fashion. Too, I found it stimulating knowing that if I did not please him he might punish me.

I bit on the meat he had dropped into the trunk and I had grasped. I had not been punished. Rather, I had been rewarded.

I was pleased at how well I had done. I wondered if, as Publius, of the house of Kiomenes in Corcyrus, had thought, I might be a natural slave.

I had discovered, at least, that I was a slut. I did not know if, beyond that, I might also be a slave.

I chewed on the meat.

I was no longer a virgin now. My virginity had been taken from me by Speusippus of Turia. When he had grown angry and would seize me and throw me beneath him, making me helpless, he would then, without further ado, imperiously, with little regard for my feelings, have me. Well then was I, held helpless and penetrated, reminded who held the final power. In these assaults on me, of which there had been three, I was firmly and fixedly had. On the other hand, in spite of his clear conquest of me, and my physical and psychological acknowledgement of this fact, I did not feel as much as I had thought I might. Perhaps this was because he had taken too little time with my body. On the other hand, I was excited and aroused, just from serving him. For example, my body had received him swiftly and obediently. Too, I responded emotionally and psychologically, in a rather global sense, to what he had done to me. The last time, however, I had been frightened, for that time I had begun to sense, deep within me, terrifying me, something that began to hint at what might be the nature of a slave's yielding. I now lay in the trunk, in the darkness, helpless, finishing the piece of meat. No longer was I a virgin. I had now been opened, as the Goreans might say, for the uses of men. Speusippus of Turia had done it to me. I finished the meat. I was uneasy and restless in my small prison. I tried to thrust from my mind the memory of that insinuative, incipient sensation, that rudimentary physiological hint, that primitive, inchoate anticipation of what it might be possible for a woman to feel. I must never permit, I vowed, slave fires to be lit in my belly. I began to anticipate how inutterably piteous and helpless they might make a woman. I rubbed my thighs together. I did know I wanted to have more experiences of the sort I had had tonight. Speusippus of Turia was despicable. He was detestable. Why, then, I asked myself, was I hopeful that I had been pleasing to him, why did I find myself, undeniably, wanting to be pleasing to him? He was even going to shear me in the morning. I wondered why he was going to do that. Perhaps it had to do with his vengeance on me. Too, perhaps he was greedy, and was eager for even the little bit of money my hair might bring him. On the other hand, doubtless he did not want me to be recognized. Shearing would presumably help to prevent that. It might be a good idea to be sheared. At any rate, the decision was his, not mine. He knew my secret. He knew who I was. He, therefore, could do with me as he pleased. Similarly I, though a free woman, because of this power he held over me, must serve him as a slave. I clenched my fists, angrily, in the trunk. I was suddenly almost overcome with the humiliation of what was being done to me. I was not a slave! I was a free woman! Yet I must serve him as a slave! How rich, how glorious, was his vengeance on the Tatrix of Corcyrus. In the morning, he would even shear her like a slut!

I suddenly cried out with rage and struck at the insides of the trunk.

Speusippus, awakened, came over to the trunk, and, frightening me, beat on its top with something heavy, perhaps a staff or club.

"Be silent in there," he said, "or I will pour two inches of water through the air holes."

"Yes, Master!" I cried. "Forgive me, Master!" The sound of the object beating on the trunk had been fearfully magnified inside it. I had been almost overwhelmed by the sound. I had tried to cover my ears with my hands. My ears still hurt.

I now lay shuddering on the blanket in the bottom of the trunk. How absurd my outburst had been.

What a fool I was. Did I not know I was in his power? What did I need to convince myself of that, a marked thigh and a band of steel, which I could not remove, locked on my neck?

I lay there on the blanket. I lifted it, briefly, about my face and nose. I inhaled deeply. Yes, there was the smell of other bodies on it, bodies probably as small, and soft and curved as mine. But those bodies, I suspected, had worn brands and had had their necks encircled with collars. Slaves, doubtless, had lain here. Now it was my turn, that of the Tatrix of Corcyrus. I smoothed out the blanket and paid close attention to its texture and the feel of it against my cheek and body. The sweat and odors which I might leave in this cloth, I thought, would probably not differ much from those of my predecessors. I might be free but here, in this confinement, it would do me no good. Here I, the Tatrix of Corcyrus, doubtless to the amusement of Speusippus, would squirm, and sweat and stink no differently from a slave. Indeed, from the point of view of a new occupant, any lingering traces of my sojourn here would doubtless be interpreted as indicating the earlier tenancy of merely another slave, no different from others.

I felt the blanket lightly with my finger tips.

It excited me, somehow, that I lay where slaves had lain. I

touched my neck. I wondered what it would feel like to feel a collar there, and know that I belonged to someone.

I remembered serving Speusippus and then, quickly, I tried to force from my mind the memory of that incipient sensation which, in his third having of me, I had started to feel. I twisted in the trunk. I was restless. I moaned.

I was the Tatrix of Corcyrus!

And yet I had been worked like a slave, and used like a slave, and had served as a slave!

I had been degraded and humiliated. I was a free woman. I was not a slave! I was not a slave!

I remembered the sensation I had begun to feel. I moaned, from somewhere deep within me.

I touched the inside of the front side of the trunk with my finger tips. I had done this on a thought. Sure enough, as I had thought might be the case, I felt there the furrowing of fingernails. I then lay back in the trunk, on my back, my knees up. I had heard of such things. The marks did not seem to be connected with any desperate effort at escape. They seemed more like the helpless scratchings of a woman in frustration. One or more women, I suspected, at one or more times in the past, had crouched inside this trunk scratching at its interior wall, perhaps whining to be released, that they might serve the pleasure of Speusippus of Turia. How horrifying to be so much at the mercy of men, I thought.

I then, in terror, tried to force the memory of that rudimentary sensation, that merest hint of a sensation, from my mind.

"I am not a slave!" I told myself. "I am not a slave!"

I lay then again on my side on the blanket. I hoped that Speusippus was not displeased with me. I must try to please him better, I thought.

## 20

# THE STREAM; THE STONE

I knelt on a flat rock near the side of a small stream, pounding and rinsing a tunic. This one belonged to Speusippus. There were other girls, too, along the banks of the stream. It was a campsite about twenty pasangs west of the Viktel Aria. There were several wagons back from the stream, including that of Speusippus. Two slave girls, naked, stood downstream, splashing and pouring water on themselves, washing. I rinsed the tunic of Speusippus and took up another, one of several which were thrown there, beside me. He had, as at the previous campsite, volunteered my services as a laundress generally to men who did not have slaves with them. For my services he received small gratuities, such as tarsk bits and swigs of paga. It amused him putting me, the Tatrix of Corcyrus, to work in this fashion. He did not, interestingly enough, similarly make me available for more general services. Had he done so, I would have been obedient and dutiful.

"Your master is a beast, Lita," called a girl down the way, picking up her laundry. "You will never be finished."

"I will finish," I laughed, dipping and rinsing another tunic.

She then went her way.

I was pleased that we were no longer traveling south on the Viktel Aria. Last night I had begged Speusippus on my knees not to take me to Ar. He had seen how terrified I was to go to Ar. "I will not take you to Ar," he said. He had then permitted me to lick and kiss his feet in gratitude.

This morning we had turned west off the Viktel Aria.

Five days now I had been in the charge of Speusippus of Turia. Interestingly enough, he had not made intimate use of me since the first night in the shack. I had stayed rather close to him, when possible, particularly after my first full day in his power. I sometimes brushed against him, or touched him, seemingly inadvertently. Yesterday I had knelt behind him and licked at the back of his knee, then looked up at him. But he had only walked angrily away. "Remember that you are the Tatrix of Corcyrus, and not a slave," he had later said to me, when I was humbly serving him his supper. "Yes, Master," I had said, lowering my head, as a slave. But surely, except in the modalities of intimacy, except in the forcings from me of helpless yieldings, and such, he had dealt with me as a slave. He had even made me do slave exercises, that my body might be as shapely, firmed and vital as that of a slave. I had been treated as a slave, worked as a slave and even abused as a slave. He cuffed me when it pleased him. Once I had even seen him toying with a whip. I then redoubled my efforts to be pleasing to him. It must have amused him to see the Tatrix of Corcyrus so zealous to please him, so much in his power. But, except for the first night, he had not put me to his intimate pleasures. How fortunate that was for me, I thought. How lucky I am! Then, at night, I would sometimes moan and whimper, locked in the trunk, kept now in his wagon.

"Greetings, Lita," said a girl, coming with some laundry, to kneel down near me.

"Greetings, Tina," I said. She was a curvaceous little brute, owned by Lactantius, a teamster from Ar's Station. Recently they had been coming north from Ar; then they, too, had turned west. I had met her earlier, around supper time, back among the wagons. She, like some of the other slaves, initially, had been frightened of me. I was not branded and collared. Might I be free? I had assured them, however, lying well, I thought, that I, too, was only a slave. It was only that my Master had not yet seen fit to collar and brand me. Somewhat to my surprise they, looking at me, and once assured of my bond status, seemed to find no difficulty whatsoever in accepting the premise that I was indeed a slave. To them, slaves themselves, I looked like a slave. Looking at me, I realized, and somewhat to my consternation, they saw me easily, unquestioningly, naturally, and obviously, as a slave. "I knew even before I was told," had said one of the girls. "You could see it." How amusing I had later thought, irritatedly, that they could not tell the difference between me and them. Surely to a discerning eye it must be clear that I was free, and they bond. How stupid they were. But then, of course, they were only slaves.

"Your master is surely one of the ugliest men I have ever seen," said Tina.

"He is not so bad," I said, lifting a tunic, dripping, from the water.

"How your skin must crawl when he forces you to his intimate service," she said, dipping a tunic in the water.

"I do not think his whip would permit that," I said, wringing out the tunic.

"It must be horrifying to have to serve him," she said.

"No," I said. "Not really."

"He is not bad?" she asked.

"No," I said. Surely he had been strong with me, and had made me obey him well.

"I suppose there could be some pleasure in being forced to serve, and totally, such a twisted, despicable little brute," she said, "the domination of you, the disregard of your will and preferences, the reminding of your femaleness that it is enslaved, that it must do what it is told, that it must, no matter what, be pleasing, and perfectly so, to the master."

"He is not really that bad," I said, "really." I did not see any reason to tell her that I had, yesterday, knelt behind him and licked at the back of his knees, begging his touch. Similarly I did not see any reason to tell her that it had been denied to me.

"That is interesting," said Tina. "It is sometimes so hard to tell about a master."

"Yes," I said.

We then continued our work.

I wore the brief gray tunic which Speusippus had let me put on, and had then ordered me to remove, the first night in the shack. My ankles were chained; some ten inches of chain separated them; the chain was fastened on them by means of two padlocks. I was the only girl in camp, as far as I knew, who was shackled. During the day, when the wagon was moving, my ankles were not shackled. Then, however, he would chain my wrists, a chain running from them then to the back of the wagon. I would walk then, generally, behind the wagon, chained to it. The road was fairly well traveled. Today, lifting my chained wrists, I had waved to the girls in an open slave wagon. Individual neck chains went to a common chain in the wagon. Interestingly enough, they, too, were sheared. Sometimes I would sneak a ride in the back of the wagon. Then I no longer did this. He caught me once there and informed me that if I did this again I would be punished. Thereafter I rode in the back of the wagon only when I had received his permission, generally after begging for it. This permission, however, he was usually lenient in granting. It was almost as though he did not wish me to be exhausted. It was almost as though he wanted to keep me fresh, almost as though he intended to deliver me somewhere.

I wrung out another tunic and placed it behind me, on the rocks.

It was hot and I rubbed my hand back over my head, feeling there the short, bristly stubble of hair. As he had promised, he had, on the first morning of my captivity, sheared me.

"Lactantius," said Tina, "is merciless with me. In his chains he makes me kick and scream with pleasure."

"That is nice," I said.

"Does your master force slave yieldings from you?" she asked.

"He does with me what he pleases," I said. "He is the master. I am the slave." I was not even sure what slave yieldings were. I gathered they might be some peculiarly helpless form of orgasm.

I looked to the side, to a small pool of water, wherein I could see my face reflected. I again touched my head, feeling the short stubble of hair there. He had sheared me very closely, to within perhaps a quarter inch of my skin. In the days since the shearing the hair had not appreciably lengthened. I wondered if he would permit my hair to grow out, perhaps to cut it again in a few months, to add more of it to his stock, or if he would, perhaps for his amusement, or to keep my identity a better secret, keep me closely sheared. The decision, of course, was his. I was to him, in effect, as his slave.

I wondered if the shortness of my hair, the result of the shearing, made me less attractive to Speusippus. I wondered if that were why he had not snapped his fingers and commanded me to his pleasure.

"Am I ugly, Tina?" I asked.

"No," she said.

"My hair?" I asked.

"It will grow back," she said.

"Do you think any man could want me, as I am?" I asked.

"Surely you have seen the teamsters looking at your ass?" she said.

"No!" I said.

"You have a pretty ass," she said.

"Thank you," I said.

"You are very pretty as a whole," she said. "You have a curvaceous figure, though a little short, and a lovely face. Have no fear. You would make a nice armful for a man. You are a piece of well-curved slave meat. You are a tasty pudding."

"Thank you," I said. How scandalized I was to hear these things! I was not used to hearing myself spoken about in terms of the graphic simplicities often applied to slaves. To be sure, she did not know that I was not a slave. Tasty pudding, indeed! I wondered if I were a tasty pudding. Perhaps, I thought. I did know I was small and curvaceous, and could easily be picked up by men, and carried about, and, if they wished, overpowered and put to their purposes. Perhaps to them, small and helpless, and desirable, I did look like a tasty pudding. Thinking of myself in those terms made me feel weak, vulnerable and excited.

"Your master is not contenting you, is he?" asked Tina.

"No," I said.

"Have you displeased him?" she asked.

"I have tried not to," I said.

"Have you begged?" she asked.

"Yes," I said. Surely, in licking at him, as I had, I had begged for his touch. "But he has scorned me."

"Interesting," said Tina. "Are you so unskilled, so inert, so like a free woman that you are not even worth having?"

"I do not think so," I said.

"I do not understand it," she said. "Surely he wants you to become more of a slave and not less of a slave."

"That is perhaps it," I said, frightened. I recalled his words to me at supper yesterday evening. "Remember that you are the Tatrix of Corcyrus, and not a slave," he had said.

"What?" she asked.

"He may want to keep me more like a free woman," I said.

"Why would he want to do that?" she asked. "That would be stupid, since you are a slave."

"He has not branded me, or collared me," I pointed out.

That he had not done these things I had hitherto supposed was merely in accord with his avowed purposes of shaming and humiliating me, making me serve as a slave in spite of the fact that I was free. But now, I feared, these omissions might have a more complex motivation.

"If he does not want you," she said, "why does he not simply sell you?"

"He may want me," I whispered, "at least for a time."

"He does not seem eager to part with you," she said. "He even has your ankles chained."

"Yes," I said. I was being kept, I now realized, under an unusual security. During the day my wrists were usually chained, often even to the wagon. In the evening, at campsites, as I did now, I wore ankle chains. At night, my tunic removed, he would lock me in what served as my kennel, the trunk.

"Does he rent you out?" asked Tina. "Sometimes a man can get an offer on a girl that way."

"No," I whispered.

"The whole matter seems very puzzling," said Tina.

"Yes," I said.

I was suddenly becoming terrified. Speusippus, I feared, however absurdly, sensed that I might be a slave. He seemed concerned, then, apparently, that I not be permitted to enter too deeply into my slavery. But, why not? Most men certainly do not interfere with the natural growth, the progress and development of a woman in her bondage. Most men, at least of Gor, permit her to achieve this self-fulfillment; some of them, within certain latitudes of discipline, even permit her to proceed largely at her own pace, gradually coming to understand, incontrovertibly, that she, loving and obedient, has always been a slave to the core.

I was not a slave, of course! But, if I happened to be, why was Speusippus acting as he was? I doubted that he would deny me the collar out of spite. More likely he would put it on me and then try to make me regret I wore it. Too, if I were not a natural slave, was it not now time that he put me in a collar? I, a free woman, had been forced, to my humiliation and shame, to serve as though I might be a slave. Surely the next natural step in his vengeance would be to make me a legal slave and own me. Would it not be a splendid jest, now, to take Sheila, the Tatrix of Corcyrus, to the shop of a metal worker, to see her writhe and scream under the iron, to have her fitted with a collar and then lock it on her throat, to make her an actual slave? But he did not seem to have any intention of doing so. What fate, then, I wondered, might Speusippus of Turia have in mind for me?

I wrung out the last tunic, and rolled it up, and put it with the others. They could be unrolled and laid out to dry on the wagons.

"What is the news, Tina?" I asked.

"About what?" she asked.

"About anything," I said.

"There is not much," she said. "There is some fear for the Sa-Tarna crop, because of the great deal of rain. There is going to be a celebration in Ar because of the birthday of Marlenus, the Ubar there. Lactantius thinks that is important."

"Is there any news from the west?" I asked.

"The usual," she said.

"What is that?" I asked.

"You have heard about the escape of the Tatrix of Corcyrus?" she asked.

"No," I said.

"That is strange," she said. "It happened some days ago. There is a great search on for her."

"I did not know that," I said. "Where do they think she went?"

"No one knows," said Tina.

"Oh," I said.

"There is now a reward of a thousand gold pieces for her," she said.

"That is a great deal of money," I said. I felt sick.

"Tina," I said.

"Yes?" she said.

"Lactantius, your master, is from Ar's Station. What is he doing on this road?"

"He picked up freight in Ar," she said. "He is taking it west."

"Where?" I asked.

"To Argentum," she said. "What is wrong?"

"Nothing," I said. "What is he doing on this road?" I asked.

"What do you mean?" she asked. "He is doing exactly what he is supposed to be doing."

"What road is this?" I asked.

"It is the road to Argentum," she said.

I pretended to be dissatisfied with one or two of the tunics I had washed. I dallied by the stream until Tina had finished her work and returned to the vicinity of her master's wagon. Then, when no one was looking, I bent down and picked up a small, sharp stone from the edge of the stream. This I inserted in the hem of my slave tunic. Later I would hold it in my mouth, for the tunic would be taken from me before I was put in the trunk. The trunk, though sturdy, was not an iron or steel slave box. It was a trunk, made of wood, banded with iron.

## 21

# THE ROAD

I fled along the stone road, eastward, back toward the Viktel Aria.

The road was wet. The night was cloudy.

It had taken me two nights, with the sharp stone, to cut through the wood, under the blanket, in the trunk. I had begun by drawing deep, even scratches. The scratches had then, repeatedly, been deepened, slowly and carefully. I had worked only with great caution, and very silently, and even then only when I was assured that Speusippus was asleep. By day I hid the stone in the blanket, and the blanket itself covered the traces of my work. I rejoiced that Speusippus was not more fastidious about the conditions of my confinement. Yesterday morning, before dawn, the bottom of the trunk had been loosened and, rolling to one side, I could get my fingers beneath it. Tonight, a few Ahn ago, I had lifted it, inside the trunk. I had then, tipping and lifting the trunk, been able to slip between the two iron bands which reinforced its strength, bands which joined with the hardware of the two locks, making it impossible to cut or saw around the locks. I had then eased the trunk back into place, slipped from the wagon, sneaked from the camp, and run.

I was naked again, as I had been, in the camp of Miles of Argentum. I did not know where my slave tunic was, as, each night, Speusippus would put it somewhere after I had been locked in the trunk. There was no clothing of a free woman in the camp as far as I knew. It was a camp of free men and slaves.

I made my way eastward, gasping, and walking and running, on the Argentum road, back toward the Viktel Aria. I did not think they would expect me to keep to the road. Yet, of course, on it, I could make my best time. Too, I did not think they would expect me to retrace the route to the Viktel Aria. Not only would this bring me into areas of greater population concentrations but, too, it would take me closer to Ar. This would be almost as bad from my point of view, they would suppose, as moving toward Argentum itself. They would expect me, I supposed, to follow the stream, wading in it, and then, a few pasangs later, strike out northward. Speusippus would recall that I had, on my knees, begged him not to take me to Ar.

I hurried on.

An additional reason for keeping to the road was that I thought, on the hard, wet surface, it might be more difficult to follow my sign, if sleen were later used. Also, of course, my sign would be confused, or I hoped it would, with that of other travelers. To be sure, there were no sleen at the campsite and Speusippus might not be able to rent one for days. By that time, especially with the rains, it might be impossible, even for such fine, tenacious hunters as sleen, to follow my scent. Too, I did not think he would have anything that would be particularly useful for setting sleen on my trail. I had deliberately left the blanket in the trunk. It would bear not only my own scent but that of numerous other women as well. The tunic I had worn, too, had been worn by others, presumably slaves, before me. Also, in the evening I had washed it thoroughly and, not donning it, handed it humbly to Speusippus before I had entered the trunk, presumably to be locked helplessly in it.

It was becoming more cloudy. I felt a few drops of rain.

Speusippus might not even rent sleen. By the time he could do so, he would recognize, as a rational man, that the scent presumably would have faded. Too, he had little of practical value in giving such beasts the initial scent. Too, it is expensive to rent sleen, and Speusippus, who was a poor man, might even lack the means to do so. It is much more expensive, for example, to rent a sleen than a slave. Sleen are often rented by the Ahn. Slaves are commonly rented by the day or week. One of the greatest advantages I had, I thought, was that Steusippus, being an intelligent man, would presumably keep the secret of my identity. It would do his coin box little good if I fell to the chain of some burly huntsman from the foothills of the Voltai. Besides, who would believe that he had ever had the Tatrix of Corcyrus in his keeping? They would surely think him mad. If authorities should search for me, I was sure it would be only as the girl of Speusippus, a runaway slave named Lita.

It now began to rain more heavily. I welcomed the rain, hoping it would diminish and wash away the scent my body and bare feet might be leaving behind me.

There was another reason I was retracing our steps on the Argentum road. Yesterday I had seen another open slave wagon, a long, wide wagon much like I had seen a few days ago. It, too, had contained several girls, their individual neck chains strung to a common central chain, their hair cropped as insolently short as mine. The similarity of the two wagons and the chaining arrangements suggested that a single company was involved. I had made inquiries. These were girls of the sort sometimes referred to as female work slaves. It is a very low form of slave, indeed, perhaps the lowest. Seldom can they aspire even to the status of the kettle-and-mat girl. They do not bring high prices. They are usually sold in multi-item lots in cheap markets and are usually purchased to be used in such places as the public kitchens or laundries, and the mills. From these applications, they are sometimes referred to, naturally enough, as "kitchen girls," "laundry girls," "mill girls," and so on. These particular girls, it had been conjectured, had been obtained from markets in the north, where prices are often cheaper. They were now being brought south and east, probably, from their shearing, for work in the mills. It was my hope that I could make secret contact with these women, and obtain food, and perhaps advice, from them. I was naked, ignorant and illiterate. I was little better off than when I had escaped from the yard of the inn several days ago. Surely they would feed me, and be kind to me. Even though I was far superior to them, as I was free and they were mere slaves, it was my hope that they would be kind to me in my need. We shared a common sisterhood in the sense that we were all ultimately helpless women on a world where men had never relinquished their sovereignty.

Toward morning the rain stopped and I, fearful of discovery as it grew lighter, left the Argentum road.

## 22

# THE WAGON; CAUGHT!

"Please, do not make any noise," I whispered.

"Who is there!" said the woman, frightened. I heard the movement of a chain.

"Please be quiet," I whispered. "I will not hurt you."

"What is going on?" whispered another woman. I heard the movements of bodies, of chains.

"Be quiet, please," I said. I had crawled over the side of the slave wagon. I had lowered myself, in the darkness, to the interior. I felt the wood of the wagon bed, beneath a blanket, or blankets, beneath my knees. The wagon, unhitched, was drawn among some trees. Two tharlarion were tethered nearby. Also a few yards away there was a tent.

"Please be quiet," I whispered. I lowered myself to my belly in the wagon. I did not wish to risk my upper body being seen over the side of the wagon.

Although the wagon was normally open when on the road it was now, on this night on which it had rained off and on, rigged with a temporary, now-partially-rolled-up cover. The cover consisted of a tarpaulin sewn about long poles on two sides. This cover was placed over a frame which consisted of five poles; two of these poles, braced, crossed and tied together near the top, were at the front of the wagon; a similar pair was fixed at the back of the wagon; between these two pairs of poles there lay, across them, parallel to the long axis of the wagon, like a ridgepole, a fifth pole. The tarpaulin, then, was laid over this long pole and held in place by its own two poles, resting against the sloping sides of the crossed poles at the front and back of the wagon. The tarpaulin was rolled up and tied about its poles in such a way that there was a gap of about a yard between itself and the side of the wagon.

"Please," I begged. I lay on my stomach in the wagon. My body was wet; my feet were muddy.

"Who are you?" whispered a woman.

"I am one who is hungry, and in desperate need of help," I said.

"But we are naked slaves," said a woman.

"And we are chained," said another.

"Give me some food," I begged. "I must have food!" I had not eaten in more than twenty Ahn, indeed, since I had received a feeding from Speusippus, and a rather sparing one, on the evening preceding my escape. He had on the whole fed me intelligently, but seldom generously. It seemed to be his intention, through diet and exercise, in so far as he could, to see to it that my body became as shapely as that of a pleasure slave.

"There is no food in the wagon," said a woman.

I moaned in misery.

"Our food is measured out to us in small, exact quantities," said a woman, "and then we must, under supervision, consume it entirely."

"There must be food," I said.

"There is food within the tent," said a woman, "but the drivers are there, and it is kept locked up."

"You must help me," I said. "I am as sheared as you."

"What can we do?" asked a woman.

"You had best flee," said another.

"I do not know what to do, or where to go," I sobbed.

"Who are you?" asked a woman.

"I am a free woman," I said.

I heard a reaction, a shrinking back in the chains.

"Do not be afraid," I said. "I will not hurt you. Too, do not kneel, please."

"You are not a free woman," said a woman.

"You are a runaway slave," said another.

"If you were a free woman," said another, "you would not come to slaves. You would go to free persons!"

"I am hungry and miserable," I said. "I need help. I do not care whether you think I am slave or free."

"She is not branded, I do not think," said a woman. I

pulled back. I felt hands checking my left and right thighs, the two most common brand sites for a Gorean slave.

"No, I do not think so," said another woman, apprehensively.

"Some men do not brand their slaves," said a woman.

"They are fools," said another.

"Yes," said another.

"But she is sheared," said another, feeling my head.

"She must then be a slave," said another.

"Some free women have themselves sheared, to sell their hair," said another.

"I am a free woman," I sobbed.

"She is naked," said another woman.

"She doesn't even have a string on her belly," said another. I pulled back, angrily, from them.

"Free women do not run about the countryside naked, my dear," said another woman.

"Nonetheless," I said, "I am a free woman!"

"Where are your clothes?" asked a woman.

"A man captured me," I said. "He took my clothes! He sheared my hair, too, for money!"

"Why didn't he keep you?" asked a woman.

"She must be ugly," said one of the women.

"I am not ugly!" I said.

"Then why didn't he keep you?" asked the woman.

"I don't know!" I said.

"You are a slave," said a woman.

"No!" I said.

"Liar!" said another.

"I am a free woman," I sobbed. "I am a free woman!"

"If you are a free woman, and are not from this area," said one of the slaves, "I think you should flee. It is not safe for you here."

"I do not understand," I said.

"Surely it would not do for you to be caught here," she said.

"No!" I said, frightened.

"Then I think you should flee, now, while there is still time."

"Where can I go?" I asked. "Where can I run?"

"Anywhere," said a woman. "But hurry!"

"Why?" I asked.

"It is nearly time for slave check," said a woman.

"Slave check?" I asked.

"Yes," she said.

"It is too late!" whispered a woman.

I looked wildly about. Not feet away I saw a lantern approaching the back of the wagon. I quickly lay down, with the others, huddled against them, as if asleep.

I heard the wagon gate being lowered in the back. It swung down on its hinges, striking against the wagon. I heard the boards of the wagon bed creak as they were subjected to additional weight. I sensed the light of the lantern in the wagon, under the tentlike tarpaulin, illuminating bodies.

I lay very still.

"Well," said a voice, "what have we here?" I felt a foot kick me.

I turned about, blinking up into the light of the lantern, terrified.

"You have been caught, Slave!" said a woman near me, elatedly.

## 23

# THE CHAIN

"On your back," said the man, "and put your hands, palms up, where I can see them."

I did so.

"Now cross your wrists, in front of you," he said.

I did this and he, with one hand, grasped them both. In this grip I was held as helplessly as a child. He pulled me to my knees and, lifting the lantern, examined where I had lain.

He then put me again to my back and released my hands.

"I am unarmed," I said. "I have no weapons. I am utterly defenseless. Please be kind to me."

"Durbar!" he called. He then hung the lantern from a hook on the ridgepole, beneath the damp, brown tarpaulin.

"I am not what you think," I assured him. "I am a free woman. I am not a slave. I am neither collared, as you can see, nor branded, as you may easily determine."

"You are a free woman?" he asked skeptically.

"Yes," I said. "And I am desperately in need of help. It is my hope that you will be kind to me, giving me food and clothing, and money and guidance, so that I may return to my home in Lydius. That is on the Laurius river. The town Laura is east of it."

"Is Lydius north or south of Kassau?" he asked.

"North," I said.

"No," he said. "South."

There was laughter from the women.

"Your accent," he said, "suggests that you might be from Tabor."

"Yes!" I said, seizing on this. "I am. My parents had arranged an unwanted companionship for me. I fled. I now want to go somewhere else."

"Tabor is far away," he said. "Did you come all this way on foot?"

"Yes!" I said.

"That is amazing," he said, "for Tabor is an island."

Tears sprang to my eyes. The women in the wagon laughed.

"What is going on?" asked a fellow coming up to the wagon, fastening a belt of accouterments about himself.

"See what we have here," said the first fellow.

"Ah!" he said.

"She claims to be a free woman," said the first fellow.

"Of course," said the second.

"A man captured me," I said. "He took my clothes! He sheared my hair, for money!"

"If you are a free woman," said the second man, he, I gathered, who was Durbar, "what are you doing here, crawling about with slaves?"

"I was afraid," I said.

"If you are truly a free woman," said the first man, "what were you afraid of?"

"You are right," I said. "I am a free woman. I should not have been afraid."

The two men laughed, and the chained women, as well. I looked about, at them, from face to face. I saw their amusement. I saw the collars and chains on their necks. How foolish I felt. I had again been tricked. Obviously, in a situation like this, a free woman might have a great deal to fear.

"I am hungry," I said. "I am desperately hungry. I am starving. Please give me something to eat."

"Bring her something to eat," said the first man to him called Durbar, "something appropriate."

Durbar left. In a few moments he returned with a small wooden bowl filled with dried, precooked meal. He poured some water into this.

I was then handed the bowl.

Some of the women laughed.

"Mix it with your fingers," said the first man. Then he turned to Durbar. "Look about the camp," he said. "See if there are any more skulking about."

"I am alone," I told them.

But Durbar went to check.

I, mixing the water with the precooked meal, formed a sort of cold porridge or gruel. I then, with my fingers, and putting the bowl even to my lips, fell eagerly upon that thick, bland, moist substance.

By the time Durbar had returned I had finished, even to the desperate wiping and licking of the bowl, that I might secure every last particle of that simple, precious, vitalizing provender.

"You eat slave gruel well," said the first men. There was laughter from the chained women.

I put down my head. The bowl was taken from me. So that was slave gruel, I thought. I knew that it, with its various supplements, was extremely nourishing. It had been designed for the feeding of slaves, to keep them healthy, sleek and trim. On the other hand, although I had devoured it eagerly, I could see where a slave who was not starving might, after a time, desperately strive to improve her services to the master, that he might see fit, in his kindness, to grant her at least the scraps of a more customary diet.

"Do you still claim to be a free woman?" asked the first man.

"Yes," I said.

"You have the body of a slave," he said.

"It is not my fault," I said, "that I have the body of a slave."

"Can you read?" he asked.

"No," I said.

"What is your name?" he asked.

I thought wildly for a moment. Then I said, "Tiffany, Lady Tiffany!"

"What sort of name is that?" he asked.

"I do not know," I said.

"It is an unusual name," he said.

"Maybe it is a barbarian name," suggested Durbar.

"Are you a barbarian?" asked the first man.

"Maybe," I said. I saw scorn in the faces of several of the chained women.

"Look," said the first man, taking me by the upper left arm, and turning it to the light. "The barbarian brand."

I did not see how I could explain this vaccination mark to the men without making clear that my origin was not Gorean. The vaccination was in connection with a disease which, too, as far as I knew, did not even exist on Gor.

"Get on your feet, here by the lantern," said the first man. "And open your mouth, widely."

I complied.

"Durbar, come up here," said the first man. He was joined by his fellow. "Back there, see?" he asked Durbar.

"Yes," said Durbar.

As a child I had had some fillings in the molar area, on the lower left side.

"They are common in barbarians," said the first man.

"Yes," said Durbar. "But, those of the caste of physicians can do such things. I have seen them in some Gorean girls."

"That is true," admitted the first man.

These fellows must also know that doubtless such things might be found occasionally in the mouths of some Gorean men. On the other hand, of course, they would not have been likely to have seen them there. They would have seen them, presumably, only in the mouths of girls, slaves. One of the things that a master commonly checks in a female he is considering buying is the number and condition of her teeth.

"Lie back down," said the first man, "on your back, as before."

I did so.

"Are you a barbarian?" he asked.

"Yes," I said. I did not see how I could, in the light of the facts, hope to conceal this from them.

Several of the women laughed. Barbarians, I gathered, were to be held in contempt. The men, however, I noted, somewhat to my uneasiness, did not seem to be viewing me with contempt. They were viewing me, rather, with definite interest. I did not understand clearly, at that time, the rather special position on Gor occupied by barbarian slaves. Servile and low, and trained to sensuous wonders, they often brought high prices; to many Gorean men they seemed ideal objects, or among such, on which to slake their most primitive and brutal sexual lusts.

"You speak the language very well," said the first man. "I could not even place your accent. Indeed, I was not even certain it was barbarian."

"It is," I said. "Thank you."

As I lay at their feet, on the blanket, on the boards of the slave wagon, they were looking down at me. I was aware that it was very much as a female that I was being looked at.

"What are you going to do with me?" I asked.

The first man shrugged. "Turn you over to the authorities," he said.

"Please do not do so," I begged. "Please!"

They continued to look at me.

"Please," I begged. "Please, please," I whimpered. I lifted my body, piteously, to them.

"Slut!" hissed one of the chained slaves.

"Please," I whimpered. "Please!"

"We'll give you a trial," said the first man. "You first, Durbar."

I reached up for him as he crouched down, swiftly, between my legs. Durbar was not first in the camp, I realized. He would warm me for the use of the other. It was he whom I must especially please.

A few Ehn later, in the arms of the leader, the first driver, I suddenly cried out with fear and surprise. It had been my intention to be especially pleasing to him but, suddenly, it seemed as though I were being taken away from myself. "No!" I said, suddenly. "Please, stop!" But I clutched him desperately. "Stop!" I begged. "Oh, stop!" I gritted my teeth. My fingernails cut into his arm and back. "Slut!" hissed one of the slaves. "Slut!"

"The feelings!" I cried. "The feelings! Please, stop!" But the brute laughed, and did not stop.

"I cannot stand it!" I cried.

But still the beast did not desist!

The sensation that Speusippus had begun to induce in me long ago, that which had struck such terror into me, now, seemingly from somewhere deep in my belly, began to emerge irresistibly. I had not known what it would be like in its larger effect, let alone its resolution.

"No!" I cried.

And then I yielded to him.

"Slut, slut, slut!" hissed one of the slaves.

I then clutched him, startled and astounded. I could hardly believe what I had felt. I held tightly to him. "Please do not let me go," I begged. "Hold me, if only for a moment! Hold me! Hold me, please!"

"What a slut she is," said a woman.

"Yes," said another.

I held tightly to the man. I tried to cope with my feelings and understandings. It had been my intention merely to be very pleasing to him; I had desired, really, to do little but give him great pleasure. Then something had happened. It seemed somehow as though he had suddenly taken me away from myself. He had taken command of me. He had suddenly begun to make me move and respond according to his will, not mine. He had literally given me no choice. He had forced my yielding. He had made me come to him and rather, I was afraid, like a slave. I was a bit disappointed in one way. It was I who was in the position of the slave. I had wanted to serve him, to please him, to bring him pleasure. Instead I myself had been forced to feel pleasure and even, choiceless, to yield.

"Did I please you?" I asked.

"Yes," he said. I licked and kissed at his shoulder in gratitude. Even though he had given me little opportunity to please him he had still, apparently, found me pleasing. Women, I supposed, might be found pleasing by men in many ways. Perhaps that is one way for a woman to be pleasing, I thought, that the man does with her what he wishes, that he chooses, as he wishes, to please himself with her.

I kissed him, helplessly. He drew back a bit from me. I saw a chain snapped onto the common chain of the women. At the end of this shorter chain there was an open collar. It was then put about my neck and snapped shut. I touched it. I was now on the same chain with the other women.

He stood up. I lay at his feet, on the floor of the slave wagon, on the blanket, chained. I had been well had. I did not know what he would do with me now. Perhaps it would amuse him to turn me over to the authorities now. I did not know.

"Do you still claim to be a free woman, Tiffany?" he asked.

"Why?" I asked.

"Because you have the responses and reflexes of a slave," he said.

"I claim nothing," I said, vanquished and chained.

"Are you really free?" he asked.

"It doesn't matter now, does it?" I asked.

"Not at all," he said.

"What do you think?" I asked him.

"I think you are a slave," he said.

"I am not branded and collared," I reminded him, "except, of course, for the holding-chain collar."

"We will do something about that," he said, "outside of Ar."

I looked at him, startled. Quickly I scrambled to my knees before him, the palms of my hands on the floor of the wagon.

"Accustom yourself to calling free men 'Master' and free women 'Mistress,' " he said.

"Yes, Master!" I said.

"And you are low girl here," he said, "so you will address your chain sisters as 'Mistress' as well."

"Yes, Master!" I cried.

"You are a mill girl now, Tiffany," he said.

"Yes, Master! Thank you, Master!" I sobbed, and put down my head, covering his feet with kisses of gratitude.

He then withdrew, taking the lantern with him. Durbar accompanied him.

I then lay down with my chain sisters. I tried to gather my thoughts. I had been captured, and this terrified me. Furthermore I now could entertain few realistic thoughts of escape. I did not think that any mysterious men would suddenly appear to free me, as at the camp of Miles of Argentum. Similarly these men seemed to be professionals in the handling of women. I did not think they, like Speusippus, for example, would be likely to use a wooden trunk for a slave kennel. Furthermore I knew the security in the mills, behind those high, gray walls, was for most practical purposes absolute. Similarly, there presumably I would be branded, collared and, if permitted clothing, put in distinctive garb. Thus, even if one did manage to get beyond the walls, one would presumably be apprehended swiftly and returned to the mill masters. Similarly the mills had their own sleen, both for patrolling the yard at night and, if need be, trailing slaves. No, girls did not escape from the mills. Too, I was horrified at the thought of going to the mills, for they were one of the lowest and hardest slaveries on Gor. That would be the end of Tiffany Collins, I feared, a slave in a Gorean mill. On the other hand I had, honestly, and joyfully, kissed at the driver's feet for the mercy shown to me. Had he turned me over to the authorities I would doubtless have eventually been returned to Speusippus as his strayed Lita, and then conveyed by him, probably in chains, to Argentum, there presumably to be commended to the attentions of the impaling spear. As it was, in the mill, in Ar, I should be hidden and safe. There, though a slave, I would be concealed, fed and protected. I did not think anyone would think of looking in a mill for the Tatrix of Corcyrus, and certainly not one in Ar. My feelings were thus mixed in this matter. I was relieved, too, in a way, of course, that I now no longer needed fear capture. It had happened to me. I must now abide its consequences. Too, no longer now need I forage for food and shelter as an ignorant, naked fugitive, often fearful, miserable, cold and hungry. I supposed it had been only a matter of time until someone had caught me. Perhaps it was just as well that it had happened as it did.

But whatever might be the pros and cons of this matter they were now mostly academic. I had again, as a matter of fact, fallen into the power of men. I lay in a slave wagon. Their chain was on my neck.

I wondered, too, on what sort of creature it was that they had their chain.

I did not think that I was the same Tiffany Collins as I had been earlier.

The second fellow who had had me, the leader of the two drivers, had taught me much. I now knew, to some extent, what could be done to me. I did not think I was likely to forget it. I could be forced to yield myself to a man as a slave. This made me feel very helpless. Men are, I supposed, the masters. But, too, I remembered clearly that wild, surging, overwhelming sensation I had felt. I certainly, desperately, wanted to feel that again. Too, I sensed, it frightening me somewhat, but also exciting and intriguing me almost to the point of madness, that behind that sensation there might be others, indeed, that there might lie beyond that sensation almost indefinite vistas of kindred emotions and feelings. Who, I wondered, has plumbed the depths of feelings' oceans or has successfully mapped the countries of love? I found that I, and this frightened me, wanted to submit to men and yield to them as a slave. This was not a simple matter of sentience, incidentally, but involved an entire matrix of feeling, thought and emotion. I wanted to love and serve, to be fully pleasing not merely in a sexual manner but in all ways, to ask nothing and give all. But, too, it must be admitted that powerful physical feelings were also involved. I bit at the blanket and squirmed.

"Lie still," said a woman.

"Yes, Mistress," I said. "Forgive me, Mistress."

I must not let them make me a slave, I thought. I must fight these feelings, these sensations. I must try to be more like a free woman, I told myself. I must try to be inert and cold.

But what chance will I have, I asked myself, if I am branded and they put a collar on my neck, and I am subject to the whip, and to the uncompromising disciplines of Gorean masters?

I must not permit them to light slave fires in my belly, I thought.

But what can I do if they should simply choose to do so, I thought. Then they would be lit, and that would be all there was to it, I told myself. Then, Tiffany, poor girl, you would be a slave for certain. "You are already a slave for certain, Tiffany, and you know it," a voice seemed to say from within me, that voice which in the past had seemed to speak to me, too, though usually in the quarters of the Tatrix, as when it had ordered me, and I had complied, to kiss a whip or the slave ring. "Perhaps," I said to the voice, to myself.

It was near dawn now. The wagon would proceed east on the Argentum road, reach the Viktel Aria, and turn south. Then, in time, it would arrive in Ar. Soon I would be enslaved, legally. I would be, totally, legally, a slave on Gor.

I found myself looking forward to the collar and the brand. They were now unavoidable. I would have no choice in the matter. They would simply be put on me. I hoped I would look well in my collar. I hoped I would look well in my brand. Most women are stunning in them, and I did not think I would be different. I wondered if I were truly a slave.

I wondered if the collar and brand belonged on me. "Perhaps," I thought. I hoped it would not hurt too much to be branded. It was the mark that stayed, of course, not the pain.

"You are awake," whispered a woman to me.

"Yes, Mistress," I said.

"You may be pretty," she said, "and the men may like you, but do not think that you are better than us."

"No, Mistress," I said.

"You are a little slut," she said.

"Yes, Mistress," I said.

"And you are going to be a work slave, too, my dear," she said.

"Yes, Mistress," I said.

"Now go to sleep, barbarian slut," she said.

"I will try, Mistress," I said.

In a moment or two, suddenly recalling the wild sensations the driver had induced in me, I inadvertently moaned and moved.

"Be quiet!" said the woman.

"Yes, Mistress," I said. "I am sorry, Mistress!"

Then I lay there frightened, chained, on the blanket, on the boards of the wagon bed, under the overhead tarpaulin. I turned and grasped the blanket. I bit at it. My thighs moved.

I was afraid.

I feared that already slave fires had been lit in my belly.

# 24

# THE MILL

I stood in a long line, single-file, of some twenty girls. We were all naked. We were in the yard of one of the linen mills of Mintar, of Ar.

I heard the second of the two heavy gates close behind us. I looked back, and about me, across the yard, at the high walls, with their guard stations.

"Do not even think of escape, Tiffany," said a girl behind me, Emily.

"There is only one way out of here," said another girl, behind her, "and that is to please your way out."

Almost any woman, I supposed, could become pleasing. And even women who, objectively, seemed rather plain, I knew, as their attitudes changed, and as they became submissive, and yielding to their femininity, in their deepest emotions, could become beautiful. Still, of course, in a mill, few would know this. Such a woman, I supposed, aching for a man's touch, might be kept indefinitely in the mill, working her long hours of tiring labor, her left ankle chained to the loom. The mills, incidentally, like certain other low slaveries, such as those of the fields, the kitchens and laundries, serve an almost penal function on Gor. For example, a free woman, sentenced to slavery for, say, crimes or debts, may find herself, once enslaved, by direction of the court, sold for a pittance into such a slavery. Such slaveries also provide a place to utilize women who are thought to be good for little else. Most women, after a short time in such a slavery, strive to convince masters of their fuller potentialities for service and pleasure. If the woman prefers to remain in such a slavery, of course, that, too, is found acceptable by the masters.

"But that, too, is dangerous," said another girl, "for if you are too pleasing, the whip masters will hide you and keep you for themselves."

"You are all sluts," said a large, ugly woman, Luta, a few spaces back.

A whip cracked, and we all jumped, frightened. We were naked. We did not want to feel it. "No talking in line," said a man. We were then silent. Luta need not have spoken as loudly as she had. I do not think the man would have minded it if we had spoken quietly among ourselves.

I was afraid of Luta. She was large and strong, and I could tell she did not like me.

"Next," said a man at a table, and we moved up one space.

Only two of the girls in this line had been in the slave wagon on the Argentum road with me, Emily and Luta. Though Emily bore an Earth-girl name she was Gorean. On Gor Earth-girl names are commonly used as slave names. If you have an Earth-girl name it is probably, somewhere on Gor, being used as a slave name. Similarly, if you were to go to Gor and give that to them as your name they would assume immediately that you, too, bearing such a name, were a slave. And, indeed, if you were taken to Gor, I suppose you would be.

"Next," said the man at the table. We moved up another space.

I was not now collared. It had been removed from me a few Ehn ago, before I had been assigned to this line. I had worn it for only a few Ahn. Outside of Ar we had stopped at the office and holding area of a man associated with the various enterprises of Mintar, including his mills. There we were to be divided up and, with others, transferred to closed slave wagons. One does not usually take an open slave wagon on the streets of Ar, in deference to the sensibilities of free women. While others were in the holding area I was taken by Tenrak, which was, as I had later learned, the name of the leader of the two drivers, to the shop of a metal worker. There something was done to me. Then I was returned to the holding area, now a slave. At the holding area I was put in a transfer collar. The others were already in theirs. These collars were color coded for our destinations, some girls being delivered to one place and some to another. There is an ordinance in Ar, incidentally, that all female slaves must wear some visible token of bondage. This is commonly a collar. Sometimes, too, however, it is a bracelet or anklet. This was the first time I had ever ridden in a common slave wagon. My ankles were shackled about the central bar. The girls were shackled on the bar in the order of the drivers' delivery schedule, the first girls to be delivered being shackled closest to the wagon gate, and so on. Our wagon was checked at the great gate of Ar. A guardsman climbed into the back of the wagon, crouching down, doing this work. I, naked, in the colored-coded collar, my ankles chained, sheared, attracted no undue attention. I did cry out, however, for the guardsman, in leaving, touched me aggressively, and intimately. I recoiled, wildly, frightened, trying to cover myself. But he was then gone. I looked after him, shuddering. I was horrified. He had been so bold! But then, of course, I was only a slave. I saw Luta looking at me, with hatred. I dared not meet her eyes, and looked down. In a moment the wagon was passing through the great gate at Ar.

"Next," said the man at the table.

I then stood before the table, naked.

"Thigh," he said.

I turned sideways, so that he might see my left thigh.

"Common Kajira mark," he said, and made an entry on a sheet. "Face me, Girl," he said.

I did.

"Arrived sheared," he said, and made another entry. "What is your name?" he asked.

"Whatever Master wishes," I said.

"What have you been called?" he asked. "Quick!"

"I have been called Tiffany," I said.

"You are now 'Tiffany,' " he said.

"Yes, Master," I said. He wrote something down, presumably the name. He seemed to have heard it before, unlike the drivers. Some other "Tiffany" had perhaps, at some earlier time, stood where I stood. I also realized that I had now been named. I had lost the name "Tiffany Collins" a few Ahn ago, when I had been marked, when I had become slave. That name was gone, as soon as the iron, hissing, curling smoke, had been lifted from my flesh. A free person had been locked in the branding rack. A mere animal was released from it. The name "Tiffany" had now been put on me as a mere slave name, a name which might be removed or changed at the whim of masters. I wore the name "Tiffany" now as Susan had worn the name "Susan," now merely as a named animal, merely by the will and decision of masters.

"Have you had experience in a mill, Tiffany?" he asked.

"No, Master," I said.

"Come around to the side of the table and kneel here," he said. I did so. He then bent over and, cupping his left hand under my left breast, held it steady and, with a grease pencil, across it, above the nipple, inscribed four characters. "That is your mill number, Tiffany," he said, "four thousand and seventy-three."

"Yes, Master," I said.

"Now, go there," he said, indicating another table, several yards away, near the wall.

"Yes, Master," I said. Tenrak and Durbar, at the office of the man of Mintar, outside the gate, had received ten copper tarsks for me. This did not seem to me much but it was, of course, enough to give them each five nights of pleasure in a paga tavern. I recalled that Drusus Rencius had thought I might go for something between fifteen and twenty tarsks. I had gone for only ten. On the other hand it had not been an open sale. Too, of course, I was shorn and being considered in terms of utilization in the mills. Some girls, Tenrak had assured me, go for as little as five copper tarsks. Ten copper tarsks, he assured me, was a good price for a mill girl.

I now stood before a man near the wall. Behind him was a table, on which there were, aligned, several collars, all seemingly identical in appearance and design. He had an aide with him.

The man looked at my left breast, reading the characters written there.

"Four-zero-seven-three," he said. He was then handed a collar, the next in a series of diminishing rows.

"Name?" he asked.

"Tiffany, if it pleases Master," I said.

"Can you read?" he asked.

"No, Master," I said.

He then showed me the collar, indicating the engraving on it. "This is a company collar," he said. "It says, 'I belong to Mintar of Ar. I work in Mill 7. My number is four-zero-seven-three.' "

"Yes, Master," I said. The collars would differ, then, only in the Girl Numbers.

"Lift your chin, Tiffany," he said.

I did so, and the collar was placed about my neck and snapped shut. The first collar I had worn had been a color-coded transfer collar, put on me at the holding area outside the gate, probably primarily to comply with the ordinance that female slaves in Ar must wear a visible token of their bondage; otherwise we might simply have had our destinations written on our bodies. This was my first owner collar. The laws of Ar, incidentally, do not require a similar visible token of bondage on the bodies of male slaves, or even any distinctive type of garments. The historical explanation of this is that it was originally intended to make it difficult for male slaves to make contact with one another and to keep them from understanding how numerous they might be. On the other hand, male slaves are not numerous, at least within the cities, as opposed to the great farms or the quarries, and they are, in fact, usually collared. Some, however, depending on the whim of the master or mistress, may wear a distinctive anklet or bracelet. A consequence of this ordinance from the point of view of a female slave is that she cannot now even permit herself to be taken for a free woman by accident; her bondage is always manifest; it is helpful from the man's point of view, too; he always knows the status of the woman to whom he is relating; one relates to free women and slaves quite differently, or course; one treats a free woman with honor and respect; one treats a slave, commonly, with condescension and authority.

"Kneel and kiss the whip of Mintar," he said. He took a whip from the table and held it before me. "Again and again," he said, "tenderly, lingeringly."

I did so. I trembled, thrilled, forced to kiss a man's whip, and in the intimate manner of a slave. I supposed that I would never see the man whose whip I was kissing.

"What is your name?" he asked.

"Tiffany," I said.

"In what mill do you work?"

"Mill 7."

"What is your girl number?"

"4073," I said.

"Whose collar do you wear?"

"The collar of Mintar of Ar."

"Who owns you?"

"Mintar of Ar."

"Who do you love?"

"Mintar of Ar."

"Welcome to Mill 7, Tiffany," he said.

"Thank you, Master," I said.

He then replaced the whip on the table and handed me, from a basket, two tunics. They were folded, and washed, and brown. "Thank you, Master," I said. I held them close to me. I would later discover that they were rather common slave tunics, brief, with no nether closure. Too, they were sleeveless, slit at the sides, and with a plunging neckline. On the front of the left shoulder there was a design, in white and yellow, bearing what I would later learn was an inscribed "Mu." This was a design, I would later learn, which was common to many of the different enterprises of Mintar. "Mu" is the first letter of the name Mintar. White and yellow, or white and gold, are the colors of the merchants. The tunic had nothing specific to the mills, of Mill 7. Such a tunic might have been worn by girls laboring or serving in almost any of his holdings. It was thus, in a broad sense, a company tunic. I wondered how many girls Mintar owned, or were owned by the enterprises of Mintar.

"Go now, over there," he said, pointing, "and get in that

line, where you see that small yellow flag. You will be in the chain of Borkon. He will be your whip master."

"Yes, Master," I said. Borkon, I realized, whoever he was, was he whom I must now strive to please. "Is that all, Master?"

"Yes," he said. "Did you expect to be intricately measured, to be toe-printed, and such? You are not a high slave. You are a low slave, a mill girl."

"Yes, Master," I said. "Forgive me, Master." I then leapt up and ran to stand in the indicated line. In a few Ehn I was joined there by Emily and Luta. The other girls were being sent to other lines.

In a few Ehn more we were approached by a short, muscular man in a half tunic. He came walking towards us, across the yard. He had emerged from one of the mill buildings. His arms were extremely thick. There was a whip at his belt.

When he stopped near us, we knelt, a common behavior for slave girls in the presence of a free man.

"Stand," he said.

We stood. We straightened our bodies. He walked about us, slowly.

"So," he said, "it is the usual collection of she-urts and she-tarsks. Still, I see at least two of some interest. What is your name?"

"Tiffany, Master," I said, frightened.

"We are going to get on well, aren't we, Tiffany?" he asked.

"Yes, Master," I said, shuddering. He felt me.

"What is your name?" he asked.

"Emily," said the girl behind me.

"We are going to get on well, aren't we, Emily?" he asked.

"Yes, Master!" she said.

He then stepped back from us. "You are slaves," he said. "I am Borkon, your whip master. Within these walls you will be to me as my own slaves, in all ways. Is that understood?"

"Yes, Master," murmured several of the girls.

"Louder," he said, "all of you!"

"Yes, Master!" we shouted.

"You will work, eat, drink, juice, sleep, dream and excrete upon my command," he said.

"Yes, Master!" we said.

"If any of you retain any pride or courage," he said, "I

will remove it from you. It will get in the way of your being a good slave. Do any of you retain any pride or courage?"

"No, Master!" we cried.

"I do," said Luta.

"Step forth, and kneel," he said.

Luta obeyed. Although she was a large, strong woman and could have beaten any of us, smaller, weaker women, she looked small, and suddenly timid, kneeling before Borkon.

"What is your name?" he asked.

"Luta, Master," she said.

"How long have you been a slave, Luta?" he asked, removing the whip from his belt.

"A week, Master," she said.

"It is amazing that a woman such as you has survived this long," he said. "I would have thought you would have been slain by now."

"Master?" she faltered.

"On all fours," he said.

She obeyed.

He then lashed her, and she, in a moment, sobbing and gasping, disbelief in her eyes, was on her belly in the yard, a whipped slave.

"Are you not supposed to be on all fours?" he asked.

She struggled, sobbing, to this position.

"I am authorized, if I wish," he said, "to kill you, or have you killed."

She shuddered.

"I do not find you particularly pleasing," he said. "I am considering whether or not to have you fed to sleen this evening."

"Master?" she asked.

"You are a slave," he said. "You will serve and yield, or die. I will let you make the decision."

"Master?" she asked, frightened.

"The decision is yours," he said. "Choose as you will. It makes no difference to me, one way or the other."

"Please, Master!" she cried.

"Do you choose to serve and yield, or die?" he asked. "I give you ten Ihn in which to make your decision. One! Two! Three!"

"I will serve and yield!" she cried.

"Speak more clearly," he said.

"I choose to serve and yield!" she wept.

"And without reservation?" he asked.

"And without reservation!" she said.

"Do you desire to serve and yield, and with no reservations whatsoever?" he asked.

"Yes," she said, "I desire to serve and yield and with no reservations whatsoever!"

"And do you beg to serve and yield, and with no reservations whatsoever?" he asked.

"Yes, yes," she echoed. "I beg to serve and yield, and with no reservations whatsoever!"

"You may now kiss my feet," he said.

Luta, desperately, humbly, fearfully, kissed his feet.

"More," he said.

"Yes, Master," she said.

"Do you now have any pride?" he asked.

"No, Master," she said.

"Do you now have any courage?" he asked.

"No, Master," she said.

"Kiss the whip," he said, "and as a slave."

Luta did so, fearfully.

"Return now to your place," he said.

"Yes, Master," she said and, rising up, hurried to her place.

"We are all going to be pleasing, and meet our work quotas, aren't we?" inquired Borkon.

"Yes, Master!" we said, including Luta.

He then lifted his whip to the lips of the first girl in the line. "I kiss the whip of Borkon," she said.

"Who do you love?" he asked.

"Borkon," she said.

In a moment or two I felt the whip pressed, too, against my lips. I kissed it. "I have kissed the whip of Borkon," I said.

"Who do you love?" he asked.

"Borkon," I said.

In another moment or two, after Emily, he stood before Luta. She, too, kissed the whip.

"Who do you love?" he asked.

"Borkon," she said. "I love Borkon!"

In another moment or two we were following Borkon across the yard and toward one of the buildings. I knew I would have to please him well. He was my whip master.

# 25

# I LEAVE THE MILL

I saw him shaking out the slave sack in the utility room. This was not the first time I had been unchained from the loom and hurried to the utility room.

"Get in," he said.

Before he had taken the sack from its shelf he had ordered me to the floor of the utility room, to my back on the dusty boards.

"Lie there and juice," he had told me. "Waste no time about it."

I had lain there and, briefly, shut my eyes and thought of his might and power, and my helpless slavery, and then I was ready, almost in a moment, to receive him. He had had me swiftly. "Why do you keep me ugly?" I had whimpered. Only this morning he had sheared me again. The hair of the other girls was being permitted to grow out, if only until it reached a suitable shearing length. Mine, on the other hand, he had made a point of keeping short. I had been five months now in the mill. "Be silent, Slut," he had said. "Yes, Master," I had said.

I crawled into the sack, and it was pulled up, over my head, and laced shut. I then felt it dragged across the floor. He then lifted it up, partly, I now sitting in it, and left it against a wall. He then left. The confinement was not intended to be one of full security, of course. If it had been, then I would have been bound and gagged within it, that I might not be able, by fingernails or teeth, to attack seams or cut through the leather. Indeed, if I caused the least bit of damage to the slave sack, I had little doubt but what I would be well punished. Confinement in the slave sack is, incidentally, a familiar form of light punishment for a girl. I did not think, however, that I was being punished. At least I did not know of anything that I had done which might have displeased him. As always, as far as I knew, I had tried to be such to him that he would find me pleasing. Perhaps he was angry with me because of the welt on my face, but that was not my fault. Last night I had been struck by Luta. If he wanted to punish someone he should have punished her. She was very jealous of Emily and myself, who seemed clearly to be Borkon's favorites. Last night, after supper, my slave needs much upon me, I had begged to juice for Borkon. He had permitted this in his quarters. When I had been returned to the dormitory and the door had been locked behind me, she had been up and waiting. My face was still sore. It was not my fault that she did not find herself being put to Borkon's pleasure. He certainly was free to choose her, and not Emily or myself, or one of our other chain sisters. It was no secret in the mill that she regarded herself as Borkon's slave in some special sense. Ever since he had whipped and conquered her in the yard she had been very possessive about him. She was the best worker on the chain. Yet he scarcely seemed to notice her. Sometimes she would even try to be a bit dilatory or recalcitrant, to attract his attention, but commonly this only earned her a beating, and that usually from a subordinate whip master. Interestingly, in her slavery, Luta had ceased to be ugly. Her ugliness had been, it was now clear, largely a matter of expression, as it often is, expressions which had made manifest her frustration and hatred, and her misery. Though she was now no longer ugly she remained, I suppose, rather homely and plain. On the other hand, this homeliness or plainness, at times, seemed touched with a vulnerability and softness which, especially when she was near Borkon, made it seem almost beautiful. The exercises and diet of the slave, of course, had improved her figure considerably. I did not see, frankly, why Borkon did not give her a trial at his feet. I did not think she was all that bad, really. Too, he was not Gor's most handsome fellow. Too, I would think it should count for something with a man if the woman desires to serve him deeply and fully in all ways, and is in love with him.

It was hot and stuffy in the slave sack, but it was, at least, a respite from the work with the loom. It is tiring, Ahn in and Ahn out, standing, chained, by the loom, operating it. There is the raising and lowering of the warp threads to form the lines between which the weft is placed. There is the flinging back and forth of the shuttle, inserting the weft. There is the moving of the batten, attached to the reed, thrusting the weft back and locking it in place, Too, one must feed the cloth properly and remove it correctly. One must attend to the rollers, the weights and stretchers.

I suddenly became aware that hands were unlacing the slave sack.

"You are Tiffany, aren't you?" said a voice. "Come out of there."

"Yes, Master," I said. It was one of the mill officials. He was over ten work chains.

"Why aren't you at your loom?" he asked.

"I don't know, Master," I said.

"What were you doing in there?" he asked.

"I don't know, Master," I said. "Perhaps I was being punished."

"What for?" he asked.

"I do not know, Master," I said.

"Come along," he said. "Aemilianus, the nephew of Mintar, is in the mill."

"What is he doing here?" I asked.

"It is supposedly merely a surprise inspection," he said, "but one supposes there is something more to it."

I then, almost running, hurried after him, returning to my loom.

"Borkon should be trounced," he said.

"Ah," said the well-dressed young man, in the silken tunic, with the short, silken mantle, with a golden clasp at the left shoulder. "Here is the maid from Loom 40! No, do not bother to chain her. Now, child, stand here, and remove your tunic."

I quickly obeyed.

Borkon, not looking pleased at all, was standing nearby.

"Step forth, here, child," said the young man, "and turn slowly before me."

I complied, inspected as a naked slave. I saw Emily at the loom next to mine. The shackle had been removed from her left ankle. She was standing near her loom, naked. She held her tunic in her right hand.

"Borkon, you sly fellow," chided the young man, "you have been holding out on us."

He who had fetched me from the slave sack, Borkon's immediate superior, cast him a glowering look.

"You are Tiffany, are you not?" asked the young man.

"Yes, Master," I said.

"You may kneel," he said. Swiftly I did so. "You are pretty, my dear," he said. "You may open your knees." Swiftly I did so.

He then turned to Emily. "You may kneel, Emily," he said. Swiftly she knelt. "You, too, are pretty," he smiled. Swiftly she opened her knees, baring to him tender intimacies, enslaved, and the sweet interior softness of her thighs.

"Your name, 'Emily,' is very beautiful," he said. "As you probably know, it is a barbarian corruption of my *gens* name. It seems that fate has thrown us together." The *gens* name is the clan name.

"Perhaps, Master," she said, frightened. "Thank you, Master."

"And you are a barbarian, are you not, Tiffany?" he asked.

"Yes, Master," I said.

"And a very pretty one," he said.

"Thank you, Master," I said.

"Can you believe it, Borkon," asked the young man, "if it were not for hearsay information, casual remarks overheard at the office, I would not even have known that two such beauties graced our looms."

Borkon was silent.

"These are the two beauties of the mill," said the young man to a tall, stout fellow standing nearby.

"They are certainly pretty," said the stout fellow. "But we have, in my opinion, many lovely women at the looms." The stout fellow was the mill master. I had seen him only twice before in the previous five months.

"These are the best of the current crop," said the young man.

"Perhaps," said the mill master.

"Have them sent to my house," said the young man, and turned away.

Emily and I looked at one another, frightened.

Borkon looked angry. Luta was beaming.

"I beg to please you, Master," said Luta, putting herself to the feet of Borkon. The chain was on her left ankle, going behind her; by it she was fastened to the loom. She had her head down, kissing at his feet. Never before, as far as I knew, had she been so bold. It was no secret in the mill, of course, that she was the slave of Borkon. Indeed, she had been so since that first day in the yard, some five months ago.

"What need have I of a tarsk sow?" he snarled.

She lifted her head to him, lovingly, pleadingly. I saw that the diet and exercise had shaped her excitingly. Her face, in its plainness and homeliness, seemed somehow, now, in its softness, its tenderness, its vulnerability, very beautiful. "Take me then to your lair and rut with me there, Master," she said. "I beg to be the tarsk sow to your boar."

He looked down at her, startled. "Perhaps," he said.

I felt a slave bracelet closed about my left wrist. The companion bracelet, on its three links of chain, was then closed about the right wrist of Emily.

We looked at one another, frightened.

"Come along, Girls," said the fellow who had fetched me forth from the slave sack, he who was Borkon's immediate superior.

"Yes, Master," said Emily.

"Yes, Master," I said.

We then, naked, braceleted together, carrying our slave tunics, followed him down the long aisle between the looms.

# 26

# I MUST GET UP EARLY FOR SCHOOL

I tried to hold the head of the man in my hands, and kiss at him, and lick at the side of his neck, but he, engaged in conversation, brushed me to the side. I knelt back, restraining a whimper. I wanted to touch him. I was a slave. He would not permit me to do so.

Teela, first girl, from across the room, signaled to me, and I, bowing, slipped back, rose to my feet and hurried to her side.

"Wine," said she, "to the master."

I hurried to the serving table and fetched a vessel of wine. I then went behind the feasting table, behind which the men sat, talking. Some musicians were playing, at one side of the room. I knelt behind the young Aemilianus. "Wine, Master?" I whispered. "Yes," said he, extending his goblet. "Thank you, Tiffany," he said. "Yes, Master," I said, and withdrew. The courtesy of Aemilianus, a habit with him, probably a function of the gentleness of his upbringing, in no way affected the totality of the bondage in which his girls were kept. Whereas one need not thank a slave, one may, of course, if one wishes, thank them. From the point of view of the girl, since she knows she is in a collar, being treated with courtesy can sometimes be more frightening than being treated with rudeness or cruelty, or, as is more often the case, with gentle, intimate, absolutely unqualified authority. Being a slave she knows that a master's invitation to remove a garment is equivalent to a categorical command to strip. She hastens to obey.

I went then, at a sign from Teela, after replacing the wine vessel on the serving table, to the side of the room, where I knelt down beside Emily.

An Ahn or so earlier we had been in the kitchen. "Stand straighter, Girls," had said Teela, inspecting us. "You are not bending over looms now."

"You are pretty in your slave silk, Emily," had said Teela.

"Thank you, Mistress," she had said.

"You, too, Tiffany," said Teela.

"Thank you, Mistress," I had said. We both wore scarlet pleasure silk. It was diaphanous, and left little doubt as to the lineaments of our figures. We wore the collar of Aemilianus. We now belonged to him. Twelve copper tarsks for each of us had been transferred to the accounts of Mill 7. On our left ankles we each wore a tied string of slave bells. These jangled sensuously when we moved. On our upper left arms we each wore a coiled, barbaric, snakelike armlet.

"Although you have been purchased as house girls," said Teela, "and surely we need more of them around here, you will also be expected upon occasion, as tonight, to serve at dinner. Indeed, I suspect that the Master has more in mind from you than simple domestic services."

Emily and I looked at one another.

"The musicians are already playing," said Teela, " and the other girls are on the floor. I shall soon send you both out, too, on the floor."

"Yes, Mistress," said Emily.

"Yes, Mistress," I said.

"Remember that you are not lofty free women," she said. "Remember that you are only female slaves. You exist for the service and pleasure of men. When you go out there drip with obedience and sensuousness. Let every glance, every look and movement, signify to men the promise of untold pleasures, and if any of them should so much as snap his fingers, see that you fulfill that promise and a thousand times more."

"Yes, Mistress!" we said.

"There will be no free women present," she said. "That will make things easier."

That was a relief for us. The frustrations and chilling hatred of free women for their imbonded sisters, and their power to inflict pain on them, tended naturally to preclude, or inhibit, the performances of slaves. Their presence, too, of course, tended to have an adverse effect on the satisfactions obtainable by the free men present. If a free woman is present, for example, one is scarcely likely to tear the silk from a laughing, squealing slave and rape her on the table. Female slaves commonly wear relatively modest garments and serve unobtrusively and decorously when free women are present. Except for the perfection of their service, and their collars and the relative brevity, openness and looseness of their garments, one might not even know they were slaves, unless perhaps, of course, one looked into their eyes, or touched them.

"Remember the many things I have told you," said Teela.

"Yes, Mistress," we said.

"Are we not too scantily clad, Mistress?" asked Emily.

"Not for pleasure slaves," said Teela.

"Yes, Mistress," said Emily. We addressed Teela as "Mistress" for she was, in the house of Aemilianus, first girl.

"You are distressed to appear before the master so exposed?" asked Teela.

"Yes, Mistress," she said.

"Because you like him?" she asked.

"Yes," she said.

"And I think he likes you, too," said Teela.

"Do you, Mistress?" begged Emily, eagerly.

"Yes," said Teela, "but remember that you are to him only as a slave."

"Yes, Mistress," she said.

"Surely he saw you naked when he bought you," said Teela.

"Yes, Mistress," said Emily, her head down. Men do not buy clothed women.

"Then you have nothing to hide," said Teela. "Similarly, as a slave, your body is public."

"Yes, Mistress," said Emily.

"Put aside all concern with your own self-image," said Teela. "Your only concern now is the pleasing of your master."

"Yes, Mistress," said Emily.

"Please him well," smiled Teela.

"I shall try, Mistress," said Emily.

"Tiffany," said Teela.

"Yes, Mistress," I said.

"Do you enjoy the house?" she asked.

"Yes, Mistress!" I said. Though I had been here only two days, some forty Ahn, I reveled in its contrast with the mills. It was clean, and spacious and quiet, and had lovely grounds, surrounded by a high, white wall, in which was an ornate, barred gate. Here I was well rested and well fed. My duties were light, usually those of a maid, dusting and cleaning, making beds, tidying rooms, and such. Sometimes, too, I helped in the kitchen. I did not have to wear the mill uniform, bearing the sign for the enterprises of Mintar, but wore, instead, usually, a light, white house tunic, similar to that often worn by tower slaves. I even had access to a bath. Similarly my kennel was comfortable and, for a kennel, spacious. I could not stand erect in it but there was more than enough room to stretch out and roll about. The gate in the kennel was a small one. It was barred, and set in the barred side of the kennel facing the corridor. It is common to have one side of a kennel open, except for the bars. The girl is always, you see, to be available to the eyes of the master. He may look upon her whenever he chooses, day or night. The small gate is also common in slave kennels. The girl, commonly, accordingly, enters and leaves the kennel on all fours. She is, after all, an animal. Too, it is useful in various leashing and chaining arrangements. In this house, as in most, the girl is kept naked in the kennel. I did not mind the tiny gate of the kennel, however, or my observability and nudity within it. I much preferred its semi-privacy to the locked dormitory at the mill. Too, its comforter, blankets and pillow were a welcome change from the flat, straw-filled mat and thin blanket on the cement floor of the dormitory.

"Do you want to go back to the mill?" asked Teela.

"No, Mistress!" I said.

"It would be well for both of you, you, too, Emily," said Teela, "to remember that you are both on trial here. You have not been brought here to weave cloth on a loom. And you have not been brought here simply to dust and make beds. Your slavery in this house involves more extended services."

"Yes, Mistress," we said. We had no doubt as to what these more extended services were. About our upper left arms were golden, snakelike armlets. About our left ankles were tied slave bells. Our bodies could scarcely feel the lightness of the slave silk on them.

"You must now decide," said Teela, "whether you wish to serve the pleasures of men, and fully, or you wish to return to the mill. In a sense, you must decide, really, what you are, and how you wish to live. I commend to your attention the noble alternative, to be chosen by all truly free women, of returning to the mill, of returning to the back-breaking, repetitious labor of the loom. The alternative, of course, is so dreadful I scarcely dare mention it. It is to serve men, to belong to them, to be at their beck and call, to be their willing, obedient, eager, shameless, helpless slave."

Emily and I regarded one another.

"Sluts choose the collar and the helpless service of men," she said. "Women who are truly noble and free choose the mill." She looked at me. "Tiffany?" she asked.

"I choose the service of men," I said.

"Then you are a slave and a slut," she said.

"Yes, Mistress," I said. This admission seemed to me very liberating.

"Emily?" asked Teela.

"I, too, choose the service of men," she said, "especially that of Aemilianus!"

"You, too, then, are a slave and a slut," said Teela.

"Yes, Mistress," said Emily.

"But that you would shamelessly choose to be pleasure slaves over noble mill girls does not mean that masters must see fit to accord you such a slavery. It is up to you to prove to them that you have the aptitude, the talent, the dispositions, the desires and reflexes to be even considered for such a slavery."

"Yes, Mistress," we said.

"I am going to send you forth now on the floor," said Teela. I heard the slave bells on my ankle jangle. The sound, sensuous and barbaric, startled me. "If you are not both found sufficiently pleasing," she said, "both of you, and certainly you, Tiffany, will be back in the mill by tomorrow night."

"Yes, Mistress," we said. I found myself wishing that Aemilianus had found me as fetching as he apparently had Emily. I thought my trial was likely to be harder than hers.

"Mistress!" said Emily.

"Yes?" asked Teela.

"Tiffany and I are self-confessed sluts and slaves. You have forced us to face this truth about ourselves, and admit it."

"Yes?" said Teela.

"What of you?" asked Emily. "You are lovely, and beautiful, and in a collar. What are you?"

"A bold question," said Teela.

"Forgive me, Mistress," said Emily.

"I, too, of course, am only a slave and a slut," said Teela. "And I love it!" Then she kissed us both. Then she drew back from us. "You will be slaves out there before free men," she said. "Too, there will be no free women present. Revel in your womanhood and manifest it shamelessly!"

"Yes, Mistress!" we said.

"Go forth, Slaves," she said.

"Yes, Mistress!" we said and, with a jangle of slave bells, hurried to join the other girls on the floor.

"Your knees," I whispered to Emily, "open them."

"Thank you, Tiffany," said Emily, spreading her knees. The knees of the pleasure slave, when she is in a kneeling position, are to be kept open before the master, and, indeed, before all free men. Emily, in the same room with Aemilianus, was still struggling with her modesty. In the mill, of course, Aemilianus had had her open her knees before him.

We knelt side by side at one side of the room. What little serving was being done was now being attended to by the other girls. How beautiful they were. And how natural, and perfect, and right and fitting it seemed that they, in their slightness and beauty, were serving men. I knelt there, with Emily, to one side, my knees open, in pleasure silk, a collar locked on my neck, a barbaric, golden, coiling ornament on my upper left arm, slave bells tied on my left ankle. I knelt there, ready to serve. How strange it was, I thought. How far I had come! How far away, now, seemed the perfume counter in the department store on Long Island, the photographer's studio, my apartment. I remembered that pretty, mercenary, greedy little clerk at the perfume counter. She was no longer free. She had now been made a collared slave girl. She had once been Miss Tiffany Collins. She was now an animal, and nameless in her own right, but masters had seen fit to put the name "Tiffany" on her.

"Tiffany," whispered Emily.

"Yes," I whispered.

"Isn't Aemilianus handsome?" she whispered.

"Yes," I said.

"I want to crawl to him," she whispered, "and beg to serve his pleasure."

"Do not break position," I warned her.

"No," she whispered.

"Perhaps he will let you serve him later," I said.

"I hope so," she whispered. "I hope so!"

"You like him," I observed.

"I think that I am his love slave," she whispered.

"It is too early for you to know something like that," I said. I did not know, of course, whether it was or not. Sometimes these things can be told at a glance.

"I want him to whip me," she said.

"Why?" I asked.

"Because I love him," she said.

Then, at a glance from Teela, across the room, we were both quiet.

I was somewhat upset. The men had had, on the whole, a very decorous supper. I had thought, given our garb and bells, that we might have been expected to serve in more exacting and intimate fashions than we had been called upon to do. The supper, on the other hand, had apparently been a rather normal one. To be sure, the men, being men, and no free women being present, had had the supper, for their pleasure, served to them by beautiful, revealingly clad women, collared slaves.

I glanced over at Emily. She could not keep her eyes off Aemilianus.

Some women desire occasionally, or at least once, to be whipped by the man they love. This has to do, it seems, with deep psychological feelings, feelings probably connected with the woman's desire to submit and fulfill her biological destiny, this perhaps being a manifestation, within the human species, of the dominance/submission ratios endemic in nature. This involves, of course, an intense sentient interaction with the lover. Intense emotions, sensations and feelings are involved. In this situation the woman, who desires to surrender and yield, understands that she is now at the mercy of the lover, and is helpless under his will. It gives her an opportunity, too, of course, to show the lover that she, in her love, and in the intensity of her feelings, offers herself up to him.

I had once been Tiffany Collins, of Earth. I was now a collared slave girl on Gor. I touched the collar. It was light, but, too, it was efficient and inflexible. I supposed it would not do to tell anyone but I loved it on me. I felt, somehow, it belonged on me. It was right, I felt, somehow, on me. But, too, sometimes I was terrified to wear it. I knew that it meant that I was owned, and at the mercy of men.

I knelt there. I was no longer free. I could now be bought and sold. I must obey.

My major fear now was that I might be sent back to the mill.

I, and, indeed, the other girls, had been given little or no opportunity to prove to the masters that the slave bells tied on our ankles were not an inadvertence or a mistake. At various times during the supper I had tried to be attentive to one man or another, and as a slave, and as my belly had seemed to beg, but, each time, I had been brushed away or dismissed. I had been rejected. This stung my vanity, as well as increased the frustrations of my scorned femininity. I feared, too, it betokened that I, perhaps found insufficiently pleasing, might soon be returned to the mill.

I watched the men, talking, and finishing their liqueurs. I watched, too, the one or two girls still in attendance on them. They were beautiful, in their grace and serving. How perfect and natural it seemed that they should be serving. I touched my collar. Women by nature belong to men, I thought, and I am a woman. Why had men on Earth, I wondered, allowed themselves to be tricked out of their sovereignty by man-hating and vicious women, abetted by frustrated, weakling males? When will they take us again in hand, I wondered, and own us? But the men on Earth, with few exceptions, I feared, were lost to manhood.

Teela came and knelt down beside us, only another slave girl.

"May I speak?" I whispered.

"Yes," she said.

"I have tried to be attractive," I said. "I have tried to be desirable. I have tried to serve well. But no one has taken me. No one has used me."

"No one has been taken. No one has been raped," she said. "The men talk politics and business."

"May I inquire as to the nature of these discussions?" I asked.

"The usual rumors about a truce between ourselves and Cos," she said. "In business, the master is sounding out his colleagues about the plausibility of a venture involving feast slaves."

"What are they?" I asked.

"Girls, maids, entertainers, dancers, rented in groups to private individuals or organizations for feasts, and such," she said.

"Such enterprises exist now, do they not?" I asked.

"He is considering the desirability of investing in the area, and perhaps forming his own company to enter the field."

"I see," I said. "But trained girls are expensive, are they not?"

"Yes," she said.

"But mill girls are cheap, and might be trained," I said.

"Precisely," said Teela.

I trembled.

"Emily! Tiffany!" called Aemilianus, sitting behind the long, low table, with his friends.

We quickly leapt up and ran to kneel on the tiles before him.

"These are mill girls?" asked a man.

"Yes," said Aemilianus, "but now, as you can see, they are not in the company uniform."

"Some silk, some cosmetics, makes quite a difference," said a man.

"They cost me only twelve copper tarsks each," said Aemilianus.

"But that is scarcely fair, Aemilianus," said a man. "You purchased them from your uncle's mill. Had you bought them in an open market they doubtless would have cost you more."

"Something more, doubtless," said Aemilianus.

"It is nice to know that such girls occasionally come to the mills," said a man.

"I see that I shall have to make more inspections of uncle's mills," said another young man, one whom, I gathered, must be a cousin of Aemilianus.

"It is not that rare, actually," said Aemilianus. "Too, remember there are several mills. Too, almost any girl, with the proper diet, exercise and training, and properly costumed and made-up, and knowing herself subject to the whip, can become of considerable interest."

"That is true," said a man.

"Pausanias, who is the mill master in Mill 7," said Aemilianus, "has informed me that, in his opinion, there are many lovely girls even in Mill 7."

"Interesting," said a man.

"Are these two," asked a man, "from Mill 7?"

"Yes," said Aemilianus. "They are the two best that I found there."

"You needn't depend on the mills, of course," said a man. "You can buy in the market."

"You could also buy trained slaves to begin with," said a man.

"They are more expensive," said a man.

"That is true," he agreed.

"I shall show you one advantage of the mills," said Aemilianus. "Emily," he said, "do you wish to be returned to the mill?"

"No, Master!" she said.

"Tiffany?" he asked.

"No, Master!" I cried.

"The motivation of mill girls, as you can see," said Aemilianus, "is high. Accordingly, they may be expected to train swiftly, desperately and superbly."

"Have you discussed your ideas with Mintar?" asked a man.

"Yes," said Aemilianus, "and he has given me license to proceed."

"Would this be involved with the enterprises of Mintar?" asked a man.

"No," said Aemilianus. "It would become one of the enterprises of Aemilianus."

"I see," said a man.

"My uncle, of course, will extend the initial loans at nominal rates," said Aemilianus.

"I see," said the man.

"I am not sure this is practical," said a man.

"It will be a difficult field to break into," said another man.

"It is a question," said Aemilianus, "of providing a quality service at competitive prices."

"Perhaps," said a man.

"Emily, would you please come around the table and kneel here, beside me?" asked Aemilianus.

Emily instantly leapt to her feet and scurried to kneel in the indicated position.

This left me, somewhat disconcerting me, alone before the table.

"Would you please stand up and remove your silk, Tiffany?" said Aemilianus.

Immediately I stood and slipped from the silk. I held it, dangling, from my right hand.

"That is a mill girl?" asked a man, skeptically.

"Yes," said Aemilianus.

"Those are slave curves, if I have ever seen them," said a man.

"True," said another.

"You are very pretty, Tiffany," said Aemilianus.

"Thank you, Master," I said.

"How long have you been enslaved?" he asked.

"Some five months, Master," I said.

"And are you trained?" he asked.

"Only by the instructions of some men who have used me," I said, "and, of course, to work the loom."

There was laughter.

"We may then say, may we not," asked Aemilianus, "that for most practical purposes you are untrained."

"Yes, Master," I said.

"Drop the silk," he said.

I did.

"Now get on your belly on the tiles, Tiffany," he said.

Immediately I lowered myself to my belly on the tiles. I looked up at them, the palms of my hands on the floor.

"Are you familiar with floor movements, Tiffany?" he asked.

"A little, Master," I said. "I saw some once in a slaver's house." This had been in the house of Kliomenes, when I had been taken on a tour there long ago by Drusus Rancius. I had been free then, of course. Now I was as much a slave as the girls I had seen there at the time.

"I am going to signal to the musicians, Tiffany," said Aemilianus. "When they begin to play, you may begin your performance."

"Yes, Master," I whispered. When I had seen such movements in the house of Kliomenes I had never dreamed that they might, horrifyingly enough, one day be required of me. In few modalities is a woman's slavery made clearer or more manifest than when she must perform floor movements, than when she must, in effect, dance before men, never rising higher than her knees.

Then the music began.

Almost as soon as I had begun to dance I saw Emily tear back her slave silk, exposing her breasts to Aemilianus, and try to kiss him. He held her against him with his left arm about her body and held her two hands, their wrists crossed, in his grip, captured, across his body. He held her in this fashion, helpless. And both, then, were watching me.

Once I had been Tiffany Collins. I now writhed, a Gorean slave, at the feet of men.

I do not know how long the music lasted, perhaps only about four or five Ehn. Then, swirling and climaxing, it suddenly ended. I lay, gasping and sweating, on my belly on the tiles. I looked up. I hoped that I had pleased the masters.

"Very good, Tiffany," said Aemilianus.

"Superb," said one man. "Superb!" said another.

"What do you want for her?" asked a man.

"I will give you a silver tarsk," said another. I looked wildly at him. I wondered if I would be sold. A silver tarsk! I wished Drusus Rencius had heard that! He had thought I would only bring fifteen or twenty copper tarsks! And I was not even trained!

"You did very well, Tiffany," said Aemilianus.

"Thank you, Master," I said.

"Did you see, Gentlemen," asked Aemilianus, "and she only an untrained mill girl."

"Yes, Aemilianus," said a man. "Yes," said another. "Yes," said yet another.

"Teela," said Aemilianus.

"Yes, Master," she said, quickly.

"Take Emily to my room and chain her by the neck to the foot of my couch."

"Yes, Master," she said.

"Thank you, Master," cried Emily.

"On your feet, Slave," said Teela to Emily. "Cross your wrists, touching, behind your back, close your eyes and put down your head. You will uncross your wrists and open your eyes only when you feel the locking of the couch collar on your neck."

"Yes, Mistress," said Emily.

She was then led from the room, bent over, by the hair, her eyes closed and her wrists crossed, and touching, behind her back.

"You are going to be sent to school, Tiffany," said Aemilianus.

"Thank you, Master," I said.

"Does that please you?" he asked.

"Yes, Master," I said. "I have never been taught to read."

There was laughter.

"It is not that sort of school," he said.

"Oh," I said.

"Gentlemen," said Aemilianus, "and kind sirs, I thank you for your presence here this evening, and for your kind attention. Your comments, your thoughts and your counsel have been much appreciated. If any of you wish to remain the night, feel free to make use of the rooms which were put at your disposal before supper. Similarly if any of the slaves interest you, any of those who served you, or any other in the house, with the exception of our little Tiffany, take her to your room. She is yours for the night. If you are not fully pleased in the morning, let me know and I will have her thoroughly punished, and then sent to you for the week, that she may learn to improve her service."

"I will take this one," said a man, indicating one of the girls.

"And I will take this one," said another.

These two girls ran to their masters of the evening and knelt before them.

"I would like to have the one you call 'Teela' licking at my feet," said a strong, mature fellow.

"She will be sent to your room," said Aemilianus.

"My thanks, Aemilianus," he said.

"It is nothing," said Aemilianus.

"And what of this meaningless, squirming little pleasure-bundle?" asked one of the men looking at me.

I was now kneeling before the table. I blushed. I did not know if I appreciated being referred to as a meaningless, squirming little pleasure-bundle. On the other hand, these were Gorean men and I knew that I, in their hands, if they wished, would find myself transformed into little more than just such a squirming pleasure-bundle. I had learned this from Tenrak on the floor of a slave wagon.

"With your permission," said Aemilianus, "I would rather she did not serve tonight. I would like her to get a good rest. I would like her to get a good start in the morning."

"As you wish, Aemilianus," said a man.

"I am not to serve tonight, Master?" I asked.

"No," he said. "You must get up early tomorrow."

"Master?" I asked.

"You must get up early for school," he said.

"Yes, Master," I said.

# 27

# SCHOOL

I was pulled to the post, close to it and facing it. The heavy belt, with the ring on it, through which the loose post strap passed, that strap looping the post and threaded through the belt ring, was put about my belly, and buckled shut, tightly, behind the small of my back. I could now move easily about the post but, given the post strap and the belt ring, I could not be further than six inches from it.

"When you are more experienced, you will not need the harness," said the whip master. "Too, we will let you try it sometimes with your hands tied behind you."

"Yes, Master," I said.

"Address yourself now to the post, Tiffany," he said. "Make it sweat. Make it cry out with pleasure."

"Yes, Master," I said.

"Next," said the whip master.

I approached him and knelt before him. "I wear your chains, Master," I said, lifting them. "Do with me as you will."

"Again," said the man.

I rose to my feet and, facing him, head down, backed away a few paces. Then I lifted my head again.

"Remember, Tiffany," he said, "he will."

"Yes, Master," I said.

I again approached him and knelt before him. "I wear your chains, Master," I said, lifting them. "Do with me as you will."

"Better," he said. "Next."

"See how Tiffany uses the cushion," said the whip master. "That is good."

A girl must know how to use the cushions, just as the chains and furs. These cushions are usually large and soft. These are the sorts of cushions which are sometimes found at the foot of, or in the vicinity of, thrones and curule chairs, generally intended for the use of slaves. They may also, of course, be found in private dwellings. Sometimes a slave must remain on her cushion. Sometimes she is sent to it for punishment. She is taught to kneel upon it, to curl seductively on or about it, to lie across it, on her stomach or back, to hold it in certain ways, and so on.

"Good, Tiffany. Good," said the whip master.

"You are all slaves," said the whip master.

We all sat facing him, our backs against the wall of the training room. The palms of our hands were flat on the floor at our sides and our legs were extended before us, the ankles crossed, as though bound.

"If you doubt that you are slaves, examine your thighs and consider your collared necks."

We looked at one another. We were not in doubt that we were slaves.

"The only question now is whether you will be adequate or inadequate slaves," he said. "This question, now that you are true slaves, is basically a question of whether you will choose to live or choose to die. That is your basic question. I suggest that you face it. Each of you must make your own choice. I caution you against one mistake, one common to stupid or uninformed girls. That is the mistake of thinking that you can escape the full implications of your position by merely adopting what you think is slave behavior. That is not true. Authentic slave behavior is motivated from within, and is the natural manifestation of the yielded slave herself. The will and consciousness within is that of a slave. This, then, issues in authentic slave behavior. There are many ways, responses to physical and psychological tests, and subtle behavioral cues, to tell if slave behavior is authentic or not. The choice, thus, is, in effect, one of whether you choose to become a total slave, surrendered and obedient, in your mind as well as your behavior, or die."

"And this cut," said the woman, herself a slave, though permitted a brief tunic, "is called the slave flame. See how it comes down the back, swirling." She illustrated this with a kneeling girl whose hair had been cut, trimmed and shaped in this fashion. "This," she said, moving to the next girl, "is an upswept fashion. It appears sophisticated. It is a hair-do favored by some free women, but it is not outlawed for slaves. Its pretentiousness, suggesting superciliousness and arrogance, contrasts nicely with the actual reality of the slave. The girl who wears this must watch her step, lest the master grow impatient with her. If you are permitted to wear this hair-do, make certain that you, after an initial resistance, if he permits it, yield to him as a particularly low and helpless girl. This hair-do here, on Crystal, with the bun in the back, is favored by many free women of the scribes. It, too, however, like the upswept hair-do has not been outlawed for slaves. Its apparent severity contrasts nicely with sexiness required of the slave. She may be freed of its severity, and brought into the natural modality of her yielding and submissive femininity, with as little as a single tug, thusly. In contrast, regard Tiffany, who has the shorn look. Some men like this in a woman. To be sure, her hair is now growing out a bit. This is to be contrasted again, of course, with the shaven head, commonly inflicted only on a girl as a punishment or to protect her from lice in close confinements, such as on a slave ship. Again, in the matter of hair-dos as in all my instructions to you, whether having to do with perfumes, silks, cosmetics, ornamentation, or whatever, you are to consider the total effect, the entire ensemble."

"Well done, Tiffany," he said. "You bring the whip well."

He took it from between my teeth.

"Thank you, Master," I said.

"Next," he said.

I knelt before him, my head down, the palms of my hands on the tiles, in the fashion which Ligurious had required of his girls. "I beg for love, Master," I whimpered. "I beg for love!" I licked at his feet. "I beg for love, Master!" I said.

"You do it very well," he said.

I lifted my head, tears in my eyes. "But I do beg for love!" I said. 'I have not been contented in weeks!"

"How many of you other girls," asked the whip master, regarding the class, "beg for love?"

"I, Master!" cried a girl. "I, Master!" cried others.

"How many?" he asked.

And there was not one girl, naked and in her collar, in the entire class who did not raise her hand.

"Good," said the whip master. "Then you are hungry."

Our training then continued.

"No two masters are the same," said the whip master, "except in so far as each is the total master, just as no two slaves are the same, except that each is a total slave."

We all sat facing him, our backs against the wall of the training room. The palms of our hands were flat on the floor at our sides and our legs were extended before us, the ankles crossed, as though bound.

"You must, accordingly, strive to understand, relate to, serve and please the unique master in each man. You must bring your own individual personalities and talents to bear on this challenge. Try in your uniqueness to be perfect and special for him in his uniqueness. Read him. Learn him. Become acutely aware of him. Be sensitive to his moods, and their changes. Find out what he wants from you, and then see that he gets it, and more. Find out what he wants you to be, and then be it, beyond his wildest dreams. Remember that you are the slave. You exist for his service and pleasure."

"That is it, Tiffany," he said. "Stretch your limbs. Examine their fairness. Now look at the master. That is how you take a bath before a man. Will he drag you forth and have you on the slippery tiles or will he take you in the bath itself?"

"Do not forget to kiss the sandal, humbly, before eyeing it on his foot," said the whip master, "just as, when you remove them, you kiss them, before putting them away."

"Yes, Master," I said.

"Gently, Tiffany," said the whip master. "You are not rubbing down a tharlarion."

"Yes, Master," I said.

"Use the sponge well," he said. "Remember that it must not only clean but caress, and do not forget, in this service, to fondle and kiss the master, humbly and lovingly."

I kissed the wet shoulder of the man in the bath, and then kissed his cheek, through the wet canvas hood drawn over his face. He moaned. He was a male slave.

"Similarly," said the whip master, "do not forget to press your body sometimes against that of the master, sometimes seemingly inadvertently. Along these lines, for example, it is easy, seemingly accidentally, to brush his lips with a pendant breast. If his lips should part you might then press it more closely against him, begging. You might then be cuffed back in the water, but later you will doubtless be well used."

I knelt before the whip master, anxiously lifting the tray to him. He picked up one of the biscuits. He turned it over. "This biscuit is burned on the bottom," he said. "If this happens again, you will be whipped."

"Yes, Master," I said. "Forgive me, Master."

"Good, Ruby," said the whip master. "That is how to remove a man's tunic. Make it a sensuous experience for him, in which you show him your slavery and your eagerness to serve. You may replace your tunic, Abdar."

"Yes, Master," said the hooded slave.

"You next, Tiffany," said the whip master.

"Yes, Master," I said.

"These biscuits are acceptable," he said. "In fact, they are good."

"Thank you, Master!" I said.

"Good, Tiffany," said the whip master. "That is how you belly to a man. Put your head down, now. Let me feel your lips and tongue." "Master," I whimpered. "Good," he said.

"Later, too, when your hair reaches a suitable length, make certain that it falls about the master's sandals." "Yes, Master," I said.

I sensed that our training was coming to an end. We were returning to various basics, almost as elementary as scales to the musician, such things as basic kisses, caresses, position, attitudes and movements.

"Good," he said.

I had once been Miss Tiffany Collins, of Earth. I now lay on my belly on the tiles, naked and in a collar, licking and kissing at the feet of a Gorean male. It was my hope that he would find me pleasing, totally.

"Attention, Class," said the whip master.

We all straightened up, sitting, facing him, our backs against the wall of the training room. The palms of our hands were flat on the floor at our sides and our legs were extended before us, the ankles crossed, as though bound.

"The results of your tests, your examinations, are now in. It is my pleasure to inform you that you have all passed."

We dared not break position, so well trained we were, but we cried out with pleasure. We had worked hard. We did not wish to be fed to sleen, or, perhaps, if our internal slavery was adequate, but our external performances insufficient, being sent to a laundry or returned to a mill, where we might have to remain perhaps indefinitely.

"It is an excellent class, one of the best I have had," he said.

"Thank you, Master," said several of the girls.

"Too," he said, "there is not one of you, as the tests have shown, who is not an authentic slave; there is not one of you who, from the bottom of her pretty belly, does not belong in a collar."

I knew this was true of me. I did not know, of course, if it were true of the other girls or not. And last doubts on the rightness of the collar on my neck had been dispelled in my training. I now knew it belonged there. I was pleased to have been brought to Gor where I, whether I wished it or not, with absolutely no compromise, would be put in it.

"I am proud of all of you," said the whip master. "You are all luscious and exciting sluts. Indeed, I think there is not one of you would not bring a silver tarsk on the open market."

We cried out, elated, to hear this. We looked at one another, joy in our faces. I almost lifted the palms of my hands from the floor and uncrossed my ankles, but, of course I did not do so. How pleased we were. What high praise this was. We had not understood how valuable we might have become as women.

"But, remember," said the whip master, "you have, really, learned only a little. You have been familiarized with only a small selection of basic skills, apprised of only a handful of fundamentals. Your education, when you leave here, is not complete, but only begun. You may learn more in your first few days out of school, in the practical contexts of bondage, under the control and whips of masters, than you have here in five weeks. But even then, remember that you, in your collars, are still amateurs at slavery. You could not begin to compete with an experienced girl. Continue to apply yourself, to learn, to work, to love and serve. Some years from now you may begin to grasp an inkling of what can be the skills, the sensitivities and talents, the emotions, the depths of feeling, of the slave. The other side of the coin of freedom is bondage. One cannot exist without the other. The master is free and you are slave."

We looked at one another. There was much in what he said. We must strive desperately to please. We were, for most practical purposes, new girls, untutored in our collars. Most of us, even, were from the mills. We would be zealous to please. Most masters are sensitive to this. They are likely to be kinder to an unskilled girl zealous to please than a skilled one who permits her performances to lapse from standards of perfection. She may, of course, at the master's whim, by various correctional devices, be swiftly restored to zealousness. Sometimes, too, of course, she is merely sold into a lower slavery, that she may earnestly endeavor, perhaps through years of effort, to work her way up again to, say, a single-master-single-slave relationship. The mistake of even minutely relaxing or reducing the quality of her service is not one a girl is likely to make twice.

"All that remains now," said the whip master, "is to give you some experience in the types of situations in which you are likely, at least in your initial bondage applications, to find yourself."

# 28

# SCHOOL; I HAVE GRADUATED

"I am so tired," I said.

"So, too, am I," said Crystal.

"We all are," said Tupa.

It was now late at night. We had been serving this mock banquet, under the directions of a floor manager, our whip master generally to one side, looking on, since early morning. It was done in the training room, with tables set up. We did not serve actual food, of course, though we carried trays and dishes, and such.

"You are Tiffany?" asked the floor manager.

"Yes, Master," I said.

"Fruit, there," he said, pointing to a place at the table. One of his aides was there, playing the role of a banqueter.

"Yes, Master," I said. I, and the rest of the class, was naked, save for our collars and strings of slave bells tied about our left ankles. It was not thought necessary to soil slave silks in what, in effect, was a successive series of rehearsals. The floor manager did wish to make certain, of course, that we moved well, belled. The floor manager, or banquet manager, or feast master, as one may think of him, is extremely important in this type of affair. He controls the arrangement and order of the banquet, the catering, if any is required, and the musicians, dancers and serving slaves. Our class, twenty girls, were acting as the serving slaves. Another class, the next cycle in the training program, was kneeling to one side, observing. I wanted desperately to talk to one member of that next class. The musicians were no longer playing now. Similarly the dancers were off to one side, many of them now sleeping. The musicians were free. Musicians on Gor, that is, members of the caste of musicians, are seldom, if ever, enslaved. Their immunity from bondage, or practical immunity from bondage, is a matter of custom. There is a saying to the effect that he who makes music must, like the tarn and the Vosk gull, be free. This is a saying, however, which I suspect was invented by the caste of musicians, to protect itself from bondage. For example, there are many musicians on Gor, not members of the caste, who are enslaved. For example, it is quite common on Gor to train a slave girl in the use of a musical instrument, that she might be more pleasing to masters. It never seems to occur to anyone that she should then be freed. Indeed, it is felt that since she is in a collar, it will make her performance, her playing, and perhaps her singing, even more superb. Too, some male slaves are fine musicians. The only other caste on Gor which is generally considered, for most practical purposes, as immune from bondage is the caste of players. These are the fellows who make their living from the game of Kaissa, playing it for prizes, charging for games, giving instruction and exhibitions, annotating games, and so on. They are usually poor fellows but generally have little trouble securing a night's food and lodging for a game or two. The general affection and respect which Goreans feel for the game of Kaissa is probably the explanation for the practical immunity from bondage commonly accorded the members of the caste of players. Slaves are seldom permitted to play Kaissa. In some cities it is against the law for them to do so. It is often thought to be an insult to the game to even let them touch the pieces. The dancers, on the other hand, several of whom were sleeping to the side, were all females, and slaves. Few free women, I suspect, would dare to dance the dances of Gor before strong men. If they did so, how long could they expect to remain free? Any woman who dares to appear so before men, and dance, it is said, is in her heart a slave. Let her then be collared! Whatever may be the truth in these matters it is a fact that almost all of the dancers on Gor are slaves. Indeed, many of the most beautiful and exciting slaves on Gor are dancers. They bring their masters much gold.

I now knelt before the low table, before the floor manager's aide. I carried a round, empty silver platter, about eighteen inches in diameter. The floor manager accompanied me to the place, and crouched down, beside me, watching.

I lowered my head and body, from the waist down, humbly, and then, slowly, gracefully, lifted my body and head to where I might look up into the eyes of the aide. I then lifted the tray upward and toward him, proffering it to him, as though it might contain luscious fruit, at the same time lifting my body subtly to him. "Fruit, Master?" I asked.

"How did it look?" asked the floor manager.

"Good," said the aide. "Do you wish to take this perspective?"

The floor manager stepped over the low table, going behind it. "Again, Tiffany," he said.

I withdrew and, again, performed.

"Yes," he said. "That is good." It must be understood, of course, that the girl is offering not merely the luscious fruits on the plate to the guest but, too, if he should be interested, the fruits of her beauty. Similar offerings and invitations are ingredient in such expressions as "Meat, Master," "A tender morsel, Master," "Viands for your delectation, Master," and so on. An almost classical instance of this sort of thing occurs when the girl approaches from the side and back, and whispers "Wine, Master?" into the man's ear. This is to be contrasted with the common wine service in which the girl kneels, knees wide, before the man, kisses the cup, if permitted, and then, head down, humbly, arms extended, submissively, proffers it to him. In both services, of course, it is clear that the girl is a slave, and is at the disposal of the master, in all senses.

"Suppose, now," said the floor manager, "he reaches out and touches you."

I closed my eyes, and parted my lips. "Yes, Master," I whispered. "Thank you, Master! Please, Master!"

"You must be capable of variations on that," said the floor manager.

"Yes, Master," I said. I wished he had let the aide actually touch me. I was starving for the touch of a man.

"Perhaps what you have to serve is of interest," said the aide, playing the role of a banqueter. "I do not know. Display it for me."

I then put the tray down on the table and slipped back, on my knees, a foot or two. I looked at the aide. I pretended to slip slave silk from my shoulders. I then, sometimes on the floor, and never rising higher than my knees, displayed my limbs, and moved and turned before him, showing myself to him in various postures and attitudes. In this type of display expressions, too, are quite important, and being keenly alert to the possibilities of interactions with the master. For example, how do you act when you see his eye roving you, and you note indications of interest? Do you dare to seem to express outrage or resentment under his frank examination, do you feign boredom and mechanical compliance, that he may be tempted to turn you into a squirming slut begging for his least touch, are you brazen in your display, an insolent slave, are you proud to exhibit the beauty of your master's merchandise, do you show fear before this strange man, before whom you must so vulnerably perform, do you permit him to glimpse needs, do you beg him, in your performance, for his touch, and so on. On Gor it is the whole woman who is enslaved, in the fullness and depth of her intelligence and emotions. On Gor it is the whole woman who is collared. Gorean masters will have it no other way. I performed then before the floor manager's aide, totally a slave. In short, I put myself through slave paces before him, presenting myself as a total female for his interest and consideration.

Though it was late and we were tired I saw sweat on the brow of the floor manager's aide. I saw his hands move, the fingers wiping sweat from them.

"Very good, Tiffany," said the floor manager. "You may rest now."

"Thank you, Master," I said.

I then retrieved the tray and withdrew. As soon as I had replaced the tray on the serving table, I hurried to where the girls from the next class, that which was next in the training cycle, knelt.

I knelt down with them. "Emily," I said. "What are you doing here?"

"How beautiful you all are," said Emily. "We will never be able to be so beautiful."

"Nonsense," I said. "You, too, will be beautiful. It is just that you have not yet been trained."

"Perhaps," said Emily. Her eyes seemed red with weeping.

"Why are you here?" I asked.

"I do not know," she said. "I must have displeased Aemilianus. Men came for me. I was taken from the house. I was brought to the school yesterday."

"Do you still wear his collar?" I asked.

"Yes," she said. "He still owns me." She looked about herself, at the other members of her class. "Like the others," she added.

"I thought he liked you," I said.

"I thought he did, too," she smiled.

"Do you like him?" I asked.

"I love him," she said, "but he has sent me away."

I nodded. Such may be done with a slave. She is completely at the master's will.

"He is young," I said. "Perhaps he feared your love."

"Perhaps," she smiled.

We watched Crystal displaying herself, after the pretended serving of fruit.

"How beautiful you girls are," said Emily.

"We have been taught our collars," I said.

"I wonder if we can ever become as beautiful," said a girl, one in Emily's class.

"Of course you can," I said.

"I am almost jealous of you, Tiffany," said Emily, "how you look, how you move, how you carry yourself, how exciting and beautiful you have become, how owned, how slavelike!"

"I am the same Tiffany I was," I said.

"No," she said. "You are not."

"Perhaps not," I said.

"Musicians and dancers may leave," called the floor manager. "Tupa to serve fruit. Tupa to the table."

The musicians were soon filing out of the room. The dancers, eleven of them, put on a light neck-chain, dangling between them, followed them.

Another whip master, not he who had supervised the training of our class, appeared. "Class, rise," he said. "Form a single line."

Emily and her class rose and quickly formed a line. Later, I supposed, later in their training, the line would have an exact order, probably being arranged in order of height, with the tallest girls first.

"I wish you well, Emily!" I said.

"I wish you well, Tiffany!" she said.

We kissed.

"March to the cages," called the whip master.

I watched Emily leaving. I wondered if I would ever see her again.

I watched Tupa perform for a moment or two, and then, exhausted, I lay down on the floor.

"Very good, Tupa," I heard the floor manager say. He, too, was weary.

"On your backs, all of you, on the floor," said the whip master, "right knees raised, hands at your sides, palms of your hands facing upwards."

We assumed this position. We felt the tiles on our backs. We had worked hard. We were exhausted. The whip master then conversed with the floor manager and his aide. While they talked we lay on the floor, resting, but each of us, by the will of the whip master, in exactly the same position, a slave position.

"We will take delivery," I heard.

In a few moments the whip master walked amongst us, stepping over a girl here and there, and went to the door.

In another moment or two, two large men had entered. One of them, over his left shoulder, carried several loops of light chain.

"Line!" called the whip master.

We sprang to our feet and swiftly aligned ourselves, single-file. The line was arranged in order of height. In it we each knew our place. I was toward the back of the line. I heard snaps behind me. My left wrist was pulled back. I must keep my eyes ahead. Then I felt the manacle close on my wrist. It was snug. I felt a light chain, dangling, brush my thigh. Then the man was ahead of me, pulling back the left wrist of the woman ahead of me, her eyes, too, fixed forward. I saw the manacle close on her wrist. Then he was moving forward again. I looked down at my wrist. It was locked in a small, shining, steel manacle, chain extending to it, attached to a ring, from the rear, and from it, from another ring, to the front. I was in coffle. We were trained girls and would not be likely to bolt, but, still, as in common practice, we were shackled from the back to the front, eyes forward. The lead girl, Claudia, was now shackled. This completed the coffle. On the chain there were precisely twenty wrist shackles. That, too, exactly, was our number.

"Take them to the agency," said the whip master. "Tomorrow they will begin work."

At a sign from the coffle master, the larger of the two men, he who had not carried the loops of chain, we stepped forth with our left foot, as is common in beginning movement in a coffle.

We were then marched forth, naked, chained slaves.
I looked back once at the school.
We had graduated.

# 29

# HASSAN, THE SLAVE HUNTER

"Oh, no," I begged. "Please, not him, Master!"

"This is not like you, Tiffany," said the floor manager, the feast master. "You are one of our best girls. What is wrong?"

"He terrifies me, Master," I wept. I knelt suddenly before the feast master, with a jangle of slave bells, and kissed his feet. I looked up at him. "Please, no, Master!" I begged.

"He has indicated interest in you," said the feast master.

"Please, no, Master," I begged.

"To him, Slave," he said.

"Yes, Master," I said. I then rose to my feet, trying to compose myself. The feast master had turned away.

It was now two months since we had graduated from the school. It had been, on the whole, a wonderful two months. In the beginning we had had to serve at a feast or banquet only every third or fourth day, or so, but, as our reputation had spread, our engagements had multiplied dramatically. It had now become necessary for the slave masters of Aemilianus to insert open dates in our schedule, that we might remain fresh and rested. Even as of now our services had to be arranged several days in advance. There had apparently been a readiness or need for crews or teams of competitively priced feast slaves in the city. Aemilianus, with that sense of business which seemed to run in his family, had been sensitive to this. Thanks to Aemilianus the luxury of the high feast could now be enjoyed more widely in Ar than heretofore. No longer did one have to have a household filled with slaves to mount such a feast or the wealth of a "Mintar" to arrange for musicians, caterers, serving slaves and dancers. To be sure, we did not come cheap. I, like most of the other girls, was, on the whole, very pleased to be owned by Aemilianus and to be held in this form of slavery. Our work was light and, since we were often used at these feasts, and well, and sometimes many times, it was not necessary to spend much time whimpering and clawing in our kennels. Too, after the first week in the agency, in which we were kept in chains when not serving, we had received a great deal of freedom. Now, during the day, we were generally free to wander about the city as we might please. We needed only obtain the permission of the agency's doorkeeper and be certain to return in the early evening, by the time to report to the feast master. Slave girls, generally, incidentally, enjoy a great deal of freedom. Our requiring the permission of the doorkeeper, or of another free person, before being permitted to leave the agency, incidentally, is a very familiar sort of thing. Slave girls must commonly obtain the permission of a free person before leaving a house or domicile. Once outside the agency, of course, we might wander about almost as we might please. It seemed we could go almost anywhere. To be sure, we would not be permitted outside the gates unless in the company of a free person. In these jaunts we would normally wear loose, modest, white tunics. To be sure, the throats of these tunics must be open, that our collars would always be in plain sight. This is in accord with an ordinance in Ar. Sometimes, incidentally, we would serve at feasts at which free women were present. At such feasts, of course, we would be modestly garbed and serve decorously. Similarly, the dancers would be garbed rather differently than they usually were for an all-male audience, and a similar adjustment or accommodation would be evident in the dances which they performed.

I looked at the man at the table, he who had supposedly indicated an interest in me.

I found him terrifying. Why could he not have wanted Claudia, or Crystal, or one of the other girls?

He was the guest of honor at this feast, a feast held by Eito, an Oriental, a member of the caste of merchants, a citizen of Ar, a dealer in salt, one with connections with some of the towns near the Tahari. Some of his salt was said to come even from Klima, somewhere deep within the Tahari itself. The guest of honor was from the river port of Kasra, on the Lower Fayeen. Kasra lies west of Tor, which lies at the northwestern edge of the Tahari, the great desert, the Wastes.

I was not certain as to the race of the guest. He may have been Oriental, like Eito, but, too, he may have been a mix of Oriental and Tahari stock. He was, at any rate, quite different in appearance and carriage from Eito. Eito was gracious, civilized, polite, humane and affable. The guest was huge, ugly and merciless. His chest was largely bared. He wore black, heavy, leather, studded wristlets. His head was shaven, except for a swirling knot of jet-black hair just behind and below the crown. He was not of the merchants. He made his living in another fashion. He was here presumably because he was something of a celebrity. Too, he was from Kasra. Much salt passes through Kasra. Although his race might be Oriental his name was not. He had a reputation on Gor. I had heard of him in the school. His name was spoken in fear by slaves. He was Hassan, the Slave Hunter.

I wiped the tears from my eyes with a bit of slave silk. I straightened my body. I then hurried to the vicinity of the guest, who was sitting at the right hand of Eito, the host. I knelt before the guest, putting the palms of my hands on the floor and my head to the tiles. I then lifted my head, keeping the palms of my hands on the floor. "Did Master indicate an interest in Tiffany?" I asked.

"Strip," he said, "and come about the table. Address yourself to my pleasures."

"Yes, Master," I said.

In a moment I, naked, kneeling beside him, behind the table, he sitting cross-legged there, began, somewhat timidly, to lick delicately at him, and to softly kiss and caress him. He paid me little attention in this. He continued to drink, his goblet replenished from time to time by Crystal, to eat, from foods served by the other girls, and to talk with Eito. I was only an attentive slave, pressing softly, closely, about him. His back was broad and the muscles of his arms and shoulders were large and powerful. There was little hair on his body.

"It is said that you have the finest hunting sleen on Gor," said Eito.

"They are good hunters," said Hassan. "They have been bred for it."

"The trail of the slave Asdan was said to be two months old," said Eito.

"That of the slave Hippias was three," said Hassan.

"Amazing," marveled Eito.

I pressed myself against the shoulder of Hassan, and kissed and licked, softly, at the side of his neck.

"What brings you to Ar, if I may ask," asked Eito.

"I am hunting," said Hassan. "I, my men, and the animals."

"And what luckless slave is now your quarry?" inquired Eito.

"No slave," said Hassan, chewing on the leg of a roasted vulo, tearing meat from it with his teeth.

"I thought you hunted only slaves," said Eito.

"Kassim, the rebel pretender to the throne of Tor, whom my animals tore to pieces, was no slave," said Hassan.

I shuddered. Then I again kissed him, softly, almost unobtrusively, about the shoulder. I did not wish to intrude my presence too obviously upon him. This was not merely because I feared him but had to do also with the situation in which I found myself. It was not my role, in a situation of this sort, to truly distract him. I must not interfere, truly, for example, with his conversation. I must be in the background, almost like background music, in a situation of this sort, unless summoned forth. Yet, in spite of my will, I felt heat and moistness between my thighs. I could not deny that his closeness, and his might and power, in spite of my fear and my will, were arousing me. I was close to him, and servile and soft, and was becoming excited. How small and soft I seemed next to his might and power. Here there could be no confusion of natural relationships. It was obvious that such as he were the masters and such as I were the slaves. I restrained a whimper. How conscious his presence made me of my nudity, and my collar. My entire body was becoming extremely sensitive. I had been a free woman, on Earth, tutored in the false myths of my culture. Here, in a natural world, I found myself in my place, a collared slave, in attendance on a master.

"Who, then, is your quarry?" asked Eito. "Who is he?"

"It is not a 'he,' " said Hassan, tossing the vulo bone on his plate. "It is a female."

I drew back from Hassan, frightened.

"One who is well-known?" asked Eito.

"Yes," said Hassan.

"May I inquire who?" asked Eito.

"It is no secret," said Hassan.

"Who?" asked Eito.

"Sheila," said Hassan, "the former Tatrix of Corcyrus."

I drew back even further. I began to tremble, uncontrollably.

"But why are you in Ar?" asked Eito. "Surely she would not be in Ar. Ar would surely be one of the last places in the world in which one would expect to find her."

"That is what she, too, will think," said Hassan. "That is why I am certain she is here."

"I understand there is a high reward for her capture," said Eito.

"Yes," said Hassan. "It is now fifteen hundred gold pieces. But I am interested in more than the money. I have heard much of this proud, haughty woman. I intend to bend her to my will."

"I see," said Eito.

Hassan then turned and regarded me. "Lie down," he said, "and split your legs."

"Yes, Master," I said.

"Excuse me," said Hassan to Eito.

"Of course," said Eito, then directing his attention elsewhere, beginning to engage in conversation with the fellow on his left.

"What is wrong?" asked Hassan, bending over me.

"Forgive me, Master," I said. "I am afraid of you. Too, I fear for poor Sheila, the Tatrix of Corcyrus."

"I noted your responses," said Hassan.

"I know your reputation as a huntsman, Master," I whispered. "I fear she has little more chance than a slave."

"She is a proud, free woman," said Hassan, "but I will hunt her like a slave."

I moaned.

"What is your concern with her?" he asked.

"We are both, ultimately, women," I said, "who must fear and serve men."

"It is not my fault," said Hassan, "that you are both, ultimately, of the slave sex."

"No, Master," I said.

"You are a pretty slave," he said.

"Thank you, Master," I said. "Are you going to hurt me?"

"Are you going to be absolutely compliant and fully pleasing?" he asked.

"I will be absolutely compliant," I said, "and I will attempt to be fully pleasing."

"Good," he said.

"Am I to be hurt, then?" I asked.

"It will be done with you as I please," he said.

"Yes, Master," I said.

"It is interesting," he said. "Earlier you seemed warm and ready. You were weak and almost panting. I could smell you. Now you seem cold, and tight."

"Forgive me, Master," I said.

"Do you juice well?" he asked.

"Usually, Master," I said.

"Perhaps I can warm you," he said. He then began to touch me. I dared not resist that touch, and I was helpless under it.

"Have you ever seen the Tatrix of Corcyrus, Master?" I asked, beginning to twist under his hands.

"No," he said.

"Ohhh!" I said. His touch was now reminding me, clearly, that I was in a collar.

"I think you are going to juice," he said.

"Yes," I said. "Yes!"

"I have received detailed descriptions of her, of course," he said. "For example, it might be interesting to you to know that you, apparently, at least in general outlines, resemble her." He drew back from me, regarding me. "It is interesting," he said. "You would probably resemble her rather closely."

"Master?" I asked.

"There is the same eye color and hair color, and general coloring," he said. "Too, your figure would seem to be quite similar to what hers was conjectured to be, and you would certainly seem to be quite similar to her in general size, with respect to height and weight, Too, there would seem to be a similarity in such things as conjectured wrist, ankle and collar sizes."

"You seem to have been furnished with rather complete descriptions," I said. I was surprised that he had been furnished with estimations of wrist, ankle and collar sizes. One does not usually think in terms of such things where free women are concerned. On the other hand, such measurements, I supposed, are pertinent to any woman. An experienced slaver, incidentally, can usually tell a woman's wrist, ankle and collar sizes almost at a glance. I took a number-two ankle ring and a number-two wrist ring. I took a ten-hort collar. These are common and standard sizes. The most commonly worn wrist and ankle rings are the twos and threes. The most common collar sizes are the ten-, eleven- and twelve-hort sizes.

"Yes," he said. "And you seem to fit these descriptions rather well."

"Perhaps I am she," I suggested.

"Perhaps," he said. He then again bent over me. I turned my head to the side. I felt his hands on me.

"How do you know I am not she?" I said. "Oh, Oh!"

"It does not seem likely that she is a squirming slave," he said.

"Oh!" I cried. "But you have never seen her," I said.

"No," he said.

"How, then, will you know her?" I asked.

"I will not know," he said. "The sleen will know."

"Master?" I asked. I tried to hold myself tense. I tried not to feel.

"In Corcyrus," he said, "I was furnished with clothing which she had worn. It is with me, even in Ar now, as are my men and the sleen. The hunt begins tomorrow."

"But Ar is a great city," I said. "It must contain, surely, more than a million people." It must contain then, older and newer, some more faded, some fresher, millions of trails. Surely it would be impossible to pick out single trails from among such eroded, collapsed and jumbled strata of scent.

"It is true that it will not be easy," said Hassan.

"She may not even be in Ar," I said.

"She is here," he said, his hands then again on my body, forcing me to feel.

"Please be gentle, Master!" I begged.

Then, suddenly, he was gentle with me. I leaped gratefully under his touch. Then again he was strong with me, reminding me that I was owned.

Then I reared helplessly to him, at his mercy.

"How are you going to yield to me?" he asked.

"However Master wishes," I cried.

"Do not try to resist me further," he said. "I do not like it."

"No, Master!" I said.

"Feel," he said. "Feel, deeply."

"Yes, Master," I said. Then I began to feel, and feel

deeply, as a helpless, commanded slave. I felt him beginning to turn me inside out with sensation. I began to moan and whimper. Then I could no longer even think of resisting him. I sobbed, and begged for his penetration.

"Your resemblance to the Tatrix of Corcyrus is interesting," he said.

"I beg to receive you, Master!" I wept.

"Quite interesting," he said.

"You have done this to me," I wept. "You have conquered me. Now claim me. I beg to be claimed! Have me, own me, claim me, make me yours. I beg to be made yours, Master!"

"It is uncanny," he said, "the same eye color, the same hair color, the general coloring, all the other things."

"You will never find her," I cried out, angrily, through gritted teeth.

"It will not be easy," said Hassan, condescending to enter me, as I held out my arms eagerly to him, "but I will find her."

I then held him to me, desperately. I scarcely dared move. I was a surrendered slave. I sensed myself on the brink of a submission orgasm such as I had never suspected existed.

"Resist me now," he said.

"I cannot!" I sobbed. "You have brought me too far! You know you have brought me too far! You know that resistance is now impossible!"

"Struggle to resist," he said.

"Yes, Master," I sobbed. Then, with various rhythms and depths, he began to subject me to the torture of the withheld submission. "Please," I begged him. "Please!"

"Very well," he said, after a time, and I cried out, yielding to Hassan, the Slave Hunter.

Afterwards he had me clean him, with my lips and tongue, and I, naively, did so, not understanding what he intended. Then I was startled by his vitality. Then I found myself again had. They had taught me nothing of that in school. Then Hassan finished with me, drew his tunic again about himself and returned to conversation with Eito. I crept away and retrieved my slave silk. I then lay down on my side at the side of the room, my knees drawn up, the bit of slave silk clutched to me. I was half in shock. I felt small and helpless, and had. I had been devastated by Hassan, the Slave Hunter. Never before, and particularly the second time, had I yielded so helplessly, so slavishly, to a man. Never before had I been taught so thoroughly, so incontrovertibly, that men are the masters. Yet never before, too, had my femaleness felt so deeply real. Conquered and taught, informed and grateful, I lay there; I found myself rejoicing in my femininity; I found myself treasuring my womanhood; how glad, how very glad I was, that I was a woman.

The feast was now finishing and most of the guests, including Hassan, the guest of honor, had gone home.

"Are you all right, Tiffany?" asked the floor manager, the feast master.

"Yes, Master," I said.

He was a kind man. He did not make me serve further.

I lay there, resting, and recovering from the emotional consequences of Hassan's uses of me. I gradually began to feel a surprising elation. I had been in the very arms of the man who sought Sheila, the Tatrix of Corcyrus, and he had not recognized me. Even Drusus Rencius, perhaps, or Miles of Argentum, too, men who had actually seen me, I thought, might not recognize me now. Perhaps even little Susan would not recognize the lofty Sheila, the Tatrix of Corcyrus, in the collared, branded, trained, lascivious pleasure slut, Tiffany, a girl of Feast Slaves, of the Enterprises of Aemilianus, the Plaza of Tarns.

I was safe.

I did not fear the sleen of Hassan. They could never find me in Ar.

I was safe.

## 30

# SHEILA, THE TATRIX OF CORCYRUS

"Why are you fearful?" asked Claudia.

"They are coming this way," said Crystal.

"They were supposed to have left the city a week ago!" I cried.

"Apparently they did not do so," said Tupa.

"There is a crowd with them," said Claudia, excited. "Let us join them, and see where they go!"

"No!" I said. "No!"

Claudia looked at me, puzzled. We were on the Street of Hermadius, off the Plaza of Tarns. We all wore draped, sleeveless white tunics. These tunics, though brief, were rather modest in appearance. To look at us you might not have known that we were feast slaves. We were barefoot. Our collars were in plain sight. In his good taste, Aemilianus did not require us to wear advertising on our backs.

"What is wrong with you?" asked Claudia.

"Nothing!" I said. I looked back up the street. The crowd, indeed, as Crystal had observed, seemed to be coming this way. They had turned into this street from the plaza itself.

I looked down at the street. It seemed dirty. This was not usual for Ar. Usually, once a week, the streets are swept and washed down. This is usually the responsibility of those whose buildings face the street, the larger avenues, squares and plazas, and such, being cleaned by state slaves. Two days ago the smaller streets, such as the Street of Hermadius, should have been cleaned. Slave girls, who often go barefoot, tend to be very much aware of this sort of thing. I saw a slave girl, in a brief, brown tunic, standing near a wall, outside of a shop. She did not seem to be going anywhere and was not chained there. I thought, then, she might belong to the owner of the shop. Perhaps she had just emerged from the shop. She was shading her eyes, and looking down the street. Probably she had heard the crowd in the distance, and had come out to see what might be afoot.

"Mistress," I said to her, to flatter her.

"Yes, High Girl," she said.

"I am not a high girl," I said.

"You wear a high girl's tunic," she said.

I swiftly knelt before her. "Are you owned by the shopkeeper here?" I asked.

"Perhaps," she said.

I looked back at the crowd, some two or three blocks away, approaching.

"Answer me a question, Mistress," I begged.

"Perhaps," she said.

"Please," I said.

"Kiss my feet, High Girl," she said.

I did so.

"What do you want to know?" she asked.

"Two nights ago," I said, "one would have expected these streets to be cleaned. Were they?"

"Is this important to you, to know this?" she asked.

"Yes," I said.

"Kiss my feet again, High Girl," she said.

I did so.

"More deferentially and lovingly," she said.

"Yes, Mistress," I said. Then I looked up at her.

"No," she said. "We received commands from the Central Cylinder itself, from the very palace itself, not to do so. Even the great squares were not washed down this week."

"Thank you, Mistress," I said. I leaped to my feet, sick.

Claudia, Crystal and Tupa were looking down the street. The crowd was now only about a block away. In the front of the crowd, their snouts down to the ground, almost on the paving stones themselves, were two gigantic gray sleen. Their ears were laid back against their heads. Each was being restrained by two men, a stout chain leash in the hands of each man. Even so the sleen, in their eagerness, were almost dragging their keepers. Behind the sleen, huge and menacing, his chest bared, a long, coiled whip in his right hand, was Hassan, the Slave Hunter. With him were some armed men, probably his. With them, too, were some officers of Ar. With them I saw, too, one uniform of Argentum. Behind these all, eager and excited, pressing about, spilling forward about the sides, some running and pushing, was the crowd. I fled away, down the street. "Tiffany!" I heard Claudia call, from behind me. I ran.

I turned from the Street of Hermadius into Silver Street and ran from there to the avenue of the Central Cylinder. Then I was running along the western edge of the concourse, under the trees. I leaned against a wall, gasping.

"Do not loiter here, Girl," said a man.

"Forgive me, Master," I said, bowing my head and backing away, then turning and hurrying a few yards further down the avenue.

I came to a fountain, one of many on the avenue. It had two bowls, an upper bowl and a lower one, closer to the walking level, the water from the upper bowl spilling over into the lower. Free persons might drink from, or draw water from, the upper bowl. The lower bowl was for animals and slaves. Sweating and breathing heavily I put myself to all fours by the fountain and, bending down my head, lapped at the water.

Then, wiping my mouth with the back of my hand, I stood up.

I saw sleen, and those with them, turning onto the avenue of the Central Cylinder.

I cried out with misery, and again fled.

I looked wildly about.

I saw no signs now of the crowd and the animals.

I stood at the northwestern corner of the Teiban Sul Market, at the intersection of Teiban and Clive. I had come west from the avenue of the Central Cylinder on Clive.

I looked back up Clive. I saw no signs of the crowd and animals.

I began to breathe more easily.

By now, surely, they would have been coming west on Clive. They must have lost my trail.

"Suls, Turpah, Vangis!" I heard a woman call, sitting amidst baskets, hawking her produce.

I had gone to the avenue of the Central Cylinder and had kept to busy streets in the hope that the sleen would lose my scent, it being mingled with that of so many others.

Now it seemed I had been successful.

Then, from some two hundred yards away, I heard the

shrill, excited squeal of one of the animals. I looked wildly south, down the Boulevard of Teiban. The sleen, and those with them, had come west on Venaticus. As Clive borders the Teiban Market on the north, so Venaticus borders it on the south. To my horror, I saw the sleen, and the crowd, turning right, north on Teiban. They were proceeding toward me. I did not understand this. Why had they not come down Clive? Then, suddenly, sick, I remembered that I had, two days ago, taken Venaticus west to Teiban. It must be that trail, two days old, that they were following. I swiftly fled west, continuing on Clive. In a few minutes I had come to Clive and Hermadius. It was on Hermadius, less than an Ahn ago, that I had first seen the sleen. I continued west on Clive, and turned left, south, on Emerald. This street, like Hermadius, leads to the Plaza of Tarns. But I was not seeking the Plaza of Tarns and the agency. I turned right, off Emerald, when I came to Tarn-Gate Street. This is the street which leads directly between Ar's west gate, called the Tarn Gate, and the Plaza of Tarns.

When I came to the west gate I knelt before a citizen. "Master," I said, "may I accompany you through the gate?"

"No," he said.

I rose to my feet, and looked behind me.

Then I approached the gate more closely. The security here seemed unusually strict today. I did not understand this. Wagons were being inspected even to the point of prying up the lids of boxes and slitting open sacks. I saw a slave girl who was hooded stopped and unhooded, and examined carefully. Then she was rehooded and, on her leash, in the company of a master, allowed to proceed.

I walked boldly, nonchalantly, toward the gate.

Then I was stopped, crossed spears before me. "Forgive me, Master," I said, bowing my head, and quickly moving back, then turning away.

A few yards from the gate I stopped and turned again, and looked at it. Tears sprang into my eyes.

I then fled north for a few blocks on the Wall Road, and then turned right, east, to make my way back to Emerald. I saw no sign of the sleen or the crowd on Emerald. In this fashion I had doubled back on my trail. I hoped this might confuse the sleen. I continued to walk north on Emerald. The streets, I noticed, everywhere, had apparently not been swept down and washed. That injunction against their cleaning had apparently not been confined to a given district. It seemed to have been citywide in its scope.

I was bewildered, and confused and miserable. I did not know if I had eluded the sleen or not. I did not know what to do. I was afraid to return to the agency and afraid not to return to it. My trails would presumably be particularly rich and numerous in that vicinity. Certainly I left that building in the morning and returned to it in the evening. On the other hand, if I did not return to it, I did not know, then, what I should do. I could not leave the city and, if I remained within it, it seemed obvious that I must be apprehended, if not by the sleen then by free citizens, probably guardsmen. I did not think it would be difficult for them to do so. I would stand out. I was garbed as what I was, a slave, and my collar, which I could not remove, clearly identified me. Indeed, as soon as it became dark I would become suspect as a runaway slave. Slave girls, with the exception of coin girls, lure girls for taverns, and such, are generally not permitted to walk unaccompanied about the streets of a city after dark. I did not have the common garb of such slaves, such as the bell and coin box chained about my neck, of the coin girl, or the tavern silk, with its advertising, of a tavern's lure girl. My absence from my kennel would presumably be reported by midnight, the twentieth hour of the Gorean day. By morning guardsmen would be alerted to be on the lookout for me. How, too, could I live in the city? I might try to live by begging and scavenging garbage for a time as do those vagrant free women sometimes called she-urts, but I, being collared, could never pass for one. The she-urts often wear tunics almost as short as those of slaves. This is supposedly to make it easier for them to flee from guardsmen. On the other hand the guardsmen usually ignore them. Sometimes they will catch one and bind her helplessly, just to let her know that she can be caught, if men wish. These she-urts have their gangs and territories. I had little doubt but what they might set upon me and bind me, and turn me over to guardsmen, hoping for some small reward. I, being a slave, could hope for no mercy from them. They would hate and despise me. As low as they might be they were a thousand times higher than I. They were free women. Once or twice a year, particularly when there are complaints, or they are becoming nuisances, many of them will be rounded up and taken before a praetor. Their sentence is almost invariably slavery. Interestingly, once branded and in the collar, and knowing themselves helpless and under suitable male discipline, it is said they become joyful and content. It is almost as if they had adopted their mode of life and slavelike costumes because, in some part of themselves, perhaps some deep, hidden part, they were begging men to take them and make them slaves. They thought they hated men but they were, in fact, only begging to be put at their feet.

"Hold, Slave!" called a voice. "Do not look back! To the wall! Not so close! Back further! Now lean forward, putting the palms of your hands against the wall. Spread your feet, widely. More widely!"

Swiftly, frightened, I complied. Then I felt his foot kick my feet yet farther apart.

I was helpless, leaning against the wall, my feet, very widely, terribly uncomfortably, apart. My own weight held my hands against the wall. If I were to remove a hand from the wall I would fall against it; from such a position, so awkward and helpless, it is difficult to regain one's balance quickly and smoothly. In such a position one is much at the mercy of the one behind one.

"Oh!" I said.

He swiftly determined that I was unarmed. To be sure, this is not a difficult determination to make when one is in a slave tunic.

"Oh!" I cried.

"You are not wearing the iron belt," he said.

"No, Master," I said.

"You may kneel," he said.

I struggled to the wall, and then turned and knelt before him. He was a guardsman.

"Who are you?" he asked.

"Tiffany," I said, "of Feast Slaves, of the Enterprises of Aemilianus, the Plaza of Tarns."

I dared not lie to him. He could check my collar. I carried my identification about with me. It was locked on my neck.

He crouched down before me and took my wrists in his right hand, holding them together. He then, with his left hand, pulled my head back. He checked the collar. I had not thought he would have done so. I was now especially pleased I had not tried to lie to him. Had I done so I suspected I would immediately, on such suspicious grounds, after a summary beating, have been braceleted and leashed.

He rose to his feet.

"You are a long way from the Plaza of Tarns," he said.

"Yes, Master," I said.

"What are you doing here, alone?" he asked, not unkindly.

"Walking, Master," I said.

"You are not in the iron belt," he said.

"No, Master," I said.

"You are far north on Emerald," he said. "You are not now on Hermadius or the avenue of the Central Cylinder."

"No, Master," I said.

"I advise you to stay away from the lesser-known streets in this area," he said. "I would stay on Emerald or return south. These are not strolling areas for pretty slave girls, particularly for those not in the belt."

"Yes, Master," I said. "Thank you, Master."

He then turned about and left me. I rose to my feet. He had been very kind to me, considering that I was a slave. Tomorrow; of course, if certain pick-up orders were issued, he would doubtless recall that a slave named Tiffany, with short blond hair and blue eyes, had been encountered in this area.

I looked down one of the side streets. Some of these streets, like many streets in Gorean cities, did not even have regular names. One finds one's way about by knowing the area or inquiring for directions from those who do. Some streets are known informally by descriptions such as "the street where the leather worker Vaskon has his shop," "the street where the poet, Tesias, wrote such and such a poem," "the street where you can find the house of the general, Hasdron," "the street of the tarsk fountain," and so on. Irritatingly enough the same street is sometimes known by different names to different people. It is fairly common, for example, for a given street to be commonly known by one name at one end of it and another name at the other end of it, and perhaps by even another name or two, or three, along its length. For example, at one end people might think of it as the street where Vaskon, the leather worker, has his shop, and at the other end people will think of it as the street where Milo the Baker has his pastry shop. Sometimes incidents seem to give names to streets as well, such as "Fire Street," "Flood Street," "the street of the Six Raped Slaves," and so on. There seems to be a natural development, in many cases, from an unnamed but familiar street, to a street which is usually thought of under a given description, to a street which finally receives a name in a fairly ordinary sense. For example, "the street where the Initiates have their temple" is not unlikely to become "Temple Street"; "the street where you can find the brewery" may well become "Brewery Street," and so on. For example, one would expect, eventually, that the streets where Tesias wrote such and such a poem, or set of poems, such as, say, the *Oracles of the Talender,* will become more simply something like "Tesias Street" or even, as Tesias himself might have preferred, "Talender Street." Street signs in Gorean cities, where they exist, incidentally, are not mounted on poles. They are commonly painted a few feet above the ground, on buildings at corners. Many buildings at intersections in Ar, incidentally, particularly where the streets are narrow, have rounded corners. This is to enable fire wagons speeding through the streets to make faster turns.

Frightened by the guardsman's warning, and not wishing to retrace my steps on Emerald I turned to my left, to take a side street to the Wall Road, which I assumed would be safe. Surely the Wall Road, which followed the interior circuit of Ar's walls, was only some four or five blocks west. But I could not reach it directly. I took one street into another, and then another, and the streets seemed to be becoming narrower and more dingy. It was hot in the afternoon now and there were few people abroad on them. In a few Ehn I became confused, and suddenly came to realize that I was lost. I did not know the streets by name in this area and even had I been able to read the signs, there were none written here on the corners of the buildings. I was no longer fully certain even, with the shadows, the narrowness of the streets, their many turnings, of my general orientation. I could not even, because of the twistings of the streets, walk in a given straight direction. I saw a youth lounging against a wall. I put my head up and walked past him.

After a few yards I looked back. He was watching me, but he had not moved. I hurried on. I made the only turn I could, right, at the end of the street.

In a few moments, I rejoiced. I could see the wall, beyond the end of the street. This street, too, was wider than the others. It was bright and hot. It seemed deserted. Happily I hurried forward.

"Greetings, Pretty Slave," he said.

He was in front of me. I stopped, suddenly. He must have come somehow, between or through the buildings. He must have known the way I would have to come.

"Do not kneel," he said.

He took me by the arm.

"Master?" I said.

He held me by the arm. He looked up and down the street. It was empty.

He then began to conduct me, holding me by the arm, toward an alley.

"Do not make any noise," he said, "or I will slit you like a larma."

He took me into the alley, and, in a few moments, we came to a recessed place, between two buildings. He took me into this place and there pushed me back against a wall at one end of it. I could see the alley behind him. I felt the brick wall at my back. He was standing very close to me. He was much larger than I. He read my collar. "A feast slave, eh?" he said, much pleased.

"Oh!" I said, softly.

"And not belted," he grinned.

He then turned me about and pushed me against the wall. I felt my hands jerked behind my back and casually looped with cord. Then the loops grew snug. Then the knot was jerked tight, quite tight. I was helpless. I gathered that I was not the first girl he had brought to this place.

"Turn around," he said. "Face me."

I did so. I could feel one end of the cord dangling from my wrists brush against the back of my ankles. I knew the meaning of this. He did not intend to be soon done with me.

"You may now kneel," he said.

I did so, bound before him.

"Please me," he said.

"Yes, Master," I said. I bent down. I would begin at his feet.

Later I lay on my side in the recessed place off the alley. My ankles were pulled up behind me and tied to my wrists. He was sitting nearby, resting back against a wall.

"Please, Master," I said. "Let me go."

He crawled over to me and untied my ankles.

"Thank you, Master," I said.

Then he thrust them apart.

"Oh!" I cried. Then my tunic was thrust up to my waist.

He looked down at me.

"Master?" I said.

"Say, 'I am an expensive feast slave,' " he said.

"I am an expensive feast slave," I said. I supposed it was true. I would probably bring at least a silver tarsk in most markets. I was comely, and was now trained.

" 'But I beg on my back, with my legs spread, for your use,' " he said.

"But I beg on my back, with my legs spread, for your use," I said.

"Again," he said, "with more feeling."

"I am an expensive feast slave," I said, "but I beg on my back, with my legs spread, for your use."

"Very well," he said. Then he had me.

After he was finished he turned me to my belly and untied my hands.

"You may thank me," he said.

"Thank you,. Master," I said.

He then slipped away. By the time I rose unsteadily to my feet and stumbled from the recessed place into the alley he was nowhere in sight. He had taken the cord with him. Perhaps he thought it was lucky. Perhaps he thought he might have further use for it, if another slave, alone, unwary, undefended, might stray across his path. I left the alley. I smoothed down my tunic. He had not even removed it. It was now in the late afternoon. I saw the wall, over some buildings, in the distance. I began to walk slowly toward it. I must have been preoccupied. My first awareness of the nearness of the sleen was that wild, hissing, excited squeal not more than a hundred yards behind me. It was the kind of noise they sometimes make when eager upon a scent but are being restrained. They wish to lunge ahead but are not permitted to do so. It serves to signal their keepers of the strength of the scent, and perhaps to some extent ventilates their frustration and expresses their excitement.

"There she is!" I heard someone cry.

I swiftly looked about and saw the two sleen, each with its two keepers, and Hassan and his men, and the others with him, and, following them, perhaps some one or two hundred of the citizens of Ar, both men and women.

I fled before them.

"Loose the sleen!" I heard someone say.

If the sleen were unleashed they would doubtless be upon me in a matter of Ihn. I ran wildly down the street. I looked about. The sleen had not been unleashed, at least as yet. Had they been I would have knelt down and covered my face with my hands. I would not have wanted to see them leaping towards me, eyes blazing, fangs bared, jaws sopped with salivation, to seize me. I stumbled on, down the street, before the animals, before the hunters, before the eager crowd. I saw one or two men on the street back against the buildings. They did not wish to be in my vicinity, it seemed if the sleen should close with me. I continued, wildly, to run. The sleen and the hunters, efficiently, patiently, must have been trailing me for Ahn. Too, they must have switched trails, picking up my fresher trail. For example, if they were following my trail of two days ago, where I had come west on Venaticus instead of Clive, they would not have been in this area. This was my first time in this part of the city. Accordingly, they must have switched trails, probably in the vicinity of the Plaza of Tarns. It is natural for a sleen placed on a scent to follow its strongest traces.

I heard the crowd crying out with eagerness. They, or many of them, some perhaps leaving the group and others joining it, had been long on the hunt. Now it seemed they eagerly anticipated its conclusion.

I sobbed, and fled ahead of them. None ventured to stop me in my flight.

I heard the sleen squealing behind me.

Soon I began to gasp and stumble. I fell, and leaped up, and ran again.

I ran blindly, terrified, gasping. It seemed I had spent the day in flight, in terror. Then I had been caught and bound as what I was, a slave, and forced to give pleasure. Then I had been forced to beg on my back, with my legs spread, for my raping which then, insolently, had been administered to me. I had even had to thank the rapist for his attentions to me. Now, again, sleen behind me, I ran.

"No!" I cried, suddenly. "No!"

Before me was a wall, with a high wooden gate. It must surround the courtyard of some private house. Buildings hemmed me in. There was no way through or around the buildings. There was no opening here to the Wall Road, which must, judging from the proximity of the wall, be only forty or fifty yards behind the building.

I turned wildly about.

Escape was cut off.

I sank miserably to my knees beside the gate, sobbing. I covered my eyes with my hands. I did not want to see the sleen.

I heard the squealing of the sleen, and shouts of the crowd, the chain leashes on the beasts' collars, the scratching of the beasts' claws on the paving, the shouts of men, and was conscious of bodies swirling about me. I shrieked as the snout of one of the sleen thrust snuffling against me, and then it turned away.

"What are you doing here, Tiffany?" asked Claudia. Crystal and Tupa were with her. "I thought you did not want to follow the hunt."

"You should not have run," said Crystal. "Some of those in the crowd thought you were the quarry."

"That was stupid of you, Tiffany," said Tupa. "Suppose the sleen had been excited and struck at you."

I looked about, bewildered, stupefied. Men were breaking the gate at the dwelling. I saw it splinter in. The beasts with the hunters, and others, the crowd, entered the yard.

"Come along!" cried Claudia. "Hurry!"

Shaking, scarcely able to stand, I followed Claudia, and Crystal and Tupa, into the yard.

"Back!" shouted Hassan to the crowd. "Move back!"

The crowd, some two hundred of us, perhaps, pressed back around the interior walls of the yard.

Five of Hassan's men struck down the door of the dwelling and, blades drawn, entered.

The sleen now, arrested in their hunt, crouching down, tails lashing, their chain leashes firmly grasped by their keepers, lay on the flagstones of the courtyard, waiting.

The door of the dwelling hung awry on its hinges. Within, two brackets, on one side, the right, had been literally broken away from the wall.

In the yard, here and there, were patterned areas of grass, and plantings. There was, too, a table there, with two benches. The inhabitants of the dwelling, thus, if they wished, might, without bringing their garments into contact with the ground, eat here on warm evenings. In some places, low platforms of polished wood, often roofed, serve a similar purpose. In more sumptuous houses such dining may take place on porticoes or verandas.

We looked at the empty threshold.

Hassan's whip was now on his belt. It was hooked there, on the whip ring, the coils secured in the snap strap.

He looked at me. I did not think he even recognized me. I had been only Tiffany, a naked slave, a girl from whom, one evening, he had taken some pleasure. He had devastated me, overcoming and totally vanquishing me, making me more henceforth, from those moments, a slave than I had ever dreamed a woman could be. He had changed me, teaching me my true womanhood, ruining me forever for freedom.

He looked away.

He had done much to me.

He did not remember me.

We suddenly heard the clash of steel from within the house. Then, a moment later, there was a crashing of glass.

Then, once more, everything was quiet.

We watched the empty threshold, the door hung awry on its hinges.

In a few moments the figure of a woman, in robes and veils, pushed from behind, appeared in the threshold.

The sleen, squealing, lunged forward. The woman threw her hands before her face, and tried to turn back, to run into the building. The crowd shouted. The beasts' keepers struggled, with their hands in half gloves, to hold the chains attached to those wide, studded collars.

The woman was not permitted to re-enter the building. Rather she was thrust, half stumbling, down the stairs, to the yard. Behind her, in the threshold, stood men of Hassan.

She stood, half crouching, terrified, at the foot of the stairs. The chains on the collars of the sleen were taut.

Hassan moved swiftly between the animals and took the woman by the arm and flung her against the wall of the house. Quickly he positioned her, the palms of her hands against the house, her feet far back and very widely, very uncomfortably, spread. It was the same position the guardsman had placed me in earlier. Then, while she stood helplessly in this position, Hassan's knife stripped her, veils and all, as naked as a slave. He even cut the thongs of her sandals, and pulled them away from her.

He stepped back for a moment to regard her, braced helplessly, leaning forward, against the wall, his naked, barefoot captive. Then he brushed her hair forward, in front of her shoulders. The hair color, I noted, was very similar to mine. She, on the other hand, had long, beautiful hair. She had not been shorn.

He then took a collar from one of his men. It was not an ornate or expensive collar. It was a common collar, one such as any slave might wear.

I do not think she realized clearly, positioned as she was, what he was going to do. Perhaps she expected merely to be leashed. Then, suddenly, she wore a slave collar.

She stumbled suddenly at the wall, almost striking it, and then had her feet under her.

"No!" she screamed. "No!"

She spun about, facing Hassan, who had now withdrawn a few feet.

"No!" she screamed, crouching there. "No! No!" She tore and jerked at the collar, frenziedly. She even tried, irrationally, to thrust it up, over her head, but it stuck, of course, tightly, far back, under her chin.

She ran toward Hassan, and, hysterically, sobbing, struck upon him with her small fists. He let her do this for a moment or two, until she, looking up at him, realized how absurd and futile it was; then he took her by the upper arms, turned her about, and flung her back, yards back to the wall. Stumbling, she struck forcibly against it, and then slipped to its foot. She turned then, on all fours, to regard Hassan. He removed the whip from his belt.

I could hardly believe what I was seeing. It was almost as thought I, too, on all fours, was at the foot of the wall. I could see many differences between us, but, still, the resemblances, in hair and eye color, in general coloring, in figure, in size and weight, and so on, were so close as to be almost frightening. We could easily have been taken for sisters, and perhaps even fraternal twins.

"No!" she cried.

Then the lash fell upon her. She was struck to her belly on the stones, by the wall. There was disbelief in her eyes, blood at her back.

"Do you object?" he asked. "Many times, surely, you have ordered the whip upon the back of others."

She lay on the stones, gasping and shuddering.

Then he struck her twice more, summary blows, instructive blows. They were swift and perfunctory but I think she learned much from them. It seemed she was trying to press herself down into the flagstones. Her fingernails had scratched at them. Hassan replaced the whip at his belt. He pulled her up by the upper arms and placed her against the wall, facing it. He jerked her hands behind her. There were two decisive, metallic snaps. She was fastened in slave bracelets. He then took her by the upper arms and conducted her, half carrying her, to the table in the yard.

"What are you going to do?" she cried.

Then she was flung on her belly half over the table.

"I am a virgin!" she cried. Then she was no longer a virgin. As she still lay half across the table, shuddering, half in shock, a leather collar, with a ring and attached leash, was buckled about her throat, over the snugly fitting steel collar. She was then pulled from the table and, stumbling, with faltering steps, terrified, was drawn by Hassan between the snarling sleen.

He stopped, just within the ruined gate to the yard. He took up the slack in her leash until, it looped in his hand, and with a turn or two about his fist, he held her by it not six inches from him.

She was naked, braceleted, collared and leashed. Eager, restless sleen who had not yet been distracted from her scent with the exact command word, and meat, were only feet away.

Hassan looked deeply into her eyes, as a master might look into the eyes of a slave.

"Who are you?" she begged.

"I am Hassan, of Kasra," he said, "called by some, Hassan, the Slave Hunter."

"No!" she wept.

"I am he," said Hassan.

"I am in the power of Hassan, the Slave Hunter," she said, fearfully, disbelievingly.

"Yes," he said.

I feared she might faint.

"What are you going to do with me?" she asked.

"I am going to take you to my lodgings in Ar," he said, "but we will make a stop first, on the way. Then, helpless, in a golden sack, you are to be taken to Argentum."

Then he held her weight by the leash, and lowered her, gently, to the ground. She had fainted. He bent down and scooped her up and, flinging the leash back, put her over his shoulder, her head behind him. He then, with his men and the sleen, took his leave of the place. I assumed she would soon awaken, on his shoulder. When she did so she would find herself being carried as a slave.

The crowd, then, too, and most of the officers of Ar, began to leave.

I myself, but days ago, had lain, mastered, in the arms of Hassan, the Slave Hunter. "How, then, will you know her?" I had asked Hassan. "I will not know," he had said. "The sleen will know." He had had clothing, from the Tatrix, furnished to him from Corcyus, presumably from her very chambers. It was this which had been used to put the sleen on the scent, only recently in Ar. That clothing, I knew, could not have been mine. The sleen had rejected me. They had sought another. Dozens of things now, suddenly, began to come clear to me. I had been told that I was Sheila, the Tatrix of Corcyrus, that this, here, on Gor, was to be my identity. Perhaps, in a sense, then, I had been Sheila, but, obviously, there must have been another as well, the real Sheila, so to speak. The experience which I had originally taken to be a dream, when I had been drugged, early in my stay in Corcyrus, I now understood had probably not been a dream at all, but my recollection of being inspected, in my half-conscious, drugged state, by Ligurious and Sheila. Doubtless she had been curious to see me. Susan, too, once, had seemed terribly startled to find me in my chambers. She had, presumably, in spite of their precautions, caught a glimpse of the other Sheila, elsewhere in the palace. Naturally she had taken her for me. This, then, would explain her surprise at finding me, so soon and unexpectedly, from her point of view, in my chambers. This explained, too, my unusual and checkered schedule, so to speak, the certain times I must be in my chambers, and so on. These were times when the real Sheila was abroad in the palace, and doubtless attending to the governance of Corcyrus. It made sense, too, now, that I had been kept from the conduct of important business and the making of significant decisions. It was not, really, that I was not ready for such things, but, rather, that it would be absurd that I, not being the true Tatrix of Corcyrus, should concern myself with them. I remembered, too, that I had never been able to understand, really, the fear and hatred with which the Tatrix was viewed. I had done little or nothing, as far as I could tell, to inspire such feelings. These feelings, it now seemed clear to me, would doubtless have been the results of the acts and policies of the true Sheila, the real Tatrix. Unknowingly, I now realized I had seen her in the small room off the great hall on the day that the forces of Ar and Argentum had entered the city. I had known there was a woman somewhere who resembled me. Ligurious had, once or twice, told me as much. He had seemed much enamored of her. That was the woman, doubtless, and I had assumed as much, whom I had seen being leashed and disguised as a capture in the small room. She, apparently in the custody of soldiers of Ar, was to be carried to safety. What I had not realized until now was that she must also have been the true Tatrix of Corcyrus. In the great hall, before his departure, Ligurious had told me that I would soon serve my purpose. "What purpose?" I had said. "That purpose which we feared might one day have to be served," he had said, "that purpose, or major purpose, why you were brought to Gor." Only now, in a yard in Ar, did I fully realize how duped I had been. I had been brought to Gor in the event of just such a contingency. If things should go badly in Corcyrus for Ligurious and the Tatrix, if the people should rise, if the projected war for the mines of Argentum, which must have been truly theirs, turned out badly, they might escape, leaving behind them a pretty little proxy, a naive surrogate, on which enraged multitudes or menacing enemies might vent their wrath. How well they had planned. They had brought me to believe, even, that I actually was Sheila, the Tatrix of Corcyrus, that that, on Gor, at least, was my identity. Surely Susan had believed it, and Drusus Rencius, and many others. How well they had planned! My features, even, had been frequently and publicly exposed in Corcyrus. Thousands would be able to identify me as the Tatrix! But their plans had gone awry. That purpose, or major purpose, for which I had been brought to Gor, had not been served. I had been freed from the cage in the camp of Miles of Argentum. I had managed to escape. Thus, instead of the matter of Sheila, the Tatrix of Corcyrus, supposedly being concluded with an impalement on the walls of Argentum, following which Ligurious and the real Sheila, under new identities, and doubtless with salvaged riches, might proceed almost wherever they might please, an intensive and gigantic search had been initiated. Ligurious and Sheila had expected me to be identified as the Tatrix and shipped under lock and key to Argentum, there to be impaled; they had not expected me to escape; they had not counted on sleen. How unfortunate these events had turned out, at least for the real Sheila, now helpless in the bracelets of Hassan, the Slave Hunter. I thought of the impaling spear and regardless of what she was, or might have been, or what she and Ligurious might have intended for my fate, I could not help but feel sorry for her.

I felt a hand close tightly on the back of my neck. I could not even begin to think of escape.

"Turn about, Slave," said a voice.

The hand released me, and I turned about.

"Do I not know you?" asked Miles of Argentum. It had been he, apparently, in the uniform of Argentum, with Hassan, his men, the sleen, the officers of Ar. I had noted such a fellow with the others as long ago as Hermadius, where I had first seen the sleen.

"I do not think so, Master," I said.

"You look very familiar to me," he said. "Drusus," he called.

One of the officers came towards us.

I gasped, inadvertently.

"Do you know him?" asked Miles of Argentum.

"I do not think so, Master," I said.

"Why did you respond as you did?" he asked.

"It is only that he is such a strong and handsome officer, and I am only a slave," I said.

"Look here, Drusus," said Miles of Argentum. "See what we have here."

"A slave," said Drusus Rencius, dryly, shrugging. I suspected then that Drusus Rencius had seen me in the crowd but had not drawn me to the attention of Miles of Argentum. There was not the least glimmer of recognition in his eyes. It was as though he had never seen me before. I tried to give no sign of this, but I was almost overwhelmed with relief and gratitude. Then I wondered if, perhaps, he truly did not recognize me.

"Look more closely," said Miles.

"Yes?" asked Drusus.

"To be sure," said Miles, "this woman has apparently been shorn within the last three or four months."

"Yes?" asked Drusus.

"Surely you can see the striking resemblance," said Miles.

"To whom?" asked Drusus.

"To Sheila, the Tatrix of Corcyrus," said Miles.

"Yes," said Drusus. "There is a resemblance."

I was confident now that Drusus Rencius recognized me. In the first instant I had seen him, mingled with my surprise, had been incredible joy at once more seeing him. I had had to restrain an impulse to throw myself, licking and kissing, to his feet. I wondered if I were his slave. I wondered if he owned me.

"Is this Sheila, the Tatrix of Corcyrus?" asked Miles.

Drusus lifted up my tunic, on the left, casually, as a Gorean master. He did this with no more thought than one might have lifted up a corner of a tablecloth, or a curtain or drapery. I now realized that whatever might be the feelings of Drusus Rencius toward me I was now a slave to him. Once I had boasted to Drusus Rencius that I knew well how to torture a man. Now, of course, that I was a slave, the tables had been well turned. Now it was I who was at the mercy of men. They could do with me as they pleased. If there were any tortures to be administered, either physical or psychological, it was now I, and not they, who must fear them. I must set myself to be totally obedient and absolutely pleasing. He dropped the tunic back into place. He then stood before me and, with two hands, checked my collar. It was a standard collar. It was well on me. He then took me by the upper arms and, holding me, looked into my eyes. I restrained an impulse to try to press myself against him and kiss him. I wondered what he saw in my eyes, fear, perhaps, and bondage, and that I was his.

"Is it Sheila, the Tatrix of Corcyrus?" asked Miles of Argentum.

"No," said Drusus Rencius. "It is only a slave."

"I see," smiled Miles of Argentum. He put his hand under my chin. "Lift your head, Girl," he said. I did so. He withdrew his hand. I kept my head up. "Stand straighter," he said. I did. I saw that he enjoyed commanding me, as a slave.

Miles of Argentum regarded me. He grinned. "I think," he

said to Drusus Rencius, "this may be Sheila, the Tatrix of Corcyrus."

"Sheila, the Tatrix of Corcyrus," said Drusus Rencius, "has been captured."

"Has she?" asked Miles.

Drusus Rencius was silent.

"Come here, Girl," said Miles. I did so. He read my collar. I felt utterly helpless. By the collar I was clearly identified. I could not leave the city. I could not flee.

"You may go," said Miles, dismissing me.

"Thank you, Master," I said, and, with tears in my eyes, fled through the gate of the yard.

Outside I found Claudia, Crystal and Tupa. They had been waiting for me.

"What did the soldiers want?" asked Claudia.

"One was a general," said Crystal.

"Nothing," I said.

"What was the other?" asked Tupa.

"He was from Ar," said Crystal. "He was a captain."

"Where was the other one from?" asked Tupa.

"Argentum," I said.

"Where is that?" asked Tupa.

"To the south and west," I said.

"What did they want?" asked Claudia, again.

"Nothing," I said.

"Let us hurry back to the agency," said Claudia. "We do not want to be late for check-in."

"No!" said Crystal.

The doorkeeper was a friendly fellow and we did not fear being a little late. On the other hand, we did not wish to risk being switched or lashed across the back of the thighs. Similarly it is no fun to be put on one's stomach and have one's feet, by the ankles, fastened over the six-inch-high, seven-foot-long metal tying bar, and then to have them spanked with a light, springy board.

The other girls were in no doubt as to the route home. They did not even proceed to the Wall Road. They retreated on the street a bit, and then went south and east for a few streets, and then, suddenly, turning right, we found ourselves on Emerald. This was the route, I took it, which had been followed by Hassan, the sleen, and the others. Moving south on Emerald we came, after about an Ahn, to the Plaza of

Tarns. In a few moments, then, we had re-entered the agency.

"You are just in time," said the doorkeeper to us.

We lined up, single-file, at his counter. There was a cup and a pitcher of Bazi tea on the counter. Bazi tea is a common beverage on Gor. Many Goreans are fond of it. I was last in line. He took our disks from the out-board and hung them, one by one, in their places, on the in-board.

"You had best hurry along and get something to eat," he told us.

"Yes, Master," we said. "Thank you, Master."

Along the corridor a bit I turned and watched him lock the agency door. This was fastened with two bars and locks. I then watched him swing shut and lock the gate to our corridor. He then returned to his place behind the counter. From somewhere behind the counter he took out a wrapper and placed it on the counter. It contained a lunch. He also poured himself a cup of Bazi tea. He then began to eat.

I looked at the locked agency door, and the locked corridor gate.

I considered who I was.

I was Tiffany, of Feast Slaves, of the Enterprises of Aemilianus, the Plaza of Tarns. I knew this. Many people knew it. Anyone would know it who read my collar. Miles of Argentum, for example, knew it. I thought of Miles of Argentum. He had let me go. But he had risked nothing. He knew exactly where to find me, if he should care to do so. I was a helpless, imprisoned slave, totally at the mercy of masters.

But doubtless he was not interested in me.

I then went down the corridor, to the kitchen, to get something to eat.

# 31

# ARGENTUM

"Remove your silk," he said.

I did so.

"Kneel," he said.

I did so.

"Straighten your body," he said.

I did so. I knelt naked before Miles of Argentum, before his thronelike chair, on the tiles in his quarters, in Argentum.

"Your knees," he said.

I spread my knees even more widely before him.

"You are now known as Tiffany, I believe," he said, "of Feast Slaves, of the Enterprises of Aemilianus."

"I am Tiffany," I said, "of Feast Slaves, of the Enterprises of Aemilianus."

"I never forget a face," he said.

I was silent.

My entire group had been brought from Ar to Argentum, as though to entertain. This had been done at the expense of Miles of Argentum. Furthermore, much to the surprise and displeasure of the girls, who were perhaps by now somewhat spoiled, we had been brought under heavy security. We had never, from the time we had left the agency in Ar to the time we entered the grounds of the palace in Argentum, been out of chains of one sort or another. I supposed that it was only I, of all the girls, and perhaps of all those on the staff of the agency itself, who suspected the reasons for this trip to Argentum and the rationale of the security. I did not think Miles of Argentum was particularly interested in feast slaves, *per se.* Surely such might be rented in Argentum itself. I think rather he was interested particularly in one feast slave. Tonight I had been brought to him, leashed and braceleted. My keeper, a fellow from the agency, had then, in his quarters, freed me of these bonds and turned me over to him. He had rented me for the night.

"Thrust out your breasts, Tiffany," he said.

"Yes, Master," I said. I lifted and straightened my body even more, sucking in my gut and putting back my shoulders, this lifting the softness of my bosom brazenly to him, as that of a slave girl, for his consideration or attentions.

"You are pretty, Tiffany," he said.

"Thank you, Master," I said.

"I enjoy commanding you," he said.

"Yes, Master," I said.

"Are you a good lay, Tiffany?" he asked.

"Some men have found me acceptable, Master," I said.

"We are going to play a little game, Tiffany," he said.

"We are going to pretend that you are Sheila, the Tatrix of Corcyrus," he smiled.

"But I am Tiffany," I said, frightened, "of Feast Slaves, of the Enterprises of Aemilianus!"

"But we are going to pretend, aren't we?" he asked.

"As Master wishes," I said, frightened.

"Stand," he said.

I did so.

"Straighter," he said.

I straightened up, even more.

He then, from a chest at the side of the room, fetched forth a lovely, yellow, silken sheet. This he draped, regally, about my shoulders.

"Who are you?" he asked.

"Tiffany!" I said. "Tiffany, of Feast Slaves, of the Enterprises of Aemilianus!"

"But we are playing, aren't we?" he asked.

I shuddered.

"Now," said he, "who are you, really?"

"Sheila," I murmured. "Sheila, the Tatrix of Corcyrus."

"I thought so," he said.

I looked at him wildly, frightened.

"Sit in the chair," he said.

"I dare not!" I said. The thought of sitting in such a chair terrified me. It was the chair of a free person. I was a slave. I might be whipped, or slain, for sitting in such a chair. The greatest honor I might expect in connection with such a chair was to be permitted to crouch or lie at its foot, or, perhaps, to be chained by the neck to its side.

"Is a command to be repeated?" he asked.

"No, Master!" I said. I hurried to the chair and, small and frightened, sat down within it.

"Sit up more straightly, more regally, and put your hands on the arms," he said. "Good."

Then he came over to the chair and, bending over, carefully adjusted the sheet about me. He then stepped back. "Good," he said. Then he sat, cross-legged, on the tiles, a few feet from me. "Yes," he said. "Good. That is it." As he sat, he was below me. The angle would be similar to that which he had had from the floor of the great hall, or from the lower steps of the dais, looking up at me on the throne.

"I never forget a face," he reassured me.

I was silent.

"Who are you?" he asked.

"I am Sheila," I said, "the Tatrix of Corcyrus."

"Yes," he said, "you are."

He then rose up and approached me. He drew away the sheet and folded it, horizontally, again and again, until it formed, with several folds, a thick, long, narrow band, about six inches in height and the sheet's length, about seven feet, in width.

He then passed this band about my waist and about the back of the chair. He then tied me, snugly, back in the chair. He then resumed his place on the floor.

"Yes," he said, "clearly, at least a silver-tarsk girl." I recalled that he had conjectured in the great hall, much to the fury of many of my retainers, that that might be about my value in a slave market.

He then rose up, again, and approached the chair. I tried to back, even further, against the back of the chair. My hands and arms were free but the thick, yellow band, knotted tightly behind the back of the chair, held me helplessly in place.

"You are not going to interfere, are you?" he asked.

"No, Master," I said.

Then he began to caress me.

"There was quite a search for you," he said.

"Yes, Master," I said.

"It was lucky that I found you in Ar, wasn't it?" he asked.

"Yes, Master," I said.

"It is convenient that the addresses of many slaves are on their collars, isn't it?" he asked.

"Yes, Master," I said.

"It was thus easy to find you," he said.

"Yes, Master," I said.

"What is wrong?" he asked.

"Nothing, Master!" I said.

"You are squirming," he said.

"Yes, Master!" I said.

"Did you have a nice trip from Ar?" he asked.

"Yes, Master!" I said.

"Were you in chains all the way?" he asked.

"Yes, Master!" I said.

I tried to hold my body still. I dug my fingernails into the arms of the chair.

"It seems that you have been shorn," he said.

"Yes, Master," I said. "It was done last to me a few months ago by Borkon, my whip master, in Mill 7, of the Enterprises of Mintar."

"I see," he said.

"Oh," I sobbed. "Oh!" Then I could no longer control my body.

"You are squirming again," he said.

"Yes, Master," I moaned. I writhed, helplessly, uncontrollably, held in place by the tight band of the sheet, my fingernails digging into the arms of the chair.

"You respond like a slave," he said.

"Yes, Master!" I said.

"Who are you?" he asked.

"Sheila," I said, "Tatrix of Corcyrus!"

"I know," he said.

I tried to lift my body more to him, to make it easier for him to touch.

"That is enough for now," he said. He removed his hands from my body.

I looked at him wildly, piteously, pleadingly. He must not stop now! Surely he knew what he was doing to me.

"Now," he said, "Lady Sheila, you are going to be leashed, and then you are going to perform on your leash, and superbly, and, after that, you are going to beg to please me, and as a slave."

"Yes, Master," I said.

He then went to a chest and from it fetched forth a high, thick, plain, black-leather collar with a lock closure. There was a sturdy ring attached to this collar, and, attached to the ring, there was a long slave leash of black leather. It was some fifteen feet in length. In most leadings, of course, this amount of length would not be used, but would be coiled in the grasp of the master. The length is useful if the slave is expected to perform leash dances, is to be bound with the leash, or if, it doubled at the master's end, it is to be used to train or discipline her.

I sat back in the chair, held helplessly there by the thick bond of the yellow sheet. I watched him approach, with the collar and leash. He then stopped before the chair.

"I am now going to leash you," he said.

"Yes, Master," I said.

"Lift up your chin," he said.

"Yes, Master," I said. I then felt the high, thick collar put about my neck, over the collar of Aemilianus. I could feel it snug under my chin. It was then snapped shut.

"You are leashed," he said.

"Yes, Master," I said.

He then untied the sheet from the chair. I had not been freed of that bond until after I had been leashed. This sort of thing is almost second nature with Goreans in the tyings and chainings of slaves. This is reasonable, I suppose, at least in many instances, that one security should be kept in effect until it has been replaced by another. He folded the sheet twice and dropped it beside the chair.

"What is a woman in a slave leash doing on such a chair?" he asked.

"Forgive me, Master," I said. I did not leave the chair, however. I did not know what he wanted me to do.

"Slip from the chair now," he said, "and go to all fours, and then, in this fashion, crawl ten feet away, and then turn and, in this fashion, face me."

I hastened to obey. Then, in a moment or two, I faced him on all fours, the leash dangling from the collar, its end, as I had crawled, and turned, in front of me, a few feet from the foot of the chair. He had now taken his place on the chair. How right he seemed there, how lordly and masterful.

"You will note," he said, "that you wear a common slave leash and collar. There is nothing unusual or valuable about them. The collar, for example, is neither set with sapphires nor is it trimmed with gold. The leash, similarly, is of plain, sturdy material. Both devices are quite ordinary, but, of course, quite efficient."

"Yes, Master," I said.

"It amuses me to put you in such common articles," he said.

"Yes, Master," I said.

"You are now going to make as complete a circuit of the room as is practical," he said. "You will, where practical, kiss the walls at the corners, on each side of the corner, about five horts from the corner and about ten horts from the floor. Where you come to chests or furniture, you will treat them as extensions of the wall, kissing them at the corners, and so on. You will then return exactly to your present position."

"Yes, Master," I said.

"You may now leave," he said.

"Yes, Master," I said. "Thank you, Master." I then began my journey. The kissing of inanimate articles, such as a master's sandals, or the tiles on which he has walked, is useful in teaching a girl respect and reverence. There was something of this involved in his command, the having to kiss the walls of his room, the furniture there, and such, but the form of the command was presumably motivated primarily by the consideration that compliance with it would guarantee a full and adequate negotiation of the room's interior perimeter.

I was then, after a time, again where I had been before, on all fours, some ten feet from his chair, facing him. The leash, dangling from my collar, was now trailing behind me, between my legs.

"Lift your head," he said.

I did so.

"Come forward five feet," he said, "and keep your head up."

I complied.

"Put your head down," he said.

I complied.

"To your belly," he said.

I went to my belly.

"Up again," he said, "to all fours."

I complied.

"Lift your head," he said.

I did so.

"It is pleasant to have the Tatrix of Corcyrus naked and on my leash," he said.

"Yes, Master," I said.

"You may now bring me the end of the leash," he said, "—in your teeth."

"Yes, Master," I said. I went back to the end of the leash and, putting down my head, to the tiles, picked it up in my teeth. I then, on all fours, brought it, between my teeth, to Miles of Argentum.

He took it from me. I looked up at him, from all fours.

"Does Sheila, the Tatrix of Corcyrus, beg to perform on her leash for Miles, general of Argentum?" he inquired.

"Yes, Master," I said.

He stood up, then, and, with a snap, shook out the leash, and then, looping it, drew it back a bit towards him. He would play it out, or draw it in, as it pleased him, varying his perspective, and my distance from him, as I squirmed, and writhed and posed, from as little as an inch or two to the full length of the leash, something in the neighborhood of a full fifteen feet.

"Perform," he said.

"Yes, Master," I said, and performed.

I performed as excitingly and seductively as possible.

"More lewdly," he would sometimes say, "more salaciously, more lasciviously!"

"Yes, Master!" I would cry, and try to please him even more.

He kept me on the leash for at least twenty Ehn and, in the latter portion of this time, commanded me. It seemed as if he made me move, and posed me, in almost every way in which a strong-drive male might desire to see a human female, and I, of course, must conform perfectly to his wishes on my leash. He even took me about the room and to his couch. He made me do such things as grind my belly against the wall of the room and throw myself, on my belly and back, over the great storage chest, wooden and iron-banded, at one side of the room. I remember the feel of the wood and iron. Too, he permitted me, even ordered me, upon his couch, there to continue my performances. I must first, of course, kneel at the lower left side of the couch and kiss the covers before being permitted to creep upon it. Then he drew me from the couch to the floor at its foot, near the slave ring. With one hand he flung covers to the floor there, on the tiles. He then pointed to a place on the tiles, out from the covers, but in front of them. "A free person has walked here," he said. "Yes, Master," I said. I then, kneeling, put down my head and kissed the indicated place three times.

I looked up at him.

"Crawl here," he said, indicating a place at his feet.

I did so.

"You may now kiss my feet," he said.

I did so.

"You may now beg to be used as a slave," he said.

"I beg to be used as a slave, Master," I said.

"Lit there," he said, indicating a place on the covers, near the slave ring, "on your back."

"Yes, Master, " I said.

He then knelt near me, and took the leash and tied it about the slave ring. He left some four or five feet of leash between the collar ring and the slave ring. That would allow him the slack he might need to move me about, if he wished, kneeling me, say, with my head down, or throwing me to my side or belly.

He then knelt across my body and held my hands, by the wrists, helplessly down, above and to the sides of my head.

"I greet you, Lady Sheila, Tatrix of Corcyrus," he said.

"Greetings, Master," I said.

"Struggle, squirm, attempt to escape," he said.

I struggled briefly, predictably futilely. "I cannot escape," I said.

"Are you in the power of a man?" he asked.

"Yes, Master," I said.

"Completely?" he asked.

"Yes, Master," I said.

"You are completely in the power of what man?" he asked.

"I am completely in the power of Miles of Argentum," I said.

"Long have I dreamed of having you in my power," he said.

"Yes, Master," I said.

"Are you the woman who begged to perform on a leash, and then so performed?" he asked.

"Yes, Master," I said.

"You did well," he said.

"Thank you, Master," I said.

"As I recall," he said, "you also begged, kneeling, and after kissing my feet, to be used as a slave."

"Yes, Master," I said.

"It will be done with you as you requested," he said.

"Thank you, Master," I said.

He then released my hands and, changing his position, knelt on my right.

He then began to touch me, artfully and deftly. After a moment or two I realized I would not, eventually, be able to resist him, even if he were to give me permission to try. His hands were sure. He knew what he was doing. It was only a matter of time. I lay there, helplessly, and felt my slave reflexes beginning to be triggered. I bit at the covers. I saw that he intended that I would yield to him as a sobbing, pleading, subdued slave. In this I saw that I was to be given no choice.

"You are very lovely, Lady Sheila," he said.

"Thank you, Master," I said.

"And you have the reflexes of a female slave," he said.

"Yes, Master," I said. "Thank you, Master." I did not think it would be long now. I suddenly jerked back my body from his touch. He had made it so sensitive. He did not cuff me, nor chide me, but, too, he did not give me quarter. He continued, not hurrying, patiently, relentlessly, with the process of reducing me to a man-dominated, orgasmic, conquered female slave. He now held me, his left hand at the small of my back, in place.

I gritted my teeth. What men can do to us, I thought, angrily. Then I wanted only to feel, beggingly, piteously.

Then again, desperately, I strove to resist. The high, black, leather collar cut at the bottom of my chin.

I could feel the tiles beneath the covers. I had not been granted the dignity of the couch's surface. I would be had at its foot, by the slave ring.

I squirmed. I looked at the slave ring. The leash on my neck ran to it, and was tied to it.

I was leashed!

I felt his hands.

I must resist! I must resist!

"Oh, please, Master," I wept, "let me yield to you as a conquered slave!"

I must resist!

"I beg to yield to you!" I wept.

"In time," he said. "In time."

The beast! The beast! I would show him! I would resist him! I would refuse to feel! I would not let him do this to me!

"Please have pity on me, Master!" I cried. "I acknowledge that I have been conquered. I am vanquished! I am now yours, and as you want me, as a slave, fully! I beg now only to be permitted to yield to you abjectly and shamelessly. Let me tender to you now the helpless surrender of an orgasmic slave!"

Who was it who cried out so shamelessly, so helplessly and brazenly for a master's mercy? And I realized that she who cried out was I.

"Please, Master," I whimpered, sobbing, surrendered, wholly then one with myself, and wholly at his mercy. "Please, Master. Please!"

"Does Lady Sheila, the lofty and proud Tatrix of Corcyrus, desire to yield to me as a slave?" he asked.

"Yes, Master," I moaned. "I beg it! I beg it!"

He then entered me suddenly and fiercely.

I clutched him.

"Please!" I whispered.

"Not yet," he said.

After a few minutes I again begged for his permission to yield. "Not yet," he said. I moaned. He, by varying his rhythms and movements, brought me again and again to the point of yielding, and then stopped short, letting me go back a greater or lesser distance, and then bringing me forward, at one speed or another, again. In this he not only showed his power over me but took much pleasure from me.

"It is pleasant to enjoy the Tatrix of Corcyrus," he said.

"Yes, Master," I sobbed, bitterly.

Yet I could not deny that he was forcing me, too, to experience much pleasure, its nature and amount depending completely on his will.

A quarter of an Ahn must have passed.

Then again, for I do not know what time, he brought me to a point of almost unbearable tension.

"You may now yield, Lady Sheila," he said, "as you have begged, as a slave."

"Thank you, Master!" I cried, and threw my head back in elation and gratitude, and freed myself of feeling, and, as he mastered me, cried out my slave's submission to him.

Afterwards he stood up and looked down, regarding me. "It is pleasant to have had the Tatrix of Corcyrus," he said.

"Yes, Master," I said. I lay, had, at his feet.

He then crouched down, next to me, and rolled me to my stomach. He then jerked my hands behind my back and casually braceleted me. "You will spend the night braceleted," he informed me. "Yes, Master," I said. He then shackled my left ankle and chained me, by means of it, to the slave ring at the foot of his couch. He then unlocked the leash collar and freed me of it and the leash. These articles, with the key, he then replaced in one of the chests at the side of the room. He then took most of the covers and threw them back on the couch. He did leave me a sheet on the tiles. I lay on half of it. The other half, folded, he threw over me. He then retired. Toward morning, in the early hours, he summoned me to his bed and again made use of me. I knelt beside the bed, kissed the covers and crawled into it. He knelt me and turned me about, and pushed my head down. He was quick with me. He was half asleep. I suppose I should have been grateful that I was permitted the honor of the couch. I do not think he, half asleep, wished to leave it. He did not bother unbraceleting me. Then, with his foot, when he was finished, he thrust me from the couch. At the foot of the couch, on the tiles, with my teeth I readjusted the sheet about me, as I could. I then lay there, wide-eyed, for a time, not sleeping.

How far I was from my small apartment, from the perfume counter in the department store on Long Island. That mercenary little chit was now, on this natural world, a braceleted slave at the foot of a man's couch. No longer, now, was she, in the prerogatives of freedom, permitted to give men nothing, or frustration; now she must serve them with perfection and provide them, to the best of her ability, at their merest whim, with fantastic pleasures. At least now, I thought, I am good for something.

How casually Miles of Argentum had just used me! But I did not object, for I was a slave. This form of casual use, this off-handed employment of us, while perhaps inappropriate for a free woman, was acceptable for a slave. We did not have to be the subject of elaborate and tiresome preparations and pretenses, of complex rituals of attention and respect. We could, at times, be mere conveniences to the master, and, in this, too, we find something honest, natural, straightforward and lovely. There are times when the master simply wants us, and now. At such times, too, as we are slaves, it pleases us to serve.

To be sure, the use to which Miles of Argentum had just subjected me, and I was well aware of this, had not been merely casual, a simple convenience use. It had, too, been a spurning use. Though he had not spoken to me, save to summon me imperiously to him, I had little doubt that he was still thinking of me in terms of Sheila, the Tatrix of Corcyrus. What a rich joke on the proud Tatrix! What a splendid lesson for the captured sovereign, to be subjected to a mere convenience use in the early morning, and then to be spurned to her place at a slave ring. But even so I did not object. Something in the woman of me responded to the masterful authority in this treatment. It made clear to me, once again, the delicious, terrible domination to which I was subject on Gor. I wanted men to be my superiors and masters, as they were on Gor. I wanted to be owned by them, as I was on Gor. I wanted to love them, and obey them, as I had to, without choice, on Gor.

I thought of Miles of Argentum.

How skillful he was at teaching a woman her slavery. How well he had put me through my paces on the leash, and then later in his arms. And, but moments ago, he had simply ordered me to him and had then, wordlessly, before taking me, positioned me precisely as he wanted me, my head even down.

I considered my compliance with his wishes and desires. I had obeyed him perfectly. I would not have dared to do otherwise, of course. He was not a man of Earth, or a typical man of Earth. He was a Gorean male.

I twisted a bit on the tiles, carefully, so as not to dislodge the sheet. I moved my wrists a little, they locked helplessly behind my back in their slave bracelets.

How men do with us as they please, I thought. How they master us!

I pulled for a moment, angrily, futilely, irrationally, against the slave bracelets, but I could not, of course, free myself.

What a glorious world this is for men, I thought, that here women such as I must serve and please them!

But then I squirmed with pleasure and joy.

And what a glorious world for women, I thought, that here we must so serve and please!

I felt then the raptures of my bondage, from the tranquillities of selfless service to the ecstasy of a slave's sexual surrender to the dominant male, the master. How perfect I was for bondage; how perfect bondage was for me. I had been designed by nature for bondage. This was clear in my body, and in my nature and dispositions. I rejoiced that I had been brought to a world in which I was free to fulfill, and, in certain circumstances, would have no choice but to fulfill, this implicit destiny. Here, on Gor, there were none of the confusions, the denials, the lies and ambiguities of Earth; here there was clarity, structure and truth. Here civilization did not war with nature; here slaves were slaves, and masters masters. Here I would be what I was, and without compromise, a slave. I did not object. Rather was I thrilled with this, as I had now learned, my natural fulfillment.

But I was frightened of Miles of Argentum.

He seemed to think of me not as the helpless and lowly slave I was, a mere girl rented for his pleasure for an evening, but as though I were a high lady and free captive, Sheila, the Tatrix of Corcyrus, who was then, perhaps in his vengeance on her for her escape from his camp, to be humiliated and humbled, and forced even, in her now unbreakable captivity, to perform and serve as a slave.

Certainly he had taken much pleasure with me.

But he must know that the true Sheila had fallen to Hassan, the Slave Hunter. Only recently he had brought her to Argentum in a golden sack. Even now, for his amusement, he kept her for several Ahn a day in that sack, suspended, tied shut, in the throne room, while business was conducted. The sack was to be opened, and she was to be presented to Claudius, Ubar of Argentum, and the high council, and high citizens of Argentum, at the climax of a great feast, to be celebrated two days from now.

So what interest had Miles of Argentum in me?

Surely he did not think that I might be the real Sheila.

In his treatment of me, and in calling me Sheila, and so on, surely he had been only playing a game with me.

He could not remember me that clearly, I hoped, from his appearance before me in the great hall, when I had sat upon the throne, for from the time when he had had me locked, naked, a captive, in a golden cage.

No. He was only playing with me.

I was merely Tiffany, a feast slave, brought to Argentum with others to serve at the victory feast.

It was not my fault if I bore some remote resemblance to Sheila, the Tatrix of Corcyrus.

I reminded myself that Miles of Argentum did not own me.

I reminded myself that he had only rented me for an evening, for a night, as men may rent women such as I. In a few

Ahn, in the morning, I would be returned to my keepers. He would then forget about me. In a matter of days, probably some three or four days, I would be on my way back to Ar, with the others. I had nothing to fear.

He did not own me. That was what was most important. He could not even harm me, at least seriously, or permanently, without paying some form of restitution to the Enterprises of Aemilianus. I was, after all, their girl property, not his.

I then, toward morning, fell asleep.

I awakened rather late. It must have been around the eighth Ahn. The room was flooded with light.

There had been a knock at the door. It must have been my keeper coming for me, I thought. I struggled to my knees. It is in such a position that a slave girl commonly greets a free man. I did not wish to be kicked or cuffed for discourtesy. Braceleted as I was, I could not keep the sheet on me. It fell across my thighs. But it was someone else, I saw. Miles of Argentum, dressed and shaved, answered the door.

"She will be with you shortly," he said. I did not understand that remark. He then closed the door. I gathered the man might be waiting outside. I did not recognize him.

"I see that you are up, Lady Sheila," he said.

"Yes, Master," I said.

"It is just as well," he said. "It is now past the eighth Ahn."

I did not understand, at that time, the reference to the eighth Ahn. Was that supposed to have some significance to me?

I was then startled. I felt Miles of Argentum, from the back, pressing a tiny key into my collar.

"Master!" I cried.

He then, to my astonishment, opened the collar and removed it.

"Master," I said, "what are you doing? How can you do this? Where did you get the key?"

"In Ar," he said, "several days ago, the first day after I saw you in the city. I paid for you then, but the transfer of ownership, as specified in the contract, as I wished, did not become effective until this morning, at the eighth Ahn. A few Ehn ago, unknown to you, you became mine."

"Surely you jest, Master," I wept. "Feast Slaves would not

wish to sell me in this fashion. I am needed. There is no replacement here for me. There is no girl to attend to my duties!"

"I did not realize one serving slave was so significant," he said, amused.

"They like to have a full complement of slaves on hand," I assured him. "If I were to be sold to you, they would have sent out an extra girl, an addition to my group."

"And so they have," he said, smiling, "though separately, as I requested. Her name is Emily. Perhaps you know her?"

I looked at him, aghast.

"Do you know her?" he asked.

"Yes, Master," I said. "She was trained in the cycle after mine. Apparently they have now transferred her to my group."

"Doubtless as your replacement," he grinned.

"Yes, Master," I whispered. I looked at him. "Then I belong to you, truly?" I asked.

"Yes," he said, "every inch, every hair, every freckle, every drop of sweat, every drop of intimate oil."

I shuddered.

"Here is your new collar," he said, displaying it for me. "Isn't it lovely?"

"Yes, Master," I said. It was an attractive collar of gleaming steel, with a sturdy, heavy lock at the back. In it I would be marked as well, and confined as efficiently as I had been by the collar of Aemilianus.

"See here?" he asked. " 'I am the property of Miles of Argentum,' " he read.

"Yes, Master," I said, miserably.

"Lift your chin," he said.

I did so.

He then snapped the collar about my throat. I wore the collar, then, of Miles of Argentum.

"It is a perfect fit," he said.

"Yes, Master," I said.

"It is the same size as the other collar," he said. "I had your collar size from the Enterprises of Aemilianus."

"Yes, Master," I said.

"You do not seem pleased," he said. "I do not understand that. I thought you would be overjoyed."

"I am overjoyed, Master," I whispered.

"Good," he said. "I like my girls to be happy."

"Yes, Master," I said.

"I paid fifteen silver tarsks for you," he said.

I was startled. "That is too high a price for me," I said.

"I do not think so," he smiled.

"I am not worth anything like that," I said. For such a price one might get a fine dancer. Some of the lesser girls in a Ubar's pleasure gardens might not have cost so much.

"You are to me," he said.

"I will endeavor to see that you get your money's worth," I said.

"Have no fear," he said. "I will."

I began to tremble, uncontrollably. He freed my left ankle of its shackle, that which had fastened me to the slave ring.

"Stand," he said.

I stood.

"You are not very tall, are you?" he said.

"No, Master," I said.

"But you are well curved," he said.

"Perhaps, Master," I said. "Thank you, Master."

"This is the key to your slave bracelets," he said. He showed me a key, on a string. He slung the string over my head and, by it, hung the key about my neck. It fell between my breasts. Much good it did me. I could not reach it with my braceleted hands.

"I am going to turn you over now to Krondos, my slave master," he said. "You will find him a kindly and fair man. On the other hand, your least imperfection in either discipline or service will be severely and promptly punished."

"Yes, Master," I said.

"As I am an indulgent master," he said, "you will be accorded clothing from your first day in my ownership."

"Master is generous," I said. I was not speaking ironically. Sometimes a girl, particularly a new girl, must strive for days to earn even a narrow strip of cloth and a piece of string.

"It will be a tunic appropriate to the girls of Miles of Argentum," he said.

"Yes, Master," I said. He was a soldier. He probably would have a distinctive tunic, in effect, a uniform, for his females. I had no doubt, too, he being a soldier, that it would display us well.

"Clothing privileges, of course, may be quickly revoked," he said.

"Of course, Master," I said.

He picked up my silk, that which I had worn to his quarters last night, before I had removed it at his command, and wrapped it about my old collar and its key. These things he placed on the foot of the couch. They would be returned, doubtless, to a representative of Feast Slaves, currently in the palace.

"After you, Lady Sheila," he said, gesturing graciously toward the door.

I preceded him to the door, where I stopped.

"May I speak, Master?" I asked.

"Of course, Lady Sheila," he said.

"Fifteen silver tarsks," I said, "is a great deal of money to pay for a mere feast slave."

"Yes," he said, "fifteen silver tarsks would be a great deal of money to pay—for a mere feast slave."

"Master understands clearly, I trust," I said, "that that is all I am, that I am only a feast slave."

"Do you really think," he asked, "that I would have paid fifteen tarsks for you, and had you brought here with your group, all the way from Ar, if you were only a feast slave?"

"But that is all I am," I said, "only a feast slave!"

He spun me about, to face him. He stood but inches from me. I was naked. My hands were braceleted behind my back.

"Kiss me," he said.

Obediently I stood on my toes and kissed him.

"Do you call that a kiss?" he asked.

"Permit me to try again, Master," I said. I then kissed him again, but this time as a slave.

"Very good, Lady Sheila," he said. "From the first time I saw you, I thought there was a slave in you."

"I do not understand," I said.

"That is interesting," he said.

"Why do you call me 'Lady Sheila'?" I asked, protestingly.

"It amuses me," he said.

"Who do you think I am?" I asked.

"You are now, as I own you," he said, "whoever and whatever I wish you to be, but the most interesting thing about you, from my point of view, is who you once were."

I looked at him, with fear. "And who do you think I was?" I asked.

He took me and threw me against the wall. I turned, and faced him, the wall at my back.

"You look well," he said, "my former regal slut, now reduced to total slavery, naked and in slave bracelets."

"No," I whimpered. "No, no." I shook my head, helplessly, trying to deny his accusation.

"To my lips," he commanded.

I fled to him, and kissed him, deeply, as a slave. I drew back. I saw that I had kissed him too well. "No, no," I whimpered.

He took me by the upper arms and, thrusting me from behind, forced me across the room. He then put me over one of the large chests at the side of the room. I felt the wood of the chest, and the iron bands. The key about my neck, on its string, made a small sound as it struck the wood.

"It is not my fault if I bear a resemblance to Sheila, the Tatrix of Corcyrus," I said.

"You kissed well," he said.

"Oh!" I cried, entered.

"Very well," he said.

"Thank you, Master," I moaned. Sometimes a slave girl does not understand the incredible power she exerts over men, what she can do to them with a kiss, with a glance, with a smile, a gesture, a touch. My wrists twisted helplessly in the slave bracelets.

"I cannot help it if I resemble her!" I said.

"You do more than resemble her," he said.

"Master?" I cried.

"You were she," he said.

"No, no!" I cried.

"We do not wish to keep Krondos waiting, do we?" he asked.

"No, Master," I moaned. "Of course not!"

"I have discussed your work schedules with him," he said. "You will be worked hard for some five Ahn a day. Your tasks will be such things as laundering, scrubbing floors, and working in the kitchens. These seem suitable tasks for the former Tatrix of Corcyrus. Do you not think so?"

"Yes, Master," I moaned. "Oh, Master!"

"You respond well," he said. "I always thought you were a slave."

"Yes, Master," I sobbed.

"During most of the day," he said, "you will have the run of the palace and the grounds."

"Yes, Master," I said.

"But escape, of course, will be impossible for you."

"I understand, Master," I sobbed. Slave girls did not freely enter and leave the palace grounds. Within the walls I would be efficiently imprisoned, presumably promptly and conveniently summonable to the feet of the masters.

"Oh," I said. "Oh. Oh!"

"It seems that the former Lady Sheila, now in her collar, has become a hot slave," he said.

"You did not buy me merely for this," I gasped, "for wench sport, to make me cry out and sob, and yield to you. What do you truly want of me? What are you going to do with me?"

"At the moment," he said, "only this."

"Oh!" I cried. And then he made me sob, and yield to him. Then I lay helpless, sweating, devastated, over the chest. My tears were on its wood. He then jerked me back and to my feet, and turned me to face him. The key to the slave bracelets, metal and tiny, dangled now again between my breasts. He held me close to him, by the upper arms. I, trembling, looked up into his face, that of my master. "Tomorrow night, at the great victory feast," he said, "you will be turned over to Claudius, my Ubar, and the high council."

"No, please!" I wept.

He then dragged me stumbling by the arm to the door and flung it open. A man was waiting there. He thrust me to him. I was not even permitted to kneel. I stood there, shuddering, only just had by Miles of Argentum, my arm now locked helplessly in the tight grasp of the new fellow.

"Sheila," said Miles of Argentum.

"Come along, Sheila," said the new fellow, dragging me along the corridor, by the arm, beside him.

"Yes, Master," I sobbed.

# 32

# THE THRONE ROOM

The throne room in the palace at Argentum was now cool and dark. I entered, fearfully, a slave girl frightened to be in such a place. It had a lofty ceiling. I walked barefoot on the tiles to the vicinity of the dais and throne.

I turned, suddenly, fearfully, as the door closed behind me. I could not see, in the shadows, who had shut it.

"Master?" I asked. I knelt, not knowing what else to do. This was the afternoon of the day of the great feast, that for which, purportedly, feast slaves had been brought even from Ar. No longer now, of course, was I a feast slave. I was now a work slave and pleasure slave owned by Miles of Argentum. Tonight, at the feast, I was to be presented naked and in chains to Claudius, the Uber of Argentum, and the council. I looked up, toward the ceiling. Suspended there, some forty feet from the floor, on a long rope, almost lost in the shadows, was a golden sack. The sack, weighted, hung heavily on the taut rope. Sometimes, with a creak of rope, it swung slightly. I was reminded of an almost immobile pendulum.

I heard a sound in the shadows, near the door. I looked quickly in that direction.

I could see nothing in the darkness.

"Master?" I called.

A girl had told me that I was to report to the throne room. She was conveying this message on behalf of a free man. She did not recognize him. He had seemed important, authoritative. As she had hesitated to obey him, in relaying his message, so, too, I would not hesitate to obey him, in complying with it. Neither of us could guess his office or status. That he was within the palace, however, a free man, clearly suggested to us his possession of some privilege or power. As we were slaves, we obeyed. The man had been described to me by the girl, who had seemed shaken by her encounter with him, merely as one who was obviously a natural master of women such as we, slaves.

I could see him now, dimly, in the shadows, as my eyes adjusted to the light. He was standing near the door. He was a large man. "Head down," he said, "palms on the floor."

I immediately assumed this position. The voice sounded familiar, but I could not place it. It sounded, too, somewhat tense or feigned. I wondered if that were its natural sound, or if it were being disguised.

I heard steps coming around behind me. Then, from behind, my head was pulled up, by the hair. I now knelt, with my back straight. My tunic, then, the tunic of Miles of Argentum, that brief, trim tunic, of brown, trimmed with yellow, with the plunging neckline, and slit at the sides to the rib cage, was stripped away from me, from the back.

"Master?" I asked, not daring to turn.

My hands then, with two loops of a thong, were tied behind me.

"Master?" I begged. Then I could not speak. A heavy wadding was thrust into my mouth and secured there with a folded strip of cloth, drawn deeply back between my teeth, knotted tightly behind the back of my neck.

I was then turned about and put on my back before my captor, on the tiles at the foot of the dais on which reposed the throne of Argentum.

I squirmed in terror. I uttered muted, tiny sounds.

"Yes," said he. "It is I, Ligurious, once first minister of Corcyrus."

I looked up at him, in terror.

"I, and two others," he said, "escaped the raid in Ar." I recalled I had heard swordplay, and the crashing of glass. "I see that you are now a branded, collared slave," he said. "It is appropriate. That is not the major or primary reason you were brought to Gor, but it was the minor or secondary reason. You were destined, from the beginning, if not for the impaling spear, then, eventually, for the collar."

I looked up at him, terrified, over the gag, naked and helplessly bound before him.

"You are a natural slave," he said. "Perhaps you know that by now. The brand and collar are perfect on you. You are a thousand times more beautiful as a slave than you were as a free woman."

I squirmed, his bound prisoner.

"I wonder how you escaped from the camp of Miles of Argentum," he said. "You certainly upset our plans in that particular. We had not even considered the possibility of such a thing. But it seems that now the former Miss Collins of Earth may yet prove useful in our plans."

I uttered tiny, helpless sounds.

"I have not been captured," said Ligurious, "nor have I entered the palace surreptitiously. I am here of my own will. In return for immunity I have volunteered to give evidence for the state of Argentum in the identification of the Tatrix of Corcyrus. Who would know her better than I? My two retainers, those two of all the others who have remained faithful, and with me, those who escaped with me from the house in Ar, have been entered into the palace in the guise of envoys from distant Turia. As I will have my business here, so, too, will they have theirs. There is some dispute, you see, as to who is the true Tatrix of Corcyrus, she who is even now suspended in the golden sack near the ceiling in this very room, or yourself, helpless now before me on the tiles. Witnesses will give testimony. Drusus Rencius, for example, has come here from Ar. He will doubtless identify you as the true Tatrix, as he did before. We saw to it that he, like several others, knew only you as the Tatrix. Similarly I have had clothing smuggled out of Corcyrus, clothing which you wore. This will be presented to Claudius, the Ubar, and the high council, as the clothing of the Tatrix of Corcyrus. You will be identified as the former wearer of the clothing, of course, by sleen. The work of Claudius and the high council, of course, will be made somewhat easier by the fact that when the golden sack is opened at the banquet it will be occupied not by the true Sheila, but by you, her dupe and double. We will not encounter objections by Hassan, the Slave Hunter, as he will not appear at the banquet. My two men will see to it that he is detained. Similarly, objections will not be encountered by Miles of Argentum. He will receive information, purportedly from Hassan, that he had the wrong girl and that you, as he now recognizes, are the true Tatrix. Accordingly he has placed you in the sack and, in his embarrassment, and fearing a loss of honor, has left the palace, taking the other girl with him, she then to be consigned to some suitable slavery or other. In this fashion we expect Miles of Argentum to be satisfied. He, in any case, is convinced, as you probably know, that it is you, and not the other woman, who is the Tatrix. This, of course, is because we saw to it that he, like certain others, would know only you as the Tatrix. He will identify you as the true Tatrix, for he knows you as such, with the same conviction as Drusus Rencius, and others. All this is in accord with our plans. And, of course, I, too, shall identify you as the true Tatrix. You may depend on it. Meanwhile, of course, the true Sheila will be concealed in my quarters, later to be smuggled from the palace in the guise of a free woman, that of a companion of one of my retainers, supposedly an envoy from Turia. The slave brought in with him in this role, put back in proper slave garb, has already been sold to an officer in the palace guard. He could not resist the superb price on her."

There were tears in my eyes. I pulled futilely against the thongs on my wrists.

"You are very pretty, as a slave," he said, regarding me, musingly, his hands on my ankles. He moved my ankles, tight in his grip, slowly, widely apart. I could not prevent this. Then angrily, he closed them. "No," he said. "It would be too much like having her." Then, with a loop of thong, he crossed my ankles and tied them together. I could not rise to my feet now. He then looped a thong from my ankles to a slave ring near the foot of the dais. I could not now even squirm from my place. "Doubtless she will be naked in the sack," he muttered to himself, "as naked as a slave. The inhuman beasts will have done that to her. I must try not to look at her more than is necessary."

He then, quickly, rose from my side and went to the side of the room. He loosed the rope there, that rope going up to a ring in the ceiling, and then down to the sack.

I fought frenziedly to free myself. I could not do so.

Hand by hand, he lowered the golden sack to the tiles. He then opened it and drew forth from it the vulnerable, quivering body of a naked woman. She looked wildly at him. She was bound head and foot. She was gagged.

"They have put you in a collar!" he said. "How dare they have done this!"

She struggled to kneel to him. I do not even know if he, in his agitation, realized this.

The collar, of course, was the collar of Hassan. He had put it on her in Ar, and had apparently never removed it.

"No!" cried Ligurious. "The beasts! The beasts! They have put your fair thigh under the iron!"

I recalled that Hassan, in Ar, had informed her that they would make a stop first, before proceeding to his lodgings. That stop, I now realized, must have been the shop of a metal worker. There the slave mark would have been burned into her thigh. It would already be on her, thus, when she was carried over his threshold, naked and on his shoulder, as a slave.

The hands of Ligurious fumbled at the cords on her ankles, and then on her hands. He was sweating. She knelt, frightened, her back to him.

"What have they done to you!" he cried. "What have they done to you!"

She knelt with her back to him, her head down, frightened.

Could he not see what they had done to her?

She was not the same woman he had known. He had known a cold, supercilious, arrogant woman, one who had been petulant and harsh, one who had been cruel, severe and demanding, an imperious and haughty slut. This, now, was not she.

There were many differences. For example, she knelt now, rather than stood, and she was now naked, rather than regally robed and bedecked. Too, of course, on her neck, now, there was a locked, close-fitting, steel slave collar, and on her thigh, of course, might be found a certain meaningful mark, one apprising all who might find it of interest of her status, that it was bond. Too, for those who might find such things interesting, it might have been noted that her master, Hassan, apparently had her on a careful diet and exercise program. Her body was now vital and healthy, and excitingly curved, far beyond anything that one commonly expects in a free woman. But all of these things, in their way, were perhaps rather trivial or external. The most important differences about her now were internal differences, deep, profound differences, differences which manifested themselves beautifully and unmistakably in such things as appearance, carriage, attitude and behavior. These differences were doubtless consequences of having been helplessly in the hands of Hassan, the Slave Hunter. These were the major differences in her. She was now soft and vulnerable; she was now extremely feminine; she was now informed and mastered; she was now, in the thousand ways in which this can be true of a woman, a slave.

Ligurious tore the gag from her.

"Master," she sobbed.

"You know me," he said. "I am Ligurious!"

"Yes, Master," she said.

"Do not call me 'Master,' " he said, his voice throaty with emotion. I saw that he was only too eager to hear this word from her. He was fighting himself. But even this innocent title, doing little more than recognizing the place of his maleness in the order of primate nature, and surely a suitable expression on the lips of a female slave, such as she now was, alarmed him. Too long had he idolized this woman. He was not yet ready to see that she had become real; it seemed he desperately wished to keep her as some remote, cherished illusion. On the other hand, there was a painful ambiguity in his relationship to her, probably one that she had once fully exploited. This had been evident in his attitudes toward me. He had, at various times, I had understood, seriously considered subjecting me to his pleasure and, rather clearly, I think, in the modality of the uncompromising master. In this, he had, I think clearly evidenced his desire to use her in the same fashion. He had wished to use me as a proxy for his longed-for domination of her. Our resemblances, however, had apparently been too close. Each time he had refrained from doing so. I do not think he truly desired me, or at least not other than as a man might casually desire a girl he sees in a paga tavern or, say, one of the girls he might notice chained in a row on their mats on a side street, but he did desire her. Ligurious was truly a master; he had proved this with other women; similarly, in most circumstances, had he so much as snapped his fingers at me, I would have thrown my legs apart for him; this was not the modality though, for whatever reason, in which he related to this other woman; he seemed to see her as some frosty ideal of perfection, as something finer than and different from all other women, as something of which he might scarcely be worthy, as something to which he should perhaps dare not aspire, as something almost untouchable and abstract. In his mind he condemned her to perfection; in this fashion he kept her from being a woman. Hassan, of course, did not see her in this fashion. In his arms she would not find herself cheated of herself. This is not all that unusual, incidentally. A woman revered by one man as an icy goddess is often another man's pleading, licking slave. Ligurious, to his fury, as a timid swain, would never get a hundredth from her of what Hassan, her master, might command with a casual word. But this, of course, was only to be expected. She was, after all, Hassan's slave.

"But you are a free man," she whispered. "What are you doing here? What are you doing? Where is Hassan, my master?"

"Do you wish to be impaled?" he asked.

"No!" she said.

"Your body!" he suddenly cried, looking at her. "It is that of a slave!"

"Yes, Master," she wept, trying to crouch down and cover her breasts with her hands.

"And the collar on your throat, and the brand, superb!"

"Thank you, Master," she wept.

"No," he suddenly cried, much to himself. "It cannot be!" Then, not looking at her, he angrily pointed to the tunic, on the tiles near me. "Put that on," he said. "Be quick! In the halls they will think you are she."

"Yes, Master," she said.

I struggled again to free myself, and could not do so.

In a moment Ligurious had freed my ankles of the thong that fastened me to the slave ring and dragged me by the arm across the tiles to the golden sack. There, putting me to my stomach, he began to replace my bonds with those she had worn. This, presumably, is what Hassan would have done had he himself been effecting this change of slaves.

"It is so small," she said, pulling down at the sides of the slave tunic.

I looked up at her, angrily. It was the slave tunic Miles of Argentum put us all in. We all wore it, all of his girls. To be sure, in it she was well displayed, and as what she now was, a slave.

My gag was then replaced with the one which she had worn. The wadding was packed into my mouth. It was still wet from her saliva. It was then secured in place. I was then thrust feet first into the golden slave sack. My head was thrust down. The sack was tied shut over my head. In a moment I felt myself, bit by bit, helpless in the sack, being hoisted upward. The rope was then secured, and, miserable and frightened, I swung slowly back and forth in the darkness of the sack until, eventually, there was little more movement than that connected with the tension of the rope, and my own small, occasional movements.

I felt the sack being lowered.

I do not think I had been in it for even an Ahn. Surely it was not yet time for the great feast.

Then the sack was on the floor.

It was opened.

My eyes widened. I could not cry out, gagged. I was drawn from the sack by Drusus Rencius. Behind him, naked, bound hand and foot, gagged, kneeling, was Sheila, the former Tatrix of Corcyrus.

Drusus Rencius removed my bonds and, lastly, my gag. "Be silent," he said.

I nodded, and knelt before him, as the slave I was, before a master.

I then saw him, and not gently, replace the bonds on Sheila, she now on her belly on the tiles, with those I had worn, even to the gag, packed then tightly in her mouth, wet and sopping, and secured there. He then thrust her in the sack, tied it shut and, in moments, had hoisted her high to the ceiling, its enclosed and helpless prisoner.

I reached out, timidly, to touch Drusus Rencius. "May I speak?" I whispered. I did not wish to be cuffed.

"Yes," he said.

"I am not the Tatrix of Corcyrus," I said.

"I am sure you are not," he said. "I have been a dupe and a fool, as I am sure so, too, have been many of us."

"Where is Ligurious?" I asked, frightened.

"He is with his cronies from Corcyrus, those pretending to be envoys from Turia," he said. "Fortunately they did not see me. I recognized them, of course. Indeed, I have been keeping a close eye on Ligurious ever since I discovered he was in the palace. I saw him, for example, enter the throne room, and saw you enter later. I then, later, saw him leaving the throne room with the other woman, she whom, after he left his quarters, I took the liberty of replacing in the sack where she belongs. He was in his banquet robes when he left his quarters. Accordingly I do not think he will discover her new whereabouts until the sack is opened."

"It is intended," I said, "that the cohorts of Ligurious detain Hassan, and prevent him from attending the banquet."

"Hassan, I am sure," said Drusus Rencius, "can take care of himself."

I looked at him, wildly.

"Stand," he said.

I did so.

"I believe this is yours," said Drusus Rencius, lifting the skimpy tunic which, doubtless but shortly before, he had removed from Sheila, probably binding and gagging her.

"Yes, Master," I said.

"Put it on," he said, throwing it against my body.

I caught it. "Yes, Master," I said. In a moment I was in it. It does not take long to don such a garment. I adjusted it on my body. Then I straightened up. I saw I was being inspected, as a slave.

"Turn, slowly," he said.

I did so, displaying as well as I could one of the properties of Miles of Argentum.

"Have you been named?" he asked.

"Yes, Master," I said.

"What is it?" he asked.

" 'Sheila,' Master," I said.

He smiled. "That would seem appropriate," he said, "at least from the point of view of Miles of Argentum. That, too, incidentally, is the name of the slave in the sack. It was put on her in Ar by her master, Hassan, the Slave Hunter."

I nodded. I had not known that. He could have named her anything, of course. Daphne, Jean, Wanda, Marjorie, Tarsk Nose, Excrement, whatever he pleased. It had apparently amused him, however, perhaps as an irony, to put her old name back on her, this time, of course, as a mere cognomen in bondage, a convenience by means of which to refer to the animal she now was, a slave name.

"You are very pretty, Sheila," he said.

"Thank you, Master," I said. That was my current slave name.

"The other Sheila, too, is very pretty," he said. "It will be interesting, tonight, to compare you, when you are both, naked and in chains, side by side, presented to Claudius and the high council."

"Doubtless, Master," I said. In such a situation, men might, I supposed, make their appraisals and determinations under almost ideal conditions. The conditions would be almost as favorable as those of a slave market. We might even be measured and posed. When I was exhibited before him in this fashion it was my hope that Drusus Rencius would like what he saw.

He held me by the upper arms and looked down, into my eyes. "It is a long time since Corcyrus," he said.

"Yes, my master," I said.

His hands tightened, mercilessly, on my arms.

"Forgive me, Master," I said. "I meant, 'Yes, Master'!" The expression 'my master' is not an uncommon one among Gorean slave girls but it is almost invariably reserved for use with a legal master. How naturally and inadvertently it had slipped out in my response to him. But I was not his slave. I was another man's slave!

"You are clever," he said.

I looked at him with tears in my eyes.

"Perhaps you are the Tatrix of Corcyrus," he mused. "Could it be?"

"No, Master," I said. "No!"

"It is a long time since you tortured me as a free man," he said.

"Forgive me, Master," I begged.

"Doubtless you have been less successful at that sort of thing since being collared."

"Yes, Master," I sobbed. I was now a slave.

He spun me about, rudely, and thrust me towards the door. "What are you going to do with me?" I sobbed.

"I will see that you safely reach the slave quarters of your master, Miles of Argentum," he said.

"I was not the Tatrix of Corcyrus!" I said.

"Tonight," said he, grimly, "a determination will be made on that matter."

"Yes, Master," I sobbed.

# 33

# THE INQUIRY; THE OUTCOME OF THE INQUIRY; I AM THE SLAVE OF MILES OF ARGENTUM

The dancers had now scurried away with a jangle of bells. The musicians were quiet. The floor, between the tables, was cleared. The feast slaves had drawn back, behind the tables. At these tables were Claudius, the Ubar of Argentum, and members of the high council. There were numerous other dignitaries there, as well, both from Argentum and from other cities. Miles of Argentum was there, and Drusus Rencius, and Ligurious. Interestingly enough, Aemilianus of Ar, who had once been my master, was there, and Publius, who had been the house master in the house of Kliomenes, in Corcyrus. Hassan, the Slave Hunter, I noted, however, was not present. Toward the back of the room, at one of the lesser tables, there was a hooded guest, a medium-sized man. I did not know who it might be. It was much too small to be Hassan. I was naked, in slave chains, behind a beaded curtain. I would be produced when Miles of Argentum, my master, wished it Because of my proximity to the narrow, linear spaces between the beading, I had little difficulty in seeing well into the hall. The guests, on the other hand, given the closeness of the beading and their greater distance from it, could detect my presence there only with difficulty, and, even then, presumably, they would be able to tell little other than the fact that the individual there, as might be discerned from the vaguely detectable form, was a stripped or scantily clad female, probably a slave.

"It is now time," said Claudius, the Ubar of Argentum, "to come to the major business of the evening. Let the golden sack be brought forth."

Two soldiers, from a side room, dragged the golden sack

across the floor and put it before the central table, that table where sat Claudius, the members of the high council and other significant guests. At this table, too, sat Ligurious, Miles of Argentum and Drusus Rencius.

"This feast," said Claudius, "is one of victory, one of triumph. Months ago the unprovoked aggression of Corcyrus, seeking the silver of Argentum, was repelled. Further, to ensure our security, and to prevent a repetition of this form of aggression, we fought our way to, and through, the gate of Corcyrus itself. There, abetted by the people of that city, we defeated the forces of the Tatrix of Corcyrus and overthrew her tyrannous regime."

There was Gorean applause at this point, the striking of the left shoulder with the palm of the hand. Even Ligurious, I noted, politely joined in the applause.

"The ties of Corcyrus with Cos have now been severed," said Claudius. "She, now, like Argentum, is a free ally of glorious Ar."

Here there was more applause.

"And fortunate is this for her," said Claudius, "for Ar, as she has demonstrated, stands by her allies!"

Again there was applause.

"As her allies stand by her!" he added.

There was more applause.

Ar, of course, had substantial land forces. She had, doubtless, the largest and best-trained infantry in known Gor. The land forces of Cos, on the other hand, were probably not superior to those of a number of Gorean city states, even much smaller in their populations than the island Ubarate. These balances tended to be reversed darmatically in sea power. Cos had one of the most powerful fleets on Gor. The sea power of Ar, on the other hand, was negligible. It consisted largely of a number of ships on the Vosk River, largely wharfed at Ar's Station.

"The villainess in this matter, the culprit, the instigator of these hostilities, was Sheila, the cruel and wicked Tatrix of Corcyrus."

"Yes, yes!" cried several men.

"She was captured in Corcyrus but, en route to Argentum, escaped. A great search was organized and conducted. A handsome reward was posted. Still, for months she eluded us. Then Hassan, the Slave Hunter, he of Kasra, consented to take up her trail. Her days of freedom were then numbered. In Ar, not two weeks ago, she fell to his bracelets."

There was applause.

"He then saw fit to bring her to us in his own inimitable fashion, in a wagon, like a common girl, tied naked in a slave sack."

There was laughter.

"This time," laughed Claudius, "she did not escape!"

There was more laughter. I saw Ligurious smile.

"It is now time," said Claudius, "to have Sheila, the former Tatrix of Corcyrus, presented before her conquerors, to await their pleasure!"

There was applause.

"Ligurious," said Claudius, turning to him.

Ligurious rose, and walked about the table, to stand before it, and near the sack.

"Many of you know me," said Lugurious, "if only by reputation, as the former first minister of Corcyrus. What many of you may not know is that I was also the secret leader of the resistance in Corcyrus to the rule of Sheila, the Tatrix. For months within her very government I strove to dissuade her from endeavors hostile to the great state of Argentum. I attempted to assert a persistent influence in the directions of harmony and peace. Alas, my efforts were frustrated, my counsels were ignored. The best that I could hope for was to prepare the way for the victorious forces of Argentum, which I managed to do. You may recall the ease with which you took the city, once the great gate was breached."

Drusus Rencius was smiling.

"In this time, of course, I was often in close converse with the Tatrix. In my efforts to convince her of the futility and madness of her policies I was in almost constant proximity to her. I think it may well be said that there is no man on Gor better qualified than I to recognize her, or to identify her for you."

"Thank you, noble Ligurious," said Claudius. "Now," said he, "let Sheila's captor, the noble Hassan, of Kasra, have the honor of presenting her before us, that she may await our pleasure." It was quiet. Men looked about. "Where is Hassan?" asked Claudius.

"He is not here," said a man.

Ligurious looked down, smiling.

Claudius shrugged. "He is perhaps indisposed," he said. "Let the sack be opened!"

Ligurious looked about himself, pleased. He scarcely bothered to note the opening of the sack, and the drawing forth of its helpless, gagged, bound, stripped occupant. She was knelt then, bound hand and foot, naked and gagged, before Claudius and the council.

Ligurious looked about. "Yes," he said, "I know her well. There is no doubt about it." He pointed at the kneeling figure, dramatically, but scarcely looking at her, directing his attention more to the audience. "Yes," he said, "that is she! That is the infamous Tatrix of Corcyrus!"

She uttered wild, tiny, desperate, muted sounds, shaking her head wildly. How well Goreans gag their prisoners and slaves, I thought.

"Do not attempt to deny it, Sheila," said he, scarcely noting her. "You have been perfectly and definitively identified."

She continued to make tiny, desperate, pleading noises. She continued to shake her head, wildly. Tears flowed from her eyes.

Ligurious then, perhaps curious, regarded her closely. Even then, for a time, I do not think he recognized her. I think this was because of our very close resemblance, and, too, perhaps, because he found it almost impossible to believe that I was not the woman who had been drawn forth from the sack, who now knelt helplessly before Claudius and the council. Then, suddenly, he turned white. "Wait!" he cried. He crouched down, then, and took the woman's head in his hands. Her eyes looked at him wildly, filled with tears. "No!" he cried, suddenly. "No! This is not she!"

"I thought," said Claudius, "that you identified her as Sheila, perfectly and definitively."

"No, no!" said Ligurious. He was shaking. There was sweat on his forehead. "I made a mistake! This is not she!"

"Then where is she?" asked Claudius, angrily.

"I do not know!" said Ligurious, looking wildly about.

"Hassan, of Kasra!" called the feast master, from near the door, announcing the arrival of Hassan in the hall.

"I am sorry I am late," said Hassan. "I was temporarily retained. I was attacked by two men. They are now outside my quarters, where I put them, tied back to back. Their arms and legs are broken."

"See that the assailants of Hassan are taken into custody, and attended to," said Claudius.

"Yes, Ubar," said two soldiers, and swiftly left the room.

I saw Sheila, at the appearance of Hassan in the hall, immediately put her head down to the tiles. Hassan trained his women perfectly.

"Is this the woman you captured in Ar?" asked Claudius, pointing to Sheila.

Hassan walked over to her, pulled her head up by the hair, and then, holding her by the arms, put her to her belly, and then turned her from one side to the other, examining her body for tiny marks.

"Yes," he said, "this is she."

The Gorean master commonly knows the bodies of his women. They are, after all, not independent contractual partners, who may simply walk away, but treasured possessions. They receive, accordingly, careful attention. Many women, indeed, are never truly looked at by a man until after they are owned.

He then put Sheila again on her knees before the council.

"Do you believe her to be the Tatrix of Corcyrus?" asked Claudius.

"I believe that she was the Tatrix of Corcyrus," said Hassan, "yes."

"He has never seen her!" shouted Ligurious.

"She was identified by sleen," said Hassan.

"But from false clothing!" cried Ligurious. "She is not the true Tatrix of Corcyrus! But the true Tatrix of Corcyrus is here, somewhere! I am sure of it!"

"How do you know?" asked Claudius.

Ligurious looked down, confused. He could not very well inform the assemblage of the exchange he had attempted to effect earlier in the throne room. "I have seen her here in the palace, somewhere about," he said quickly. "It was she whom I thought was to be withdrawn from the sack."

"My Ubar," said Miles of Argentum, rising to his feet, "reluctant as I am to agree with the former first minister of Corcyrus, and doubtless one of the finest liars on Gor, I think it not impossible that he may have seen Sheila about in the palace, perhaps on her hands and knees scrubbing tiles in a corridor, the type of task to which it has amused me to set her."

Men looked about, wildly, at one another.

"With your permission, my Ubar," said Miles of Argentum. Then, suddenly, sharply, he struck his hands together twice. "Sheila!" he snapped. "Forth!"

Startled, frightened, I parted the beaded curtain with my chained hands and, with the small, measured, graceful steps of a woman whose ankles are chained, hurried to him. I knelt on the tiles before the table, before his place, my head down.

"Lift your head," he said.

I heard cries of astonishment.

"Go, kneel beside the other woman," he said.

"Yes, Master," I said.

"There," cried Ligurious in triumph, "that is the true Sheila, the true Tatrix of Corcyrus!"

"Do you not think you should examine her somewhat more closely?" asked Drusus Rencius.

Ligurious threw him a look of hatred and then came closer to me. He made a pretense of subjecting me to careful scrutiny. Then he said, "Yes, that is the true Sheila."

"Let them be identically chained," said Claudius.

Miles of Argentum gestured to an officer. He had apparently anticipated this request.

In moments Sheila, freed of the gag and cords, wore chains. We now knelt naked and identically chained, side by side, before Claudius, the Ubar of Argentum. Each of us had our wrists separated by some eighteen inches of chain. Each of us, too, had our ankles separated by a similar length of chain, only a little longer. Another chain, on each of us, ran from the center of our wrist chain to the center of our ankle chain. This central, or middle, chain was about three and a half feet in length.

"It is a remarkable resemblance," said Claudius, wonderingly.

"They could be twins," said a man.

"You can tell them apart," said a man. "One has shorter hair."

"That is not important," said another.

"There are other differences, too," said a man, "subtle differences, but real differences."

"Yes," said the man, "I see them now." That was he who had suggested that we might be twins. Had we been twins we, at least, would not have been identical twins. Fraternal twins, separate-egg twins, two boys, two girls, or a boy and a girl, are not likely to resemble one another any more closely than normal siblings, except, of course, in age.

"If you did not see them together, however," said a man, "it would be extremely difficult to tell them apart."

"Yes," said another.

"I submit, my Ubar," said Miles of Argentum, "that the woman on your left, she with the shorter hair, is she before whom I appeared in Corcyrus, when I brought, at your request, the scrolls of protest to that city."

"Are you certain?" asked Claudius.

"Yes," said Ligurious. "That is true. She is Sheila, the former Tatrix of Corcyrus."

"That is not the one whom the sleen selected," said Hassan.

"I have witnesses who will identify her," said Miles. "I myself am the first such witness. She is Sheila, the Tatrix of Corcyrus."

"How do you know?" asked Drusus Rencius, rising to his feet.

I was startled. How dared he speak?

"The captain from Ar is out of order," said Claudius.

"Please let him speak, noble Claudius," said Miles.

"Is it your intention to speak on behalf of the shorter-haired slave?" asked Claudius.

"Yes," said Drusus Rencius.

There were cries of astonishment in the banquet hall. Even the feast slaves, in the back, girls such as Claudia, Crystal, Tupa and Emily, looked wildly at one another. I moved in my chains. I was thrilled.

"You may do so," said Claudius.

"My thanks, Ubar," said Drusus Rencius.

"Is it your intention to jeopardize our friendship, old comrade in arms?" inquired Miles of Argentum.

"That is no friendship, beloved Miles," said Drusus Rencius, "which can be jeopardized by truth."

"That is the woman whom I saw in Corcyrus when I carried there the scrolls of Argentum," said Miles, pointing to me. "That is she who was on the throne. That is she whom I captured after the fall of the city. That is she whom I had locked in the golden cage!"

"I do not dispute that," said Drusus Rencius.

"You grant, then, my case," said Miles.

"No," said Drusus Rencius. "I do not dispute that you saw her in Corcyrus, that you later captured her, that you had her placed in a golden cage, and such things. What I dispute is that she was the Tatrix of Corcyrus."

"The captain from Ar," said Miles, "has apparently taken leave of his senses. He is being foolish. Would he have us believe that the true Tatrix was off somewhere, polishing her nails perhaps, while someone else was conducting the business of state in her place?"

There was laughter. Drusus Rencius clenched his fists. He was a Gorean warrior. He did not take lightly to being mocked and chided in this fashion.

"My second witness," said Miles of Argentum, "is the woman who served her intimately in her own quarters, who bathed her and clothed her, and combed her hair, who was to her as her own personal serving slave, now one of my own slaves, Susan."

Susan was summoned forward. How exquisite and beautiful, and well displayed she was, in the trim, tiny tunic that was the uniform of the girls of Miles of Argentum. We now wore the same collar. He owned us both.

She knelt before him, his.

"Is that the woman whom you served in Corcyrus?" Miles asked her, pointing to me.

Susan came over to me. "Forgive me, Mistress," she said.

"Do not call me Mistress, Susan," I said. "I am now as much a slave as you."

"Yes, Mistress," she said.

"Is that the woman whom you served?" asked Miles.

"It is, Master," she said.

The members of the high council and many of the guests looked about at one another, nodding.

"As this girl is the property of Miles of Argentum," said Claudius to Drusus Rencius, "you may move that her testimony be discounted or be retaken, under torture."

In Gorean courts the testimony of slaves is commonly taken under torture.

Drusus Rencius looked across the room to Miles of Argentum.

"I will withdraw her testimony," said Miles of Argentum. "If she is to be tortured, it will be at my will and not that of a court. In this, however, I make no implicit concession. I maintain that the truth which she would cry out under torture would be no different from that which you have already heard freely spoken."

"Well done, Drusus Rencius," said a man, admiringly.

I saw that Miles of Argentum did not wish to have Susan subjected to judicial torture, perhaps tormented and torn on the rack, even though it might validate her testimony and strengthen his case. But she was only a slave! Could it be he cared for her? I suspected it was true. I suspected that the little beauty from Cincinnati, Ohio, in his collar, had become special to him, that she was now to him perhaps even a love slave.

"I do not ask that her testimony be discounted or withdrawn," said Drusus Rencius, "only that it be clearly understood."

There were cries of astonishment from those about the tables.

"Susan," said Drusus Rencius.

"Yes, Master," she said.

"Do you think this woman is wicked?" he asked.

"I think she can be nasty and cruel," she said, "but, in a collar, she will doubtless be kept well in her place."

"From what you know of her," he asked, "do you think she could be guilty of the enormities and crimes commonly charged against the Tatrix of Corcyrus?"

"No, Master," she said, happily.

"Mistresses sometimes have different relationships to their serving slaves, or friends, than they do to others," said Ligurious. "It is well known that great crimes can be committed by individuals who are, to others, kindly and affectionate."

"And," said Drusus Rencius, "that a man who is a wrathful master to one woman may be little better than the obsequious pet of another."

"Perhaps," said Ligurious, angrily.

"You know that this is the woman whom you served, Susan," said Drusus Rencius, indicating me, "for you are familiar with her, and have no difficulty in recognizing her. What I am suggesting is that you do not really know that she was the true Tatrix of Corcyrus. You suppose she was because that is what you were told, and for certain other reasons, such as others took her also for such, and you saw her performing actions which, you supposed, only the Tatrix would perform, such things as holding audiences with foreign dignitaries, and such."

"Yes, Master," said Susan.

"But is it not possible," he asked, "that she might have been reported to be the Tatrix, and might have done such things, without being the true Tatrix?"

"Yes, Master," Susan granted, eagerly.

"Do you regard it as likely, Susan," asked Miles of Argentum, "that that woman was the Tatrix of Corcyrus?"

"Yes, Master," she said.

"Do you regard it as extremely likely?" he asked.

"Yes, Master," she whispered.

"Do you doubt it, really, at all?" he asked.

"No, Master," she sobbed. She put down her head.

"Remain here, Susan," said Miles.

"Yes, Master," she said.

"I call my next witness," said Miles of Argentum, "located in Venna by my men, and brought here, Speusippus of Turia."

To my amazement Speusippus was conducted forward. He seemed cringing and obsequious in the presence of such a noble assemblage. No longer, now, did he seem as detestable to me as he once had. Too, I was now a slave and a thousand times lower than he. Too, it was he who had taken my virginity. Too, I now realized that my femaleness had shown his maleness too little respect. I was a woman. Yet, in spite of that, I had not properly related to him. I had not shown him the deference which, in the order of nature, it was proper for my sex to accord to his. He was a member of the master sex; I was a member of the slave sex.

"You were, several months ago, were you not, found guilty of certain alleged commercial irregularities in the city of Corcyrus, and banished for a time from the city?"

"Yes," said Speusippus.

"As the reports have it," said Miles, "you were marched naked from the city, before the spears of guards, a sign about your neck, proclaiming you a fraud."

"Yes," said Speusippus, angrily.

"Who found you guilty, and pronounced this sentence?"

"Sheila, the Tatrix of Corcyrus," said Speusippus.

"Is she who was the Tatrix of Corcyrus in this room?" asked Miles of Argentum.

"Yes," said Speusippus.

"Would you point her out for us?" asked Miles.

Speusippus, unerringly, came to my side. He pointed to me. "This is she," he said.

"Thank you," said Miles. "You may now go."

"I had her in my grasp," cried Speusippus, "but she escaped. The reward should have been mine!" This reward had originally been one thousand pieces of gold. It had later been increased to fifteen hundred pieces of gold.

"It is not my fault if you could not hold a slave," said Miles.

"She was not then a slave," said Speusippus. Then he turned to me, with hatred. "But I got something from you, you slut," he said. "I took your virginity away!"

"Am I to understand," asked Miles of Argentum, "that you are confessing to the rape of a free woman, one who was even a Tatrix?"

Speusippus turned white.

"May I speak, Masters?" I asked.

"Yes," said Claudius.

"After he had captured me," I said, "I presented myself to Speusippus of Turia naked and as a slave, and begged for his use. As a true man he could not do otherwise than to have me."

Speusippus looked wildly at me.

"Very well, Speusippus of Turia," said Miles of Argentum, "you may go."

"Forgive me, Master," I said to Speusippus of Turia. "I muchly wronged you. I was stupid and cruel. I showed you too little respect. I now beg your forgiveness, as a woman, now a slave."

"You seem much different now from before," he said.

"I have now learned that I am a female," I said. Then I put my head down and did obeisance to his maleness, kissing his feet.

He crouched down and lifted my head. He looked into my eyes. "Fortunate is the man who has you under his whip," he said.

"Thank you, Master," I whispered. He then kissed me, rose to his feet and hurried away.

"Slave!" snarled Drusus Rencius, looking angrily at me.

"Yes, Master," I said. "I am a slave."

"Let it be noted," said Miles of Argentum, "that the

witness unhesitantly identified her as Sheila, the former Tatrix of Corcyrus."

"It is noted," said Claudius.

"He, too," said Drusus Rencius, "could have been mistaken in this matter!"

There was some laughter from some of the members of the high council, and from some of the others about the tables.

"I call now my fourth witness," said Miles of Argentum, "Ligurious, former first minister of Corcyrus. He, if no one else, should know the true Tatrix of Corcyrus. I now ask him to make an official identification in the course of our inquiry. Ligurious."

Ligurious unhesitantly pointed to me. "I know her well," he said. "That is Sheila, who was the true Tatrix of Corcyrus."

"Have you further witnesses, General?" asked Claudius of Miles.

"Yes, noble Claudius," smiled Miles, "one more."

"Call him," said Claudius.

"Drusus Rencius," said Miles.

"I?" cried Drusus Rencius.

Men looked at one another, startled.

"Yes," said Miles. "You are Drusus Rencius, a captain from Ar, are you not?"

"Yes," said Drusus Rencius, angrily.

"The same who was on detached service to Argentum, and was engaged in espionage within the walls of Corcyrus?" asked Miles.

"Yes," said Drusus Rencius.

"I believe that while you were in Corcyrus," said Miles, "one of your duties was to act as the personal bodyguard of Sheila, the Tatrix of Corcyrus."

"I was assigned the post of guarding one whom I at that time thought was Sheila, the Tatrix of Corcyrus," said Drusus Rencius. "I no longer believe that she was the true Tatrix. I think that I, and many others, including yourself, were confused and misled by the brilliance of Ligurious, Corcyrus's first minister. She was used as a decoy to protect the true Tatrix. In effecting this stratagem she was educated in the identity and role of the Tatrix, in which role, part-time at least, she performed. The success of this plan became strikingly clear after the fall of the city. She fell into our hands and, as the supposed Tatrix, was stripped, chained and caged. The true Tatrix, meanwhile, eluded us, escaping in the company of Ligurious and others."

"Ligurious?" asked Miles.

"Preposterous," said Ligurious.

"Is the woman whom you believed to be the Tatrix of Corcyrus, and whom you testified in Corcyrus was the Tatrix, before the very throne itself, in this room?"

Drusus Rencius was silent.

"As you may have noted," said Miles, "Publius, the house master of the house of Kliomenes, of Corcyrus, is in the room. I think that he, with the practiced eye of his profession, skilled in the close scrutiny and assessment of females, can render a judicious opinion as to whether or not she whom you brought to the house of Kliomenes, she whom you were guarding, is or is not in the room."

"How did you know of this?" asked Drusus Rencius.

"In the search for the Tatrix," said Miles, "the records of hundreds of slave houses were checked, to see if a woman of her description might have been processed. In this search, in the records of the house of Kliomenes, we found entries pertaining to your visit there with a free woman, purportedly a Lady Lita. Descriptions of this 'Lady Lita' were furnished by several members of the staff. There was no difficulty with these descriptions. They were splendidly clear, and usefully and intimately detailed, even to conjectured shackle sizes, just as one would expect of descriptions of a female in a slave garment. The descriptions tallied, of course, with those available of the Tatrix of Corcyrus."

"I did not know," said Publius, rising to his feet, "that it was for such a purpose I was invited to Argentum. As Miles of Argentum knows, I am the friend of Drusus Rencius. I will not testify in this matter."

"You can deny, of course," said Miles of Argentum to Drusus Rencius, "that she whom you took to the house of Kliomenes was the same woman you were guarding as the putative Tatrix. In that fashion, even if Publius can be encouraged to testify, his testimony could do no more than confirm that she here chained is the same as she whom you then brought to the house of Kliomenes. You can still deny that she who is here chained is she whom you then took to the Tatrix of Corcyrus."

Drusus Rencius was silent.

"We have, of course, independent identifications."

"We do not require the testimony of Drusus Rencius in this matter," said Claudius.

"I do not refuse to testify," said Drusus Rencius.

Men looked at one another.

"Let me then repeat my question," said Miles of Argentum. "Is she whom you believed to be the Tatrix of Corcyrus, she whom you identified as the Tatrix in Corcyrus itself, before the very throne of Corcyrus, in this room?"

"Yes," said Drusus Rencius.

"Would you please point her out?" asked Miles.

Drusus Rencius pointed to me. "That is she," he said.

"Thank you," said Miles.

"The matter is done," said a man.

"In making this identification," said Drusus Rencius, "I do no more than acknowledge that I was once the dupe of Ligurious. Can you not see? He is making fools of us all!"

Ligurious looked down, as though grieved by some irresponsible and absurd outburst.

"By the love I bear you, and by the love you bear me," said Drusus Rencius to Miles, "hear me out. That woman is not the Tatrix! She sat upon the throne! She appeared in public as the Tatrix! She sat in court as the Tatrix! She conducted business as the Tatrix! She was known as the Tatrix! But she was not the Tatrix!"

"Let us not ignore the evidence," said Miles of Argentum. "The evidence, some of which you yourself have presented, clearly indicates that she is the Tatrix. What sort of evidence would you wish? How do we know, for example, that you are really Drusus Rencius, a captain from Ar? Or that I am Miles, a general from Argentum? Or that he is Ligurious, who was the first minister in Corcyrus? How do we know anyone in this room is who we think? Perhaps we are all victims of some elaborate and preposterous hoax! But the question here is not one of knowledge in some almost incomprehensible or absolute sense but of rational certainty. And it is clear beyond a doubt, clear to the point of rational certainty, that that was the Tatrix of Corcyrus!"

There was applause in the room.

"I recall an earlier witness," said Miles of Argentum, "my slave, Susan."

"Master?" she asked, frightened.

"In your opinion, Susan," he asked, "did the shorter-haired

slave, she kneeling there in chains, she whom you served, regard herself as Sheila, the Tatrix of Corcyrus."

"Yes, Master," whispered Susan, her head down.

I, too, put my head down before the free men, the masters. It was true. I had regarded myself as Sheila, the Tatrix of Corcyrus. Indeed, even now, there was a painful ambiguity in my mind in this matter. I supposed that, in a sense, I was a Sheila, who had been a Tatrix in Corcyrus. I was, I supposed, one of the two Sheilas, who, in their different ways, had been Tatrix there. I knew, of course, that I was not the true Sheila, or, at least, the important Sheila, the Sheila in whom they were particularly interested. I, too, in my way, had been a mere dupe of Ligurious.

"She herself," said Miles of Argentum, "regarded herself as the Tatrix of Corcyrus. She accepted herself as that! She did not deny it or dispute it! Why not? Because that is who she was!"

"No!" cried Drusus Rencius.

"Why do you think she was not the Tatrix of Corcyrus?" asked Miles.

"I do not know," cried Drusus Rencius. "I just know!"

"Come now, Captain," said Miles, patronizingly.

"I know her," said Drusus Rencius, angrily. "I have known her from Corcyrus. She is petty, and belongs in a collar, and under the whip, but she is not the sort of woman who could have committed the enormities and outrages of the Tatrix of Corcyrus. Such things are not in her!"

"Has the good captain from Ar," inquired Miles, "permitted the glances, the smiles, the curvaceous interests of a woman to sway his judgment?"

"No," said Drusus Rencius.

"I think you have succumbed to the charms of a slave," said Miles.

"No!" said Drusus Rencius.

"She has made you weak," said Miles.

"No!" said Drusus Rencius.

I looked at Drusus Rencius. I was only a naked slave, and in chains. How could I make such a man weak?

"The evidence is clear," said Miles of Argentum to the Ubar, Claudius, to the members of the high council, to the others in the room. "I rest my case." He then pointed to me. "Behold she who was the Tatrix of Corcyrus!"

There was much applause in the room. Drusus Rencius turned angrily away. He stood to one side, his fists clenched.

"That is not the one whom the sleen selected," said Hassan.

Drusus Rencius spun about. "True!" he said.

"May I speak?" inquired Ligurious.

"Speak," said Claudius.

"I anticipated some difficulty in the matter of the sleen," he said. "First of all, we must understand that the sleen are merely following a scent. They recognize a scent, of course, but do not know, in a formal or legal sense, whose scent they are following. For example, a sleen can certainly recognize the scent of its master but it, being an animal, does not know, of course, whether its master is, say, a peasant or a Ubar. Indeed, many sleen, whereas they will respond to their own names, do not even know the names of their masters. I am sure the type of point I am making is well understood. Accordingly, let us suppose we now wish a sleen to locate someone, say, a Tatrix. We do not tell the sleen to look for a Tatrix. We give the sleen something which, supposedly, bears the scent of the Tatrix, and then the sleen follows that scent, no differently than it might the scent of a wild tarsk or a yellow-pelted tabuk. The crucial matter then is whether the sleen is set upon the proper scent or not. Now fifteen hundred gold pieces is a great deal of money. Can we not imagine the possibility, where so much money is at stake, that a woman closely resembling the Tatrix, as this woman, for example, might be selected as a quarry in a fraudulent hunt. It would not be difficult then, in one fashion or another, to set sleen upon her trail. A scrap of clothing would do, a bit of bedding, even the scent of a footprint. The innocent woman is then captured and, later, presented in a place such as this, the reward then being claimed."

Claudius, the Ubar of Argentum, turned to Hassan. "Your integrity as a hunter has been impugned," he said.

All eyes were upon Hassan.

"I am not touchy on such matters," said Hassan. "I am not a warrior. I am a businessman. I recognize the right of Claudius and the high council to assurances in these matters. Indeed, it is their duty, in so far as they can, to protect Argentum against deception and fraud. Much of what Ligurious, the former first minister of Corcyrus, has told you is true, for example, about sleen, and their limitations and utilities. These are, even, well-known facts. The crucial matter, then, would seem to be the authenticity of the articles used to provide the original scent. When I was in Corcyrus and I received from Menicius, her Administrator, clothing which had been worn by the Tatrix, I divided it into two bundles and had each sealed with the seal of Corcyrus. A letter to this effect, signed by Menicius, and bearing, too, the seal of Corcyrus, I also obtained. One of these bundles I broke open in Ar, and used it to locate and capture the former Tatrix of Corcyrus."

"She whom you claim is the former Tatrix," said Ligurious.

"Yes," said Hassan.

"Do you still have the second bundle, unopened, and the letter from Menicius, Administrator of Corcyrus, in your possession?" asked Claudius of Hassan.

"I anticipated these matters might be sensitive," said Hassan. "Yes."

Hassan was truly a professional hunter. I had heard the name 'Menicius' somewhere before, but I could not place it. He, whoever he might be, was now apparently Administrator in Corcyrus.

Claudius regarded Hassan.

"I will fetch them," said Hassan, rising to his feet.

"I, too, have clothing from Corcyrus," said Ligurious, "but it is authentic clothing, clothing actually once worn by the true Tatrix of Corcyrus."

"Please be so kind as to produce it in evidence," said Claudius.

"I will be back shortly," said Ligurious.

"Bring guard sleen and meat," said Claudius to one of the guards in the room.

In a few Ehn Hassan and Ligurius had returned. Too, but moments later, two sleen, with keepers, had entered the hall. The feast slaves and dancers shrank back against the walls. Such beasts are used to hunt slaves.

I, too, shrank back, fearfully, in my chains. I, too, was a slave.

"As you will note," said Hassan to Claudius and the high council, "the seal on this bundle has not been broken. Here, too, is the letter from Menicius."

The letter was examined. Claudius himself then broke the seal on the bundle and handed clothing to one of the sleen keepers. One soldier came and crouched down behind me, holding me from the back by the upper arms. Another so served Sheila, to my left. We were not to be permitted to move from our places. I saw one of the keepers holding the clothing beneath the snout of one of the sinuous, six-legged beasts. The specific signals between masters and sleen, signals which, in effect, convey such commands as "Attack," "Hunt," "Stop," "Back," and so on, are usually verbal and private. Verbality is important as many times the sleen, intent upon a scent, for example, will not be looking at the master. The privacy of the signals is important to guarantee that not just anyone can start a sleen on a hunt or call one away from it. The signals to which they respond, then, are idiosyncratic to the given beast. They are generally not unique, however, to a given man and beast. For example, in an area where there are several sleen and several keepers, the keepers are likely to know the signals specific to the given beasts. In this fashion any beast may be controlled by any of the associated trainers or keepers. These signals, too, are usually kept written down somewhere. In this fashion, if a keeper should be slain, or change the locus of his employment, or something along those lines, the beast need not be killed.

Suddenly the beast, on its chain leash, leapt towards us. Sheila and I screamed, pulling back. I actually felt the body of the beast, its oily fur, the muscles and ribs beneath it, brush me, lunging past me. Sheila tried to scramble back, wild in her chains, but, held, could not do so. She threw her head back, her eyes closed, sobbing and screaming, begging the masters for mercy. The frenzied sleen tried to reach Sheila. Its claws scratched and slipped on the tiles. It snapped and bit at her, its eyes blazing. Its fangs, long, wild, white, moist, curved, gleaming, were but inches from her enslaved beauty.

A word was spoken. The sleen drew back. It was thrown meat. Sheila, her eyes glazed, hair before her face, looked numbly at the animal. She was still held by the soldier. Had she not been I think she might have slumped to the tiles. How helpless we are, naked and in our chains, before masters. How they can do with us whatever they wish!

"The clothing with which the sleen was put on the scent of the woman on our right could have been imbued with her scent at any time, of course," said Ligurious. "For example, it could have been put in the sack with her for a night, when she was being brought to Argentum. I have here, however, and I now break the seal, clothing which is actually that of the former Tatrix of Corcyrus. See? Already she cringes and shrinks back. She knows that by this clothing she will be exactly and incontrovertibly identified as the former true Tatrix of Corcyrus."

I watched in horror as Ligurious tossed the clothing, piece by piece, to one of the sleen keepers. One of the pieces was the brief, sashed, yellow-silk robe I had been fond of. It was the first garment I had ever worn on Gor.

"That one garment," said Miles of Argentum, indicating a scarlet robe, with a yellow, braided belt, "appears to be that in which she put her curves on the day of my audience with her, that having to do with the scrolls of protest."

"It is," Ligurious assured him.

I also saw there garments which looked like those I had worn to the song drama with Drusus Rencius, and had worn later with him on the walls of Corcyrus.

"Surely you recognize that garment?" asked Ligurious, indicating a purple robe with golden trim, and a golden belt.

"Yes," said Miles of Argentum. "That is the garment she wore when she was captured."

"By you," said Ligurious.

"Yes, by me," said Miles.

"But she did not wear it long, did she?" asked Ligurious.

"No," he grinned. There was laughter from the tables.

I did not doubt but what these garments were genuine. The last garment, for example, was undoubtedly really that which had been taken from me in the throne room of Corcyrus, before the very throne itself, before I had been taken naked and in chains outside, into the courtyard, to be placed in a golden cage. These garments, Ligurious had informed me in the throne room of Argentum, before placing me in the golden sack, from which I had been rescued by Drusus Rencius, had been smuggled out of Corcyrus. He had probably paid much to obtain them.

The last pieces were all items of intimate feminine apparel, which had been worn next to my body.

I was embarrassed to see them. Now that I was a slave, of course, I would have been grateful to have even so much to wear publicly. But when I had worn them they had been the garments of a free woman. Thus, when I saw them now it was as one who had once been a free woman that I was embarrassed. Few free women care to have their intimate garments exhibited publicly before men.

I then saw the sleen, a different sleen, thrust its snout deeply into the pile of garments. I could hear it snuffling about in them. I saw the keeper, too, take the intimate garments, wadded in his hand, and thrust them beneath the animal's snout. He then held one of the longer, sliplike garments open from the bottom, and, to my horror, I saw the beast, sniffing and growling, thrust its snout deeply into the garment. My scent, from my intimacies, would doubtless be strongest in such a place.

I shrank back, even further. The hands of the soldier behind me, on my arms, forbade me further retreat.

In a moment the sleen leaped forward. I closed my eyes and screamed. I felt the hot breath of the animal on my breasts. I seemed surrounded by its snarling. I heard the scratching and slipping of its claws on the tiles, the rattle and tightening, and rattle and tightening, again, of the links of the chain leash, in its lunges toward me. I sensed its force, its terribleness, its eagerness. I heard the snapping of its jaws. Could the keeper judge the distances unerringly? Could he hold the animal? What if the chain broke? I opened my eyes. In that instant the beast was again lunging toward me. In that instant, in a flash, I saw the cavernous maw, the fangs, the long, dark tongue, the blazing eyes, the intentness, the singlemindedness, the power, the eagerness of the beast. I threw back my head and screamed miserably. "Pity!" I begged. "I beg mercy, my masters!" I cried, a terrified slave, addressing them all, in my terror, as though they might be my legal masters.

Then the sleen, with a word, was withdrawn, and thrown meat. I trembled. Were it not for the hands of the soldier behind me, on my arms, I might have collapsed. I saw Drusus Rencius looking at me with scorn. I did not care. I was not a warrior. I was a girl, and a slave.

"Thus, you see," said Ligurious, "who was the true Tatrix of Corcyrus."

"Each woman, it would seem," said Claudius, "has been identified as such, one in virtue of the articles of Hassan and one in virtue of the articles with which you have furnished us."

"Examine the seals," said Ligurious, triumphantly. "See which bears the true seal of Corcyrus!"

The broken seals were brought to Claudius. He put them

on the table before him. Members of the high council crowded about him.

"The seal broken from the package of Ligurious," he said, "is the seal of Corcyrus."

"That cannot be," said Hassan.

"Perhaps you will be given two Ahn in which to leave Argentum," said Ligurious.

"I have the letter from Menicius!" said Hassan.

"It, too, doubtless, will bear the same seal as was on the package," said Ligurious.

"Yes," said Hassan.

"I, too, have such a letter, but a genuine one," said Ligurious, "describing and authenticating the garments I have produced for you. That letter bears the signature of Menicius and is marked with the true seal of Corcyrus." He reached within his robes and produced a letter, wrapped with a ribbon, the ribbon and the flaps of the letter secured with a melted disk of wax, this wax bearing the imprint of a seal.

The seal was examined.

"It is the seal of Corcyrus," said Claudius.

The letter was opened and examined.

"The descriptions tally with the garments brought to us by Ligurious," said one of the members of the high council.

"Who has signed the letter?" inquired Ligurious.

"Menicius," said one of the members of the high council, looking up.

"I think not," said a voice.

All eyes turned to the back of the room. There, the guest who had been hooded rose to his feet.

"Who would dare to gainsay me in this?" inquired Ligurious.

With two hands the guest brushed back his hood.

"I think that I am known to several in this room," he said. "Some of you were present at my investiture as Administrator of Corcyrus."

"Menicius!" cried more than one man.

Ligurious staggered backwards.

"My dear Ligurious," said Menicius, "your confederate in Corcyrus is now in custody. He has confessed all. I deemed, accordingly, it might be of interest to venture incognito to Argentum. I did so with the papers of a minor envoy, bearing my own signature."

How startled I was! I now recognized, and clearly, the

hitherto unknown guest. I had known him as Menicius, of the Metal Workers. He was the man whòse life I had spared, when he had spoken out so forcibly against the Tatrix, on that day, so long ago, when I had been in the palanquin with Ligurious, that day in which, in the glory of a state procession, we had been carried through the streets of Corcyrus. Doubtless Drusus Rencius, who had prevented him from reaching the palanquin, remembered him well, for his courage and his opposition to the rule of the Tatrix.

"I was interested to hear that you were the leader of the opposition to the rule of the Tatrix," said Menicius to Ligurious. "I, myself, had thought that that honor was mine."

Ligurious looked about himself. He took one or two steps backward.

"I suggest that that man be put in shackles," said Menicius.

"Do it," said Claudius. Two guardsmen moved swiftly to Ligurious. In a moment his wrists had been shackled behind him.

"The seals," said Menicius, "on the package and letter of Hassan were genuine. It is natural, however, that they were unfamiliar to you. They are imprints of the new seal of Corcyrus. It was discovered, after the institution of the new regime in Corcyrus, that the old seal was missing. Presumably it had been taken by Ligurious in his flight from the city. That now seems evident. For this reason, and also to commemorate the rise of a new order in Corcyrus, it was changed."

Ligurious, shackled, looked down at the tiles.

Manicius came about the tables. He stopped before Sheila and myself. We, slaves, put our heads to the tiles. "Lift your heads, Slaves," he said. We complied.

"We meet again," said Menicius to me.

"Yes, Master," I said.

"Who are you?" he asked.

"My master is Miles of Argentum," I said. "He has named me 'Sheila.' "

"You look well in slave chains, Sheila," he said.

"Thank you, Master," I said.

He turned to Sheila. "Who are you?" he asked.

"My master is Hassan, of Kasra," she said. "He has named me 'Sheila.' "

"You look well in slave chains, Sheila," he said.

"Thank you, Master," she said.

He then, from his robes, removed a package and, opening it, exhibited soft and silken contents.

She drew back, shuddering in her chains.

"These are further garments from Corcyrus," he said. "They were taken from among the belongings of the Tatrix of Corcyrus, found in her suite of rooms in the palace." He turned to regard Sheila. "Perhaps you recognize them?" he asked.

"Admit nothing!" called Ligurious.

She looked wildly at Hassan. His face was expressionless. She then, a slave, obeyed Ligurious, a free man.

"Consider the nature of these garments," he said. "They are clearly, in a fashion, slave garments. This may be determined from their lightness, their softness and tininess. On the other hand, there are some anomalies here. For example, note that here there is a nether closure. That would certainly be unusual in a garment permitted by a Gorean master to a female slave."

There was laughter here.

"They are barbarian garments," he said. The garments he was exhibiting to those at the tables were undergarments of sorts common to free women of Earth. I had not really thought before of how feminine they were and how appropriate to slaves. Who but a slave would permit such delicious, delicate and silken things to touch their bodies?

"But few barbarian girls, as nearly as we can tell, come to Gor clothed and, if they do, they are seldom permitted to retain their clothing, or the bits of clothing left to them at that point, past the sales block, on which, one supposes, it might be removed from them."

There was some acknowledgement of this from the tables. There is a Gorean saying that only a fool buys a woman clothed.

"The Tatrix of Corcyrus, on the other hand, though a barbarian, was apparently permitted to keep this clothing. Similarly she was permitted to keep her freedom. That was removed from her only recently by Hassan and Kasra."

Men at the tables looked at one another.

"Some of us," said Menicius, "are familiar with the rumors, the frightening rumors, that there are forces on Gor, and elsewhere, who would challenge the power of the Priest-Kings themselves, rulers of Gor from time immemorial."

Men looked at one another, fearfully. Sometimes it seemed

likely to me that the Priest-Kings were mythical entities. Surely they mixed, as far as I could tell, little in the affairs of Gor. On the other hand, it was also clear to me that someone, or something, must be in opposition to the forces which had brought me to Gor. Those forces, for example, had mastered space flight. Surely Goreans, with their swords and spears, by themselves, could not have resisted them. Their clandestine efforts, for all their power, suggested the existence of a formidable counter-power. That counter-power, I suppose, for want of a better name, might be referred to as that of Priest-Kings.

"It seems likely to me, thus," said Menicius, "that such forces might bring wealth and barbarian agents, perhaps, with no Gorean allegiances, to our world, laboring in their behalf. Too, of course, they might recruit native Goreans for their purposes. How, except for such power, could a barbarian woman, such as Sheila, the former Tatrix of Corcyrus, come to power in a city such as Corcyrus? I suspect, also, that the true motivation of the attack on the mines of Argentum was not to fill the coffers of Corcyrus, already a prosperous city, but to supplement the economic resources of these other forces. They intend, perhaps, failing success in outward aggression, to subvert our world, city by city, or to form a league of cities, that may become dominant among our states. This might be accomplished, presumably, within the weapon laws and technological limitations imposed upon Gorean humans by Priest-Kings, for whatever might be their purposes."

Men looked at Sheila. She put her head down, trembling.

"Preposterous though those ideas may sound," said Menicius, "there is some plausibility to them. Too, further evidence comes from two sources. Outside of Corcyrus, in a great field, have been found burned grass and three large, deep, geometrically spaced depressions, as though something of great heat and weight, perhaps some giant, heated steel insect or fiery mechanical bird, had alighted there. Too, within the palace itself, in a subterranean chamber, we found the smells, the spoor and traces of some large, unknown beast which, apparently, perhaps from time to time, resided there. It had apparently removed itself from those premises, however, well before the downfall of the city."

Ligurious was looking at the tiles. He did not look up.

"Ligurious?" asked Claudius.

"I know nothing of these things," said Ligurious, shrugging.

"Shall we see whose garments these are?" inquired Menicius, lifting the delicate undergarments of Earth clutched in his fist.

"Yes, yes," said various men in the room.

"Please, no, Master!" wept Sheila. Then she lowered her head, cringing, for she had spoken without permission. The soldier behind her looked to Hassan, who nodded. He then cuffed her to her side from behind with the back of his hand, and then ordered her again to her knees, to which position she struggled in her chains. Menicus, meanwhile, had thrown the garments, in a silken, fluttering wad, to one of the sleen masters who thrust them beneath the snout of the beast. In a moment it was moving swiftly about the room its nose to the floor, and then, suddenly, taking the scent, lunged murderously, claws slipping on the tiles, toward Sheila. Inches from her body, the chain on its collar jerked taut, it was held back. She screamed but could not withdraw, held mercilessly, immobilely, on her knees, in place, by the soldier behind her.

"The identification is made," said Claudius, and, with a wave of his hand, signaled the sleen keeper to divert and pacify his beast. A word was whispered. The sleen, suddenly, in the superbness of its training, drew back. It seemed suddenly calm. Its tail no longer lashed back and forth. Its tongue, from the heat of its activity, lolled forth from its mouth, dripping saliva to the tiles. I could see, too, the imprint of its paws, in dampness, on the tiles. The sleen tends to sweat largely through its mouth and the leathery paws of its feet. It fell upon the meat which it was thrown.

Sheila, released by the soldier, struggled to remain upright. She sobbed, then, gasping, shuddering, her head back, half in shock. I was pleased that it had been she and not I who had been the object of this second identification. I felt sorry for her. I saw that she now, like I, was only a slave. Not only are there masters on Gor, but there are sleen. We strive to be pleasing. We do what we are told.

"May I speak, Master?" asked Sheila of Hassan.

"Be silent!" said Ligurious.

"You may speak," said Hassan to his slave.

"I confess all," she said. "I was the true Tatrix of Corcyrus! The woman next to me is innocent. She was brought to Gor as an unwitting dupe, one selected to serve as proxy for me in case our plans should go awry. She had no true power, save a pittance which we, for our purposes, were sometimes pleased to accord to her. What crimes there are here are mine, or those of the free woman I once was. It will not be necessary, therefore, to impale us both. I alone am she whom you seek. I was captured in Ar by Hassan, of Kasra, who is now my master. The reward of fifteen hundred gold pieces is thus rightfully his. I am prepared now to be turned over, as a slave, to Claudius, the Ubar of Argentum, and the high council of Argentum, to face their justice."

"Fool!" cried Ligurious. "Fool!" He struggled in his manacles. They held him well.

I regarded Sheila wildly, almost disbelievingly. She had acknowledged her identity. I was now an exonerated slave, at least of her crimes, if not of mine, those of pettiness, of pride, of selfishness and cruelty, crimes for which a woman on Gor can be regarded as fittingly enslaved.

"You have me naked and in chains now before you, I who was once Sheila, the Tatrix of Corcyrus, your enemy," she said. "I am now yours to do with as you please."

"Fool!" cried Ligurious.

"What of the speculations of Menicius," inquired Claudius, "those having to do with affairs of worlds, of the business of Priest-Kings and others."

"They are sound, Master," she said.

"Be silent!" said Ligurious.

"Speak," said Claudius.

"Hold, Caludius," cautioned a man. "Consider whether or not it is proper for mere mortals to inquire into such matters."

"Such thoughts are surely to be reserved for the second or third knowledge," said another man.

"I am a man," said another. "I repudiate the distinctions between knowledges. Knowledge is one. It is only knowers who are many."

"We are not Initiates," said another man. "Our status, prestige and livelihood do not depend on the perpetuation of ignorance and the propagation of superstition."

"Heresy!" cried a fellow.

"I shall inquire into truth as I please," said another. "I am a free man."

"It is our world, too," said a fellow.

"Surely it is permissible to inquire into such matters," said another, "if we do so with circumspection and respect."

"I think," said Claudius, "in these matters both our fears and our noble, belligerent vanities are out of place. Gods, for example, I trust, do not have need of the silver of Argentum, nor do they have need of fiery ships for plying the long, dark roads between worlds. Gods, I trust, do not leave spoor in subterranean chambers nor deep wounds in remote turfs. These things of which we speak, I think, are things which can eat and bleed."

"We do not speak, then, of Priest-Kings," said a man, relieved.

"Who knows the nature of Priest-Kings?" asked a man.

"Some say they have no form," said a man, "only that they exist."

"Some say that they have no matter," said a man, "except that they are real."

"Surely they are like us," said a man, "only grander and more powerful."

"Let us not waste time in idle speculations," said a man.

"Speak," said Claudius to Sheila.

"There are two worlds involved, Master," she said, "Gor, and the world called Earth."

"Lying slave!" said a man. "Earth is mythical! It is only in stories. It does not exist."

"Forgive me, Master," she said, "but Earth is real, I assure you. I am from Earth, and so, too, is the slave to my right."

The man looked at me, closely.

"Yes, Master," I whispered, frightened.

"That Earth is real is in the second knowledge," said one of the men, a fellow wearing the yellow of the Builders, a high caste.

"I was taught that, too," said the fellow with him, also in the yellow of the Builders. "Do you think it is really true?"

"I suppose so," said the first man. The classical knowledge distinctions on Gor tend to follow caste lines, the first knowledge being regarded as appropriate for the lower castes and the second knowledge for the higher castes. That there is a third knowledge, that of Priest-Kings, is also a common belief. The distinctions, however, between knowledge tend to be somewhat imperfect and artificial. For example, the second knowledge, while required of the higher castes and not of the lower castes, is not prohibited to the lower castes. It is not a body of secret or jealously guarded truths, for example. Gorean libraries, like the tables of Kaissa tournaments, tend to be open to men of all castes.

"Gor, and the world called Earth," she said, "are prizes in a struggle of titantic forces, the forces of those whom you call Priest-Kings and of those whom you think of as others, or whom we might think of as Beasts."

"And what is the nature of these Beasts?" asked Claudius.

"I have never seen one," she said.

"Ligurious?" asked Claudius.

"I choose not to speak," he said, sullenly.

"Continue," said Claudius to Sheila.

"Both Priest-Kings and Beasts possess powerful weaponry and are masters of space travel," she said. "Intermittently, it is my understanding, for generations, they have been involved in combat. Probes and skirmishes are frequent. As yet outright force has been unable to prevail. In many respects Priest-Kings seem to be tolerant and defensive creatures. For example, they permit native beasts on Gor, marooned beasts, and such, provided such obey their laws, particularly with respect to weaponry and technology. And never have they pursued the beasts to their steel lairs in space, pursuing temporary advantages in these perennial conflicts. The beasts, it is my surmise, having hitherto failed to win Gor by overt conquest, attempt now to obtain power on this world by specific and detailed subversions, mixing in, and influencing, the politics and affairs of cities. Indeed, in this way, perhaps they, too, hope to prepare the way for an eventual full-scale invasion, one which could then be supplied and supported by a number of strategically located cities, or leagues of cities. I know little more, specifically, in these matters than my own role. By means of the wealth of beasts and the influence of Ligurious, the first minister of Corcyrus, I was brought to power in Corcyrus. There, supported by the influence and wealth of beasts, and abetted by Ligurious, I ruled. I grew soon fond of the throne. Testing my power I found it real. I was exhilarated. I became ambitious to expand the sphere of Corcyrus's influence and, in particular, to obtain, if possible, for my own wealth, the mines of Argentum. In these things I exceeded my authority. Ligurious, against his better judgment, at least initially, pleaded my case with beasts and protected me from them, convincing them to accept my proposals. Ligurious was smitten with me. I seduced him to my projects. I played with his feelings. I toyed with his emotions. I exploited his sentiments. I made him dance like a puppet to my will. I deprived him of his leadership and manhood."

I looked at Ligurious. His face was dark with anger as he looked down at Sheila, now another man's slave.

"These projects, to be sure, were dangerous," she said. "Too, I was a valued agent. Thus, through Ligurious, an order was placed with the beasts, that a double might be obtained for me. The girl selected was the collared slave to my right, now the slave, as I understand it, of Miles of Argentum. She was brought to Gor and taught that she was Sheila, the Tatrix of Corcyrus. She came to accept this identity. Some knew me as the Tatrix. Some knew her as the Tatrix. That there were actually two women involved was a carefully guarded secret, known only to a handful of trusted followers. We miscalculated seriously in at least one matter. We did not think that Ar would honor its treaty commitments with Argentum, that it would risk all-out war with the Cosian Alliance, in which Corcyrus was implicated. As it turned out, of course, Ar did support Argentum and, as it also turned out, we were not supported by Cos. Defeated in war and in the face of an uprising, too, within our own city, Ligurious and I, with some others, fled. The slave on my right, she who was brought to Gor as my double, was left behind on the throne, to be captured and, in my place, bear the wrath of the enemy. As you know, she escaped. A vast, intense and lengthy search was undertaken to recover her. In this search, as you know, as well, both of us were eventually apprehended. Now both of us, she who was the Tatrix and she who was her double, now both no more than slaves, kneel stripped before you, helpless in your chains." She put down her head.

"Speak further," said Claudius.

The slave lifted her head. "You may put me under tortures, Master," she said, "but, woe, I know little more than I have spoken. The beasts keep us much in ignorance so that, if captured, we can reveal little of their strategies and plans. What details there are beyond those I have given you would, I fear, be meaningless or trivial to you, such things as descriptions of the appearances of agents on Earth, where I was first contacted, and such."

"As beasts may be allied with men," said Claudius, "so, too, I suppose, might men be allied with Priest-Kings."

"Yes, Master," she whispered.

"Are there not, then, on Gor, places where such men may be found?" asked Claudius.

"There are several, doubtless, Master," she said.

"Name one such place," said Claudius.

She turned white. She looked to Hassan, her master. His eyes forbade hesitation. Neither mercy nor lenience were to be shown to her.

"The house of Samos, in Port Kar," she whispered.

Claudius looked to Menicius.

"That rumor, too, I have heard," he said.

Claudius then regarded Ligurious.

"I choose not to comment on these matters," he said, straightening himself. He seemed very strong. He was the sort of man, it seemed to me, who might serve as master to the slave in almost any woman. Many times, I knew, I had felt the helpless desire and fear of a slave in his presence. Sheila did not meet his eyes. No longer was she a Tatrix. She was now naught but a stripped and chained slave.

"Tortures, doubtless," said Menicius, "might be brought to bear upon your resolve."

"True," said Ligurious, "but only at the cost of sacrificing the honor of Argentum."

Claudius looked at Ligurious.

"Claudius?" asked Menicius.

"Ligurious, it is true," said Claudius, "came to us a free man, of his own will. He has been guaranteed immunity in Argentum, and has been guaranteed a safe conduct from her walls."

"He has sought to misdirect our inquiries and has distorted and misrepresented evidence," said a man.

"Perjurious abominations he has uttered!" cried a man.

"Impale him!" cried another.

"Impale him!" cried yet another. Men rose to their feet, shaking their fists.

"Impale him!" cried several.

Ligurious smiled. The victory was his. What a small thing would be his impalement compared to the stain on the escutcheon of Argentum. His freedom was guaranteed.

"Remove the former first minister of Corcyrus from our presence," said Claudius, "lest I be tempted to betray the pledge of my city. Let his shackles be removed only in his own quarters, to which he is to be closely confined."

Two soldiers seized Ligurious by the arms.

"We have matters to inquire into," said Claudius to Ligurious, "and resolutions to be made. It is possible we may have need of you for further testimony, asseverations germane to our proceedings. In any event, your presence will be retained for our pleasure until our deliberations have been concluded. Then, and then only, will the pledge of Argentum be honored."

"Such a reservation is fully in accord with our original arrangements," said Ligurious loftily. "I abide by your decision as willingly as I must also abide by it, perforce."

"Postpone the deliberations a thousand years!" cried a man.

"That is not the way of Argentum," smiled Claudius.

At a gesture from Claudius Ligurious was conducted from the room.

"Do you object, Menicius, my friend?" asked Claudius.

"I had not realized the guarantees extended by Argentum," said Menicius. "You have, of course, under the circumstances, no choice."

"I feel sorry for him in a way," said Claudius, looking after Ligurious. "He is a strong man, ruthless and powerful, proud and strong, but he permitted himself to be the dupe of a female, to be wound about the finger of a woman."

Claudius then pointed to Sheila. "Bring that slave forward," he said.

With a whimper Sheila was dragged to her feet, pulled forward and, with a rattle of chain, thrown to her knees before Claudius.

"This woman," said Claudius, pointing to Sheila, "has been proved by evidence and testimony, both written and oral, to be the former Tatrix of Corcyrus. Indeed, this fact has been acknowledged, ultimately, even in her own admission."

He looked down at Sheila. "Who captured you and brought you here, Slave?" he asked.

"Hassan, of Kasra, Master," she said.

"The reward, then," said Claudius, "clearly belongs to Hassan, of Kasra. Let it be brought!"

An officer left the room. Hassan came forward, about the tables, to stand near the kneeling slave. In a few moments the officer had returned. He carried a heavy, bulging sack over his shoulder which he lowered gently, heavily, to the floor before the table. It must have weighed between ninety and one hundred pounds.

"In this sack," said Claudius, "carefully counted, but assure yourself of the matter, are fifteen hundred pieces of gold, stamped staters of Argentum, certified by the mint of the Ubar."

Hassan looked down at Sheila.

"Shall scales be brought?" asked Claudius. "We will take no offense. If any discrepancy be found, perhaps the result of some inadvertence, we shall see that it is made good."

"No," said Hassan. "Weights and balances, the chains and pans, need not be fetched forth."

"Accept then the reward," said Claudius. "You have well earned it."

"What fate do you intend for this woman?" asked Hassan.

Claudius shrugged. "The mounting for the impaling spear has already been prepared," he said. "The spear itself has been sharpened and polished."

"Fifteen hundred gold pieces," said Hassan, "seems a great deal of money for a mere slave."

"It was you yourself, as I understand it," smiled Claudius, "who neck-ringed her and, shortly thereafter, with a blazing iron, marked her slave."

Hassan smiled. "I seem to recall something to that effect," he said. He looked down at Sheila. "Are you a slave?" he asked.

"Yes, my master," she said, "and only you know how much a slave."

I was thrilled to hear her say this. Every woman, in her deepest heart, wants to find a man whom she must serve perfectly, a man who will bring out the fundamental and profound slave in her, a man who will bend her uncompromisingly and helplessly to his will. In Hassan Sheila, obviously, had found such a man.

"Are you prepared, now," asked Hassan, "to be turned over to Claudius and the high council?"

"Yes, Master," she said. "I ask only, first, to be permitted one last time to kiss your feet in respect and reverence, and, in doing so, to express, too, my gratitude for the joy you have given me in these few days you have owned me. They have been the most precious of my life." She then, tenderly, kissed his feet, extending obeisance and love to the man who had made her a slave. There were tears in my eyes.

Hassan laughed, a roar of a laugh. She looked up, startled.

"Do you truly think I brought you here," he laughed, "to turn you over to Claudius and the high council?"

"Of course, Master," she said.

"No!" he laughed.

There were cries of astonishment from those about.

"Kiss my feet fifteen hundred times, you luscious baggage," he laughed, "at least once for every gold piece you are costing me!"

"Yes, Master," she cried, startled, putting down her head.

"This woman was the Tatrix of Corcyrus, was she not?" laughed Hassan.

"Yes," said Claudius, startled. "That has been established, even by her own admissions."

"And I have, thus, earned the reward, fully and clearly, if I should wish it?" asked Hassan.

"Certainly," said Claudius, puzzled.

"That is all I wanted," said Hassan. "Indeed, it is all I ever wanted."

"I do not understand," said Claudius.

"For years," said Hassan, "I have heard of the Tatrix of Corcyrus, of her tyranny, of her fabled pride and beauty. I found such a woman intriguing. Then, wonder of wonders, she fell. None could find her. I was curious to know what it would be like to have such a woman in my collar, a fair-skinned, golden-haired Tatrix of the north, to make her crawl, and cry and serve, to make her a man's woman."

I looked at Sheila. She was weeping with joy at his feet, kissing them, and his ankles and legs. "I love you, Master," she wept.

"So I captured her and made her a slave, mine," said Hassan.

"It was never your intention, then, to deliver her to us?" asked a member of the high council.

"No," said Hassan. "Had that been my intention I would not have removed her virginity from her and enslaved her."

"Had you never any doubts on this matter?" asked a man.

"Had I any," smiled Hassan, "they disappeared the instant I saw her. I knew then I would keep her for my own slave."

"But why did you bring her here?" asked a man.

"That you might see her humbled and helpless, and for my own glory," said Hassan.

"It is pleasing to see the former Tatrix of Corcyrus as a humbled slave," said a man.

"Yes," said Hassan.

"What if we take her from you?" asked a man.

"You will not do so," said Hassan. "That would be theft."

"But what of her crimes?" asked a man.

"Those were the crimes of a free woman," said Hassan. "She is no longer a free woman. She is now only a slave."

"I love you, my master," whispered the slave, her head at his feet.

"Sheila," said Hassan.

"Yes, Master," she said, lifting her head.

"You may continue your obeisances and services in the privacy of my chambers," he said.

"Yes, Master," she said. She rose to her feet, her head humbly lowered.

"Conduct her to my quarters," said Hassan to a soldier, he who held the key to her chains, "and chain her to the slave ring at the foot of my couch."

The soldier glanced to Claudius, and then nodded. "Come, Slave," he said.

"Yes, Master," she said, and was conducted from the room.

"It has been an interesting evening," said Hassan, lifting his hand to the assemblage. "I wish you all well!"

"We, too, wish you well, Hunter," said Claudius.

"Hail, Hassan!" called a man.

"Hail, Hassan!" called others.

The men rose from about the tables, saluting and applauding Hassan. He, lifting his hands, and turning, waving to them, took his leave from the hall. I think he was eager to begin the instructions of a slave.

Men, then, in twos and threes, began to take their leave.

Menicius stood before me. He put out his hands and I lifted my chained wrists to him. He took my hands and turned them over, looking at the snug wrist rings locked on them.

"If I had my tools," he said, "I could have these off of you in a matter of Ehn."

I looked up at him, startled. I knew, of course, that he was of the metal workers.

"But without a key, or such help, you are absolutely helpless in them, aren't you?" he asked.

"Yes, Master," I said.

He smiled.

"You!" I said. "It was you who freed me in the camp of Miles of Argentum!"

"Once," he said, "you spared my life, in Corcyrus. It seemed only fitting, then, that I might, if it were within my power, grant you some small favor in return."

"But how could you have gained entrance into the camp," I said. "And there were two of you! There was another, as well, one who must have had influence, one who must have been trusted, one who must have been more highly placed!"

I saw Drusus Rencius looking at me.

"You," I whispered. "It was you!"

"Perhaps," he said.

"But you are an officer of Ar," I said. "How could you do such a thing?"

He looked at me, angrily. "I know you," he said. "Whatever might be your frailties, your weaknesses, your pettinesses, your cruelties, I could not believe you were guilty of the crimes of the Tatrix of Corcyrus. Such things I could not believe were in you. Thus, I did not free the Tatrix of Corcyrus. Rather, to prevent a miscarriage of justice, I assisted in the escape of an innocent woman. In this sense I could even regard my act as having been performed in the line of duty."

"You did not know, truly," I said, "that I was not the Tatrix, nor that I could not be guilty of such crimes. Indeed, in Corcyrus, you even identified me, explicitly, as the Tatrix!"

His face clouded with anger.

"Your motivations were more complex," I said, "and deeper, and more painful and more cruel. It was not within your province to determine my innocence or guilt. That responsibility was that of Claudius, the Ubar of Argentum, and the high council. In no way was it incumbent on you to risk your commission, your future, your honor, your life, on what must at best have been little more than a remote possibility."

He regarded me with fury.

My heart leapt with joy. "You love me!" I whispered. "You love me!"

I feared for a moment he might strike me. But he did not do so. I was another man's slave.

"I love you, Master!" I wept. "I have loved you from the beginning, when I first met you!"

He regarded me, wildly. Then he sneered, "Lying slave!"

"No, Master!" I protested. "I love you! I do love you! I love you with my whole heart!"

"What is going on here?" asked Miles of Argentum, coming over to us.

"Nothing," said Drusus Rencius.

Menicius was smiling.

Miles of Argentum took the key to my chains from the soldier who had held it. He freed me of those stern impediments, so suitable for the confinement of women such as I, slaves.

"Slave," said he.

"Yes, my master," I said.

"Go to the quarters of my women," he said.

"Yes, my master," I said and, tears in my eyes, fled to the quarters of his women.

## 34

# LIGURIOUS IS SERVED BY TWO SLAVES

I lay naked on the couch of Ligurious, in the palace in Argentum. His touch had already reduced me, more than once, to a quivering slave.

"Wine," he said.

"Yes, Master," I said, and struggled up, turning. I fetched him the goblet from a small, low table near the couch and, in a moment, after kissing the goblet, head down, kneeling, arms extended, proffered it to him. He sipped a bit of the wine, a Ka-la-na of Ar, and then returned the goblet to me. I kissed it again, and then replaced it on the table. With a gesture he indicated that I might once again crawl onto the couch. This was the last evening Ligurious was to spend in Argentum. In the morning he was to receive safe conduct from the city. I had been assigned to serve him tonight, in accord with the generosity of Gorean masters. Another girl, too, was to serve him, but I did not know who she was.

There was a knock at the door.

"Kneel, and grasp your ankles," he said.

I did so. I was then helpless, bound by his will.

He went to the door and opened it.

A slave was there. She was naked. Her wrists were behind her back. About her neck, tied, was a key, doubtless to her bracelets, and a whip. There were two guards at the portal, but they were those who had been guarding it. The girl had apparently come alone through the halls to the portal, obediently, as I had.

Ligurious indicated that she should enter. She did, and he closed, and locked, the door behind her.

He freed her of the bracelets and tossed them, and the key, to the side. He then removed the whip from about her neck. He regarded her. Their eyes met.

There was a long moment of silence.

"Kneel, Slave," said Ligurious, defining the relationship between them.

"Yes, Master," she said.

"Is that the fashion in which I have my women kneel before me?" he asked.

"Forgive me, Master," she said, and put her head down to the tiles before him, the palms of her hands flat on the floor.

"Lift your head," he said.

She did so.

"Kiss the whip," he said. "Again, lingeringly!"

"Yes, Master," she said.

"Now lick and kiss it," he said.

"Yes, Master," she whispered.

He then hurled the whip from him. It slid back across the tiles, until it stopped, at the door.

"Fetch," he said.

The girl, on her hands and knees, went to the whip. She put down her head at the heavy, locked door and picked up the whip, delicately, in her teeth. She then, the whip in her teeth, turned from the door and, head down, on her hands and knees, returned to the center of the room.

"Kneel," he said, "in the position of the pleasure slave." She knelt, then, back on her heels, her knees spread widely, her back straight, her shoulders back, her belly sucked in, her head up, her hands on her thighs. Between her teeth was the staff of the whip.

"Whip," said Ligurious.

She gave him the whip, extending her head towards him, opening her mouth, letting him take it from between her teeth. She then, unbidden, resumed the erect, graceful, beautiful position of the Gorean pleasure slave.

He shook out the blades of the whip and dangled them before her eyes.

She swallowed, hard.

"Face that direction," said Ligurious, pointing.

She rotated her body about a hundred degrees to her left.

"To your belly," he said.

She went to her belly, her hands at the sides of her head. He changed his position a little. He was now a bit behind her, and to her left. He was right-handed.

She began to tremble.

He looked down at her.

I, kneeling, tightened the grasp on my ankles. I was sweating.

I looked at the branded female on the tiles.

Sheila, who had once been the Tatrix of Corcyrus, now a slave girl, lay at the feet of Ligurious, who had once been her first minister, positioned.

How she had used him, and tortured him! How cleverly she had manipulated him, how insidiously and cunningly she had exploited him!

He let the blades of the whip, idly, brush her back. She whimpered.

I recalled her words, two evenings ago, in the banquet hall, how she had said that she had made him dance like a puppet to her will, how she had deprived him of his leadership and manhood.

He drew the blades back, away from her body.

"What are you?" he asked.

"A slave, Master," she said.

"And what else?" he asked.

"Naught else, Master," she said.

I wondered if she retained power over him yet. I saw the whip swing back now, and to the side. He held it with both hands. On Earth a woman may reduce, diminish and destroy a man with impunity. This, however, was not Earth; it was Gor. I saw the whip pause at the height of its arc. I wondered if she retained power over him yet. Then I saw his eyes. In them I saw that the spell which she had exercised over him was broken.

I cried out and averted my eyes, swiftly, as the whip fell. The beating lasted only a few moments.

Then I looked back. Sheila was on her side, her body flaming with burning stripes; she was gasping and sobbing; she looked wildly up at Ligurious, a Gorean master. Then she looked away from him, not daring to meet his eyes. She, a female, lay now at the feet of a male, he totally dominant over her. She was now in her place in nature.

"Do you wish to be whipped further?" he asked.

"No, Master!" she sobbed.

"You will serve well, and yield perfectly," he said.

"Yes, Master!" she said, fervently.

Ligurious turned to face me. "You may break position," he said.

Swiftly I released my ankles and slipped from the surface of the couch, to stand beside it.

"Bring furs from the surface of the couch, and spread them here, on the tiles," he said.

"Yes, Master," I said. I saw that, in his use of her, he would not permit Sheila the dignity of the couch.

"Kiss the furs," said he to her, "and crawl upon them."

She did so.

"On your back," said he to her, "split your legs, part your lips, lift your arms to me."

The slave complied. He forced her to hold the position for a few moments and then he crouched down near her and took her head in his hands, pulling her up to a seated position, and crushed her lips beneath his. She murmured and moaned, and then, when he thrust her back, I saw there was blood at her mouth. She whimpered, frightened. I think he had waited years for that kiss. Then, patiently, and with uncompromising authority, he addressed himself to her beauty. In moments, choiceless, she was a sobbing, aroused, begging slave.

"You amuse me," he said.

"Please, Master," she begged. "Please!"

But he continued to tease and torment her, toying with her emotions and passions. She writhed in his arms, pleading, helpless and needful, performing and commanded. She might have been a paga slave or a girl rented on a mat in the back streets of Argentum.

"You juice well," he informed her.

"Thank you, Master," she sobbed. "Please, Master! Please!"

I lay on my side, at the edge of the furs, near them. I

watched with fascination, learning what a man could do to one who was now no more than one of my sisters in bondage.

Then, after a time, at last, he permitted her her slave's yielding, and in it she cried out her slavery, and her submission to men, and, specifically, to he who was her master of the evening.

Then she lay in his arms, softly and tenderly, an overwhelmed, submitted slave.

I thought the vengeance he had taken on her had been exquisite. In his arms she had found her bondage well confirmed upon her.

Ligurious, Sheila in his arms, looked over at me.

I then lay, my belly sucked in, my legs slightly flexed, my toes pointed, as seductively as possible before him. I, too, was a slave, and at his disposal this evening.

He rolled to his back, looking up at the ceiling.

"I did not know that you were such a man," she whispered.

"Nor I," he smiled, "that you were such a woman."

"You were harsh with me, Master," she smiled.

"Do you object?" he asked.

"No," she said.

I then crawled to him, and kissed him gently on the thigh. I did not wish to be forgotten.

"A fortunate man am I," said Ligurious, "to be served by two Tatrices."

"Two slaves, Master," she smiled.

"Yes," he said, "two slaves."

Twice more that night did he make use of her, and, at various times, he had one or another of us, and sometimes both, please and serve him. Toward morning, when she slept, he made use of me again, and I yielded to him once more, gasping softly, as a slave to the master.

Then later we lay together, quietly. It felt good to lie close to such a strong man, a master.

"Sheila will make Hassan a fine slave," he said.

"He will see to it," I smiled.

"She loves him," he said.

"With the profundity of the slave," I acknowledged.

"He loves her, too, I think," he said.

"I think so, too, Master," I said. "Do you love her?"

"No," he said. "That infatuation was an illness. I am cured

now. I retain, however, of course, a fondness for her, as might anyone for a pleasing slave."

"Then, too," I said, "it is my hope that you have some fondness for me."

"Yes," he said, "I am also fond of you."

"May I speak?" I asked.

"Yes," he said.

"It is a long time since I was brought to Gor with steel on my ankle."

"Yes," he said. That band of steel had been removed from me in Corcyrus. It was, I gathered, a device by means of which slavers, or those in league with Beasts, or those opposed to Priest-Kings, marked women brought to Gor for their purposes.

"The major purpose for which I was brought to Gor, I gather," I said, "was to serve as a precautionary double for Sheila, one who might then, particularly in the event of the failure of your plans, serve to confuse or deceive enemies, one who might, say, divert attention from her true whereabouts, one who might even, perhaps, be caught and sentenced in her place, that she might then make good her escape."

"Yes," said Ligurious, "that sort of thing, precisely, and well would you have served such purposes had you not managed to escape from the camp of Argentum."

"Do you begrudge me my escape, Master?" I asked.

"No," he said, "for had you not escaped I would still be not as a master to a woman but as, in effect, her slave."

"If there was a major purpose for which I was brought to Gor," I said, "then it seems evident, and I think you have stated or implied as much, that there must have been a minor purpose, or purposes, as well." I recalled I had gathered something of this sort even from the agents I had met on Earth.

"Yes," he said, "of course, and to understand it, and well, you would need only to regard yourself, and closely, in the mirror. In particular, note the beauty of your face, its intelligence and sensitivity, and your softness and femininity, so different from that of more masculine women, those with larger amounts of male hormones, and the lusciousness of your slave curves. There was indeed a minor purpose for which you were brought to Gor, that purpose which I called to your attention in the throne room, here in Argentum, that purpose which you now, you little she-sleen, obviously wish to hear explicitly reiterated."

"Oh?" I asked, innocently.

"That purpose for which most women are brought to Gor," he said.

"And what purpose might that be?" I inquired, innocently.

"That purpose which you now, from your hair to your toes, manifest so perfectly," he said.

"Oh?" I asked.

"That purpose?" he said. "Is it not obvious? It was to be made a female slave."

"Yes, Master," I said, and kissed him.

For a time we lay quietly side by side, not speaking. Each of us, I think, had our thoughts.

"Master," I whispered.

"Yes," he said.

"May I speak again?" I asked.

"Yes," he said.

"Sheila and I have our collars," I said. "We must go where masters wish, heeding them and doing their bidding. But what of you? Tomorrow you will have your freedom. What will you do? Where will you go?"

"Away," he said. "I do not really know." He kissed me, softly, and I kissed him back, gently.

Then he fell asleep.

I lay there for a time. Sheila was owned by Hassan, whom she loved. I, like many women, was owned by Miles of Argentum, whom I admired and respected, and feared, and to whom I could not help but yield helplessly and promptly, but whom I did not love. Tears sprang into my eyes. Then, after a time, I, too, fell asleep.

# 35

# I AM PROVEN A NATURAL SLAVE BEFORE DRUSUS RENCIUS, WHOM I LOVE; THE SILVER TARSK

"Here," said Drusus Rencius, angrily, to Publius, of the house of Kliomenes.

I jerked the bit of slave silk tightly, defensively, about my body, and backed from the soldier.

I could not help responding as I had!

"It is as I told you, long ago, in Corcyrus," smiled Publius.

"Yes," said Drusus Rencius. He then placed a silver tarsk in the hand of Publius.

"Do not withdraw, Slave," said Publius to me.

"Yes, Master," I said, and knelt, on the broad stair leading up to the serving dais in the private dining room in the palace at Argentum.

"It is not wise to wager against a slaver in such matters," said Publius. "We can tell such matters at a glance."

"I had thought, then, at least, that she was different," said Drusus Rencius.

"She is too vital and healthy, and has too strong drives to be different," said Publius.

I knelt on the broad stair, embarrassed, holding the slave silk about me. On this same stair, and on the floor below, and on the surface of the dais itself, before the long, low, small table, I had been ordered to writhe, to the music. Then I had been ordered to stand, my knees flexed, with my hands clasped behind my neck. Then a soldier had been ordered to feel me. I had jerked and almost screamed from his touch.

The man had smelled his hand, and laughed.

"You are right," had said Drusus Rencius to Publius. "She is a slave, and a natural one."

Such things may be told from movements, dispositions and reflexes.

"Yes," had said Publius.

I put down my head and stared, angrily, at the carpeting on the stair.

I had known for months, of course, that I was a natural slave. It is not hard for a woman to know this. It can be made clear to her in many ways, for example, from dreams and fantasies, and from wishes, desires and needs. It is one thing for a woman to know this, of course, and quite another for her to find it made the subject of a public demonstration.

"You see," said Publius, "is it not as I told you?"

"Yes," granted Drusus Rencius, good-naturedly.

I looked down, almost in tears, a proven natural slave. How unworthy I was of Drusus Rencius!

"May I withdraw, Masters?" I asked.

"No," said Publius. "Continue with your service, Sheila."

"Yes, Master," I said, and rose to my feet. In a few moments, again, I was serving the men, bringing them food and drink, seemingly as though nothing had happened.

This matter went back to the time when I was a free woman, and had been taken for a tour to the house of Kliomenes by Drusus Rencius. In Publius's office he had made the wager, while I knelt in the light to one side. Drusus Rencius had accepted it.

"Cakes, Masters?" I asked, kneeling near them, proffering them the tray.

"Yes," said Drusus Rencius.

"Yes," said Publius.

Drusus Rencius and Publius did not have slaves of their own in Argentum. Susan and I had been volunteered by our master, Miles of Argentum, to serve them.

With a movement of Publius's finger I was dismissed from the side of their table.

I replaced the tray of tiny cakes on the nearby serving table.

Susan then approached the diners. "Black wine, Masters?" she asked.

"Yes," said Drusus Rencius.

"Yes," said Publius.

Susan then turned to me and snapped her fingers. "Sheila," she called.

"Yes, Mistress," I said. I took the vessel of black wine, removing it from its warmer, and put it on its tray, that already bearing the tiny cups, the creams and sugars, the spices, the napkins and spoons. I then carried the tray, with the black wine, hot and steaming, to the table and put it down there. Susan then, as "first slave," took the orders and did the measuring and mixing; I, as "second slave," did the pouring. Afterwards I returned the tray to the serving table, and the vessel of black wine to its warmer. I then joined Susan, kneeling beside her in the vicinity of the serving table.

"When it comes time to serve the liqueurs," said Susan, "you will serve those of Cos and Ar, and I will serve those of Turia."

"Yes, Mistress," I said. The liqueurs of Turia are usually regarded as the best, but I think this is largely a matter of taste. Those of Cos and of Ar, and of certain other cities, are surely very fine. I had little doubt that Drusus Rencius, of Ar, and Publius, at least once of Ar, would prefer those of their own city. Susan, I suspected, knowing my feelings for Drusus Rencius, was trying to be kind, giving me the liqueur that he was almost certain to choose. On the other hand, did she not know that now I could scarcely bear to face him, that I, only Ehn ago, had been proven before him to be a natural slave!

"You are not a free woman," whispered Susan. "Suppose the men look this way. Get those knees apart!"

"Yes, Mistress," I said. Susan was younger and smaller than I but she, having seniority over me among the women of Miles of Argentum, was dominant over me. I must obey her as though she owned me, as though she was my Mistress. In such ways is order kept among slaves. It is in accord with the precisions and perfections of Gorean discipline.

But the men did not soon call for their liqueurs. Twice more, rather, talking and sipping, did they call for black wine, and twice more did two slaves, Susan and Sheila, serve it to them.

Eventually it grew late, and the musicians were permitted to withdraw.

Still the men drank and talked.

"Why are you crying?" asked Susan.

"It is nothing," I said. I gasped, and half choked. I held back sobs. I restrained my tears. I wiped my eyes with slave silk.

Before the man I loved I had been stripped to the core. The one thing I had desired most fervently to conceal from him, above all men, had been made clear to him. My secret was revealed. My deepest and most secret self had been casually disrobed and displayed for his consideration. I had been publicly proven, before the man I loved, to be utterly worthless. I had been publicly proven to be a natural slave.

"They are ready for their liqueurs," whispered Susan.

We then brought them to them, on the two small trays.

"Liqueurs, Masters?" asked Susan.

"Liqueurs, Masters?" I asked.

"Yes," said Drusus Rencius.

"Yes," said Publius.

Publius, to my surprise, selected a liqueur of Turia. "Those of Turia are the best," he said to Drusus Rencius, smiling, almost apologetically.

"Perhaps," smiled Drusus Rencius, "but I prefer those of Ar."

"In the judgment of liqueurs," said Publius, "patriotism is out of place."

"I have never confused objectivity with municipal pride," responded Drusus Rencius.

"Perhaps," said Publius. "But you also thought that this woman was not a natural slave."

"That is true," laughed Drusus Rencius.

I looked at the silver tarsk on the table near Publius. It seemed very large and very heavy. It glinted softly in the light. I could see, in the light, a dark, crescentlike shadow on one side about its rim, on the wood. He had not yet placed it in his pouch. He had won it from Drusus Rencius.

"Look at me, Slave," said Drusus Rencius.

I struggled to lift my head. I met his eyes. Then I lowered my head, ashamed.

"I was wrong about you," he said.

"Yes, Master," I whispered.

"You are indeed a natural slave," he said, "and an obvious one."

"Yes, Master," I said.

I looked again at the coin near Publius. Drusus Rencius had made a wager. He had lost the wager. He had lost the bet.

"You may leave, Slaves," said Publius.

"Thank you, Master," said Susan.

"Thank you, Master," I said. Then I turned and fled from the room, sobbing.

Behind me I heard Publius laughing, a great, roaring laugh. He was well pleased, it seemed. Doubtless he should have been. He had won his bet.

## 36

# IN THE QUARTERS OF MY MASTER

I was thrust, laughing and stumbling, down the hall before Drusus Rencius. I wore nothing but a steel collar locked on my neck.

I preceded him, pushed and thrust toward his quarters. I laughed with joy. He was not gentle with me. He was angry.

"To your belly!" he snarled, at the entrance to his quarters.

Then, in a moment, as I lay on the tiles I felt my hands jerked behind my back and tied there, tightly. In another moment, I felt his strong hands cross my ankles and loop them with binding fiber. Then, by the loops, they were drawn closely together. Through my ankles I felt the jerking tight of the knots. I then lay there at his feet, helplessly trussed. He flung open the door, angrily. He then scooped me up as though I might weigh nothing and threw me over his shoulder. I was then, as a capture and a slave, carried helplessly over the threshold. Within he put me on the floor, on the tiles, near the foot of the couch, near the slave ring. He then closed and locked the door behind us. He then came and stood near me, looming over me, looking down at me.

This morning, early, I had been sent stark naked, even collarless, to the courtyard, that I might bid farewell to my friends of Feast Slaves, who were now leaving for Ar. I had spoken with them, and kissed them, shedding tears. My favorites among them were Claudia, Crystal and Tupa, with whom I had been close friends. I watched them all, one by one, naked, ankle-chained, then climbing into the wagon, threading their chains about the opened central bar, then taking their places. Many times had I, too, similarly secured, en route to various destinations, usually in the city of Ar itself, been similarly secured and transported. Then the wagon was creaking away. The canvas had not yet been put in place, to be tied down, stretched over the frame, to its rings on the outside of the wagon bed. It was cool, and early. That could be done later to protect the girls from the sun. They, rising to their knees in the wagon, lifted their hands, waving me farewell. One girl was not with them, Emily. Two days ago she had bidden me farewell. She was leaving early with her master, Aemilianus, for Ar. We had thought that he had come to Argentum on business, or perhaps to observe the performances of his Feast Slaves in this allied city. On the other hand, it now seemed clear that he had come to Argentum, astoundingly enough, on the account of a mere slave, that he had come to Argentum merely to reclaim Emily, to get her again in his personal collar. I did not think he would be likely to let the lovely slave, once from the mills, go again. Much did it seem they loved one another. She went with him happily, helpless in his bracelets.

I watched the gates to the palace being opened for the passage of the slave wagon.

Speusippus had left Argentum on the day after the banquet, that in which the identity of Sheila had been determined.

Five days ago Ligurious had left. The next day Hassan, of Kasra, his men and sleen, and the slave, Sheila, had left. At the suggestion of Menicius who, at the same time, had returned to Corcyrus, Hassan was to take Sheila to Port Kar, for interrogation in the house of Samos, this with respect to matters having to do with Priest-Kings and beasts. I had little doubt but what she, now in a collar, would prove eager and cooperative. If she survived the interrogation, as I expected she would, she was then to be taken back to Kasra by Hassan. In that city, near the Tahari, on the Lower Fayeen, I had little doubt she would learn her collar well, and love.

The wagon went through the palace gates. They were then closed behind it.

I lowered my hand.

I stood, tears in my eyes, naked, collarless, on the flat stones of the courtyard.

I felt much alone.

"Do not kneel," said a voice behind me.

I almost knelt, my knees flexing. It is common for girls such as I to kneel automatically, immediately, upon being addressed by a male voice.

"You are naked," observed the voice.

"Yes, Master," I said. The voice was that of Drusus Rencius.

I had not been given permission to turn.

"Where is your collar?" he asked.

"I do not know, Master," I said. "It was removed from me this morning."

"Why?" he asked.

"I do not know, Master," I said. "I suppose it is to be changed."

"That is true," said the voice.

"Master?" I asked.

"You are going to be put in a new collar," he said.

"Master?" I asked.

"I have it here," he said.

"You, Master?" I inquired.

He stepped about, in front of me. He showed me an opened collar, graceful and slim, and of inflexible steel.

"Read it," he said, indicating the legend which, in small, graceful letters, was incised in the metal.

"I cannot read, Master," I said. "I have never been taught."

"Oh, splendid," he said, irritably. "An illiterate slave!"

"Some men think they are the best kind," I said, not a little irritated myself. I was not illiterate in English, of course, only in Gorean. I had not been taught to read in Corcyrus, probably in order to better keep the politics of the city from me, and in order to guard against my better understanding my position there. Many Gorean slaves, of course, are illiterate, and deliberately kept so. In that fashion, for example, she may be used to carry messages about, even having to do with herself. The common way in which a girl carries a Gorean message is on foot, with her hand braceleted behind her. The message is then inserted in a capped leather tube tied about her neck. Given the braceleting, of course, even a literate girl may be used to carry messages in this fashion, which may or may not have to do with herself. Some men feel that if a woman is taught to read and write, particularly after she has been made a slave, she may come to think that she is important. This delusion, of course, may be swiftly removed from her by the whip. For what it is worth, literacy commonly increases the value of a slave. It may usually be depended upon to add a few copper tarsks to her value, much like the ability to play a musical instrument or to dance, or to cook and sew. Some men enjoy owning educated slaves and some do not. Needless to say, the slave, when she is in the power of a Gorean master, whether she is educated or not, will serve as a full slave. Indeed, most men expect far more of an educated slave than of one who is not educated.

He then went behind me, again.

"Lift your hair," he said.

"What are you going to do?" I asked.

"Must a command be repeated?" he inquired.

Swiftly I thrust up my hair, baring the back of my neck. My hair, at least, extending over my nape, was now long enough to require this.

"What are you going to do?" I asked. I felt the steel of the collar under my chin, then its being adjusted on my neck.

"Put you in this collar," he said. Then he snapped it shut. I was collared.

"By what right?" I asked.

"You may lower your hands," he said.

I did so, brushing my hair back over the steel. "By what right?" I asked. I did not dare turn to face him.

"By every right," he said.

I was bitter. "Doubtless you told my master, Miles of Argentum, of the results of your experiment last night, that in which I was conclusively proven to be a natural slave."

"I did see him last night," said Drusus Rencius.

"I see," I said, bitterly.

"But he has had you leaping in his arms, several times, apparently last night, and earlier, on various days," he said. "I told him nothing he did not already know."

"I see," I said. Last night, after I had served Publius and Drusus Rencius, I had been ordered to the couch of Miles. There, in spite of my feelings and my distress, I had been forced, three times, to serve him well. The last time, unable to help myself, I had cried out, surrendering myself totally to him. Miles of Argentum, as is his wont, such a man, when he wishes, takes everything from a woman. I had then, a few Ehn afterwards, been sent back to the slave quarters. Apparently it had been later the same night, perhaps in the neighborhood of the Twentieth Ahn, when Drusus Rencius had seen him. I had not seen him since earlier this morning, when I had knelt before him, kissing his feet, gratefully, for his attentions to me last night, and he had, without explanation, removed my clothing and my collar. I had then been permitted to go to the courtyard, that I might see my friends off. Drusus Rencius had probably been informed that he might find me here.

"You seem bitter," said Drusus Rencius.

"Yes," I said.

"Why?" he asked.

"My own master has not even seen fit to change my collar," I said.

"I see," he said.

"What collar is it," I asked, "the collar of a scullery maid, of a kitchen slave?" I had not realized I had been so displeasing last night.

"Neither," said Drusus Rencius, "or, perhaps, in a sense, both, and that of other slaveries, as well."

"I do not understand," I said.

"What is so hard to understand?" he asked.

"You have been empowered by Miles of Argentum to change my collar, have you not?" I asked.

"No," he said.

I touched the collar, fearfully. "I do not understand," I whispered. I feared for Drusus Rencius. I feared he had committed a crime.

"I do not need that power," he said.

"Why not?" I asked.

"Because it is my collar," he said.

"Yours!" I cried. I almost turned about.

"Yes," he said. "I bought you last night."

I fainted.

I lay now naked, save for my collar, on the tiles of the quarters of Drusus Rencius, in the palace at Argentum.

I had apparently not long been permitted the luxury of unconsciousness in the courtyard. I had awakened, held in a sitting position, my face, stinging, seeming to explode, being jerked, by blows, first with the flat of a hand, and then with its back, from side to side. Gorean men are not always indulgent with their female slaves. I scrambled to my knees and looked up at my master, Drusus Rencius, of Ar. "To my quarters, and swiftly, Slave," he snarled.

"Yes, Master!" I had cried, joyfully.

I had then preceded him to his quarters, moving swiftly, but scarcely swiftly enough, it seemed, from the point of view of Drusus Rencius, striding fiercely behind me, like some impatient, grumbling larl. It seemed he could not wait to get me alone. Many times was I hurried, pushed and thrust from behind. I was even twice kicked. It was not my fault that I was a woman, and that my legs were shorter than his! Then, at his portal, I had been ordered to my belly. I had then been bound, hand and foot. I had then been carried into the room, over his shoulder, as a slave, helpless. He had put me down on the tiles, near the foot of his couch, near the slave ring. He had locked the door. He was now standing near me, looking down at me. I pulled, futilely, at the ropes on my wrists and ankles. I was bound, perfectly. The door was locked. I was a slave girl alone with her master. I was utterly helpless.

He stepped back at bit. His face was unreadable.

"Whip me!" I begged. "I love you! Teach me that you own me!"

He took a step, further back.

"I beg the lash, Master," I said. My heart was filled with joy and love.

His face was expressionless. He did not speak.

"Let me kneel before you," I said, "and beg to be beaten with a slave whip."

He did not speak.

"Whip me!" I begged. "I love you! I love you!"

"Slave," he sneered.

"Yes, Master," I said.

"Natural slave," he said, angrily.

"Yes, Master," I said.

"I did not know you were a natural slave," he said.

"You knew it before you bought me," I said. "You knew it from last night."

"Yes," he said.

"But still you bought me!" I said.

"Yes," he said.

"I love you!" I said.

"You are a natural slave," he said. "Your love is worthless."

"It is, at any rate, real," I assured him.

"I wonder," he said.

"You paid for it," I said. "You must have wanted it."

"Perhaps," he said.

"Master?" I asked.

"Perhaps I have purchased you not for your love, but for your hate," he said.

"I do not understand," I said.

"You have caused me much grief and pain," he said, "particularly when you were a free woman, in Corcyrus."

"I am sorry, Master," I said.

"And well you might be," he said, "as you are now my slave."

"I am sorry anyway," I said.

"Perhaps it is my intention to humiliate you, to debase and degrade you, to abuse you, to teach you, at my hands, fear, misery and pain!"

"You may do with me as you please," I smiled. "I am your slave."

"I wonder how you will like it," he mused, "in your collar, hating me, but utterly helpless, knowing that you must obey me, absolutely, and serve me, in all things, with total perfection."

"I do not hate you," I laughed. "And you need not concern yourself with obedience and service. As I am a slave, you may depend upon them. Too, I shall render them to you eagerly, not only from the meaning of my collar but from the bottom of my heart."

"Perhaps I should debase and degrade you," he said.

"The more you debase and degrade me, Master," I said, "the more I shall love you."

"How you tortured me in Corcyrus!" he said, angrily, looking down at me.

"I was cruel and petty," I said.

"Much misery did you cause me," he said, angrily.

"I am sorry," I smiled. I was not completely displeased, of course, to learn of his discomfort.

"You are not truly sorry, are you?" he asked, a smile about his lips.

"Not really," I admitted, shrugging in the ropes.

"Why?" he asked.

"I am a woman," I said.

"Women enjoy taunting men, and tormenting them with desire," he said.

"Some women, sometimes," I said.

"You, then," he said.

"Yes," I said, angrily, rising to my elbows, "I, then!"

"I thought so," he said.

"It is a flattering tribute to a woman's power," I said, "her capacity to arouse desire!"

"Doubtless," he said, bitterly.

"I only wish I had known how important I was to you at the time," I said. "That would have made the matter much more amusing!"

"I see," he said.

"I am glad to learn, even now," I said, "how much I had disturbed you. Thank you for confessing it to me!"

"You're welcome," he said, quietly, perhaps too quietly.

"I'm glad I made you miserable!" I said, angrily. "I'm glad I made you sweat and squirm, when you could not have me!" I was glad, too! In Corcyrus he, though desperately attracted to me, I think, had resisted my advances. This had caused me great frustration. I had, as a consequence of this spurning of me, taken a woman's vengeance upon him. I had, in a thousand ways, in glances, in small words, in smiles, in tiny gestures, in movements, in seemingly careless proximities, in seeming inadvertences, tormented him. I had seen to it, many times, that passions would flash and flame in Drusus Rencius, which I would then, haughtily, refuse to satisfy.

"But those days are gone, aren't they?" said Drusus Rencius.

I lay back on the tiles. "Yes, Master," I said. I swallowed hard. I was very conscious, then, of my nudity, and of the tight binding on my wrists and ankles, making me absolutely helpless.

"Things are different now, aren't they?" he asked.

"Yes, Master," I said. I was now a slave. The least discontentment a girl causes her master can be taken out of her hide. I was now at his disposal, completely. I must now ready myself for him, and please him fully, at as little as a glance or a snapping of fingers.

"Get on your knees," he said.

"Yes, Master," I said. I struggled to my knees. It was not easy, bound as I was. He did not help me. I then knelt before him. He stood then, his arms folded, some feet from me, across the tiles.

"You look well on your knees, bound as a slave," he said.

"Thank you, Master," I said. I recalled Corcyrus, where I had been to him as a Tatrix. I was now bound naked before him, as a slave.

"There are vengeances to be taken upon you," he said.

"Do with me as you will," I said. "I am yours."

"I will," he said.

"Yes, Master," I said.

"How I despise you!" he said.

"Yes, Master," I said.

"You are utterly beautiful," he said.

"Thank you, Master," I said.

"Are you afraid?" he asked.

"Yes," I said.

"You do not seem truly afraid," he said.

"I do not think you are the sort of man who buys a woman to hurt her," I said.

"You cannot know that," he said.

"I suppose not," I said. Consider the matter of marriage. Most women, prior to their marriage, do not truly know the man they are marrying. They will come to know him, truly, only in living with him, his. It is natural, then, that a woman should enter into such a relation with a certain amount of trepidation. How much more so, then, must this be the case with the female slave, whose new master, one who will have total power over her, is likely to be a total stranger, a fellow whom she has probably never even seen before her sale. Is he going to enfold her lovingly in his arms, and master her, and cherish her as a treasure, or is he going to feed her to sleen? She does not know. You strive desperately to please him. You are his. You hope for the best.

"You do not seem convinced," he said.

"I am not," I smiled.

"Perhaps suitable lashings would convince you," he said.

"Perhaps," I smiled.

"Do you think you are never to be whipped?" he asked.

"No, Master," I said. "I know that I am a slave. I know that I am subject to the whip."

He unfolded his arms and looked at me, with fury. "How utterly, utterly beautiful you are," he said, "and how provocative, and delicious!"

"And I am yours, and you may do with me as you please," I said.

"How you infuriate me!" he cried, suddenly, his fists clenched. He turned away. I was silent. I squirmed a little in the ropes. They held me well.

He stood by the window in his quarters. "I remember Corcyrus," he said, bitterly. He put the palms of his hands on the sides of the window, looking out.

"I, too, remember Corcyrus," I said, happily.

"Slut," he snarled.

"Yes, Master," I said.

"There are vengeances to be taken upon you," he said, angrily.

"You are certainly entitled to them, Master," I said, smiling. I loved Drusus Rencius.

He looked about at me, angrily.

"Let us put our heads together," I suggested. "Perhaps, then, we can plan certain appropriate exactions, ministrations wherewith that arrogant slut, Sheila, may be well punished for her stupidities."

"You seek to divert my wrath," he said.

"Perhaps," I smiled.

He leaned back, wearily, against the wall, by the window, looking at me.

"Surely a girl cannot be blamed for hoping to do that," I said.

"I suppose not," he smiled.

"Oh," I said, "I forgot! I am no longer Sheila, am I? My collar has been changed!" I looked at Drusus Rencius. "I do not have a name now, do I?" I asked.

"No," he said.

"Is master going to name me?" I asked.

"I will, if it pleases me," he said. "I will not, if it does not please me."

"Yes, Master," I said.

"I am a fool," he said.

"I shall maintain a judicious silence," I said. "If I agree I would seem to proclaim my master a fool. If I disagree, I should, at the very least, contradict him."

"I am a fool!" he said, miserably.

"I do not think so," I said, "but, of course, I am only a slave, and I could conceivably be mistaken."

"I should sell you," he said.

"You may do with me as you wish," I said. I had no fear, however, that he would sell me. It was not for such a purpose, I was confident, that he had bought me.

"You do not fear me, truly, do you?" he asked.

"Not, ultimately," I said.

"Why?" he asked.

"Must I speak?" I asked.

"No," he said, angrily. "You need not speak."

He turned wearily, angrily, away.

"Master?" I asked.

He turned again to face me. "You are a beautiful, complex woman," he said.

"I am a simple slave," I said, "a man's toy, a bauble for his pleasure."

"Simple or complex, you are a slave," he said. "There is no doubt about that."

"Your slave," I reminded him.

"Why did I buy you?" he asked.

"I can think of several reasons," I said.

"Do you mock me?" he asked.

"I tease you," I said. "I do not mock you."

"I care for you," he said, suddenly, bitterly.

"I know," I said.

"And you only a slave!"

"Yes, Master," I said.

"What a fool I am!" he cried.

I was silent.

"You did it to me," he said.

"I?" I asked.

"Yes," he said, "you, with your intelligence, your beauty, your vulnerability, your sensuousness, your glances and movements, your bondage skills, your insidious slave wiles, the perfections of your servitude, made it impossible not to desire you, not to lust for you, inordinately, not to want you, not to demand you, to the point of madness, for my very own!"

I was silent, bound before him. There was some truth, of course, or at least I thought so, to these charges. At least I hoped there was. I had tried, with all the skills I had been taught, and with all the devices, and instincts, of the natural slave, which I was, to attract and lure him. The outcome of such a campaign, of course, if successful, is that the girl becomes the man's slave. She is then, of course, subject to whatever vengeances he might be pleased to take upon her.

I squirmed in the ropes. I belonged to him. I began to sweat. For the first time I felt genuine fear.

"You wrapped me about your finger," he said. "You manipulated me!"

"Forgive me, Master," I said.

"Gloat in your power, Slave!" he said.

"Forgive me, Master," I whispered.

"Even last night," he said, "in your writhing on the steps, you made me wild for you. You made me want to tear off your silk and hurl you beneath me, then to have you, uncompromisingly, like the luscious slut and slave you are!"

"Yes, Master," I whispered.

"I saw your body jerk in the hands of the soldier!" he said, accusingly.

"I cannot help what I am!" I cried, looking up at him, angrily, tears in my eyes.

"You are a slave!" he cried.

"Yes!" I cried. "And had you been there you could, later, have seen my body jerk in the hands of Miles of Argentum. That night he made me, three times, serve him well, and the third time, writhing, I cried myself his, a submitted slave. In the morning I kissed his feet in gratitude!"

"Slave, slave!" snarled Drusus Rencius.

"And do you not make women respond like that," I said, "the girls in the taverns, the girls on their mats, the girls thrown to your feet, for your sport, at the house of a friend?"

"Yes," he said, angrily. "I make them grovel and scream!"

"And why, then," I asked, "should you object if other men make me respond in the same way?"

He regarded me, with fury.

"Am I different?" I asked.

"Apparently not," he said.

"I am not!" I said.

"They are slaves," he said.

"So, too, am I!"

"I had hoped you might be more," he said.

"What?" I asked.

"A free woman," he said.

"I have been a free woman," I said. "Do not laud them to me!"

"Do you speak ill of free women?" he asked.

"No," I said, "for I do not wish to be whipped!"

He glared at me.

"Look at me," I said. "I am naked and bound before you! Would you really prefer that I was a free woman?"

"No," he said, and my blood almost froze in my veins.

"You see?" I whispered.

"Yes," he said, angrily.

"I am a thousand times more than a free woman," I said, "both to a man and, in my heart and emotions, to myself."

"How is that?" he asked.

"I am a slave," he said, simply.

He looked down, sullenly.

"You take free women into companionship," I said, "but you dream of slaves. You even dream of the free woman as a slave. I doubt that any glandularly sufficient male does not want us as slaves. If he doesn't, then I think he must be very short on imagination. What do you think is the meaning of your size and strength, your energy and agility, your dominance? Do you think it is all some alarming, inexplicable, statistical eccentricity? Can you not see the order of nature? Is it so difficult to disclose? Why do you think men make us slaves, and put us in collars? It is because they want us as slaves. And why do you think we make such superb slaves? Because we are born slaves."

"If I take my place in the order of nature," he said, "then, obviously, you will be put in yours."

I pulled at the ropes. "I think I am already there, Master," I said.

He looked up at me.

"I am on my step," I said. "It is now only necessary that you ascend to yours."

"You do not even have a name," he said.

"Perhaps Master will, if it pleases him, give me a name."

"Perhaps I should name you," he said. "Doubtless you might be conveniently ordered about and referred to, if you were named."

"Yes, Master," I said. The name would be a slave name, of course. Such names, like collars, are worn whether the slave wishes them or not. Some masters think of such names as being along the lines of verbal leashes, the utterance of the name, like the sudden tug of a leash, immediately calling the slave's attention to the master and his wishes. In any event, the slave name, and the knowledge that it is a slave name, deeply, and appropriately, informs the consciousness of the slave. Too, of course, it is the only name she has.

He turned away from me.

"You still hesitate to accept me as what I am, a total slave, don't you?" I asked.

"Perhaps," he growled.

"If you wish," I said, "relate to me as to a despised slut in bondage. You will discover that I will respond well to you in that role."

He spun about. "Do you think that you are not despised?" he asked.

"Master?" I asked.

"I do despise you," he said, angrily, "for Corcyrus, for your meaninglessness, for your pettiness and cruelty, for what you are, and for what you have done to me!"

I shrank back in the bonds.

"And you are maddeningly beautiful," he said. "You are excruciatingly desirable!"

I was silent.

"I am a free man!" he cried. "I am of the warriors! I am an officer! I am a citizen of Ar, glorious Ar! And I am a fool! What you have done to me! Such women as you are the downfall of men! You have cost me my respect and my honor!"

"Do you want me to pretend to be a free woman?" I asked. "I can do that. I did it for years. At times I even believed it. I can do it again! Command me, if you wish, to the pretense!"

"You are a slave," he said. "It is all you are. Do not mock me."

"Forgive me, Master," I said.

"Day in and day out, night in and night out, I fought my feelings for you," he said. "I immersed myself in duties. I adopted strenuous activities. I sought solace even in the taverns, and in the arms of others. I chided myself for my foolishness. I berated myself for my stupidity! I castigated myself for my madness! But I could not drive you from my mind! Ever more hotly burned the flames of my passion! And you are not even free!"

"No," I said, suddenly, angrily. "I am not even free!"

"A slave!" he said.

"Yes!" I said. "A slave!"

"Gloat, Slave," said he, "for you, with your wiles, and your insidious beauty, have brought a soldier, and a free man, low."

"Punish me," I said. "You own me."

"Do not fear," he said. "You will be punished, for Corcyrus, and for your insolence."

I shrank down in the ropes, trying to make myself appear

smaller. I feared now that perhaps Drusus Rencius had bought me primarily for the purposes of vengeance.

"Even now," he said, "still, when you are helpless, in my ropes, I find you exquisitely desirable, exquisitely beautiful."

"Thank you, Master," I whispered.

"You ruin me," he said. "You tear me apart!"

I put down my head, frightened.

"You make me a slave!" he cried.

"It is I who am the slave," I said.

"I hate you!" he cried.

"I do not think so," I said.

"As Sheila, who was the true Tatrix of Corcyrus, was to Ligurious, so, too, are you to me!" he said.

"No!" I said. "There is a great difference!"

"What?" he demanded.

"I love you!" I said.

"Sly, clever slave!" he sneered.

"I do love you!" I cried.

"Cunning, insidious slut," he said. "You fear for your own hide! You know that you are now, at least, within my power. You fear that it will be done to you as you deserve, that you will be thrown to sleen!"

"No!" I wept.

"Sweat and squirm now, luscious slut," he said. "Cry out your love for me. Perhaps I will be moved to be merciful, and keep you as the lowest and most worthless slave on Gor!"

"I do love you!" I wept.

"Lying slave!" he cried. He leapt across the room, and, with the flat of his hand, savagely, struck me from my knees. My right shoulder struck the tiles. I tasted blood in my mouth. I lay there, bound, frightened. It had been only a slap, but I felt as though my head might have been almost taken from me. I was awe-stricken. I had not realized how strong he was. What if he had truly struck me? I knew I must obey him with perfection.

"On your back," he said, "knees raised, heels on the floor."

I then lay before him, in a standard, supine capture position.

"You look well at my feet, Slut," he said.

"Thank you, Master," I said.

"Have you reconsidered the telling of truth?" he asked.

"I love you," I whispered.

"Lying slut!" he hissed. He then, with the side of his foot, kicked me. I recoiled, crying out. I would doubtless, for several days, bear a fine bruise there, evidence of his displeasure.

I turned to my side. I put down my head. I kissed the foot that had kicked me. Then I returned to my former position.

He turned away from me and went to the other chair in the room, a curule chair, with ornate, curved arms. I, my head turned to the side, watched him. He sat down in the chair, his hands on the arms, and regarded me.

"Should you not be on your knees, Slut?" he asked.

"Yes, Master," I said. I struggled to my knees and knelt, facing him.

He regarded me. He seemed weary.

"And thus it is," he said, "that slaves conquer warriors."

"It is I who am conquered, Master," I told him, "not you."

"You make me weak," he said, wearily.

"Unbind me," I suggested, smiling, "and I will make you strong."

"She-sleen," he smiled.

"Yes, Master," I said.

He looked to one side of the room, moodily, lost in thought. "How strange has been the course of events," he said. "I took you for a Tatrix, and my enemy. Then, as it pleased you, in the fullness of feminine cruelty, when I could not have you, when you thought me a mere guard, you amused yourself with me, taunting me with your beauty, torturing me with desire. Now, months later, you have come into my power, as my naked slave."

He turned his head slowly towards me. Then he regarded me, slowly, fully, every bit of me.

"Are you well roped?" he asked.

"I am roped perfectly, and am absolutely helpless," I said. "It was done to me by Drusus Rencius, of Ar, my master."

"It is a suitable answer," he said.

I was silent.

"Perhaps I will keep you," he said.

"Do, please," I said. I loved him.

"If I keep you," he said, "you will be kept as a slave. Do you understand what that means, my dear?"

"Yes, Master," I said. I would be kept in the absolute perfections of Gorean slave discipline. I would have to be perfect for him, in all ways. I shuddered.

"Do you believe it?" he asked.

"Yes, Master," I said.

"That is well," he said, "for it is true."

"Yes, Master," I whispered.

"You seem to be afraid," he said.

"I am," I said.

"But you were not before," he said.

"No," I said.

"But you are now?"

"Yes," I said.

"Why?"

"Because now I sense, as I did not before, that you are strong enough to control me, and to punish me, terribly, if I do wrong, or am not fully pleasing."

"Believe it," he said, quietly.

"I do!" I said.

"I wonder if you will make a good slave," he said.

"I will try my best, Master," I said.

Then he continued to look at me, appraising me.

I straightened my body.

How marvelous it must be for a man, I thought, to have such absolute power over a woman, to have her so subjected to him, even to having her in the perfection of his bonds. And how marvelous it was for me, too, to know myself so much his, to know myself, will-lessly, eagerly, at his pleasure. And what woman does not want a man a thousand times more than she, one to whom she must submit, one whom she must fear, one whom she must love?

I looked at him.

"It is different from Corcyrus, isn't it?" he asked.

"Yes, Master," I said.

He looked away, again, again seemingly lost in thought.

"May I speak?" I asked.

"Yes," he said.

"Is it truly so tragic, to care for a slave, just a little?" I asked.

"You have done enough," he said. "Do not seek further to make a fool of me."

I was silent.

He put his head down, in his hands.

How painful, complex and subtle can be the relationships between human beings. I tried to understand how he must view me. He saw me, it seemed, as one who, if she were free, and immune from punishment, and held power, would torment and scorn him, exploiting him, despising him, amusing herself with him. As far as I knew I had done little to provoke these feelings, at least until he had refused my advances. I had given him reason, to be sure, in Corcyrus, to believe me contemptible and petty. I had made certain Earth values, to his irritation, clear to him, such as an amoral expediency and a mockery of honor. My smallness, my contemptibility, I had unwittingly flaunted before him, regarding such things at that time as signs of my depth and cleverness. Too, he seemed to find me, in some way, and I did not fully understand it, maddeningly desirable. This had to do, it seemed, with some unusual and subtle relationship between us. These things, doubtless in part because of his pride and self-image, his reluctance to accept tenderness, his fear of feeling and sentiment, his lofty conceptions of the attitudes and behaviors proper to his caste, had driven him half mad with frustration. Yet, too, he had, with Menicius, risked his life in the camp of Miles to free me, and he had sought desperately to protect and defend me in the inquiry with Claudius and the high council. It was clear, I think, he cared for me deeply. In all this, of course, he regarded me as little more than a curvaceous, scheming slave, one who did not care for him, but one who, to protect herself, would do anything, even pretend falsely to love. He did not know I truly loved him.

I resolved upon a bold plan. I would attempt to get him to cure himself of the false Sheila, that the way might then be open for a poor, nameless slave who so much loved him.

"Free me," I said, angrily, pulling at the ropes.

He looked at me.

"Free yourself," he said.

"I cannot!" I said.

"Why do you wish to be freed?" he asked.

"I do not love you!" I said.

"Now, at last, you speak the truth," he said.

"Not only do I not love you," I cried, "but I hate you! I despise you! I hold you in contempt as a piteous weakling! I always have!"

He smiled.

"I am tired of trying to fool you," I said. "Now, free me!"

"Why should I free you?" he asked.

"Because I am a free woman!" I said.

"That is not true," he said. "I saw you jerk in the hands of the soldier."

"I could not help myself," I said.

"Only a natural slave could not have helped herself," he said.

"I do not want to belong to you," I said.

"I have an alternative in mind," he said. "I think I shall give you to the department of the mines. There, naked and yoked, you shall carry water."

"No!" I cried.

"Do you beg to be kept in my collar?" he asked.

"Yes, Master," I whispered.

"Then we shall let it stand at that, shan't we?" he asked.

"Yes, Master," I said. I had not counted on the possibility of being sent to the mines.

I knelt back in the ropes. I looked at Drusus Rencius. He was quite capable, I realized, suddenly, of sending me to the mines. I did not want that to happen. Too, looking at him then, I saw him suddenly not only as a man I loved but, also, independently, as a strong and powerful master. I found, then, that I had squirmed in the ropes, inadvertently, reflexively, my thighs moving. I hoped that he had not noticed.

"What is wrong?" he asked.

"Nothing!" I said. I felt the heat of the slave in me. I hoped he could not detect the signs in my body. I hoped he could not smell me.

He was silent.

"May I speak?" I asked.

"Yes," he said.

"I gather," I said, "that you intend to keep me."

"At least for a time," he said.

"I presume," I said, "that at least one of the purposes for which you purchased me was to make use of me."

"Perhaps," he said.

"I am ready," I said. "Begin my slavery."

He regarded me, not speaking.

"You see me in a collar," I said, angrily. "You know what a collar does to a woman!"

He smiled.

"I have been owned," I said. "I have had masters. They have made me this way!"

"So men do have their vengeance," he said. "The scheming beauty is needful."

"Yes!" I said.

"Speak clearly," he said.

"I am needful," I said.

"You are more than needful," he said.

"You may or may not believe I love you," I said, "but about my arousal, my need, there is no disputing."

"That is true," he said. "You are obviously, now, a needful slave."

"Please," I begged.

He left the chair and, crouching beside me, not hurrying, freed me of the ropes.

"Touch neither me nor yourself," he said.

"Yes, Master," I moaned. My body was flaming with desire.

He regarded me for a few moments. I moaned.

Then, for a brief moment, he took me in his arms. His hand was upon me, intimately. "I love you! I love you! I love you!" I cried, jerking in his hands, pressing against him, trying to cover him with kisses.

"Stop," he said. "To your belly."

Then I was on my belly, on the tiles, my hands at the sides of my head, prone, before his curule chair. He resumed his seat.

I lifted my head and upper body, wildly, agonized, to regard him.

"You are a hot slave," he said.

I regarded him wildly, pathetically, unbelievingly, speechlessly.

"Do you beg a man's touch?" he asked.

"Yes," I said, "yes!"

"Then beg," he said.

"I beg your touch," I wept. "I beg your touch! Please touch me, Master! I beg it!"

"Truly?" he asked.

"Yes," I said. "I beg your touch, truly, Master! I beg it, truly! Please, touch me, Master! Please! Please!"

"No," he said.

I collapsed then to the tiles, sobbing, helpless, quivering with need.

"And thus," said he, "may a hated slave be denied."

I then became aware that he had left his chair, that he was standing near me.

I lay at his feet, aroused, almost unbelievably impassioned, denied.

I understood then better than ever before how it was that some women could tear at the walls of their kennels with their fingernails, how they could reach out through the bars, begging piteously for the least touch of a rude guard, how they could, under the deft touches of an auctioneer's whip, scream their passion on a slave block, begging to be bought.

"You deserve this," he said.

"Yes, Master," I said.

"Do you know now what it is to be in a collar?" he asked.

"Yes, Master," I said.

"Hereafter," he said, "do not try to play stupid games with me."

"Master?" I asked.

I felt myself jerked to a sitting position, his hands on my upper arms. "How stupid do you think I am?" he asked. "Do you think I could not tell you were playing some sort of game?"

"My arousal was real!" I said, startled.

"I am well aware of that," he said.

"Oh!" I cried, as he touched me. Then he thrust me back from him.

"You are a slave," he said. "We will do things my way, not yours."

"I do not understand," I said.

"I considered this," he said, "even before I bought you. I now see, as I thought, that it is necessary."

"I do not understand," I said.

"We shall begin again," he said. "I shall make my determination with care."

"I do not understand," I wept.

"You are fortunate," he said, "that I am less stupid than you thought. Had I not seen through your subterfuges you might have been flinging yourself to the jaws of sleen, or guaranteeing the signing of your papers for the mines."

I shuddered.

He then put my wrists together, crossing them, and held them in one hand, and drew me across the tiles to the slave ring at the foot of his couch. There, cunningly, looping the chain about my throat, he fastened me, by the neck, on my knees, closely to the slave ring. He then, too, braceleted my hands to the slave ring. I could, thus, even if I were tempted to do so, do little to assuage the almost intolerable passions he had aroused in me. I looked at him, piteously. He laughed, and left. Then I was kneeling there, bewildered, alone, chained. I was a slave. I must await his return. He did not, of course, tell me where he was going or when he would be back.

"You understand, do you not," he asked, "that this is a symbolic re-enactment and that it in no way compromises your slavery?"

"Yes, Master," I said.

"For example," he said, "for your treatment of me in Corcyrus, and for various insolences, and lapses, you must still answer to me, and to my whip."

"Yes, Master," I said.

"You are now dressed, are you not," he asked, "fully in the garments of the Tatrix, even to the nature, the subtlety and delicacy of the undergarments?"

"Yes," I said.

"And beneath those," he said, "in the eccentric undergarments of Earth, in garments similar to those which you, a barbarian, doubtless once wore there?"

"Yes," I said. These undergarments had once belonged to Sheila. They had been brought to Argentum by Menicius, for the inquiry. I supposed that now, technically, they might be the property of the state of Argentum. I, at any rate, did not own them. I could own nothing. Rather it was I who was owned. Fortunately, Sheila and I were almost identically figured.

"Turn, Tatrix," said Drusus Rencius.

I turned, obediently, before him. He sat in the curule chair, across the room. I had been given the slave name, "Tatrix." I had been given no choice in the matter, and I must respond to it, perfectly.

"Good," he said. "Now walk back and forth, slowly."

I did so.

Many of the garments I wore had been those which I myself had worn, when I had been playing the role of the Tatrix. This pleased Drusus Rencius. He remembered me in them.

"Good," he said. "You may now stop."

I stood then again before him, facing him.

"Turn again," he said.

I did so.

"Good," he said.

I wore no bond. He had even removed from me his collar. It hung now on the arm of the curule chair. There was no doubt, however, that I was a slave, or whose slave I was. I was branded, and I was paid for.

"You will now strip yourself naked, slowly," he said. "I intend to enjoy this."

I reached to the pins at the side of the veil. One by one, I removed them. I then put the veil with its pins, to one side. I then, with both hands, putting back my head, brushed back the hood of the robes. I shook my head and arranged my hair. I then faced Drusus Rencius, face-stripped.

"Continue," he said.

One by one I removed the garments of the Tatrix. Then I stood before him clad only in undergarments of Earth, in a brassiere and panties.

Drusus Rencius nodded.

I removed the brassiere, and straightened my body.

"Excellent," he said.

I faced him.

"Now remove the last veil," he said.

I bent down and, in a moment, stepped from the panties. I then, again, straightened myself before him. I hoped he liked what he saw. He owned it.

"Superb," he said. "Superb!"

I smiled.

His face grew hard. "Kneel," he said.

Swiftly I knelt, in the position of the pleasure slave.

I swallowed, hard. I saw that he had no intention of permitting my beauty, if beauty it was, which had at one time apparently been so tormenting to him, when it had been inaccessible, diminish in any way the perfections of his mastery of me.

He went to a chest at the side of the room, and drew forth a small, gray garment, which he threw to me. I caught it against my body. I shook it out, happily. "You kept it, Master!" I laughed, delighted. It was the brief slave tunic, sleeveless and gray, which I had worn in the house of Kliomenes, so long ago, in Corcyrus.

"Yes," he said, "for when you were my true slave."

"I love it!" I said. To some, I suppose, it would have seemed a scandalous rag, unseemly and degrading, but I found it very beautiful, not only because of the lovely and sensitive way in which it enhanced and displayed the beauty of the female figure but because of memories with which it was associated, memories which, for me, at least, were very precious.

"Put it on," he said.

Still kneeling, I drew it happily over my head. Then, slipped into it, I smoothed it down about my body.

"You are so beautiful," he said. "Stand."

I stood, and pulled it down more about my thighs. "It is rather short, though, isn't it?" I said.

"It will be shorter," he said, drawing out a knife.

"Master!" I protested, but he, with the knife, cutting and tearing, must have shortened it by at least two horts.

I looked down, dismayed.

"Later," he said, "sewing, smooth out the hem."

"But if I take up the hem," I said, "it will be even shorter!"

"Must a command be repeated?" he asked.

"No, my master!" I said.

He then stepped back, to regard me.

I pulled down at the sides of the garment. If it had been much shorter I feared my brand might have shown!

"Stand straight," he said.

I did so, my hands at my sides.

"A great improvement," he said. "Even though it is perhaps a bit long it is now, at least, within the normal ranges for slave lengths. Yes, I think it is now, even though a bit long, acceptable for a slave, even perhaps suitable for one. Before, of course, it was suitable, intentionally, only for a free woman pretending to be a slave."

"Turn," he said.

I did so.

"Yes," he said, "I think it is now suitable, or will be, when you have attended to the hem, shortening it still further."

I knew that I must learn to go forth in such garments, the garments of slaves.

I stole a furtive glance at a mirror. The garment, I saw, to my pleasure, set me off beautifully, though, to be sure, as what I was, a slave.

"Do you like it?" he asked.

"Yes!" I said.

"You may now remove it," he said, "and kneel again, as you were before, before me."

"Yes, Master," I said.

He returned to the curule chair.

I was then again before him as I had been, naked and kneeling.

"You are aware, doubtless," he said, "that my feelings toward you are, or were, extremely complex."

"Yes, Master," I said. "And if I may speak of such matters, in my opinion, you have understood me very well in some things, and very little in others. Also, it seems you have sometimes wanted me to be, or expected me to be, things which I was not."

"Do you understand what we are doing here?" he asked.

"Yes," I said. It was now clear to me. He had seen me as a Tatrix, he had seen me stripped, he had seen me again in the garment, subsequently shortened to slave length, which I had worn in the house of Kliomenes and in the room in the inn of Lysias.

"When we have completed this symbolic re-enactment," he said, "you, regardless of what you may or may not have been, will be, in my mind and in yours, my slave, in a modality which I find acceptable."

"Yes, Master," I said. I was, of course, already his slave, legally, totally, and in my heart. I suspected that he might now have come to sense this, but that he was not sure of it. Accordingly, he would take no chances with me. I would be put through processes of enslavement, and rites of submission, the outcome of which, no matter what might be my nature, motivations or dispositions, would be to make clear to me my condition, that I was, whatever I was, scheming woman or loving female, his slave, and totally.

"Three things will now be done to you, matter-of-factly, and in order," he said.

I looked at him, puzzled.

"Down on all fours," he said, "and crawl here, head down, to the foot of the chair."

I did so and there, unceremoniously, he crouching down, behind me and to my left, I was collared. He was not gentle with me.

"Kneel back on your heels," he said, "and extend your arms, wrists crossed."

I looked at him, startled, protestingly, as my wrists, with one end of a long leather strap, were lashed together.

"Stand up," he said. I was pulled to a position at the side of the room. The long end of the strap was tossed up, through a ring fixed in a beam, and then put through another ring. Drusus Rencius then drew on the strap and my bound wrists were drawn up, above my head. He then looped and knotted the long end of the strap about a hook, on the side. I then stood there, at the side of the room, naked, in the collar, my hands bound together, held over my head. "Master," I said, "this is not like you! Where is your concern for me?"

"Were you given permission to speak?" he asked.

"No, Master," I said. "Forgive me, Master!" I looked up at my bound hands. The strap was dark on them. I jerked at it. I could not free myself. I was tied in place. My entire body, suddenly, felt very bare, very exposed, very vulnerable. I looked over my shoulder. I was frightened. This was clearly a whipping position.

"Please, Master!" I whimpered.

"Kiss the whip," he said.

I did so, fearfully.

I recalled that only an Ahn before I had begged his lash, in my joy at learning myself his. I had pleaded for the stroke of the whip that I might, in my joy and pain, in tears, reveling, experience his dominance over me, and know myself his. Now, however, this seemed very different. I had been put in place as though I might have been anyone, any slave! Did I mean so little to him? Was I so unimportant?

Then behind me, before I was fully set for it, I heard the hiss of the five supple blades. I screamed, struck, sobbing! I knew he had not struck me with his full strength. I could tell that from the sound. Still my back seemed to burst into flame. The blades had seemed, too, to encircle me, scalding and tearing at me. "No more!" I begged. Then I was again struck.

Had I stolen a pastry? Had I not cleaned my kennel well enough? Had I not pleased some master well enough in the furs?

I was struck again.

"Oh," I sobbed, in misery.

Then twice more was I struck. Drusus Rencius did not much vary the locus of the impact nor the timing. He did not exploit the psychological aspects of the whipping. It was done simply, routinely. Then it was over.

When he freed my hands of the strap I sank to my knees on the tiles under the ring. I was half in shock. I knew he had not struck me with his full strength and, indeed, I had been struck only five times. It had been little or nothing as beatings go. Had I truly stolen a pastry, or done something displeasing, I would doubtless have been much more seriously beaten. The beating had been little more than informative in nature, not even really admonitory. Still I had felt it keenly. I had now felt the Gorean slave whip. No woman who has felt it ever forgets it. If I had had any doubts about the wisdom of being pleasing to masters these blows, few and light though they might have been, would have dispelled them. The beating had been little or nothing. Still, and I knew it, I had been under the whip.

He gave me scarcely a moment to recover. Then, crawling, swiftly, crying out, half dragged, I was pulled by the hair to the center of the room.

He knelt me there.

"Put your head down, to the floor," he said. "Clasp your hands, firmly, behind the back of your neck."

"Yes, Master," I moaned. He was then behind me. He put his hands, under my arms, on my breasts, sweetly and firmly. Then he moved his hands back, caressing my flanks. My head was down. My fingers were together, behind the back of my neck. I was in his collar. It was steel, I could not remove it. I belonged to him. My body hurt, from his whip, that of my master. My head hurt, from my hair, where I had been conducted, unceremoniously, to this location. "Please, Master," I sobbed. "Not like this! Not you, please!"

"The slave is pretty," he remarked.

"Oh!" I cried. "Oh!"

"You have a lovely ass," he said.

"Ohhh!" I said.

"You may thank me," he said.

"Thank you, Master!" I said. I tried not to move. It was difficult. "Please do not treat me like this. Please do not handle me like this!"

"I will do with you as I please," he said.

"Please do not make me yield like this, please! I love you!"

"Yield or not, as it pleases you," he said, unconcernedly.

Then I began to whimper and moan.

"Do not move," he said.

"Please," I begged.

"You are a slave, aren't you?" he asked. "And a natural one?"

"Yes, Master," I said. "Yes, Master!"

"Very well," he said, "you may move."

I then, in the helplessness of my need, in shame and love, began to move. In moments I was tendering him my capitulation.

"I beg to yield!" I sobbed.

"Very well," he said.

I then, a few moments later, lay on my belly on the tiles. I tried to feel resentment toward Drusus Rencius. I failed.

I turned to my side and, the palms of my hands on the floor, regarded him. He was again sitting in the curule chair.

"You are now ready to begin your slavery," he said. "Your name is 'Lita'."

"Yes, Master," I said. I was now no longer "Tatrix." I was "Lita." I would respond well to this name. It had many memories for me. It almost turned me inside out with love for Drusus Rencius.

"You may serve me wine, Lita," he said.

"Yes, Master," I said.

A few moments later I knelt, lovingly, at the side of the curule chair. In his hand Drusus Rencius held the goblet of wine. I had even been permitted to drink from it, from the side opposite to that which had touched his lips.

"I know that you may not believe this," I said, "and I do not wish to be struck for saying it, but I love you."

"Now that you are my slave, and are in my collar," he said, "it doesn't matter, one way or the other, does it?"

"I suppose not," I smiled. "But I do love you."

"I thought you might," he said.

"Why did you resist my advances in Corcyrus?" I asked.

"You were not toying with me?" he asked.

"No," I said.

"There were many reasons," he said. "There was a discrepancy in our stations. I thought you a Tatrix. I was only a soldier. Too, deception was involved in my post. I was truly serving Argentum, and Ar, not Corcyrus. Too, though in a part of me I recognized the slave in you the first time I laid eyes on you, in another part of me, I supposed you actually, in spite of the evidence of my senses, to be a free woman.

Thus, it was important, though it tortured me to do so under the circumstances, to accord you respect and dignity."

"Rather would you have accorded me force and mastery," I smiled.

"Yes," he said. "Too, do not forget that on a certain level, or in a certain part of me, I recognized that you were, rather clearly, a slave. How then could I admit to myself that I, a warrior of Ar, might have certain feelings toward one such as you, only a slave? Too, that I discerned your pettiness, your cruelty and shallowness, dissuaded me from honestly admitting my feelings to myself. I did not wish to regard myself as a fool. Further, of course, you, seemingly so haughty and mighty a Tatrix, treated me with injustice and scorn. It is little wonder I dreamed of you in my collar, in my chains, under my whip."

"Does it still distress you that I am a slave?" I asked.

"No," he said.

"Even a natural slave?" I asked.

"No," he said.

"You lost a silver tarsk to Publius on the matter," I reminded him.

"It was a bet which, in my heart, I hoped to lose," he said.

I licked at his knee, slowly, lovingly. Then I looked up at him.

He put down the goblet on the tiles, to the right of the chair.

He took my head between his hands, those large, strong hands.

"You are a superb natural slave," he said.

"Forgive me, Master," I said.

"I do not object," he said.

"Good," I said.

"In fact, it pleases me," he said.

"Good," I whispered.

He held my head between his hands, like it was that of a dog.

"Do some men care for their slaves," I asked, "just a little?"

"Some men care for them much more than a little," he said.

"Even natural slaves?" I asked.

"Those are the best sort," he said.

"I am glad to hear it," I said.

"In every woman," he said, "if one can but find it, I believe there is a natural slave."

"I believe it is true, Master," I said.

Then I felt myself drawn to his lips, and I was drawn half into the chair, and then he, holding my head, not releasing it, turned, and I felt myself moved backwards and to the side, to my knees, before the chair, and then he was crouching before me, and then I felt myself being lowered backwards to the floor. "I love you," I whispered. "I love you, my master!"

"Do I make you weak?" I asked.

I lay now on love furs, at the foot of his couch. He had put a chain on my neck.

"No," he said.

I leaned over, and kissed him, delicately, intimately.

"Aiii!" he said.

"I see that my master speaks the truth," I said.

"She-sleen!" he said, and then, with a rattle of chain, threw me again beneath him.

"I would be a hundred slaves to you," I whispered, "a thousand!"

"You are," he whispered. "You are."

"Doubtless master is tired now," I said, "and should rest. I will stop."

"Not yet! Not yet!" he said.

"Very well," I said.

"Insatiable slut!" he growled. "Do you think I am made of iron?"

"It seemed so," I said.

"Desist," he said.

"Yes, Master," I laughed. It was hard for me to keep my hands off Drusus Rencius. He was so beautiful. I snuggled down beside him, my head at his hip. I kissed his hip. Then I lay there, quietly, beside him. "I am not disturbing you now, am I?" I asked.

"No," he said.

"Would you like to rest now?" I asked.

"Yes," he said. His hand was in my hair.

"Would you like me to relax you?" I asked.

"Very well," he said.

I crawled to my knees.

In a few moments, he said, "Is that your idea, as how to relax a man?"

I laughed, and continued my work, lovingly.

"Obviously you have been trained," he said.

"I am not one of those women who thinks her part in making love is finished when she lies down," I said.

"That is clear," he said. The slave, of course, is not permitted the ignorance, inertness and mediocrity of the free woman. She must serve marvelously and totally. Nothing less is permitted her.

"I am a woman of many talents," I assured him.

"Doubtless," he said, half moaning.

"I have attended school," I informed him. "And I am a skilled feast slave. I am also skilled at weaving on a mill loom."

"Marvelous," he gasped.

"Shall I stop now?" I asked.

"Continue," he said.

"But I thought you wished to rest?" I said.

He looked at me, menacingly.

"I shall continue," I said. "I would certainly not wish for a command to have to be repeated. That would be a reflection on my discipline. Too, I have no wish to be beaten twice in one day."

"I wonder who is the master and who is the slave," he said.

"You are the master, and I am the slave," I said. "I am clear on that."

"Would you care to mount me?" he asked.

Eagerly I did so.

"Are you now Mistress?" he asked.

"Whatever Master wishes," I laughed. I sensed, suddenly, what might be the sensations of power and pleasure a woman might experience, putting a male to her use, before she was restored to the order of nature, and her servitude. "Would you truly permit me this?" I asked.

"Of course," he said, "but, later, we will do it somewhat differently."

"Yes, Master," I said, puzzled.

Then, to my amazement and delight, grinding and tensing, watching him closely, I transformed him into a squirming slave beneath me, and then, when it pleased me, took his yielding from him.

Later in the afternoon, when we had rested, and he had had food brought in, and we had eaten, he put me again in such a place, but this time I must face his feet and my hands were held behind me. In such a way, sometimes, a captured free woman, stripped, is placed backwards on a kaiila, her hands bound behind her. This is usually done only when she is being led to slavery. In such a way, then, he used me. My slavery was again well impressed upon me. This type of position, it might be mentioned, is also used by Gorean masters with the woman facing forward, where he can see her face, but with her hands tied, say, before her or behind her, or at her collar, bound either with actual thongs or, most cruelly, "by his will," that form of "tie" in which a woman must keep her hands in a given position, for example, holding them as if bound, or, say, keeping them on her hips or clasped behind the back of her neck. If she breaks such a position, of course, she is subject to terrible discipline. She must then, as he lies slothful and recumbent beneath her, at his ease, observing her, perhaps amused, writhe upon command and thus serve, and eventually cap, his volcano. Later he taught me this sort of thing first-hand. He used the collar tie and, mercifully, with real thongs. When he was finished I had not only learned again that I was a slave but that this general sort of position, even with the female facing forward, has no intrinsic connection with female dominance. He had let me experience it in that fashion to see what it was like. He had then returned me to total bondage.

"Master," I said.

"Yes," he said.

"I have been doing a great deal of thinking," I said.

"Is that what you have been doing?" he asked.

"I mean, in the last few Ehn," I said.

"Yes?" he said.

"I have learned my collar," I said.

"Good," he said.

"You have taught it to me well," I said.

He shrugged. The Goreans have a theory that any man can teach a woman her collar, and perfectly.

"But was it necessary," I asked, "that you used me as you did earlier, after you had whipped me?"

"How was that?" he asked.

"Master!" I protested. Then I saw that he wished to make me speak. "When you made me kneel, with my head down," I said, embarrassed.

"No," he said. "It was not necessary."

"Then why did you do it?" I asked.

"It amused me," he said.

"Surely there was more to it than that," I said.

"Yes," he said, "it is a useful way to show a woman, one who may be proud, or not clear on the matter, that she is a slave."

"I see," I said. "I find it difficult to forget the experience."

"Oh?" he asked.

"Yes," I said.

"Doubtless you were appropriately degraded and shamed," he said.

"No," I said. "To be sure," I said, "it was instructive, but, as I recall it now, I found it very moving and exciting."

"You liked it?" he asked.

"Doubtless it brought my slavery home to me," I said, carefully.

"I would think so," he said. "It would doubtless be difficult to continue to think of oneself as a free woman after having been used in that fashion."

"I liked it," I said, suddenly.

"That is interesting," he said. The beast! He knew I had almost screamed with submission and pleasure!

"Are slaves often used in such a fashion?" I asked, as though unconcerned.

"Sometimes," he said.

"Might I ever again be put under such a discipline?" I asked.

"Perhaps," he said.

I looked at him.

"Perhaps if you beg prettily enough," he said.

"I will," I smiled. "I will!"

"Do you recall the position?" he asked.

"Yes," I said.

"Speak," he said.

"The girl kneels, with her head down, her hands clasped behind her neck," I said.

"You recall the position perfectly," he admitted.

"Yes," I said.

"Assume it," he said.

"Yes, Master," I said, joyfully.

"Thank you, Master," I said, softly, lying in his arms, thanking him for his touch.

It is now evening. Again he had gone to the door and summoned a slave. Again we had had food brought in and had, again, eaten.

"Ohhhh," I said softly. "Thank you. Thank you, Master. You are my master. You are my master! Thank you. Thank you, my master."

Then, later, he held me closely.

"Master," I said.

"Yes?" he said.

"I have often wondered what was the meaning of a golden cage, and why I, when thought a Tatrix, was placed in one."

"The gold," said he, "is a precious metal, is thought perhaps fitting for a free woman, in particular for one of high station, and certainly for a Tatrix. That it is a cage, on the other hand, signifies that she is taken to be, in actuality, no better than a slave, and only fit to be a slave. To place her in such a cage is then to make a clear statement as to her true and rightful nature."

"I see," I said. "And doubtless the golden sack is of similar import."

"Yes," he said.

"Yet Hassan enslaved Sheila before placing her in such a sack."

"True," he said, "and that she as a mere slave was yet placed in such a sack must have induced exquisite emotions in her, emotions of fear, of outrage and humiliation."

"Doubtless," I said.

"It was a joke on the part of Hassan," he said, "an exquisite one."

"Doubtless," I said.

"But doubtless, too," he said, "it served a useful purpose in her on-going training."

"Doubtless," I said.

"But doubtless, too," he laughed, "it seemed an appropriate modality, did it not, in which to transport a former Tatrix to Argentum?"

"Yes," I said. I shuddered.

"But I think you need not fear confinement now in golden cages or golden sacks," he said. "Cages formed of simple, sturdy bars of black iron and deep, doubly-sewn sacks of heavy, plain leather, black and thick, tied or locked shut, will now serve well enough for you, confinements suitable to the more common slave you now are."

"Yes, Master," I laughed. Such devices would suffice quite well, surely, for a common girl such as I now was.

"Master," I said.

"Yes?" he said.

"Read me my collar," I begged, "please."

"I showed it to you before," he said. "You should have read it for yourself."

"You are teasing me," I pouted. "You know I cannot read."

"Not even your collar?" he asked.

"No," I said.

"Well," he said, "do not worry about it. It is not necessary for you to be able to read your collar. All that is necessary, from your point of view, is that it is locked on you, that you cannot remove it, and that it can be read by free men."

"Are you going to teach me to read?" I asked.

"Such skills would seem to have a very low priority," he said. "For example, can you play the kalika?"

"No," I said.

"Do you know the exercises and luscious movements of slave dance?" he asked.

"Not really," I said.

"So why should you be taught to read?" he asked.

"I could spy on your mail," I said.

"I had not considered that," he admitted.

"It could improve my price," I said.

"That is probably true," he said.

"Many men," I said, "enjoy having a girl who can read. It gives them pleasure to make her serve as well, or better, than an illiterate girl."

"I shall think about it," he said.

"Thank you, Master," I said. Whether I would learn to read or not was not up to me. In the final analysis, it was up to masters. It would be done with me as they wished.

"Tell me, please," I asked, "what is on my collar."

"A speck of dust," he said. "There, I have removed it."

"Please," I said.

"It is simple," he said. "It says, 'I belong to Drusus Rencius, of Ar.' "

I kissed him. "It speaks the truth not only of my legal condition," I said, "but of my heart."

He then, again, began to touch me. "Thank you, Master," I breathed, again. I did not know whether or nor I would be taught to read. Then, in a few moments, gently, softly, I began again to yield to him.

I lay on one elbow, regarding Drusus Rencius. "What did you pay for me?" I asked.

"It is not important," he said.

"I am curious to know," I said.

"Curiosity is not becoming in a Kajira," he said.

"Nonetheless," I said, "we are notoriously curious. Doubtless the saying would not otherwise have gained such wide currency."

"That is probably true," he said.

"I would like to know," I said.

"What is the difference of a coin or two?" he asked.

"I know it was not much," I said.

"Oh?" he asked.

I laughed merrily, and he reddened. I knew I had triumphed!

"You paid for me!" I laughed. "You know what you paid! What did I cost you? What did I bring Miles of Argentum!"

"I do not recall," he said.

"Miles of Argentum," I laughed, "when he saw me in Corcyrus, thought I would bring a whole silver tarsk! He, then, too, had only seen me fully clothed, clad in the full regalia of the Tatrix. Only my face had been unveiled! Had he seen me naked he might have raised his estimate! Too, suppose he had seen me in a posture of submission or had had me writhe at his feet in slave chains! Suppose he had put me through detailed and methodical slave paces, or had had me bring him the whip in my teeth!"

"Perhaps he would have added a copper tarsk or so to your price," speculated Drusus Rencius. "Who knows?"

"You yourself," I said, slyly, maliciously, "in Corcyrus, as I recall, conjectured that I would probably bring only between fifteen and twenty copper tarsks."

"That seems about right," he said. "In a normal market, under normal conditions, of course."

"But that was untrained," I said. "Subsequently I was trained."

"Yes," he said, "that is true. I suppose it would be only fair to improve your price by a copper tarsk or so in virtue of such a consideration."

"But suppose a man particularly wanted a woman," I said. "Suppose she was, for some reason, very special to him. Perhaps she had been cruel to him. Perhaps he mightily desired her. He might then be tempted to pay at least a little more, might he not, to obtain her?"

"I suppose so," said Drusus Rencius, irritatedly.

"What did you pay?" I asked.

"It doesn't really make a difference, does it?" he asked.

"I suppose not," I said, "but I would like to know."

"I do not recall," he growled.

"Miles of Argentum," I said, "truly at one time believed me, and with good reason, from his point of view, to be the Tatrix of Corcyrus. For that reason he paid fifteen tarsks for me, fifteen silver tarsks."

"What an idiot," said Drusus Rencius, darkly.

I laughed. "Fortunately he was your friend," I said, "and for that reason would cheerfully accept a considerable loss in my resale."

"I paid more than fifteen silver tarsks for you," said Drusus Rencius.

I clapped my hands with pleasure. "I knew it must be so!" I laughed.

The face of Drusus Rencius was black with rage.

"What did you pay!" I asked. "What did you pay!"

"More than twenty tarsks," he said, angrily.

"How much!" I demanded. "How much!"

"I paid fifty silver tarsks for you!" he said, furiously.

"Fifty!" I cried.

"Yes!" he cried, in fury.

"Wonderful!" I laughed. "That is wonderful!"

He scowled at me fiercely.

"I am surely the poorest investment a man has ever made in a slave girl," I laughed. "You will have to keep me forever. You will never recoup that loss!"

"Oh!" I cried, thrown to my stomach on the love furs.

Then my legs were thrust apart. Then as I gasped and clutched at the furs, almost before I could move, from behind, handled like the slave I was, I was pinioned, held and entered.

"You need not fear I will sell you," he said. "I have waited too long to possess you."

I squirmed, impaled.

"And do not worry about the economic aspects of the matter," he said. "You are going to make your sales price up to me in value, aren't you?"

"Yes," I said, "a thousand times!"

"Is that all?" he asked.

"A thousand times a thousand times!" I gasped.

"Is that all?" he asked.

"And more, and more, and more!" I cried.

"You will now move as I direct," he said.

"Yes, Master," I said. "Yes, Master!"

"I love you. I love you. I love you!" I moaned. "I love you so much I could die with the love of you."

Then his lips were again upon me.

It was now in the early light of morning. In a few hours he would leave for Ar. I would accompany him, perhaps even in his chains, his.

"You are doing it to me again!" I moaned.

"Be quiet," he whispered.

Then I melted to him again, soft and lost, held, in his arms, and then he swept me up again, will-less, his collared slave, like a swirling leaf high into the clouds of ecstasy, and love.

# 37

# AFTERWORD

Wars, I suppose, continue.

Who knows what knives are lifted, what secret, stealthy marches may be afoot?

But these things seem far away.

Ar, in the evening, seems very beautiful.

I must conclude this narrative now. I have been summoned to my master's couch. I hasten to obey.